Rosie and Ruby

Patricia Dixon

Also By Patricia Dixon

Over My Shoulder
They Don't Know
Deaths Dark Veil

Praise For Patricia Dixon

This is a very special story of our times, which is at times both uplifting and heart breaking. Patricia's strength lies in that she never shies away from difficult subjects, is extremely aware of how people feel, think and react in certain situations and is passionate about her characters. There is a poignancy to her storytelling, but also a touch of comedy, especially when the story moves to France. The magical love story she weaves around Daisy and Adam moved me to tears on more than one occasion, so much so, I needed to keep a steady supply of tissues by my side. **Tina J – Amazon Reviewer**

Patricia has a wonderful gift and I for one am so happy that she shares it with us. **Debi Davies – Amazon Reviewer**

There are many kinds of love, and Patrica Dixon draws each one with a sensitive, uplifting, and at times heartbreaking pen. Highly recommended. **Mandy James**

I have laughed and I have cried, wow a brilliant book I couldn't put it down. I have read all her books and I think this is the best yet. Can't wait for the next one keep them coming please. **Cheryl Hooper – Amazon Reviewer**

Patricia Dixon, what are you trying to do to me? I can barely see through tears and I am an emotional wreck. The book will set you on a roller-coaster of emotions. I'm lost for words sorry. MUST READ!!! **Adele Shea – Goodreads Reviewer**

For my lovely dad.
Thank you for the memories.
I miss you every day.

x

Chapter 1

Ruby 1998

Ruby lay underneath her cold blankets, mesmerised by the flashing blue lights that illuminated her bedroom walls. Sirens wailed and tyres screeched as the police pursued the thrill-seeking low life who obviously had nothing better to do on a Saturday night, other than pinch a car and race it around the estate. It wasn't unusual to be kept awake and tomorrow there would probably be a repeat performance, or a different drama, played out in full view of the residents, albeit from behind closed doors and through murky glass. If not a car chase, then it would be Frank across the landing, shouting the odds because he'd been locked out by Carol, his long-suffering wife. Alternatively, there would be the sound of feet, running up and down the stairwell on their way to see Denzil, Openshaw's very own small-time drug baron who lived in the flat at the end of their row.

There was always noise of some description: a drunken fight, car alarms, raised voices or taxis honking their horns until the early hours. Ruby thought it amazing that despite being skint and probably on the dole, so many of her neighbours could still afford to take a cab into Manchester every weekend and get wasted but then again, most of them were up to no good or on the fiddle. None of this bothered her unduly, it was just reality and a way of life that she had grown up with, and gradually, over time, she'd become accustomed to it.

Each day on her way to and from school, she crossed the rundown estate which was once a shining example of the government's ideal; building pristine, futuristic streets in the sky.

These days, it was no better than the post-war slums they had cleared to build the concrete monstrosity she called home. It was actually a glowing testament to social housing gone wrong and inhabited by people who had no interest in being part of normal society, something she realised when a bunch of scumbags burned down their community centre, signalling the end of the old folks meeting hall *and* her youth club.

The boarded-up windows covering the smashed glass of derelict family homes, and the rows of abandoned, empty shops told their own tale of hope having left. The only viable businesses remaining were the chippy and the off-licence. The latter had bulletproof glass protecting the staff inside and the mere fact that they passed your purchases through a safety hatch said it all really. Nobody dared to go into the park unless it was to buy weed, otherwise you'd get your head kicked in for straying onto somebody else's patch. Then there was the local swimming baths – a long distant memory after being knocked down. The expanse of wasteland that remained was subsequently used for illegal fly-tipping and appeared to have been ignored by the council, despite it being a smelly eyesore and yet another blot on the landscape.

The only families that seemed to move here now were from far-off lands, some of which Ruby hadn't even heard of, and who spoke languages that both isolated and alienated them from other members of the community. The even sadder truth was that nobody seemed to care. The foreigners had little in common with the original residents and neither had anything remotely uplifting to chat about either, so they all just got on with it and ignored each other, extinguishing any hope of community spirit.

Ruby was so cold. It was February and along with the incessant rain, the temperatures had dropped to single figures and the flat was freezing at night. The whole place had a tinge of dampness and the speckled patches of green and black mould seemed to be taking over the ceilings and walls, expanding and spreading their spores, along with the unmistakeable stench of poverty. Ruby was paranoid that soon her clothes would start to smell, too. That was the last thing she needed, turning up at school with a pongy uniform, so she did her best to keep herself clean and tidy albeit without the help of her mum. Ruby had become quite independent, more out of necessity than desire, however, she quite enjoyed her trips to the launderette mainly because it was warm inside and it meant a couple of hours away from home, reading magazines and listening to the idle chatter of the caretaker and her customers.

Unfortunately, Stella, her mother, was going through another very skint period at the moment which meant they now had to dry their washing on a maiden which took forever, especially in front of the most inefficient electric fire in the world. As for the central heating, it was permanently switched off and the flat was always dark and dingy. During the winter months, Ruby became obsessed with checking the electric meter. Her worst fear was being plunged into darkness, especially when The Perv was knocking about, so she made it her mission in life to squirrel away coins here and there, and keep it fed.

She had heard that to keep warm you should wear lots of layers, which was easy if you actually possessed multiple items of clothing, but as she didn't, Ruby had wrapped herself in her dressing gown and kept her socks and fluffy slippers on. Keeping still didn't seem to help either. She'd even tucked the duvet under her feet to seal in any heat, and her nose was cold and runny. She really wanted to put her head under the covers but that would mean taking her eyes off the bedroom door. Her mum would be back soon with The Perv and from the looks of them when they went out, they were half-cut before they even got to the pub so God only knew what state they'd be in when they got home. So much for being skint.

Ruby could hear the whirring of the police helicopter as it approached the estate. This was the norm and it would be up there for ages, tracking the stolen car, shining its light on the idiot thief while he made his futile bid for freedom. The chase would be the talk of her school on Monday and the culprit would no doubt turn out to be someone's brother or cousin who'd end up being the star of the canteen and hero worshipped by all his brain-dead mates. Still, there was a small part of Ruby that wished she was in that car too, but she wouldn't waste time taunting the police and bouncing up kerbs. Instead she'd head for the nearest motorway and keep on driving until she ran out of petrol, and get as far away from home as possible.

She was just nodding off when the sound of the front door slamming jolted her into a state of awareness. Ruby listened to her mother's irritating giggling and the clip-clop of her heels on the lino as she opened and closed cupboard doors, not that there was anything inside them worth eating. They'd probably been to the chip shop, The Perv was very generous when it was in his own best interests and Ruby knew they'd soon be topping themselves up with the cans of lager they'd failed to guzzle earlier. Even though she was hungry too, Ruby would rather starve than go outside her bedroom door. The Perv would just love that, a chance to sneak a peak at her nightie and leer while her mum wasn't looking. No, she would stay there, nice and still and pretend she was asleep and hopefully, they'd drag each other off to bed and spend the rest of the night comatose.

An hour passed and Ruby had monitored every single noise they made. She'd heard her mum go into the bathroom, and then, thankfully, the TV was switched off, signalling that they'd finally gone to bed. All was quiet outside her door. This didn't necessarily mean she was out of the woods just yet. The worst-case scenario was that he'd got her mum so paralytic that she couldn't come to Ruby's rescue like last time, a thought which made her heart pound inside her chest and fear ripple through every nerve and sinew in her body. Almost paralysed by her own imagination, Ruby had no alternative than to lie in the dark, stay awake, and wait.

**

Two weeks earlier, on one normal Saturday night, almost the same thing had happened. Ruby had eventually managed to doze off despite the racket they were making, but later, she was woken from a fitful sleep by the creak of her door. As the light from the kitchen streamed into her room she could see the silhouette of Barry the

Perv standing at the end of her bed, staring silently down at her. In the horrifying seconds before she screamed, she could have sworn he was holding something in his hands and whatever it was, was definitely sticking out of his trousers. It was also quite possible that every occupant in the block heard Ruby's blood-curdling screams and, thankfully, so did her mum who was woken by the sound of her hysterical child and panicked calls for help from Barry. Ruby could hear him now, acting like he was totally innocent. Though it had to be said, he managed to put on quite a performance that night and had thrown Stella totally off the scent.

'Stella! Stella! Come quick! I think your Ruby's ill or something. She's going bleedin' daft in there. For Christ's sake, hurry up!'

When her mother eventually staggered in, stinking of lager and kebabs, as Ruby gulped for air and tried to explain what had happened, Barry intervened and made out like he was the avenging angel.

'I was sitting in there, minding my own business watching *Match of the Day* when she set off screeching like a banshee. Scared the shit out of me she did so I jumped up, thinking that someone had broken in and I legged it in here. She was raving on about someone being in her room but she must be having a nightmare cos I checked the window and there's nobody about. I'll nip outside and look around, just to be on the safe side.'

Ruby couldn't believe what she was hearing when Stella fell for his lies.

'No, love, it's okay. Just stick the kettle on and make her a brew will you? It was just a nasty dream, wasn't it, Ruby? You'll be okay once you've calmed down. Did you have a cheese sarnie before you went to bed? That's probably what did it. Now just try and forget about it and think of nice things.' Stella stroked her daughter's head and stood up before swaying slightly, then made her way to the door.

'I'll be back in a minute with your brew and I'll see if I can find a couple of biscuits as well. Won't be a min, and I'll leave the door open in case you want me.' Then she was gone.

Ruby sat in silence and disbelief as she heard her mum thank Barry for running to their rescue, then tell him how glad she was that they had a big, strong man to look out for them. By the time she came back with the tea and, inevitably, no biscuit, Ruby was pretending to be asleep. She waited for her mother to leave and the door close before bouncing out of bed. She tried to push the wooden chest, but it was too heavy so she removed the drawers and dragged it in front of her door, then put everything back inside before jumping back under her duvet. Ruby didn't sleep a wink that night. The merest noise or creak made her panic, imagining Barry creeping about outside her door.

At thirteen she'd never had a boyfriend but her best friend, Crystal, had. Ruby listened on a regular basis to all the gory details of her teenage love life so had a very good idea what Barry was doing with his hand at the end of her bed. He made Ruby's skin crawl and if she was honest, her mum was getting that way too. 'Think of something nice,' she'd said. Ruby would've laughed if the statement hadn't been so pathetic. What the hell was there to think of around here that could vaguely squeeze into the 'nice' category? Nice wasn't part of Ruby's life or vocabulary. Nice happened to other people with normal mums, not those who lived at the arse end of a rough estate, surrounded by people who didn't give a shit about anything other than their next benefit payment and watching Jerry Springer on the telly.

If she wasn't careful, Ruby thought, she'd end up as a guest on that show. Her mother certainly fitted the bill and had been through so many blokes she'd lost count. They were all a bunch of desperate losers and all cast in the same mould: divorced or kicked out by their previous girlfriends, and usually looking for an easy leg-over and somewhere to kip. Stella gratefully provided both as she seemed incapable of existing without a man for any length of time.

At first, everyone benefited from the blossoming romance as the newbie fell over himself to get into their good books and make a positive impression, bringing presents for them both and laying on the charm. For a few weeks at least, the heating was turned on, the flat was clean and tidy and Ruby even got some nice treats and home-cooked food while her mother attempted to ensnare whatever low life she'd stumbled upon this time. It never lasted though, and once the shine had rubbed off, normality soon set in. Stella inevitably got bored of domesticity and her man. Once she bled him dry and he realised she was no saint, Ruby's mother was off to pastures new and the Stag's Head on the hunt for another victim. This time though, Stella had plumbed new depths because Barry was the worst of a bad bunch.

Ruby still remembered her mother when she was pretty. She'd always had bleached blonde hair but in those days it didn't have thick black roots and resemble candy floss. Stella was the mummy in the school yard that stood out, always wearing brightly-coloured dresses and very high heels that matched her outfit. Ruby's mummy wasn't like the dowdy ones who came in raincoats and woolly hats in winter. Stella had lots of lovely make-up, black shiny boots, a see-through umbrella and a boyfriend waiting at the gates to zoom them away in his posh car and take them for tea in a restaurant.

Now, Ruby realised that what her five-year-old eyes looked up to as glamorous, the other mothers looked down on as cheap. As the years rolled by and Stella failed to find a keeper (or spoiled her chances by always looking for someone with a bigger car and a fatter wallet), time and too much vodka took its toll on her looks. In a continuous cycle of self-pity and desperation, she hoped to find salvation in another bottle from the off-licence and solace in the arms of anyone who'd have her.

***

Ruby continued to watch the door, recalling the first time Barry came into her room, and how afterwards she'd prayed really hard that he would dump Stella the very next day and be long gone by teatime. She had stayed in bed for most of that Sunday until she heard them leave, thus avoiding any contact and nearly fainted with relief when Stella came in that night alone. She looked tearful and was carrying a bottle of wine that signalled an evening of sorrow-drowning was on the cards.

'Well, that's it. He's gone. Packed his bag and disappeared into the sunset. He'll be miles away by now.'

Ruby would've done a cartwheel had there been enough space. In an attempt to feign interest and offer a smidgen of sympathy, she asked if her mum knew where he'd gone.

'Only to Ireland, he'll be back in a fortnight. He's visiting his sister. Reckons she owes him some money so when he gets back, it's party time! Anyway, there's not much in so it's soup for tea. I'd do you cheese on toast but you might have the screaming abb-dabs again and my nerves won't take it, especially as Baz isn't here to look after us. You'd best open a tin.'

But Ruby wasn't hungry anymore and making her excuses she left Stella to drink herself stupid with the rent money. Sloping off to her bedroom, she buried her head in the pillow and cried herself to sleep.

**

Remembering the events of that night still made Ruby feel sick and brought her sharply back to the present. The noises from the street outside had died down and thankfully, so had the sounds of her mother repaying Barry for an evening on the tiles and a chippy supper. It was 4am. The boy racers had finally called it a night and the helicopter had flown off into the darkness. There was still the occasional slam of a car door and the odd siren in the distance. Ruby allowed herself to doze. Surely Barry would be snoring away by now and she could get some sleep. She was dreaming of being fostered by Pippa in *Home and Away* and spending days on a caravan park or hanging out on the beach. In her dream, she really suited the red tartan dress she wore for school… and then her bed jerked and the strategically-piled books and alarm clock tumbled noisily to the floor, warning her of imminent danger and importantly, waking her from her sleep.

Ruby's eyes shot open. He was there, outside the door, silently trying to force it open but there was no way he could get in because jammed into the space between the door and her bed was a chair and a chest of drawers. Ruby's heart pounded so hard she truly thought it would explode inside her chest.

'Are you awake, Ruby? Come on, love, don't be shy. I only want a little chat to say sorry for what happened last time. Go on. Open the door for your Uncle Barry.' He gave the door one more push.

Horrified, Ruby saw his fingers appear as he squeezed his hand inside, feeling around for whatever was blocking his entrance. Leaping from her bed, sheer terror and adrenaline fuelling her movements, Ruby pounced onto the chair and then leapt on top of her cupboard before lunging at the door. Using her whole body weight she rammed it hard against Barry's wrist, causing him to groan in pain.

'You little bitch,' hissed Barry. 'I'll make you sorry when I get in there, you cocky tart.'

Spotting her pencil case lying next to where her books had been, she rummaged inside until she felt her compass. Fury, shame and terror were coursing through her veins and without a second thought, gripping tightly, she rammed the steel spike into the back of his hand. Then Ruby started to scream. If they thought she was a banshee the last time, second time around she probably woke the dead, but most importantly of all, she woke Stella.

When her mum stumbled out of her bedroom, dragging on her dressing gown and trying to force open her bloodshot, mascara-streaked eyes, she was met by the sight of Barry in his underpants. He had one hand trapped inside Ruby's bedroom while her daughter screamed hysterically from the other side.

'Mum! Mum! Make him go away. He's trying to get in my room. He's a perv, Mum. Please just make him go away.'

Stella may have been many things but she wasn't naive, and knew there and then that this time she really had picked a bad one. Without hesitating, she ran over to the draining board and grabbed the frying pan, grasping it firmly in both hands.

'Get away from my daughter you dirty bastard. It's okay, Ruby, I'm here, love.' Stella tried to sound reassuring and in control, just before she lost it completely and smashed the pan into Barry's head. 'You dirty get! What the fuck do you think you're playing at? Get away from my girl or I swear I'll kill you.' Stella was livid.

Barry didn't know what hit him (literally) when the cold metal whacked the back of his head. For a moment he couldn't figure out what hurt the most, his speared hand or dented skull. From between the crack Ruby watched as he slumped to his knees so she relaxed the pressure on the door as Barry's blood smeared fingers left red tracks all down the woodwork. The next thing they heard was the doorbell ringing and someone shouting through the letter box. It was old Mr Kenyon from next door.

'You alright, Stella love? D'you want me to ring the coppers? I heard you and your Ruby screaming.'

Stella ran to the front door, still grasping the frying pan, and flung it open to find Mr Kenyon in his pyjamas, holding a rolled-up newspaper and a plastic spatula.

'It's okay, Charlie, no need for the police, as long as this scumbag is out of here in the next ten seconds. He was trying to get into our Ruby's bedroom, the filthy pervert. Go on, get your stuff and get out!' Stella waved the frying pan menacingly as Barry scuttled off, holding his bleeding hand, too stunned and embarrassed to speak.

Returning within seconds, his shirt and jacket stuffed under his arm and holding up his trousers with his uninjured hand, Barry made his silent, shamefaced exit from the flat. Not daring to look anyone in the eye, he fled into the freezing night but not before Stella kicked him in the rear end as Mr Kenyon gave him one last jab with his rolled-up newspaper and a crack on the head with the spatula.

It was 7am and getting light. Ruby's bedroom furniture was back in its rightful place and the blood stains had been wiped off the door. Her eyes burned in their sockets from crying and lack of sleep. No matter how hard she tried she couldn't banish the image of Barry's hand poking through the door while her heart lurched when she imagined what would have happened if he'd managed to get in. Once Mr Kenyon had left, Ruby had repeatedly insisted that Stella checked the door was locked before she could relax. Every sound made her jump, fearing Barry had come back for revenge or his shoe, which Stella had chucked over the balcony when she'd found it on the landing. It must have slipped off in his panic to get away and now lay amongst the rest of the rubbish in the courtyard below.

When daylight finally peeked through her curtains and the party people of east Manchester began returning home, only then did Ruby feel able to settle. She was utterly exhausted, both mentally and physically but needed to get some sleep because later on that day she was going to go over to see Rosie, her cousin.

It was Aunty Doreen's birthday and, as with any special occasion, Ruby and her mum would make the two-bus journey to the south side of Manchester and spend time with the upwardly-mobile section of the family. Ruby knew full well that Doreen looked down her nose at her sister, Stella, and had been ashamed when she brought an illegitimate child into the family. Out of duty, Doreen had fulfilled the promise she made to their dying mother that her wayward sister had to be looked after, not rejected, and baby Ruby was to be watched over and cared for. This was something that her Aunty Doreen did begrudgingly without grace or kindness, whereas Rosie offered it unconditionally, along with friendship and love.

Even though the Wilson's home in Cheshire wasn't the most cosy or welcoming of abodes, Ruby saw her visits to leafy suburbia as a breath of fresh air and a welcome break from the bleak greyness she saw on a daily basis. The garden was beautifully pruned and surrounded by privet hedges, and even though the interior screamed out for a dash of colour it was nevertheless tastefully furnished and coordinated using an unimaginative pale green palette.

Ruby embraced all of this. To her it represented stability, and was clean enough to eat your tea from the floor but above all, it was quiet and calm. Even Uncle Jim seemed to blend in with the house, never putting a foot out of place, seamlessly merging into his armchair and the wallpaper, nodding occasionally to agree with Doreen but for the most part he kept his opinions to himself, his head down and concentrated on reading the newspaper.

Despite the bland frugality of Aunty Doreen's cuisine, Ruby knew that whenever she was invited for a sleepover or a few days in the school holidays, there would be three home-cooked meals placed before her on the starched white tablecloth and clean, fragrant sheets on her bed. But the icing on the cake was always Rosie. Never having siblings of their own, the two cousins saw in each other the sister and companion they never had. Ruby looked up to and adored Rosie while in return, being four years older, the elder cousin enjoyed her role as big sister to the fragile, wide-eyed, eager little girl who, when they were younger, held her hand tightly and hung on to her every word.

As they grew up, and despite the fact they lived miles apart, their bond managed to survive even when Doreen temporarily banned Stella from the house after her sherry-induced, bad behaviour on Christmas Day. Ruby's frequent lack of bus fares to make the trip alone was sometimes a stumbling block, but nowadays Rosie gave her the money for a return visit which she stuck down her sock and hid from Stella. Even when she got her first boyfriend, it didn't get in the way and Ruby wasn't pushed out because Rosie wasn't like that. She was Ruby's rock, always there in a crisis, someone wise to confide in, a much needed escape route.

By the time Ruby eventually slipped into the land of dreams her heart had lifted slightly, and a small smile lingered on her lips because in a few hours she would be with her cousin, and then everything in the whole world would be okay.

Chapter 2

Rosie 1998

Rosie dragged the heavy case along the pavement, its wheels getting caught between the cracks in the paving flags. Despite this and her vision being blurred by the hot tears that seeped from her eyes, she was undeterred, resolute. Her blood, which had reached boiling point a few minutes earlier, coursed through her veins, pumping her heart and fuelling the rage that burned inside. With every step, she became more determined, each stride led to freedom – a place where her mother's cruel, spiteful words couldn't hurt her anymore. The curtain twitchers would love this and Rosie was slightly disappointed that it wasn't summer when the prim front lawns would've been occupied by dedicated Sunday gardeners. One of them would have nosily, but very politely, asked where she was going and then she could have told them in no uncertain terms that she was getting as far away from her stuck-up, narrow-minded, bigoted, control freak mother as humanly possible.

As it was, on this drizzly February day, most of the inhabitants of Sandringham Avenue would probably be on the way back from church or reading the *Mail on Sunday*. Or, as in her mother's case, preparing for a birthday party that anyone with half a brain would try to avoid on the grounds it would be totally crap. Mind-numbingly boring, devoid of any life or soul and catered for by the woman with the tightest arse in Cheshire.

Rosie's cheeks burned red from the exertion of her escape. Her blonde hair was soaked and her case was really heavy because it contained all her worldly possessions and had been packed hastily after the worst forty-eight hours of her life. If only she'd seen the letter from the college before her mother got to it, then she'd have been able to get away with her double life for a little while longer. On the other hand, maybe it was meant to be because deep down, Rosie knew she couldn't live a lie forever and now it was all in the open. Decisions had been made, harsh words spoken and doors slammed shut.

As Rosie turned onto the main road and trundled towards the train station she suddenly remembered Ruby. She would be arriving in a couple of hours with Aunty Stella for the Grim Reaper's birthday party and would be upset not to find Rosie there, a thought which for a second caused even more turmoil.

Due to Aunty Stella's inability to manage her finances, their phone had been cut off ages ago so there was no way of ringing Ruby to explain about the row. Rosie made a mental note to save up and buy her cousin a cheap mobile phone. It was about time she had one and it would make keeping in touch a hell of a lot easier, but for now, she would just have to sit at the bus stop and wait for them to arrive. Then she could warn them about the party from hell and at least give Ruby and Aunty Stella her side of the story. She could only imagine how her mother would tell it and one thing she knew for sure, Doreen would be the victim and Rosie painted as an ungrateful, wayward daughter.

There was nothing for it. Rosie sat down on the bench, thankfully protected from the wind and the rain by the plastic shelter and waited patiently for the bus to arrive. It would be the longest, coldest two hours of her life but it gave her time to think and get her head straight and most tellingly, despite the freezing temperature, a numb bum and blue lips, during her time of quiet contemplation, not once did Rosie consider going home.

***

Rosie thought back to the day she started work at the hotel, maybe that's when things really began to change, or had it been a slow creep; a mixture of age, angst and rebellion or just plain and simple growing up? Perhaps you didn't have to settle for what your parents said you needed or should be grateful for. You didn't have to live the way they had or follow in their footsteps, or even tread the path they had laid out for you since the day you were born. Rosie wasn't ungrateful by any means. She knew she had a good life and certainly didn't need reminding by the Sunday school teacher to give thanks in her bedtime prayers, *or* by Doreen for that matter, every sodding birthday and Christmas. Rosie only had to look at her little cousin to appreciate that she could've ended up with someone like Stella for a mother. Not only that, following rare visits to Ruby's flat, Rosie was always truly grateful when she got home at night and rested her head on her pillow in the warmth and comfort of her clean and tidy, pastel pink bedroom.

Rosie suspected that Doreen had planned her future before she was even born and most likely kept another master plan in reserve, just in case she'd turned out to be a boy. Rosie was put on a carefully controlled, strategically thought out path that Doreen followed to the letter from day one. Sunday school, Brownies, Guides, riding and dancing lessons, a squeaky-clean life which was firmly rooted in a solid, Christian, middle-class upbringing surrounded by like-minded folk. She was privately educated at the local prep school, which hopefully would provide Rosie with an acceptable social circle and, with a bit of luck, a favourable gene pool for when she was married off to some poor boy Doreen had earmarked at kindergarten. Doreen had already settled on acceptable career paths for Rosie, all of which bordered on the far-fetched and were the polar opposite of anything her daughter was actually considering. Something senior in the medical profession was top of the list, a surgeon perhaps and then, what could only be classed in Rosie's eyes as depressingly mundane, either a barrister or bank manager.

Doreen's plans ran into trouble as soon as her daughter went off to the local high school, when it became clear that their finances didn't run to a private secondary education and, worse still, Rosie failed to win a bursary to anywhere noteworthy. Meeting girls from other walks of life, especially those not vetted or approved of by her mother, gave Rosie an insight into how the other half lived. Her new friends didn't have to conform to the nice girl image. They dyed their hair and got their ears pierced, drank cider on the park and snogged the face off unsuitable lads at the bus stop. For tea, her mates had pizza or lasagne, paella, curry or hot chilli and rice, foods from around the world that would never touch the lips of those living inside 42 Sandringham Avenue.

Doreen couldn't abide foreign food, foreign people or probably anything that had the word foreign associated with it and therefore everyone else had to suffer. Rosie longed to go abroad, even on a day trip, to Spain or France or Italy, anywhere would do, but instead, each year they went to Scarborough for two long, dreary weeks. One summer, the mould was miraculously broken and they threw caution to the wind and tried Tenby, where sadly, the Welsh accent got on Doreen's nerves so that was the end of that. Rosie could not understand why two people who were financially comfortable would want to spend a fortnight freezing their tits off on a windy east coast promenade. Not when there were passenger jets shooting across the sky whisking people to paradise – or Magaluf at the very least. Rosie still remembered sitting in the dining room of the same bleak, draughty hotel, waiting to see how the chef had managed to boil broccoli into submission and murder pork chops for the umpteenth time that week. As she picked at her tinned peaches and evaporated cream she swore that when she was old enough, she would buy a rucksack, get a passport and head for the sun and never come home again.

Maybe it was her Dad's fault. If he'd stood up to her mother now and then perhaps things would've been different. Surely he had a pair of balls hidden somewhere down his perma-pressed slacks? If he had, Rosie surmised they were probably shrivelled up from lack of use. It was common knowledge that he had long since been banished to the Land of Lovelessness, sleeping in a satin covered twin bed, nicely separated from Doreen by a bedside table and a reading lamp. Maybe he got lucky on his birthday or

Christmas as a special treat, however, Rosie was sure that, as with everything else in his life, he took the path of least resistance and stuck to reading his book.

No wonder he disappeared to play bowls at every given opportunity and volunteered for anything on the church committee. The only reason he got to vote for his party of choice was because he visited the polling station on his way to work, otherwise Doreen would be there, telling him exactly where to put his black cross. Stupidly, during yesterday's battle she had hoped for some support but true to form, he just tutted and nodded, solemnly shaking his head in all the right places until predictably and on cue, he sided with Doreen.

Rosie knew she had toes but couldn't feel them anymore. In an attempt to restore the blood supply to her feet she began pacing the bus stop, determined to stick it out and just to focus her mind, went over the events of Saturday, the day from hell. It was one she would never forget, when she had to face the consequences of deceit, the full force of Doreen's wrath and her mother finally stepped over the line.

***

When she turned sixteen, Rosie and her best friend Laura decided they needed a holiday job. It was a threefold plan. Firstly, it meant Rosie had an excuse not to go to Scarborough, secondly, she got to stay at Laura's house for two weeks which would be a holiday in itself and thirdly, they would have stacks of cash to fritter away during the summer months.

Rosie was still firmly on track and adhering to her mother's grand plan that meant staying on at school to do her A levels after the summer. For this reason, Doreen didn't put up much of a fight when both Rosie and Laura found work as chambermaids at Fairhaven Manor, a prestigious country hotel nestled in the heart of the Cheshire countryside. It was a popular venue for up-market weddings, business conferences, and romantic breaks, and used as a hideaway for anyone who was anybody.

Patricia Dixon

Once a stately home, Fairhaven's impressive sandstone walls were bordered by rolling hills, immaculate lawns and surrounded by a moat festooned with lily pads. It was picture-perfect and whilst its charms were totally lost on Laura, whose main occupation after bed making was chasing anything in pants (staff or guests, she wasn't fussy), Rosie looked back on those six weeks as one of the happiest times in her life. Without a clue of what she wanted to do with her future, apart from drink alcopops and have some fun with her friends, Rosie was happy to go with the flow and jog along in her carefree life.

Not only did she avoid Scarborough, she had plenty of money and a host of admirers amongst the waiters and porters. But apart from the many excellent social and financial aspects to her job, Rosie couldn't wait to get there each day and embraced everything. From the lavish surroundings, the constant stream of new faces, happy brides and grooms, celebrities in dark sunglasses, weekenders and golfing parties. Whether it was monotonous room changes or doing a shift in the luxurious pool and spa, she would happily fold fluffy towels and inhale the scents of aromatherapy oils as they were liberally wafted and applied to the guests.

Helping in the restaurant was like a military manoeuvre. There was even an art to laying the crisp linen and the cutlery. Rosie took pride in surveying the dining room once it had been prepared and later, as she cleared the tables, found the sound of clinking glasses and the chatter of the guests, mingled with the aromas of the mouth-watering dishes created for fine diners, all strangely soothing. Even though most days her feet ached and her back felt like it would snap from changing beds or carrying trays, Rosie didn't care because Fairhaven Manor allowed her to experience a whole new world. And although she didn't see it coming, it offered her a way out of Sandringham Avenue.

As the final week of the summer holidays approached, Rosie began to feel downhearted about leaving the hotel and even the prospect of joining the hallowed ranks of the sixth form did nothing to lift her spirits. That was, until she was called into the office by Mrs Amery, head of housekeeping. Possibly one of the most efficient, unflappable people Rosie had ever met, her boss was always groomed to perfection and emitted an air of totalitarian control amongst the staff, but unusually, she was nice with it. Mrs Amery demanded hard work and high standards which she rewarded with compliments and encouragement and the occasional cheeky wink when she caught you ogling a handsome guest, or speculating about what was inside Tony the barista's rather tight trousers.

'Well, Rosie, how have you enjoyed your time with us here at Fairhaven? We will be sorry to see you go at the end of the month. I hope we haven't worn you out, but I expect you'll be glad to get back to the classroom and have a nice rest?' Mrs Amery casually rearranged the paperwork on her desk before resting her eyes on Rosie as she waited for an answer.

'Yes, I have enjoyed it, thank you very much. But to be honest, I'll be sad to leave and will miss you all. I'm not really looking forward to going back to school either. I think I'd rather work here but my mum would have a blue fit if I didn't do my A levels.' Rosie actually surprised herself with her words because saying it out loud somehow made it true, she didn't want to leave.

'Good answer. I was hoping you'd say that because I've had a little chat with the other department managers and we were wondering if you'd like to stay on. Not full-time of course. I wouldn't want to interfere with your education *or* incur the wrath of your mother but if you are agreeable, there's always a place for a hard worker at Fairhaven and you've impressed everyone during the summer. We can find plenty for you to do at weekends and during term breaks, so what do you think, would you like to join us?' Mrs Amery sat back in her chair, twiddling her fountain pen and scrutinising Rosie's face.

Rosie's cheeks were hot from the thrill of it all, not only did they want her back, they were impressed as well. A bubble of happiness gurgled its way upwards from inside her racing heart.

Her reply came out as an over-excited giggle but she managed to compose herself and replied.

'I'd love to come back, really I would. I'm so grateful, and thank you for asking. Shall I just turn up next weekend then? I'll get the bus as usual and I'm sure my mum will be pleased, thank you so much.' Rosie knew she was rambling while Mrs Amery just smiled wryly and rose from her desk.

Indicating it was time to go by walking to the door, she motioned for Rosie to follow. 'Right then, we'll see you on Saturday morning bright and early. I'll put you on the rota and take it from there, any problems in the meantime or if you change your mind, let me know.' Mrs Amery patted Rosie kindly on the shoulder as she showed her out, feeling rather pleased as she watched their newest recruit float off down the corridor.

That was eighteen months ago and since then Rosie had spent every weekend and school holiday at The Fairhaven, in between studying for her A levels which she hated with a passion. Laura had been slightly miffed that she hadn't been asked back but bagged herself an upper-sixth boyfriend who occupied her time nicely and left Rosie guilt-free. Doreen had objected at first, insisting Rosie should concentrate on her schoolwork only to be artfully convinced that there was ample time during the week for diligent study and besides, she wanted to be an independent woman and be able to buy her mother something nice for Christmas and birthdays. How else could she repay her parents for such a wonderful upbringing? Doreen fell for it hook, line and sinker. On the understanding that Monday to Friday, Rosie would study hard and not neglect her schoolwork, she was allowed to work at The Fairhaven on weekends and holidays.

Rosie didn't rest on her laurels and went from strength to strength. The respective managers found her to have a natural way with guests, plus, she was pretty, well-groomed and professional and soon found herself spending less time making beds and more time making people smile. Whether she was giving that all important first impression at the reception desk or waiting-on in the restaurant and assisting with functions and conferences, Rosie was a hit. At the same time, she was beginning to realise that the hospitality industry might just be the one for her. There was so much to learn and from what she had seen, it could take years to climb the ladder but despite that, Rosie had no inclination to follow any of the routes her mother had planned for her. The thought of it kept her awake at night, knowing full well the trouble that any detour from her mapped-out life would cause.

The General Manager, Mr Hardy or Alfred to those he favoured (Rosie being one of them) had high hopes for his new protégée and one rainy November morning during a break for refreshments, he quite innocently fanned the flames of discontent already raging within Rosie's soul.

'Rosie, have you ever considered management training once you have completed your A levels? I only ask because I feel you will be well-suited and we would be happy to send you on the appropriate courses, maybe an apprentice type scheme, unless you have other ideas for your future.' Alfred stirred his coffee slowly, hoping for a positive response.

Rosie was stunned. It was like a dream come true. What was the point in going to university when she had absolutely no idea what she wanted to study? For all her mother's heavy-handed hints and list of preferred careers for her daughter, not one of them excited or interested her like the proposition placed before her. Alfred was offering her an apprenticeship on a plate so why be a penniless student when she could have the best of both worlds, working in a beautiful hotel with her friends *and* get paid at the same time as studying? It was perfect.

'Alfred, I can't believe you've just said that. It's been on my mind for a while now and would be a brilliant opportunity. The thing is I don't think my mum will be very pleased about it. She's expecting me to go to university next September and has sort of set her heart on it. But I'm sure once I've explained everything and all the advantages of your offer, she will understand. I'll speak to them both tonight and let you know in the morning. I'm so happy, I can hardly breathe.'

Rosie's trademark flushed cheeks had already betrayed how she felt, so Alfred just smiled and nodded and prayed that Mrs Wilson wasn't really the controlling tyrant he suspected she was.

Unfortunately, Rosie's wonderful news did not go down well at all with Doreen, in fact she hit the roof and told her crestfallen daughter that over her dead body would she go on a 'training course' and certainly not into the hotel industry. Anyone would have thought Doreen had just been told that her only child wanted to work in a brothel and needed to have pole dancing lessons, not been given the opportunity of a lifetime following a career she would love. Knowing her mother too well, Rosie realised she was on the verge of being 'banned' from going to work as it was only putting nonsense and stupid ideas in her head. Instead, she wisely acquiesced and told her mother that she was right, she hadn't been thinking straight and she would politely decline Alfred's offer. Conversation closed, or so Doreen thought as she huffed and puffed her way into the kitchen to warm up the tapioca. However, what happened when Rosie went to work the next day was a different story entirely.

After a sleepless night shedding angry tears, festering and cursing her mother then going over every possible alternative, Rosie went into work with her mind made up. As she cheerfully told Alfred that her parents were totally, one hundred percent behind her decision to go into the hotel industry, she was so convincing that she had to remind herself it was actually a big, fat lie. In reality, she was hoping that Doreen would somehow change her mind at the same time as praying for a miracle. To be on the safe side, Rosie kept up the pretence at work and at home. She applied to Leeds University to study Economics as well as applying for a course in Hotel Management, much nearer to home in Manchester.

She kept her parents happy by being a good girl and studying while diligently going the extra mile during the Christmas period at the hotel, desperate to ensure Alfred didn't change his mind. Loving every minute she spent in the garland-festooned party atmosphere, Rosie assisted the events manager with a Winter Wonderland wedding and checked in excited guests at the mahogany desk. Her eyes twinkled as brightly as the lights on the giant spruce that stood grandly at the foot of the sweeping staircase as she inhaled the glorious, festive fayre which the chef served to glamorous partygoers. As promised, Rosie provided both her parents with lavish gifts in an attempt to convince them there was actually money in changing beds and cleaning toilets. Unfortunately, despite her efforts, both remained resolute, happily ticking off the days until May when she would sit her final exams and be on the next rung of her ladder to hell.

Rosie had no way of pre-empting the course of events that followed. How was she to know that the University in Manchester took great pride in having its name emblazoned across its stationery and on that Friday morning in February when an envelope plopped onto the mat, she would be at school and Doreen's eagle eyes would spot something suspicious? When Rosie breezed into the kitchen that evening she was met by a solemn welcoming committee and an opened letter which was spread accusingly on the table top. Questions and accusations followed.

Why had she gone behind their back and applied for this course? She was deceitful, sly, underhand, a disgrace, ungrateful, stubborn, wilful, and so the list of negative adjectives went on. Doreen screamed and shouted and Rosie screamed back. Jim kept his trap shut throughout and did his nodding-dog routine. Ultimatums were given and rejected. She would leave the hotel forthwith and give up this ridiculous notion. The letter was torn in two and chucked in the bin, only to be retrieved by Rosie who tipped the contents of her school bag out in retaliation, refusing to ever step foot inside the sixth form block again unless they let her have her way. Friday night ended with Rosie stomping off to her room, Doreen was left weeping and wailing on the settee, and Jim wishing they had a dog so he could take it for a walk and escape the madhouse.

Saturday spiralled out of control when at six-thirty that morning, through the wood of a locked bedroom door, Doreen informed Rosie that she had telephoned the hotel and informed them she wouldn't be returning, ever. In a fit of rage, Rosie told her mother exactly what she thought of her, using what Jim called expletives. And just to show them how mad she really was, punched a hole in her wardrobe door. By the time she had calmed down and could breathe normally, with throbbing knuckles, Rosie plucked up the courage to ring Alfred and in between sobs and apologies explained what a mess she was in.

Rather than admonish her, Alfred calmly advised her to talk things through with her parents and even offered to have a word with them on her behalf, but she turned him down, knowing full well her mother would be vile and condescending and nothing was going to change Doreen's mind. One thing that made her smile, then cry even more, was that Alfred assured Rosie that there would always be a job for her at Fairhaven. He was only a phone call away and would help her in any way he could.

The only time Rosie left her room was to go to the loo or make some toast and grab a packet of Jaffa cakes, some Mr Kipling pies and a bottle of milk from the fridge. She would've stayed upstairs all day but she was starving. A stony wall of silence existed between all parties and continued right through Saturday night up until Sunday morning when she heard movement downstairs and smelt bacon cooking. Rosie was famished but couldn't bear to be in the same room as either of them, so left it a while and let them stew. When she thought the coast was clear, Rosie tentatively made her way downstairs to the kitchen and as she passed the lounge, spotted the cards on the mantelpiece and the ancient 'Congratulations' banner strung across the mirror above the fireplace. Then she remembered it was her mother's birthday. *'Well, she can stick her present right up her arse,'* thought Rosie sourly and carried on into the kitchen. She was pouring milk into a bowl of cornflakes and fully intended scarpering straight back to her room, already resolved to boycotting the party and making Doreen squirm, when her parents appeared in the kitchen. Her mother spoke first.

'So, there you are. I hope you've come to your senses after your silly tantrum and we'll have no more of your foul language or this hotel nonsense. I'm prepared to overlook your appalling behaviour yesterday and put the events of the past twenty-four hours behind us, however, we do expect an apology. The things you said were most hurtful.'

Rosie stood with her mouth open. Did her mother really think it was that simple? Doreen obviously did.

'Don't stand there catching flies, Rosie. And why look so surprised? I pride myself on having a very forgiving nature and I'm prepared on this occasion to give you a second chance. Besides, we have a party to cater for and you look dreadful, so pop upstairs and make yourself look decent then you can help me do the food. But first, your father and I are waiting for your apology.' As she finished her little speech, Doreen went over to the bin to throw some envelopes inside.

As her mother opened the lid, Rosie spotted something. It was one of the blouses she wore for work, scrunched up and covered with bits of egg and bacon rind, all the scrapings from breakfast. In that split second the room went red, or was it the blood simmering in her veins, swimming across her eyes? Whatever it was, it marked the crossing of a line, highlighting the very final insult and the point when Rosie knew there was no going back.

'Why is my blouse in the bin? I'm going to need that for work. Now I'll have to wash it again.' Rosie spoke calmly, letting her words sink in, waiting for her mother to receive her message, loud and clear.

'I think we've already been round the houses with this, Rosie, and you are *not* going back to that hotel. Do I make myself clear?' Doreen had turned white with anger and was visibly shaking.

Jim looked like he was going to faint.

'No, Mother, I think I made myself quite clear last night. I am *not* going to Leeds. I am going to work at The Fairhaven whether you like it or not. You can't control me forever so one way or another I will get my own way. You can't force me to do what you want anymore, do *you* understand?' Rosie gripped the bowl of cereals, waiting for her mother's reply.

'Oh, I think you will find that while you are living under my roof, young lady, you will do exactly as you are told, isn't that right, Jim?'

Rosie's dad nodded obediently, which was totally expected.

'Well, if that's the case, then I'll just have to leave, won't I? If I'm not under your roof or your control it means I can do whatever I want. Isn't that right, Mother dearest?'

Rosie made for the door but Doreen blocked her way.

'You're not going anywhere, young lady. It's my birthday and you will not show me up, today of all days. The vicar is coming and half the avenue so just stop this silly performance and grow up. You're acting like a naughty child.' Doreen folded her arms, two pink dots on her cheeks against the pallor of rage.

Rosie could not believe what she was hearing. This was about her future, her happiness, her life and all her mother really cared about was saving face, keeping up appearances and her own selfish wants and needs. Well, if her mother wanted childish, Rosie decided that was exactly what she was going to get! Letting out an eardrum piercing scream, fuelled by sheer frustration and injustice, Rosie launched her cereals at the wall, smashing the bowl and splattering Jim and Doreen in a shower of soggy Cornflakes. Then she pushed past her spluttering mother, taking the stairs two at a time and locked herself in her bedroom. Dragging her suitcase from under the bed, Rosie rammed it full of her belongings, hastily grabbing underwear from drawers and wrenching clothes off the hangers in her wardrobe. Filling a carrier bag with her toiletries she jammed whatever she could get her hands on into her case and handbag before throwing on her clothes and grabbing her coat. Making a final sweep of the room, she grabbed Humphrey, her bedraggled teddy bear and a photo of her and Ruby when they were kids, sitting on the front step with their arms linked, two happy little girls smiling for the camera.

A huge sob caught in Rosie's throat as she looked down on the image. A tear blobbed onto the glass as she remembered their childhood innocence, when life was simple and uncluttered by grown-up problems. Now look at them. Both had mothers riddled with faults who, between them, managed to make their daughters so terribly unhappy. Well, Ruby might be stuck with Stella but Rosie had had enough. The crumpled blouse in the bin was the catalyst and in some ways it represented her screwed up mother with a twisted brain. Doreen might think it was okay to pour rubbish on her blouse, but Rosie would not allow her to do the same to her life. Taking a deep breath, she rammed the photo into the carrier bag then wiped away her tears and opened the door. As she bounced her case noisily down the stairs, Doreen appeared in the hall with Jim trotting along behind, fury written across her face.

'If you leave this house, madam, don't think you will ever be coming back! You are bringing shame on this family. I'm warning you, if you disobey me, you will be sorry!' Doreen's face was incandescent with rage.

As she spoke, Rosie noticed a Cornflake stuck in Doreen's grey, bouffant, over-sprayed hair and fought the urge to laugh.

'Really, Mother? Well, for your information the way I feel about both of you right now, I don't want to come back – ever. So just move out of my way and get on with making your sad sandwiches for your pathetic party. Your guests will be here soon and I'm sure you're more concerned about making them happy than me.' Rosie grabbed the catch, opened the front door and stepped outside.

The icy air hit her flushed cheeks as she marched down the path. Flinging the gate open, she stepped into the avenue, over the line and into the land of free will. Purposely not shutting the gate as she knew it irritated the hell out of her mother, Rosie stopped and turned to see them both, stock still, staring in shock. Her father's mouth was frozen open in horror and no doubt worried shitless about the repercussions that would follow. Her mother's was a grim line, set in stubborn stone. Then Rosie realised she'd forgotten something.

'Oh, how rude of me. I totally forgot to say happy birthday, Mother, have a really, really nice day.' And then she went.

***

Rosie could see the bus approaching in the distance. It was the one o'clock from Stockport and Ruby and Stella would hopefully be on board, otherwise she might just die of hyperthermia right there in the shelter. Rosie managed a wry laugh, imagining the double dose of shame which would be heaped on Doreen if the stiff, frozen body of her errant daughter was found in the bus shelter.

The bus drew nearer and Rosie couldn't wait to explain everything, mainly so she could go somewhere warm once she'd dished the dirt. It was no secret that there wasn't much love lost between Stella and Doreen, and Rosie suspected her aunt would be on her side, nevertheless, they could make their own minds up whether to turn round and avoid the party, or face the Des O'Connor music. The main aim was to reassure Ruby that she would stay in touch and she wasn't being abandoned because no matter what happened, Rosie would always be there for her cousin. It was a promise that she would faithfully keep, and on that cold February afternoon, she had no way of knowing that in the future, how important her oath would turn out to be.

Chapter 3
Ruby 2010

Ruby wiped the crumbs off the shiny marble counter and flicked the kettle on. Marcus would be down soon for breakfast and she wanted everything to be perfect. She knew he loved the smell of freshly ground coffee brewing and had made pancakes especially. The kitchen table was set with her favourite breakfast service, crisp white porcelain with hand painted sunflowers and it was one of her favourite wedding presents. The finishing touch was the giant spray of exotic flowers which stood in the centre of the table and the scent from the colourful blooms tickled her nose every time she got close. Marcus had presented her with them when he arrived home the night before, a token of his gratitude for the lavish dinner she'd prepared.

After reminding Oliver at least a hundred times not to spill anything or dribble Coco Pops on the tablecloth, as an extra precaution, Ruby pulled Lily's highchair further away from the table, just in case she made a grab for the maple syrup or kicked out with one of her chubby legs and sent the milk jug over. Casting her eyes over the immaculate kitchen, Ruby felt pleased with her preparations. The shiny, hi-spec units gleamed and the marble floor was spotless. After a sleepless night she had risen early and, along with making pancake batter, she'd got on with some cleaning, making the most of the peace and quiet before her family awoke. Marcus didn't even hear her get up as she slid from beneath the white silk sheets; he was comatose and sleeping off a spot of over-indulgence the night before.

The previous evening, they had been entertaining and two other couples had joined them for dinner. Kevin from the office was just an underling but a major bootlicker, along with his accountant fiancée, Diana. Then, there was another associate called Roman, one of their agents based in Thailand who'd flown in for business meetings with Marcus. He was accompanied by his so-called assistant Helene, who, according to Marcus was thick as pig shit but undeniably stunningly beautiful. Roman's wife was at home looking after their four children and oblivious to his philandering.

Ruby loved to cook, it calmed her and while she was immersed in a recipe or shopping for special ingredients, it took her mind off her worries. Most importantly, she wanted to impress Marcus and their guests and always pushed the boat out with the very best cuisine she could offer. The night had gone extremely well, apart from the fact that Diana irritated the hell out of Marcus and seemed intent on trying to prove what an intelligent, successful, independent woman she was – facts that Ruby knew full well meant absolutely nothing to her husband. As for Helene, it was obvious that he thought she was common so virtually ignored her all evening and took great pleasure in doing so. Ruby wasn't sure if he did it on purpose because on the rare occasions he did take notice, Marcus referred to her as Helen, much to her thinly veiled annoyance. Other than that, it had all gone well and she was congratulated by everyone on her skills as a hostess and culinary expertise. Marcus looked like the cat that got the cream which meant she could relax slightly and try to enjoy the evening, but there's always something to do when you're the hostess with the mostest so by the time they all decided to call it a night, she was worn out. Marcus, however, having enjoyed being in the company of Roman who loved his brandy as much as her husband loved whisky, was in no mood for sleep so as Ruby had expected, her night was certainly far from over.

Hearing footsteps on the landing, Ruby began to cook the pancakes and poured the coffee before giving the table a final once over. Oliver was spooning cereal into his mouth and chattering away about the dinosaur model he was making at school. At almost five years old he embraced every day with wide, excited eyes and loved learning new things. He was bright and full of energy, had a constant bank of questions at the ready and then some in reserve, talking Ruby's socks off at every opportunity. He was kind and considerate to his baby sister and even though he could be rough and ready with his friends at school, he had a sensitive side and was still partial to a cuddle from his mummy. His dark brown, watchful eyes didn't miss a trick and Ruby admitted he could be a bit of an ear-wigger, prone to worrying about the snippets of doom he sometimes caught on the news and bordering on the obsessive about death, heaven and the monster that he was convinced lived in the laundry basket. Other than that, his main concerns in life were learning to ride his bike and being invited to Michael Patterson's birthday party. He was halfway through telling her all about what a triceratops ate for his breakfast when Marcus bounded into the kitchen.

Ruby's stomach lurched as her husband entered the room, knowing only too well how vile he could be towards everyone when he had a hangover and prayed that just this once, Oliver wouldn't give it a go and try and engage his father in conversation. True to form, her little boy who despite being given enough signs that Marcus just wasn't interested, gave it his best shot with an interesting dinosaur fact.

'Daddy, do you know what extinct means? That's what happened to all the dinosaurs that lived on this land.' Oliver's eyes were wide with expectation, his spoon was hovering mid-air, precariously overloaded with dripping milk and Coco Pops while he waited for an answer.

'Of course I know what it means, now be quiet and eat your breakfast. I'm in a rush.' Marcus was oblivious to the look of hurt that washed over his son's face as he slammed his briefcase onto the perfectly laid table.

The sudden jolt made Oliver's arm jerk and, inevitably, the spoonful of brown, milky cereal splattered all over the white tablecloth.

'Oh, for Christ's sake. Look what he's done. Are you completely stupid or are you just a baby who can't find his mouth? Ruby, don't buy that stuff again, he makes too much mess.'

Turning to Oliver who was on the verge of tears, Marcus fired off more instructions.

'Go on, take your plate to the dishwasher, you've had enough.' Oliver jumped up from the table and grabbed his bowl, sloshing milk everywhere and winding Marcus up even more. 'Right, that's it. Get upstairs and out of my sight. You're even more stupid than your mother. Go on, don't just stand there like a moron, and tears won't help either. Stop being soft.'

Oliver was like a rabbit trapped in the headlights and then Lily picked up on the tension and began to wail, prompting Ruby to quickly intervene.

'Go and brush your teeth and get your school bag ready. Just stay in your room and I'll shout you when it's time to go.' Ruby gently stroked Oliver's pale, frightened face in an attempt to reassure him. Her heart was breaking for her little boy while at the same time, fear and hate fought for first place amongst the multitude of emotions swirling through her brain.

'Great! Now she's off. Can't you shut her up or are you incapable of that too, and what's that smell, it stinks in here?'

Marcus was in full flow now as Ruby turned to see the blackened pancakes smoking in the pan because amidst the chaos, she'd forgotten all about them.

Hastily removing them from the heat, Ruby silently poured milk into his coffee and placed it on the table then took Lily out of her highchair and tried to soothe her.

'Would you like something else instead? I can make you some eggs if you prefer.' Ruby prayed he'd just go to work. She couldn't wait for him to be gone and for once, got her wish.

'No, I don't want eggs. You'll probably ruin those as well. I'll get something in town. Don't forget to pick my dry-cleaning up, either. I need those suits for my trip. Do you think you can manage that?' He took a gulp of coffee then slammed down his cup, grabbed his case and made for the door.

Having no other option, Ruby followed him out, replying to the back of his head which she could cheerfully have smashed in.

'I'll collect them on my way back from the doctors. I have two appointments this afternoon so if you ring and I don't answer it's because I'm in the surgery or with the optician. Your mother is having Lily for me while I have my examinations. I did tell you.' Ruby's heart raced in her chest, waiting for him to think of a reason to forbid her from leaving the house.

'Right, whatever. I'll be back late tonight so don't make dinner. I'm meeting with Roman and then we'll eat in town. Anything is better than the slop you feed me.'

Ruby counted to five and watched as Marcus grabbed his keys and opened the door although she knew what came next, the public show of affection for a nosey neighbour or anyone passing by.

Standing on the doorstep like the dutiful wife, Ruby waited as Marcus kissed her on the cheek and then pecked Lily on the head, tickling her leg playfully for added effect, and then he was gone. Ruby turned and slammed the door shut then carried Lily upstairs to find Oliver who was playing quietly with his dinosaur model, deep in thought.

When he saw Ruby, Oliver looked up and gave her a thin smile. She could tell he'd been crying but had long since given up trying to explain or defend her husband's behaviour. Why should she protect Marcus or lie to her little boy for him? The last thing she wanted was for Oliver to lose faith in her as well, or feel like she was betraying him by sticking up for his dad who, for the record, was nothing but a cruel, vicious bully. Instead, she placed Lily on the floor and sat by her son.

'Come on you! Give me a hug. I'm going to miss you while you're at school today. I'll bet Mrs Taylor has got lots of exciting things for you to do, and it's sports today so you'll be worn out by the time Granny picks you up later.' Ruby stroked his head and hugged his little body close, drinking in the feel of his arms which were wrapped tightly round her shoulders as she breathed in the scent of baby shampoo from his hair.

'I bet Granny takes us for cakes after school, on those silver trays with lots of sandwiches. Can I have fizzy orange?' Oliver's big round eyes stared hopefully.

How could she resist? Ruby smiled down at her lovely little boy. His ability to wash his father's bad behaviour away and look for the happy things in life was something that she envied and only hoped that he really did forget quickly and wasn't just pretending for her benefit.

'Of course you can have a fizzy orange, sweetheart, and the biggest piece of chocolate cake as well. Now let's get ready for school, we don't want to be late, do we?' As Ruby gathered them both up, she wished that a glass of pop and a slice of cake would make everything better in her world. It wouldn't, and she was starting to realise that if anything, her husband's behaviour was actually getting worse.

Ruby sat in the churchyard of St Peter's in the heart of Prestbury village. Lily had nodded off in her pram during the walk back from school and having no desire whatsoever to return to her beautiful home on the gated estate, she found herself a bench and took some time for herself. The gentle, late May sun warmed her face as she closed her eyes and listened to birdsong and engine noises from vehicles making their way up the high street. Ruby knew she was lucky to live in this prestigious village with its Saxon history and Tudor houses, where the streets were spotlessly clean and they regularly won awards for its beauty and floral displays. It was a far cry from the concrete estate where she grew up. The inhabitants of Prestbury were a million miles away from the people she used to live amongst, those who clung on tightly to the very bottom rung of society.

The affluent area was a magnet for footballers and their wives, northern celebrities and rich, commuting businessmen, her very own husband being in the latter category. Oliver went to a lovely private school and mixed with other well brought up children of rich parents. She had a brand new car and expensive clothes but apart from these and her four bedroomed, Georgian style house with its impressive pillars at the front door and a huge conservatory at the back, Ruby had nothing. No friends, no interests or hobbies and no prospect of ever breaking free from the life Marcus designed and vigilantly controlled for her and their children. She sometimes thought he might be the male version of Aunty Doreen but much nastier and with fists that punched.

The problem also lay in the fact that everything she had was approved of and paid for by Marcus. He ensured she had no money of her own apart from her child benefit which could only be used for the children, and then every penny spent had to be accounted for. He was in charge of all matters relating to the home and gave her an allowance for food. If she required new clothes or anything for herself she had to ask, then he would decide if she really needed it and provide her with an amount he deemed adequate. Ironically, if she had to entertain or appear publicly as his wife then no expense would be spared. She could languish at the beauty parlour, have her hair done at the best salon in Manchester and treat herself to a brand new outfit, even down to underwear – Marcus would insist on it. For that reason in particular, Ruby dreaded social invitations as she had no desire to dress up for her husband or as he menacingly put it, repay his generosity in bed.

Last night was no exception. The beautiful flowers were not really a gift from a loving, appreciative husband. They were just part of the smokescreen that blew about her life, proving to everyone what a fabulous, considerate guy he was. The day before, whilst out shopping for the food she was about to prepare, the futility of it all made Ruby want to weep. Knowing full well that no matter how hard she tried, how perfect the meal or how well her hostess duties stood up to his intense scrutiny, once he'd drank his whisky and wine, the guests had left and the dishwasher was loaded, her services would be required in the bedroom. Tears stung at the corner of her eyes as she tried to wipe out any memory of yesterday and his cold and brutal treatment. It had become something to just grin and bear while praying for it all to be over as quickly as possible.

In the tranquillity of the sleepy churchyard, Ruby thought back to life before Marcus. It wasn't the greatest existence but compared to this, she'd swap it in a heartbeat. She truly would. There were so many what ifs, so many things she'd have done differently. For a start, she would've paid heed to every scrap of advice and listened seriously to the warnings of those who hadn't been taken in by him. But one thing was for sure, if she could change her life in any way, there were three things she'd want to keep exactly as they were. Her two precious children and Rosie.

***

Everything began to change around the time her cousin left home. When Ruby stepped off the bus all those years ago to find Rosie sitting in the shelter, half frozen with a large soggy suitcase by her side, a brave smile on her face and a right old tale to tell, she didn't realise that being partially abandoned by her one and only true friend, would force her to stand up for herself and change the course of her own life. Stella was too hung-over to make the trip after mourning the premature and shameful departure of Barry the Perv, so Ruby made the journey alone. There was no way she was going to her aunts if Rosie wasn't living there anymore so instead, she spent the rest of the day with her cousin.

They sat in the waiting room of the train station and ate the whole box of chocolates Ruby had bought for Doreen. She couldn't believe how mean they had been but more than anything she admired Rosie for standing up to her parents and having the guts to walk out. Rosie reassured Ruby that she would keep in touch and wrote down the number of The Fairhaven and Laura's house. She had arranged to hide out at her school friend's home and take it from there. Whatever happened, nothing had changed between the two of them and once things had settled down, Rosie promised Ruby they could meet up and spend time together.

It was getting dark when they said their goodbyes. Ruby firmly refused to let Rosie go back out into the cold, assuring her cousin she was big enough to walk to the bus stop herself, so as the train pulled into the station, they had one last hug and went their separate ways.

Taking Rosie's advice, the very next day, Ruby started looking for a Saturday job. This would provide some cash to top up the mobile phone that Rosie was going to buy for her, thus enabling them to keep in touch. Also, having your own money made you independent and after what had happened to Rosie, an emergency fund was vital if you ever wanted to escape the clutches of your mother. Destiny played its hand when on the way home from school the following week, Ruby spotted a card in the window of a bakery on the outskirts of the estate. Wasting no time, she went inside and asked the kind looking lady behind the counter if she could apply for the job. As it was quiet, she got an interview there and then and after assuring Sandra, the owner, that she was reliable and hard-working, Ruby talked her way into starting that Saturday morning.

Ruby loved working for Sandra and there were many advantages to working in a bakery, especially the warmth which was much welcomed after a night in the chilly flat. Then, there was a hot bacon roll (or two if she fancied it) for breakfast and a pie and a cake for her lunch. Whether she was scrubbing bowls and tins, whisking cream or filling pies, Ruby put her heart and soul into her little job because for a few precious hours she was free from the concrete jungle and Stella.

As time went by and Sandra got to know Ruby, she was able to extract snippets of information about her home life and began to feel sorry for the skinny girl with the mousy brown hair and matching sad eyes. She knew only too well of her mother's reputation in the area and had heard a few rather unsavoury tales about Stella's behaviour and regretful choice of men. With this in mind, Sandra increased Ruby's hours to working a few nights after school and in the holidays. She was a hard grafter, and it was obvious from the state of her school uniform and the clothes she wore to work on Saturdays that any money Stella had coming in certainly wasn't being spent on her daughter. Before she went home in the evenings, Sandra always gave Ruby a carrier bag containing a few bits, cooked meats and muffins or a couple of cold pies, a tin loaf or some fruit cake. Whether she shared it with her mum or not, that was her business but it gave Sandra a clear conscience when she sat down to dinner that night with her own daughters.

Time ticked by and a year had passed. Ruby was due to take her GCSE's in the summer and for a while, life at home had been bearable. Since the Barry incident Stella had learned her lesson and kept her boyfriends away from the flat, or at least whenever Ruby was around. This was probably why, on a rainy Wednesday lunchtime when she burst into the flat after being sent home from school with a stomach bug, Ruby caught her mum and a greasy-haired bloke in an uncompromising position on the kitchen table. She'd already spent most of the morning with her head down the toilet but seeing her mum and her latest conquest, bang at it on the Formica table just made her want to chuck her guts up again, all over the dirty lino floor.

Red faced and mortified with embarrassment, Ruby stormed into her bedroom and slammed the door, disgust for her mother seeping through her veins and about to ooze from every pore in her body. Desperate to sleep and hopefully erase the images from her mind, Ruby opened her drawer to take out her nightie, and that's when she noticed something odd. Having no order or routine in her life outside the boundary of her bedroom door, Ruby had always taken pride in her room regardless of how sparse and drab it was. And most importantly, she looked after the few items of clothing she possessed and washed everything herself. Therefore, it was easy to spot that the neat row of underwear and socks had been disturbed and as she quickly pulled open the drawer underneath, Ruby found the rest of her belongings in the same state. Someone had definitely been snooping around in her things.

Rushing over to her bedside cabinet, she wrenched open the top drawer and knew instantly it had been invaded. Her heart lurched as she grabbed her purse and warily opened the zip. Ruby gasped when she looked inside, there were still a few coins in there but the twenty pounds she had saved was gone. Blind panic took over as Ruby pulled the chest of drawers away from the wall and frantically felt for the envelope that was sellotaped to the back. Relief washed over her as she ripped it free and saw that it was intact and, thankfully, still contained all of her savings. As Ruby's blood pressure began to return to normal and her heart rate slowed, she held the money to her chest. This was her escape fund and she realised now how stupid she had been to leave it in the flat so without a second thought, she shoved it down her school blouse and went outside to face her mother.

'Has lover boy gone then?' Ruby glared at Stella who was sitting at the kitchen table, smoking and casually reading *The Sun* as though nothing had happened a few minutes earlier. All Ruby could think was, '*I hope the dirty cow has wiped the table,*' as she shuddered and watched her mother with barely concealed contempt and disgust.

'Yes, he's gone, no thanks to you and anyway what are you doing at home? You should be in school. I hope you're not skiving because the last thing I need is the bloody wag police round here causing trouble.'

Stella was so brazen it made Ruby snort with laughter, even though none of this was remotely amusing.

'What do you mean, no thanks to me? For your information I've been sent home sick, not that you care cos all you're interested in is getting pissed and laid, so don't make out you give a shit about me or school. And by the way, someone's been in my room and nicked twenty quid out of my purse. Was it that scumbag or you?' Ruby was shaking with rage as she waited for Stella's answer.

The words that came out of her mother's mouth remained ingrained on her memory, etched deep for the rest of Ruby's life. It also marked the end of their already limited relationship, for good.

'You cheeky, ungrateful little bitch! No, I have not nicked your fucking money and neither has Dave. And while I'm at it, I'm sick of having no life because I have to look after you and sneak about while you're at school. I've wasted my best years stuck here, waiting on you hand and foot while you dragged me down. Well from now on if I want to bring my boyfriends back here, I bloody well will, so if you don't like it you can fuck off!' Stella stubbed out her cigarette and glared at Ruby.

'And don't turn on the waterworks, it won't wash with me. You ruined things with Barry because you act like a little tart, flouncing around in your nightie all sweet and innocent. It was probably *you* that egged him on that night, not the other way round, so if Dave doesn't come back it'll be your fault and you'll be sorry, so piss off out of my sight. I'm sick of looking at your high and mighty face. Go on. Get out!'

Stella was white with rage, even below her lined, fake tanned face which was twisted and riddled with spite. Without another word, through wizened lips she lit another cigarette and took a long drag, flicking the match into the overflowing ashtray before storming into her bedroom and slamming the door.

Tears blinded Ruby's eyes as Stella's speech settled into her brain, the stinging accusations pierced her heart and her cheeks burned with shame and shock. Unable to think of anything else to do or even say, she turned and opened the door and walked silently along the littered landing, down the filthy stairwell and into the street. Ruby had nowhere to go. She thought of going to the bakery but it was forbidden if you were poorly in case you passed your germs along. She couldn't go back to school either and it was ages till her friends would be finishing lessons, so instead she walked aimlessly towards the precinct and sat on one of the benches. Taking her phone out of her pocket Ruby rang the one and only number in her contacts list, the person she knew would understand. Ignoring the old man who came and sat by her side to eat his bag of chips and whilst the nauseating smell of grease and vinegar wafted her way, she phoned Rosie. She would know what to do.

By five o'clock that evening when Ruby returned to the empty flat, she had a post office account, two bolts and a padlock for her door, and a plan. From now her wages would go straight into a savings account. Next, she was going to ask Mr Kenyon if he would fit the locks for her while Stella was at bingo. In future, when Ruby went out, she would padlock her door from the outside and when she was at home, she could bolt herself in, just in case Dave or whoever Stella dragged back for a quickie, tried it on again. And finally, she was going to get the best GCSE's she could then find a full-time job, save every penny she earned and get the hell out of Stella's life, forever.

True to her word, Ruby began to save up hard and asked Sandra if there was any chance she could take her on full-time once she left school but it didn't look likely. Her boss had already given her as many hours and as much help as she could so she encouraged Ruby to go to college and learn a skill, catering perhaps, but she was adamant. The only way to get away from the estate and Stella was to earn money. Sandra knew Rosie was keeping her ears open for a position at the hotel, but feeling guilty, and desperate to help her young friend in any way she could, she put out the feelers and eventually came up trumps.

The best friend of her eldest daughter worked in Kendal's, the large upmarket department store in Manchester and promised to put a word in for Ruby. The saying '*it's not what you know, it's who you know*', certainly rang true. After much preparation, a smart haircut and a new outfit from Sandra's catalogue, Ruby sailed through her interview and was offered a position in Ladieswear. She was to start full-time, the week after she sat her final exam, so with warm hugs and promises to not be a stranger (and floods of tears on Sandra's part) Ruby left the bakery and started working in the city centre. It was the start of a brand-new life.

Chapter 4

Ruby

Ruby didn't even bother to tell Stella about her job until the night before she started work, or the seven very acceptable GCSEs she attained, either. Their relationship had broken down so badly that they rarely spoke or even clapped eyes on each other. Dave was unusual in the respect that he actually had a place of his own so sometimes Stella stayed there, which Ruby loved as she had the flat to herself. She bought and cooked her own food and left money towards the rent and bills on the table every week. What Stella did with it was her own business. When the lovebirds were in the flat she just locked herself in her room or went to visit one of her school friends who inevitably, she had less in common with now. It was clear that everyone was changing and beginning to move on. They had enrolled at college, started apprenticeships or like Ruby, found themselves a job. Others had nothing to do at all apart from staying at home, watching rubbish on the telly all day long and waiting for their next dole cheque.

For Ruby, work became her favourite place to be. It wasn't the most riveting job in the world and she spent most of her day removing armfuls of unwanted clothing from the changing rooms and replacing them on the rails, or working on the till, folding lovely clothes she could only dream of wearing. The up- side was that she made new friends and every so often could afford to go for a pizza or to the cinema after work. The added bonus of getting a staff discount also meant that instead of being scruffy and unfashionable, at last she could treat herself to something new from the cheaper ranges in the store. Ruby stuck rigidly to her savings regime which was fuelled by her dream of having enough for a deposit to rent a flat. She spent many a happy hour, fantasising about her very own place while unloading boxes in the stockroom.

On a rainy, Friday evening in October, she was standing at the bus stop, daydreaming and feeling particularly pleased with herself. She clung on tightly to a carrier bag containing her new jeans and jumper, which had been put away ages ago and were now, finally, paid for. Ruby was looking forward to wearing them on Sunday, it was her birthday and a group from work were going bowling to celebrate. As the bus trundled slowly towards the stop, battling its way through the rush hour traffic, a male voice broke into her thoughts. Ruby jumped, she had been so distracted by her thoughts, she hadn't noticed the man standing next to her.

'About time too. I bet you any money that two more will come round the corner, this first one will be packed and the others will be empty.' The figure stuck his hand out to signal for the bus to stop, just as two more orange and white buses appeared in the distance. 'See what I mean?' The young man smiled as he turned to face Ruby, relieved to have finally grabbed the girl's attention.

In that precise moment, at the ripe old age of almost seventeen, Ruby's orbit changed. Looking up she saw the softest brown eyes she could ever have imagined, framed by waves of sandy hair that blew uncontrollably in the wind. As the face that spoke the words waited expectantly for a response, her heart missed a beat and a flush of nerves crept up her shy face and into her cheeks. Gathering her wits, Ruby grappled desperately for something to say, anything would do, so she said the first thing that came into her head.

'Do you think we should wait for the next one then? I bet there'll be nowhere to sit on this one.' And with that short sentence, their fate was sealed.

They let the other passengers board the bus and caught the next one instead, which as they expected was almost empty. Making their way to the top deck they chose a seat at the front (only nutters and troublemakers sat at the back) and during the half hour journey home in the crawling traffic, Ruby Moore totally and unexpectedly fell hook, line and sinker in love with Dylan Hopkins.

***

Lily began to stir in her pushchair, snapping Ruby out of her daydreams and back to reality with an unwelcome thump. Standing to leave she popped the dummy back into her daughter's mouth, hoping it would soothe her back to sleep for a short while at least. As she made her way back, Ruby couldn't get Dylan out of her mind. Why, whenever things were bad, did he stalk her consciousness during the day and haunt her dreams at night? Filling her head with images and memories that she found hard to shake off gave her no comfort, it only made her sad. She had long since given up on him coming back to find her or wishing he would turn up and rescue her from the mess she had made of everything. Nevertheless, he always managed to get inside her brain, leaving in his wake a longing for the past and the happiest year of her whole life.

***

Dylan was cool. It was official. He wasn't like the boys she'd hung around with at school. Dylan was in a band and listened to rock music and wore his hair long, unlike the clean-cut boy groups on TV. He didn't care if it made him appear odd or stand out in a crowd because he was confident and comfortable in his own skin and took no notice of what everyone else was doing. They would lie in his bedroom for hours listening to music, surrounded by posters of Nirvana, R.E.M, Metallica and U2; to this day, whenever Ruby heard Aerosmith's 'I Don't Want to Miss a Thing' she would be transported back in time to Dylan's room. His arms would be wrapped round her shoulders as they lay on his Manchester City duvet, the volume turned up while they memorised every word. It was their song and sometimes even now, depending on her mood,

Ruby would either have to switch it off because the lyrics were too painful or turn the dial right up and have it blasting from her car stereo, in open defiance of the life she now lived and the man she had foolishly married.

Dylan worked part time in the café at British Home Stores in between studying for his A levels at college. He had a normal family, a friendly homemaker for a mum, named Yvonne, and a solid, dependable dad, Trevor, who worked away on the oil rigs off the coast of Scotland. He had two younger sisters, Lexie and Hannah, aged five and seven. They all sat down together for tea every evening to a proper cooked meal, and here, they would talk about their day or tease each other and laugh. That's what Ruby remembered the most. It was a house full of laughter and cooking smells and most of all, she was always welcome to sit around the table and join in.

Dylan lived just up the road in Audenshaw, so on the nights they met at the bus stop after work they would talk and hold hands all the way home, making the most of their thirty-minute journey together. If City were playing or it was band practice, they would tear themselves apart and Ruby would go back to the flat, otherwise, she would stay on the bus and spend the evening with Dylan and his family. Constantly trying to avoid outstaying her welcome or being in the way, Ruby did her best to be polite and helpful, however, she needn't have worried. Yvonne recognised a lost soul when she saw one and took her under her wing, cursing Stella for her lack of maternal care and interest.

To the relief of both parties, Ruby was invited to Dylan's for Christmas Day thus leaving Stella free as a bird and absolved of having to make a forced effort, or a decent lunch. Out of what little respect for her mum she had left, Ruby bought Stella a present and placed it on the kitchen table before she left the flat on Christmas morning. It was a bottle of perfume from the store and she'd had it gift wrapped in gold paper and fastened with a red bow.

Even though she'd had the offer to stay over at Dylan's on Christmas Eve, Ruby had declined, making up a story that she should try to make a bit of an effort with her mum and not leave her alone. In truth, she didn't want to intrude. Ruby had to swallow down a lump of self-pity and blink back tears as she looked around the scruffy kitchen, littered with empty lager cans and bottles of Lambrini, all of which Stella and Dave had noisily consumed the night before while she lay in bed behind her locked door. Earlier that morning, as she counted the minutes until she went to Dylan's, Ruby opened the cheap, floppy card that Stella had left on her bedside table. It contained her Christmas present of ten pounds. Adding insult to injury it contained no message or words of love and best wishes, just a drunken scrawl saying, 'from Mum'. Pushing the tacky card from her mind, Ruby opened the door and picked up her carrier bags, one containing some clothes and the other packed with the gifts she had lovingly chosen for Dylan and his family, purposely slamming it loudly behind her. Stella and Dave could rot for all she cared. She was staying with a real family for the whole of Christmas and New Year, and she was going to enjoy every last second of it.

Dylan and his family soon became Ruby's world, which was lucky, the one inside the concrete jungle was beginning to fall apart. The flats were due to be demolished and the residents relocated. This meant that eventually she would either have to tag along with Stella, who she presumed would move in with Dave, or find a place of her own. Mr Kenyon had already departed and was now living in an old folk's home. He was getting bad on his legs these days and refused to go to his daughter's so, as he put it, he was getting his feet under the table at The Meadows Retirement Centre before there was a mass exodus of oldies from the estate. Most of the flats were being boarded up as people gradually drifted away and, inevitably, squatters had moved in. The only upside was it made Ruby aware that there were actually people worse off than her, aside from the fact she had the crappiest mum on earth. Putting her worries and impending homelessness to the back of her mind, Ruby tried to concentrate on the here and now and being in love.

She had been sleeping with Dylan for a while and they stole precious moments when Yvonne was out shopping but terrified of repeating history, Ruby took herself off to the Family Planning Clinic and went on the pill, which she took religiously. There was no way she would make the same mistakes as Stella and bring a child into the world if she couldn't look after it properly. Ruby swore an oath to herself that when she had children, she would be in a position to give them everything, including bucketfuls of unconditional love. Otherwise she'd end up cold-hearted, resentful and poor, like her own mother.

Dylan was her first real boyfriend and apart from kissing boys from school at boring house parties, he was her one and only and she thought it would be so forever. Spring turned to summer and Ruby was thoroughly immersed in Hopkins family life. She had days out to Blackpool, a camping trip to Rhyl at Easter and had even been to Maine Road to watch Manchester City play. Taking everything in, she'd stood in the stands, listening to the chants of the fans, the deafening roar of the crowd when the team came out, and the thrill and uproar that reverberated around the ground when City scored. The bloke standing next to her lifted her off her feet, wrapping her in a bear hug, making her blush like a fool but what struck her most of all was being part of a tribe of strangers, joined together by one common bond. It was one of the most amazing experiences of her life. Looking up at Dylan who was engrossed in the game, she thanked God sincerely for sending him to her and asked that her happiness and the feeling of belonging somewhere would never end. Inevitably, because nobody seemed to listen to Ruby that much and she was quite possibly the unluckiest person in the world, for reasons beyond her control, the end came much sooner than expected.

The plan had been for Dylan to take his A levels and continue his studies in Manchester. He wanted to be an engineer and as he was intelligent and worked hard, there was no reason why this shouldn't have come to fruition. Since his dad worked away, he wanted to be near his mum, sisters and Ruby, so to everyone's relief, going away to university wasn't an option he even considered. With his exams taken, all he had to do now was await his results and then accept his place in the autumn and everything would be rosy. So on a sunny afternoon in July, as Ruby waited at the bus stop alone, not expecting to hear from Dylan until after band practice, she was surprised when she received a text from him. He asked her to stay on the bus and come straight to his and would explain when she got there.

Dylan was waiting at the stop and as soon as she clapped eyes on him she knew something was wrong – really wrong. It was obvious from his red-rimmed eyes that he'd been crying and he looked pale underneath his sun-kissed face. Naively she'd assumed that he must have had a falling out with one of the lads in the band, that's why practice was cancelled. Something told Ruby to wait and not ask questions as they walked silently to the park at Ryecroft and sat facing the empty bowling green. He was holding her hand tightly and staring straight ahead. From that day on, whenever Ruby saw a park containing the squares of green turf, the next few horrible words and what happened afterwards would come flooding back.

'My mum's got cancer. They've just told me. They've known for a few weeks but didn't want to upset me while I've been doing my exams. Anyway, she's got to have treatment and they think there's a good chance she'll get better because the hospital spotted it early. She's going to be poorly with the chemo and even though they were putting a brave face on it, I can tell my dad's out of his mind with worry.'

He squeezed Ruby's hands as she heard his voice crack.

'Oh God, Dylan, I'm so sorry, your poor mum! I thought she'd been looking tired lately but didn't seem ill or anything. But that's good news, isn't it? They've caught it early and she will get better. I'm sure she will. Please don't cry, we can all help her and I can look after the girls while she's in hospital. I could even stay over and take them to school and stuff like that. It's going to be okay, honest it is.' Ruby folded her arms around his body as she heard him sob.

'Ruby, listen to me. That's not all, there's something else.' Dylan wiped his eyes and composed himself, taking her hands in his, grasping them tightly as he looked her in the eyes.

'We're moving away, up to Scotland, it's all been arranged. Dad wants to be near her while she's having her treatment but can't afford to give up his job, and if there's an emergency he'll only be a helicopter flight away. They told me to stay here and go to uni but I can't just get on with my life when they'll need me more than ever. If Dad's on the rig, I should be there to take care of Mum and the girls. We've been round the houses with it but I'm going to go with them. I'll apply to a uni in Scotland otherwise I'll take a year out and get a job. At least that way Mum won't feel guilty as well as being ill. They're going to rent our house out until we know the score. I'm sorry, Ruby. I've been going over and over how to tell you but I promise, it won't split us up. You can come up whenever you want and hopefully we will be back here as soon as she's better.' Dylan wiped his eyes, guilt-ridden by the look on his girlfriend's face.

In Ruby's world, time had actually stopped because during those brief seconds, any happiness she knew, had been extinguished by his words. That morning, as she'd caught the bus to work, her heart had been light as she looked forward to the weekend and taking the train with Dylan to visit Rosie. The lump of lead that now rested in her chest was so heavy she thought it might actually damage her heart. Her mind raced with images of saying goodbye, Yvonne on a drip in hospital, lonely bus journeys that ended at the estate, no more Sunday dinners or evenings listening to music in Dylan's room. Her boyfriend was leaving her, the love of her life and the family she had never known – they would all be gone and she would be on her own, again.

How Ruby survived the next few weeks she would never know. The only thing that sustained her was her love for Dylan and the family that she had grown to look upon as her own. Fighting the overwhelming urge to beg to be taken with them, pride and common sense intervened. They had enough to cope with without an extra family member, so instead she helped them pack away their belongings for storage, or entertained Lexie and Hannah so Yvonne could rest.

Ruby developed tunnel vision and focused on being strong and supportive because for one reason or another, all their hearts were breaking and filled with dread. She convinced herself that if she helped them get through this terrible time and didn't make a fuss, they wouldn't abandon her. She assured her tortured heart that the sooner they went away and Yvonne got better, the sooner they could come home and life would get back to normal. The day she said goodbye and the Hopkins family set off for their rented house in Aberdeen, Dylan and Ruby clung on to each other for dear life, making promises and drenching each other's shoulders in tears. But even the best, most solemn of promises get broken and unfortunately, so did Ruby's heart.

For a while, they kept in touch. A phone call every night and hundreds of texts a week kept their love alive but as Yvonne became increasingly weak and Dylan took on the strain of university and caring for his mum and sisters, the miles that separated them forced open the cracks that were beginning to show. Where once there had been comfort and relief in hearing each other's voice at the end of the line, now their loving conversations were replaced by tension and recriminations. Ruby made only one journey to Scotland to see Dylan.

It was about two months after he moved and the much-anticipated week of catching up and being together turned out to be miserable and a complete let down. His happy, settled home now seemed dysfunctional and in disarray. The rock that was Yvonne had become reliant on others, namely Dylan, who was struggling to combine university with childcare and a needy girlfriend who was out of the loop socially and intellectually with his new friends. In short, his life had become a juggling act and he couldn't cope, so gradually, just as Ruby had always feared, they grew ever distant. After many tearful, soul searching phone calls they agreed to be 'just friends'. It was for the best they told themselves, they would keep in touch and be there for each other at the end of the phone. Although it eased the pain and made losing a limb more bearable, Ruby knew in her heart that it was over and Dylan might never come back.

Fort Beswick, as it was fondly known to everyone in the area, mainly the police force, fire brigade, assorted criminals and the unemployed majority of east Manchester, was due to be demolished and Ruby's home would soon be reduced to rubble. Still, it was the last thing on her mind as she lay in bed, night after night mourning the loss of her reason to get up in the morning. Ruby would replay every moment she'd spent with Dylan, over and over until more often than not she cried herself to sleep. The sounds of the estate could be heard less and soon, it became eerily quiet. Not so many footsteps now or sirens and late-night taxis. It was a ghost town and subconsciously, Ruby knew it was time to get out.

Lady Luck must have finally woken up from a deep sleep and decided to give Ruby a bit of a break, by encouraging Martine from the home furnishings department to place an advert for a room to let on the noticeboard in the canteen. To move things along, Lady Luck ensured that all the tables were full apart from the one situated right underneath the aforementioned card, written helpfully in bold red biro and asking for a 'single female to share four-bed house in Reddish'.

On her lunch break, bored to death and with nobody to talk to, Ruby had nothing better to do than read the posters and various advertisements on the corkboard, and with Lady Luck on her side for once, her eyes fell on the white card. Reading and rereading the words, glimmers of opportunity and excitement filtered into her brain, while hope (a sentiment she thought had previously abandoned her) egged her on. Reaching over, Ruby unpinned the card and without further contemplation, left her cold tea and cheese sandwich and headed off to home furnishings in search of Martine. She was going to make damn sure she got first dibs on that room.

For the next few years of her life, Ruby made the most of being young, free and happily single. Sharing a house with three, like-minded party girls meant that she thought of Dylan less and her heart eventually healed. The scar remained but it was less visible. They all worked and played hard, swapped shoes and clothes, ate very little (so they could buy more shoes and clothes) drank lots of whatever was on discount at the supermarket, had one-night stands and fleeting affairs, partied into the night and slept it off the next day. In between all this, Dylan and Ruby kept in touch through polite cards and the odd, perfunctory text but both knew the inevitable truth, they had moved on.

Yvonne thankfully recovered but the family decided to remain in Aberdeen and sold the house in Manchester, sealing many fates and pouring cold water on any remaining hopes of reconciliation. Stella moved in with Dave then straight out again when she met Ricky, the manager of Argos where she finally got a job. He had a bungalow in Bolton and a caravan in Morecambe so as far as Stella was concerned, she'd hit gold. Too much sludgy water had flowed under the bridge for Ruby to be interested in or care about what her mother did anymore, so she got on with her life and was contentedly living it to the full. Until the day she met Marcus.

Chapter 5
Ruby 2010

Ruby loaded the breakfast things into the dishwasher while Lily played with her toys on the kitchen floor. It was only 10.30am and she felt emotionally drained already. The build-up to the previous evening's dinner party and the events that followed in the bedroom were taking their toll. Her body ached and she had bruises on the inside and out. Shuddering at the memory, she stuffed the chocolate and coffee stained tablecloth into the washing machine and began wiping down the marble surfaces. Her mind was riddled with snapshots of the past, so many black and white images of a stupid girl who should have known better and followed her head, not her feeble heart. Most importantly, while her world was still full of colour, she should have taken note of the hints and observations made by her worried friends. As she thought back to that fateful day when she met Marcus, not for the first time, Ruby wondered how her life would have turned out if she'd just stuck to her guns and kept her head under the duvet.

***

Martine had spent the past hour trying to coax Ruby from the warmth of her bed and out into the murky September drizzle for a night on the town.

'Come on, Ruby, it'll be a laugh. This bloke's loaded and it's in a really posh bar. We won't have to pay for a thing except the taxi home, unless I get lucky, then I'm in for a night at the Midland and you can walk back. Come on, don't be a bore.' Martine jumped on the bed and tried to drag the duvet off Ruby's head, intent on changing her mind.

'Sod off, Martine. I'm knackered. I spent way too much last night so I'm skint till payday. And I've got nothing to wear either. Ask Jackie or Kay to go, I'm staying here.' Ruby was looking forward to a hot bath, a bacon sandwich and an early night.

'Please, Ruby. Jackie's still got her head down the loo and Kay's gone to the gym. Look, I'll pay for the bus to town and the taxi home. I was only kidding, I won't abandon you no matter how fit he is. It'll be champagne all the way and he might even buy us our dinner, that's way better than a bacon butty.' Martine paused then gave it her best shot. 'I'll even let you wear my red dress and the matching shoes. Come on, you know you want to, so stop playing hard to get!' Martine tickled Ruby through the duvet, using annoyance tactics as her final ploy.

'So… I can wear the red dress *and* you're paying for the taxi?' Ruby popped her tangled head and mascara smudged face out from under the covers. 'If this place is a dive, you'll be sorry and I'd better get something to eat too because I'm starving.' Ruby scowled at Martine to let her know she'd be in trouble if it turned out to be a wild goose chase.

'Scouts honour. He was flashing the cash when he came in to buy his mother a crystal rose bowl and I know he's staying at the Midland because I had it gift wrapped and sent over. He invited me and a friend for champagne cocktails, so it'll be dead classy, how many more clues do you need Miss Marple? He's loaded so get your finger out and let's get going.'

Martine, as usual, was on the money because the bar was indeed quite exclusive and when they arrived, the champagne was flowing freely. Nate spotted them more or less as soon as they entered the room and was all over Martine like a rash, which didn't surprise Ruby as her raven-haired, crimson-lipped friend was striking enough in her Kendal's uniform but when she turned up the heat with one of her extra clingy, pulling numbers, no man could resist. Ruby was holding her own in Martine's red, figure hugging, forties style dress, her fair hair styled into a high chignon. She definitely looked the more sophisticated of the pair and was attracting quite a few admiring glances from the inebriated group of businessmen who were lounging on the leather sofas.

Sipping her champagne as she people watched, while trying hard not to stare as Nate's hand became rather familiar with Martine's bottom, Ruby was enjoying the opulence of her surroundings when she was joined on the chesterfield by another suited figure. She didn't turn to look, but from the corner of her eye was aware of long legs, stretched out in front of him and the lemon smell of his aftershave. Playing it cool she continued to sip and watch, listening to the jazz music that played softly in the background. Eventually, she won the waiting game and he spoke first.

'I see your friend has met Nate. I hope she's not easily offended as he can be quite a handful when he gets going.'

The words were spoken softly in Ruby's ear, not quite a whisper but gentle enough to make the hairs on her neck stand on end, and then submit to the urge to face him.

Ruby turned her head and was captivated by the man seated beside her. She could almost breathe his scent he was sitting so close, looking deep into her soul with his dark eyes. His short ebony hair was carefully styled and swept off his face but the fringe would flop down occasionally as he spoke, giving him a boyish look, just for a second. Finding her voice which she decided should be the correctly spoken one she used at work whilst serving ladies who lunch, Ruby gave him one of her best customer service smiles before replying.

'I can assure you that Martine is more than capable of coping with your friend, in fact, he might be the one who needs rescuing at the end of the night. She can be a bit of a man-eater when she gets going.' Ruby smiled and gave a delicate wave of her fingers in the direction of Martine who returned a flirty wink.

'Mmm, you might be right there. May I refill your glass, it's looking slightly empty. Here, drink this and I'll get us another bottle, if that's okay with you, of course?' He waited politely for her answer before ordering.

While they both kept one eye on the behaviour of their respective friends, Ruby, and Marcus Cole (as he'd eventually introduced himself) spent the evening immersed in conversation. Once the bottle of champagne was empty, he suggested they go for something to eat, otherwise they would be too smashed to talk and he wanted to find out everything about her. Flattered and almost starving to death she accepted, so they left Martine and Nate to their own devices and walked the short distance to Marcus's favourite Italian restaurant on Deansgate.

He was interesting and funny, self-deprecating and attentive. Ruby in return did her best to make working in Ladieswear sound like the best job in the world while inwardly worrying about her lack of pedigree and humble beginnings. To her surprise, and because he seemed genuinely interested in everything about her, instead of glossing over the obvious differences between them Ruby opened up and was semi-honest about her background. Marcus was fascinated by her working-class roots. He confessed to never visiting east Manchester and even though she painted a slightly less vivid version of her relationship with Stella and the reasons for their state of estrangement, he was genuinely sympathetic of her situation and small family circle. He in turn had an entirely different tale to tell.

He was the managing director of the family firm which imported clothes of every description from all over the world which were then sold in catalogues and department stores across the UK. His work took him to far flung reaches of the globe, Thailand, Hong Kong, Turkey, Malaysia and he was often out of the country, meeting with buyers and manufacturers alike. His father had died many years ago leaving only his mother who lived in Prestbury in their family home, which naturally would one day be his. For the present, he lived in a loft apartment by the quays as it was more convenient for their offices in the centre of Manchester.

Ruby was impressed by everything about Marcus even though she tried desperately not to show it. She didn't gush or simper, say wow or giggle, instead, she asked interesting questions about the places he visited or the garments they produced rather than allude in any way to his wealth. He escorted her home that night and insisted on paying for the taxi. Marcus behaved like a perfect gentleman when he kissed her gently on the cheek before asking if he could see her again as soon as possible, to which she naturally agreed. And that was that, her fate was once again sealed.

Ruby's life quickly ascended into a world she never even knew existed. A few miles from the city centre where she worked and partied there were people who orbited a completely different universe. She had glimpsed it briefly during weekend visits to see Rosie at The Fairhaven, but eyeing the fabulously rich guests at the hotel with their luxury cars was completely different to rubbing shoulders with them on a regular basis. Marcus was unrelenting where Ruby was concerned and soon monopolised her every waking moment. Bouquets of beautiful flowers frequently arrived at work, making the other girls green with envy. He would collect her at the end of her shift whenever he could and whisk her off to a restaurant or back to his apartment where he would cook for her. There were luxury weekends away at beautiful hotels and parties at the golf club or the homes of his wealthy friends.

Marcus was extremely popular amongst all of his acquaintances, male and female and it hadn't gone unnoticed by Ruby that now and then, she would be on the receiving end of icy stares and contemptuous looks from beautiful women whom she suspected were ex-lovers. Despite this, when they were together he only had eyes for her and made her feel like she was the most important person in the room. Everything was going wonderfully until he announced that he would like her to meet his mother, and worse, they were invited for Sunday lunch the very next weekend. After politely accepting, Ruby went straight into panic mode, much to the enjoyment of her flatmates who teased her mercilessly, winding her up with their prophecies of engagement rings and Cheshire-Set weddings.

'That's it, Ruby. Before you know it you'll be up the aisle and producing the next Tarquins and Tabithas for the Cole dynasty. I can see you now in your Range Rover and Ralph Lauren jeans, popping off for a spot of lunch with footballers' wives, then after a couple of glasses of Chablis you'll be whizzing home to tell the chef what you'd like for dinner. I hope you won't forget your poor, loyal mates from the slums though.' Martine slurped her coffee from the mug for theatrical effect.

'Piss off, Martine! It's only Sunday lunch for God's sake. Anyone would think I was meeting the Queen the way you go on. Anyway, you've been to loads of blokes' houses to meet their mother, do you hear me laughing at you? But I can see now why you weren't asked back if that's how you drink your coffee, and get your feet off the table, you scruff.' Ruby had been raiding the wardrobes of her flatmates, desperately trying to find something suitable for the dreaded occasion.

She couldn't possibly buy another outfit from work, or anywhere. Over the past three months she'd spent every spare penny on making herself look presentable and was now totally skint. If she was honest, Ruby didn't even want to meet Marcus's mother. Things were fine just as they were and where bonding with other people's families was concerned, she had already learned her lesson the hard way. Ruby was adamant that this meeting was only a formality, out of politeness and respect to his mother, not something she would encourage or crave. As long as it made Marcus happy, that was all that mattered. Never again would she let her guard down and get close to anyone's family, she'd had a belly full of disappointment on that score.

It was for that reason, and a great pity really, that Ruby wasted the whole of Thursday night and the next two days worrying about meeting Marcus's mother. Despite her preparations and attempts to impress, it was quite clear by the time they set off in his car after brandy and mints that Olivia couldn't stand Ruby, would not be encouraging contact of any kind, and furthermore, couldn't wait to get her out of the house. Fortunately, the feeling was mutual.

Earlier, as they'd pulled off the main road lined with elegant mansions and gated properties, into a sweeping gravel courtyard large enough for at least four detached houses, Ruby held her breath in awe at Marcus's family home. It was a huge 1920's creation, with grand, squared windows whose glass glistened in the sunlight. The tall curving gables at each end gave the house a castle-like appearance with large white double doors situated in the centre, supported by grey marble pillars on either side of the impressive family motto, carved into the stone above. Perhaps Martine was right, thought Ruby nervously as she picked up her gift, smoothed down her skirt and checked her appearance in the mirror, The Queen might actually live here after all. Sensing her nervousness Marcus held her hand as they approached the front door which was dramatically swung open before they even had chance to ring the bell. Standing before them was Olivia, petite and curvaceous, she guarded the entrance in a mauve, woollen suit, beautifully cut and accessorised with a pearl brooch. Her perfectly polished shoes oozed class and showed off toned legs, encased in, what Ruby was sure were, pure silk stockings. Her hair was perfectly set and blown off her face in gentle waves of regal silver, the precision applied make-up was tasteful and masked her age well, which Ruby estimated to be in her late fifties. There was a pause, not quite an awkward silence and then she spoke.

'Ruby, how nice to meet you. Do come in.' Her cold, delicate hand shook Ruby's firmly, graciously accepting the gift-wrapped chocolates before she continued. 'Marcus has told me so much about you, here, let me take your coat and then we can go through to the drawing room and have a drink before lunch.'

Olivia hung Ruby's coat on the wooden stand before turning. There was something elegant about the way she walked that told her young guest she'd been schooled in deportment; she almost glided. They made their way into a beautifully decorated, pale yellow room, tastefully furnished with antiques and oil paintings where, with a flowing motion of her hand, she gestured for Ruby to sit in a grey velvet, high-back chair. It was strategically placed to one side of an ornate white marble fireplace that was adorned along its mantelpiece with a photographic homage to her son. Ruby thought it looked like an altar, festooned with images of Marcus the God, through the ages.

Accepting a gin and tonic from Marcus who was now playing waiter, Olivia sat opposite on an identical chair. They chatted about the weather, the waterlogged lawn, the drive over, her backgammon and bridge club which she hosted every Wednesday, and the sermon her friend, the vicar, had delivered that morning in church. The conversation droned on and on with a few polite questions thrown Ruby's way, just to keep her in the loop, niceties really about how she enjoyed her job and did she travel far to get there. Nothing too intrusive or difficult but apart from that, it was mainly the Marcus and Olivia show.

Finally, the housekeeper, Mrs Wallace, interrupted a tedious monologue about the Conservative Club Christmas Dance to inform them that lunch was ready, so once again, Olivia gestured with her hand that Ruby should rise and they followed obediently into the dining room. Lunch was bearable thanks to Olivia being a skilled and practised hostess, adept at making sure her guest had everything she needed and was enjoying the food. Apart from that, Ruby felt not one ounce of warmth or genuine interest flow along the polished, mahogany table in her direction. Olivia wasn't rude and didn't snub Ruby in any way, yet neither was she kind or welcoming. How could Marcus be related to this cold fish? He was so loving and generous and full of fun and warmth. Maybe he was adopted, thought Ruby as she despondently cut into her apple pie.

Eventually, and not before time, Ruby's ordeal came to an end. Marcus seemed oblivious to the fact that the two women he had just dined with seemed equally relieved to be saying goodbye, but it was clear to Ruby that Olivia had simply gone through the motions and probably couldn't wait for her to leave. At least she hadn't let herself or east Manchester down and had held her own with one of Cheshire's finest.

'Well, that went well. Did you enjoy yourself? I think you were a hit with my mother. She seemed to take to you straight away. And Mrs Wallace always puts on a marvellous spread. That apple pie was a triumph, don't you think?' Marcus rambled on, oblivious to his passenger's lack of enthusiasm as he sped through the country lanes, eager to get her back to the apartment for an evening of passion.

'Yes, it was lovely, Marcus, and so is your mother. I'm glad you think she liked me, and your home is beautiful by the way. I've had a lovely time.' As she said the words, Ruby knew that most of them were untrue. A feeling of deflation settled into her bones, unease made its presence felt and by the time she arrived at the apartment, self-doubt and low esteem were telling her to prepare for the worst.

The following week and to Ruby's surprise, the bad vibes she got from Olivia didn't seem to have permeated into Marcus and he was as keen as ever. The run up to Christmas was a constant round of cocktail parties, dinners and intimate soirees for two so having managed to put Olivia from her mind, she was caught on the back foot when Marcus invited her to spend the holidays with him and his mother at the family home.

Ruby was stunned to say the least. She inquired whether the invitation was directly from Olivia and whether it would be a bit of an intrusion, having a virtual stranger to stay for the festivities. She was totally unsurprised to learn that it was his idea, but Mother was thrilled and that Ruby would be more than welcome to join them. Nevertheless, Ruby had no intention of accepting his offer and, luckily, had a ready-made excuse.

'Marcus, that's a lovely idea. It would be wonderful to come to your mother's but I've already made plans. I think I *have* mentioned that I always spend Christmas with Rosie and have done for the past four years. It's sort of a tradition and I couldn't let her down. She's always been so good to me and the only close family I have left, really.' Ruby took a sip of her wine and noticed a flash of annoyance flick across Marcus's face, he recovered quickly though and placed his hand over hers.

'Darling, how stupid of me. Of course I remember, but I just wanted to make sure you had somewhere to go. I'd hate to think of you alone at Christmas so it's not a problem. What about over New Year, Mother hosts a fabulous party, perhaps you could come for that?' Marcus turned on the charm with one of his sexy, intense, straight in the eye stares.

It scored a bull's eye in her heart and Ruby was powerless to resist.

'Of course I'll come. And please thank your mother for me. I'll look forward to it. Now I'll have to find something suitably glamorous to wear for this party. I don't want to let you down.' Ruby hoped her little performance was convincing as the last place she wanted to be was in the company of Olivia and under her frosty scrutiny for days on end. And not only that, what the hell would she wear?

'Ruby, you never let me down and as for something glamorous, let me treat you. I want to make everyone at the party jealous because you're with me. We'll go shopping this weekend and there'll be no expense spared, you deserve it.' Marcus smiled and ordered another bottle of wine. He'd sealed the deal and got what he wanted.

Ruby, however, was blissfully unaware that this was merely the warm-up stages of a carefully devised plan. In the long run, Marcus fully intended to stake his claim on the young innocent before him, then take total control of his investment and make very good use of his newly acquired asset.

Everything was going well during Ruby's stay at Olivia's, mainly because they'd managed to keep out of each other's way. Olivia rose early and took long walks with her dogs, two huge black Labradors named Bertie and Boris. By the time Ruby and Marcus finally roused themselves, they were able to eat breakfast alone. Thankfully, they only used the house as a base and spent their days shopping or having lunch in one of the many country pubs dotted around the area. They were staying until the second of January and Ruby had been persuaded by Marcus to book a fortnight off work. It hadn't gone down well as she would miss the sales but seeing as she rarely went anywhere, her manager benevolently and unexpectedly relented. The change of heart by Ruby's stern manager was mainly due to the experienced persuasiveness of Marcus who telephoned to ask a special favour, not to mention the added bonus of theatre tickets and the semi-anonymous bouquet of white roses that was delivered to the office in Ladieswear.

New Year's Eve arrived and Marcus suddenly remembered he had to pop out on an errand and insisted that Ruby wait at the house and relax. Bored stiff, she sought out Mrs Wallace to ask if she could use the kitchen to make a cup of tea, still feeling like a stranger she didn't want to intrude into the housekeeper's domain. When Ruby popped her head round the door she found Mrs Wallace busily preparing canapés for that evening. She seemed like a lovely lady and always gave Ruby an encouraging smile when she was serving dinner or if they crossed paths somewhere in the house.

'Would it be alright to make some tea, Mrs Wallace? I won't get in your way. Shall I make you one, too?'

The housekeeper looked up from her chore and smiled gratefully. 'Oh, that would be lovely, Ruby dear, and there are some nice biscuits in the tin. I think I'll give my fingers a break from this and put them to good use with a piece of shortbread. Come on, let's treat ourselves.' Wiping her hands, Mrs Wallace waddled over to the biscuit tin and took it back to the table and plonked herself down on the chair, waiting for her cup of tea.

She watched contentedly as the pretty young girl with long fair hair busied herself with cups and plates. Ruby was so different from the other women Mr Cole usually brought home. She wasn't overly made up and annoyingly confident, dripping with designer clothes and jewellery and driving a sports car bought with Daddy's money. There had always been a theme running through his previous conquests but this time he'd broken with tradition and found himself someone with a bit of class, who seemed like a lovely person to boot. The only problem was that from what she'd observed, Mrs Cole didn't seem too keen on her son's choice of girlfriend, which was a bit of a shame really.

'These canapés look lovely, Mrs Wallace. You are clever. Perhaps you can show me how to make them. I wouldn't know where to start. Do you think I could have a go now and help you get ready for the party?' Ruby was fed up with reading and wandering around an empty house.

'Of course you can, my love, and I've got a few vol-au-vents that need stuffing so we can get on with those next. It'll be nice to have some company but there's no rush, let's polish off this shortbread first.' Mrs Wallace smiled and slid the biscuit tin over to her guest who smiled back.

Feeling relaxed for the first time in days, Ruby tucked in.

The party was everything that Marcus had described and more. The well-heeled glitterati of Prestbury pulled up in their expensive cars to mingle, drink champagne and dine on a sumptuous buffet prepared by Mrs Wallace. Ruby was introduced to everyone as she was guided around the room by Marcus who was revelling in the many compliments she received. The beautiful gown he had personally chosen gave her much needed confidence, its oyster, sequin and crystal beaded bodice emphasised her long neck and slender shoulders, then flowed elegantly to the ground in a swirl of sheer black chiffon. Ruby had nearly fainted when she saw the price tag of over a thousand pounds but he had insisted she have it. After their shopping spree, which included the purchase of shoes and a delicate bracelet to compliment her gown, she was taken for a makeover and given a dewy fresh look, one that Marcus said he preferred as he found overly made-up women a complete turn off. Her hair was pulled back into a sleek ponytail, secured by a simple beaded band to match her dress, and combined with her tasteful make-up and stunning gown, Ruby looked like she'd fallen off the cover of a magazine. A perfectly reproduced picture of elegance and style. Just how Marcus liked it.

As she sipped her drink, Ruby felt rather smug, remembering a conversation she'd had with Martine who had other ideas on the matter of her friend's burgeoning relationship, as did Kay and Jackie. They'd decided to have a word in Ruby's ear when they found out she wouldn't be partying with them at New Year. Everyone was getting a little fed up with their flatmate and her lack of loyalty.

'You've got to give it to him, Ruby, he sure knows how to impress but if you're not careful, he'll have you wrapped round his finger and at his beck and call before you know it. He's halfway there already. We've hardly seen you all over Christmas and you're never home anymore. I reckon you wouldn't even notice if we rented out your bedroom.' Martine was looking petulant and soon received back-up from Kay.

'Honestly, Ruby, we're really happy for you and all that but it's like he's taken over your life. We miss you and all we're saying is that you need to take a break from him, a couple of nights a week at least. And try to remember who you really are, and your mates too.'

Ruby rolled her eyes and told herself that it was jealousy talking.

Then Jackie piped up. 'It's not just your life he's taking over though, he's even changing the way you dress and how you speak. I know it's not such a bad thing because you work with the public, but it's as though he's moulding you into his idea of a perfect girlfriend. If you're not careful you'll end up being a Stepford wife.'

Ruby just shook her head and laughed along, choosing to ignore the very concerned and deadly serious look on her friend's face. So many times in the future, she would return to that Tuesday night in the house and instead of brushing their concerns under the carpet she would have sat down and listened to good advice and taken heed of erudite warnings. But she was in love with the kindest most generous and handsome man in Manchester. Nothing, not even her closest friends would spoil her happiness this time.

Ruby couldn't find Marcus anywhere. It was getting close to midnight and she wanted to be by his side when the clock struck twelve. The only place she hadn't looked was the kitchen which is exactly where she found him, right in the middle of having strong words with Olivia. Holding her breath, Ruby stood on the other side of the door in the darkness of the corridor, eavesdropping on their heated conversation.

'Mother, this is ridiculous. I'm not listening to another word. You can't tell me what to do anymore, I'm not a child!'

Ruby could hear the anger in his voice, which was a revelation in itself.

'Marcus, both you and I know so well that even as a child I had little influence on anything you did, but you will hear me out on this one. I am adamant that you do not propose to Ruby, do you hear me? She's not the one for you and for the life of me I cannot understand what you see in her. She's not your type and you are making a huge mistake!'

Ruby inhaled sharply. *'Oh my God, he's going to propose!'* Her brain went crazy at the thought of it and her heart hammered away in her chest as she listened in.

'You have no idea what my type is, Mother, and quite frankly, it's none of your business. Stop being a snob and leave me to make my own decisions. You were the one who told me to sort my life out and plan for the future so here I am, taking your advice for once.' This time, there was an element of sarcasm and a hint of ridicule in his voice.

'Don't you dare call me a snob, Marcus. I am nothing of the kind and you know it but this is all moving far too quickly and it will end in tears, you mark my words.'

Ruby could sense the fury in Olivia's voice, it almost sounded like she was losing control. Hearing footsteps behind her Ruby darted further along the corridor and tucked herself inside another doorway, shielded by a large storage cupboard. Then she heard Henry, one of Olivia's guests, calling her name.

'Olivia, there you are. Come along m'dear, it's almost midnight and we're all waiting. I've been searching everywhere. Is everything alright, you look quite flustered?' Henry had stopped in the hallway, holding the kitchen door open and casting light onto the marble floor tiles.

Ruby prayed no one would see her, it would be too humiliating. Marcus spoke next.

'Everything is just perfect, Henry, thank you very much. We were just on our way. See you in a moment, Mother. I'm going to find Ruby, if I have your permission that is?'

Ruby heard his footsteps as he marched off, followed immediately by Olivia and Henry. She couldn't hear what they were muttering but she knew it would be about her. Well, it was official then. Olivia hated her and had done her best to prevent Marcus from proposing. It was all down to him now. All she could do was wait until midnight to see if he had it in him to go against his mother's wishes and in doing so, make Ruby the happiest woman alive.

Ruby lay on her side, staring out of the window as clouds flitted across the New Year's Day moon. It was 3am and she couldn't sleep. Her mind kept going over and over the evening's events while she blinked back tears and tried to quell the feeling of impending doom. Olivia had won! There had been no proposal when the clock struck twelve and an array of fireworks streaked across the sky as kisses were exchanged and the champagne flowed. Just for a second though, Ruby thought she'd triumphed when Marcus took her by the hand and led her into the library. As they stood by the patio doors in the quiet room surrounded by books, the only sounds they could hear were screeches and bangs from the multi-coloured displays exploding in the jet black sky. Telling her he had a little surprise, Marcus reached into his pocket and her elated heart pounded with sheer joy, until he pulled out a long white envelope containing first-class tickets to Dubai. Ruby admonished herself for being the most ungrateful woman on earth but as she sobbed in the darkness while Marcus slept peacefully by her side, she couldn't banish her disappointment and her growing resentment of Olivia.

She needn't have worried though, because one week later, while they sat watching the sunset at the foot of the floodlit Safran Tower in the Al Wadi desert, gazing at the burnt orange dunes and eating Thai food, created and served by their personal chef and butler, Marcus once again reached into his pocket, got down on bended knee and proposed to Ruby. And of course, not missing a single heartbeat, she said yes.

Chapter 6
Ruby 2010

R uby carried Lily upstairs. She needed to get her changed before dropping her off at Olivia's. It was imperative that both children looked immaculate, leaving no room for criticism or the need to tell tales to Marcus – he thought she was a bad enough mother without her mother-in-law chipping in. The relationship between Ruby and Olivia was one of polite tolerance and apart from the odd glimmer here and there it hadn't warmed up with the passing of years. She came to Sunday lunch once a fortnight, sometimes alone, sometimes with Henry her companion. Ruby wasn't sure of the exact nature of Olivia's relationship with the gentle giant of a man who played tirelessly with Oliver and Lily, but one thing was for sure, Marcus hated him.

When Olivia announced over lunch her intention to move Henry into the family home, Marcus managed to keep a lid on his emotions in front of his mother. Once the coast was clear, he predictably flew into a fit of rage and began knocking back the whisky and, inevitably, knocking Ruby around their bedroom walls, too.

Henry was an old acquaintance and his relationship with Olivia went back many years. He was widowed and childless and rattled around a large house in Alderley Edge and frequently acted as Olivia's plus-one at social events. They often spent evenings together, reading and listening to Radio 4, occasionally taking day trips and weekend breaks. After he suffered a serious fall and needed care and somewhere to convalesce, Olivia kindly invited him to stay with her and during this time they realised that him moving in permanently would be a perfect solution to their oversized housing situation. Ruby knew they had separate sleeping arrangements because Oliver had told her that Henry had billions of books all over his bedroom and it smelt of pipe smoke, but Granny's room was always tidy and smelt of flowers. Other than that, they did everything together and Ruby didn't pry because for the most part Olivia kept out of her business so she willingly returned the compliment.

What surprised Ruby more than anything was that despite her opinion and observations of Olivia, Oliver and Lily appeared to totally adore their grandmother. Lily had decided to call her Golly which they presumed was a two year olds combination of Granny and Olivia, and followed her around like a lovesick puppy. Oliver couldn't wait to get out of the door fast enough when she arrived to collect them and constantly begged to sleep over at The Castle, as he called it. Ruby often wondered if his eagerness had a lot to do with the dreadful atmosphere in their own house, because most days, she felt the same and would give anything to be able to rush out of the door, jump in a car and escape. But in her case it certainly wouldn't be with Olivia.

Over Sunday lunch, her mother-in-law religiously behaved in much the same way as she did when they dined at hers. Always thankful and polite, she would offer to help Ruby in the kitchen which Marcus forbade as she was the guest, so instead, Olivia entertained the children, sending them into fits of giggles until they were inevitably told to calm down and behave at the table by their kill-joy father. She also never, ever complained or criticised Ruby's cooking but didn't over compliment her either. Olivia really was the proverbial cold fish and extremely hard to fathom.

Even where Marcus was concerned, the only warmth or contact between mother and son that Ruby ever witnessed was as she pecked him on the cheek when they said goodbye. '*Pair of weirdos*,' was the sour thought that crossed Ruby's mind on more than one occasion. She had hoped that once they were married, Olivia would thaw slightly but it wasn't to be, even the arrival of Oliver didn't do the trick so Ruby gave up trying. In her lowest moments, she imagined it would have been nice to have had a mother figure to help her choose her wedding dress or give advice about married life and baby matters, but in reality, Ruby was definitely barking up the wrong tree and remained isolated and lonely.

***

After the grand proposal, things had moved extremely quickly. It was clear that neither her flatmates nor her prospective mother-in-law were going to dance a jig following the announcement and one evening, after dinner with Marcus, she made a decision that further displeased both parties.

'So, I was thinking, now we've told everyone, perhaps we should set a date, the sooner the better as far as I'm concerned. I don't want to run the risk of you changing your mind and scooting off with someone else.' Marcus swirled his brandy around his glass, watching her intently.

'Shut up you fool! I'm not thinking of scooting anywhere, unless it's with you. But when did you have in mind, is there a proper time limit? I don't want to upset your mother.' Ruby sipped her water and waited expectantly.

'Well as it happens, I had a look at my diary and I've got quite a few trips booked during spring but I'm free for all of July, so maybe we could do it then. Is that too soon?' Marcus gave her one of his worried looks and her heart melted.

'Do you mean this July, Marcus, or July next year?' Ruby was slightly taken aback and didn't want to appear too eager.

'This year, of course. Do you think for one minute I'm going to wait forever to make you mine? I want a ring on your finger as soon as possible, but if you think it's too soon and we haven't had time to get to know each other, I have a little suggestion that might persuade you to take me on. I can tell you have reservations, so just let me explain.' A cheeky, boyish grin spread across his face as he grasped her hand, entwining their fingers.

'What if you moved in with me right now? It seems foolish that you pay rent at your place when you are always at mine, and it would be like a trial run. Then you could test drive me and whittle away all my annoying faults before we even say, "I do". How's that for a deal? Please say yes. I've thought of nothing else all day.' He ended the performance with one of his intense, smouldering stares and her answer was a foregone conclusion.

Ruby loved living in the apartment, which was a far cry from her small room in Reddish. She had a fabulous view of the city skyline from the decked roof terrace and she adored the polished black marbled floors in the stainless steel kitchen. The bathroom was sheer luxury and the lounge was filled with contemporary furniture and sleek leather sofas. Marcus said she could do whatever she wanted to put her mark on it, giving her a credit card to spend on anything she needed, especially while he was away.

The day Ruby drove him to the airport to see him off on his month-long trip to the Far East, she thought her heart would break at the prospect of being apart for so long. He in turn, made her feel terribly guilty, portraying his heavy workload and visits to factory sweatshops in the searing heat, followed by boring business meetings spent haggling down prices. Then, there'd be hideously long evenings entertaining tiresome buyers, listening to their boring drivel when all he really wanted was to be at home, in bed with her.

What Marcus was really thinking was a different story entirely. As he boarded his Singapore Airlines flight and took his seat in first class, he told himself that if he didn't score with one of the cabin crew during the flight over there would still be plenty of time to hit the brothels and nightclubs of every city that he and Roman visited on their tour. He'd done his family duty and lined up a nice wife and child-bearer, successfully reeling her in to ensure she was so grateful for the life she'd become accustomed to that she would do exactly as she was told. All he had to do now was get rid of her common, annoying friends and that cousin of hers, then he would be home and dry.

Marcus didn't want anyone interfering in his life, not even his mother but she already knew to keep her distance. Moving Ruby in was a master stroke and once they were married he'd make sure the lot of them were out of the picture. Nodding curtly to the attendant he ordered a drink and decided that until he got back, he was going to forget about his fiancée and enjoy himself. He'd earned some fun and was going to let his hair down, with anyone who was willing. Marcus knew from experience that the women over there were eager to take his money and would do whatever he wanted, literally. *'And let's be honest,'* he thought to himself as he smirked and took a swig of champagne, *'it's nothing a shot of penicillin can't cure once I get home.'*

Ruby knew that Martine and her roommates were unhappy with her news and there had been a really weird atmosphere when she packed up her things and moved out of the house. The get-together she had arranged that night was by way of an apology and an attempt to bring them onside. She desperately wanted them at her wedding, not only because they were her best friends but apart from Rosie, Aunty Doreen and Uncle Jim, her side of the registry office was going to be rather empty. She had pushed the boat out and bought plenty of wine and lovely food, and they had all agreed to stay over.

They all took a while to warm up but once they'd knocked back a few glasses of wine and embraced their surroundings, sitting on the terrace looking over the skyline of Manchester whilst eating Indian food, the ice began to thaw. Partly due to the wine and Martine's pep talk on the way over, Jackie and Kay did as they were told and let bygones be bygones and got into the swing of things, making plans for her hen night and choosing wedding outfits from magazines. Ruby was having a ball and feeling very drunk and slightly wistful, remembering nights just like these when she first moved into their house, when the phone rang bringing her straight back to reality. Trying in vain to make them shush and turn the music down she picked up the receiver to hear Marcus's voice at the other end. Placing her hand over the speaker, she ran into the bedroom where she could hear him properly.

'What the hell is going on there? It sounds like you've got a herd of screaming banshees in my apartment. What the hell do you think you're playing at, Ruby?' Marcus was furious and for once, had let his saintly mask slip.

'Marcus, calm down. It's just the girls. I invited them over for some drinks. I've not seen them for ages and I never get a chance to catch up with Martine properly at work. I'm sorry but I didn't think you'd mind.' Ruby gulped and realised she was trembling slightly. She had never heard him so angry, ever.

'Well, I'm not bloody happy about it, Ruby, and actually, I do mind. I'm out here, thousands of miles away, missing you like crazy and then I find out you're having a wild party at my expense. I'm working my backside off in this sweat box and all you can think about is your damn friends. I'm really hurt to be honest. I didn't think you were so selfish.' Marcus played his hand well and waited for Ruby's apology. He was in for a shock.

'Actually, Marcus, I think you're the one that is out of order here. Firstly, I thought this was *our* apartment now, not yours. You gave me a credit card so I could look after myself while you were away and insisted I made good use of it, so I am. I've invited my friends around to discuss the wedding and yes, they may have had one too many to drink but it's not against the law. As for work, I'm sure you are hard at it over there but it's not without its benefits, is it? I had a look at the hotel where you're staying and it's not exactly a two-star boarding house. For your information, I work hard too and I'm entitled to let my hair down once in a while. If you have any objections to anything I've said, I will give you your credit card and keys back and go home with the girls right this second, do you hear me?' Ruby's cheeks were hot and she was mad as hell.

Maybe the wine had made her brave but she meant every word she said. As she listened and waited for a response, it finally dawned on her that the line had gone dead. Walking back into the lounge she realised she may have gone too far and before she knew it, her bravado had evaporated along with her flash of indignant independence. He had obviously slammed the phone down after her rant and would be even more furious now. Taking a swig of wine to steady her nerves, Ruby went back to her friends, not wanting them to know what had gone on – she wasn't in the mood for teasing. In fact, she wasn't in the mood for anything but put on a brave face and got on with the night, despite the nauseating storm of fear and anxiety swirling around her heart.

He didn't call at all the following day or in the evening and consequently, Ruby spent a miserable Sunday cleaning and worrying and listening for the phone. She rang his hotel to apologise but was told he was out. She sent texts which he ignored, so instead, she sat it out and waited. At 10am on Monday morning as she stood at her counter folding silk scarves, a huge bouquet of lilies was delivered with a note apologising for being tired and grumpy. Marcus said that the line had gone dead mid-conversation and he needed to get to a meeting and had been crazy busy since, but he sent love and kisses and a million 'sorry's'. The tension drained from Ruby's body and relief flowed through her veins, just from knowing he'd forgiven her and even better, he mustn't have heard her drunken rant either. Instantly, she felt guilty because he was miles away from home and missing her while she'd behaved like a spoilt girlfriend and spat her dummy out. Ruby spent the rest of the day calling his hotel and leaving messages promising to make it up to him as soon as he got home.

It was music to Marcus's ears when the concierge handed him a folded slip of paper, passing on her numerous messages and simpering apology – he knew he had her on the back foot. He'd been livid when he rang the apartment and heard those slappers screeching in his home. When she dared to answer him back and threatened to leave he flew into a seething rage, slamming the phone down and storming out of the hotel. He eventually took his temper out on an unfortunate young streetwalker who regretfully invited him back to her room and paid dearly for Ruby's outburst. Later, as he made his way back to the hotel, trying to blend in with the other men who roamed the streets posing as tourists, who in reality were looking for cheap, no strings sex, Marcus realised that this time he may have gone too far. His knuckles were bruised, there was blood on his shirt and he was nervous. He just hoped the prostitute wouldn't call the police, praying that the occasional beating was just an accepted hazard of her job and she'd keep quiet.

As for Ruby, while she languished in the land of forgiveness and stupidity, arranging her flowers in the crystal vase she'd bought from Martine, she had no idea that whenever Marcus remembered her insolence she would be punished for stepping out of line that night. In addition, he was now more determined than ever to be rid of her common ex-housemates, once and for all.

The wedding went according to plan and took place on a sunny July afternoon at the registry office inside Manchester Town Hall and was attended by Marcus's cronies, extended family, and his mother's close circle of friends. Ruby had her cousin by her side as bridesmaid, along with her three ex-flatmates and with the permission of Rosie, who had made an awkward peace with her parents, Aunty Doreen and Uncle Jim made up the numbers. Ruby hadn't had any regular contact from Stella in over two years and the last she'd heard, via Doreen, was that Ricky the store manager had retired and they'd bought a place in Alicante. Presumably, her mother was busy relieving him of his life savings and topping up her tan, so Ruby thought it best all round to leave her in ignorance. There was no way on this earth that she would have invited Stella anyway, the damage had been done years ago and over her dead body would she allow anyone or anything to ruin her big day.

Surprisingly, Marcus had left the choice of wedding dress to Ruby who had unwittingly been well trained in his likes and dislikes and was therefore able to pick something she knew he would approve of, however subliminally. Owing to bad timing and cancelled arrangements, always due to Marcus's heavy schedule, Rosie finally met him during the pre-wedding dinner he'd arranged just seven days before the big day. Here, he laid on the charm and did his best to impress, flashing the cash whilst asking all the right questions and appearing terribly interested in his fiancée's closest relative. In reality, he was trying to ascertain the threat level that she posed to his relationship and on hearing she would be spending more time abroad in the future, deemed her to be of little consequence.

On the night before the wedding, as Ruby and Rosie relaxed in their luxury hotel room provided by Marcus, drinking champagne and ordering treats from the room service menu, they reminisced and laughed, and shed a few overemotional, alcohol-induced tears.

'So, tell me honestly, what do you think of Marcus? You know sometimes, I can't believe my luck. It seems like a fairy tale come true. I still have to pinch myself to believe it's all real.' Ruby lay on her back, admiring the intricate coving around the ornate ceiling.

'Well, nobody can deny that he adores you. He couldn't take his eyes off you last week at dinner and I was beginning to feel like a spare part. As long as you are one hundred percent sure that it's not too soon. It has been a bit of a whirlwind romance and my only concern is that you haven't got to know him, warts and all, yet.' Rosie was desperate not to put a downer on her cousin's happiness so voiced her concerns as tactfully and honestly as she could.

'Oh, don't you start as well, Rosie. I've heard all this from Martine and the girls. I know it's quick but we *have* been living together for the past six months and we get on so well. It's been perfect and as Marcus says, we've got our whole lives to get to know each other. So stop worrying and pour me another drink. You'll get frown lines if you carry on.' Ruby brushed off her cousin's words, determined that nothing would spoil her mood.

'Okay, you win. It's just that I've got so used to looking after you all these years and it's hard to let go and now I'm going to be travelling more, I worry that you won't have someone close by if you need anything. As long as you know that I'm always at the end of the phone and I don't care what time zone I'm in, I want you to promise that you'll ring me.' Rosie's eyes swam with tears and her heart ached for her cousin. Despite Ruby's good fortune and undeniable happiness there was something about Marcus that didn't ring true and it filled her with a niggling unease.

Ruby sniffed and reached for a tissue. 'Look, you're making *me* cry now. I promise I will ring if I need you and we will keep in touch, just like we always have. Nothing can ever come between us. But please don't worry, I've got Marcus now and he will take care of me. You can go off on your travels and forget all about me for once in your life and concentrate on having a good time.' Ruby wiped her eyes and gave Rosie a huge hug, clinging on. As the tears subsided and just about managing to stop her voice from breaking, she continued.

'I remember when we were little and you used to hold my hand when we walked to the park or went round the shops with Aunty Doreen. I used to look up at you and just knowing you were there made me feel so safe and secure. I always felt like I was a scruffy little sparrow and you were a golden eagle, sent to take care of me. That's what I picture in my mind whenever I think of us growing up and I'll never forget it, Rosie, ever. If you hadn't been there to guide me and be my friend, God knows where I would've ended up. I realise things are changing again but I want you to know that I owe you so much and you will always be my best friend, forever and ever.'

The tears fell again as they both clung on until chief bridesmaid Rosie called time and pulled rank, sensibly insisting they didn't want to turn up the next day with red-rimmed, puffy eyes and needed to pull themselves together, pronto.

Wiping their eyes and blowing noses, without further ado they spent the rest of the evening plucking eyebrows and slapping on face cream. Rosie stored away her doubts and focused her mind on making sure that her little sparrow had the best wedding day in the whole world.

Married life was mostly blissful, interspersed with melancholy shades of darkness, black moments that tilted Ruby's world from its axis before being gratefully restored to a state of harmony. The lapses were always caused by Marcus's moods and jealous tendencies, blamed always on Ruby's thoughtlessness and lack of regard for his feelings. They continued to live at the quayside apartment as it was convenient for work. Marcus did point out on a regular basis that Ruby had no need to sell dresses anymore as he could provide for both of them, to which she firmly replied that she enjoyed her independence and would be bored out of her mind all day at home. He took this on the chin for a while but gradually, whittled away any joy she took from going to work by waiting for her outside the store most evenings, thus preventing any socialising in the pub across the way or even an innocent chat with her colleagues as they strolled to the bus stop.

Ruby dreaded being invited to birthday meals or staff functions as it would inevitably end up in a row followed by one of his sulky moods which made being in the apartment unbearable. Ruby tried to reason with him by explaining that he could trust her implicitly and had no need to be jealous and there was no way that Martine could lead her astray when she had the most wonderful husband in the world.

Even mentioning the fact that he attended business lunches and dinners and frequently travelled without her was quickly brushed off as being irrelevant, it was part of his job and a necessity. Eventually though, he wore her down and she began turning down invitations as it wasn't worth the trouble at home. Soon people stopped asking, including Martine, who'd become distant and sat with the other girls in the canteen now. Before she knew it, Ruby was isolated and alone, both at work and at home which by coincidence was around the time Marcus decided they should start a family.

At first Ruby wasn't sure about the idea. She was only twenty-three and thought they should get a couple of years of married bliss under their belt before having a baby, but her life had begun to lack lustre so gradually she warmed to the possibility. Not one to let the grass grow, that October, right in the middle of her monthly cycle, Marcus arranged a surprise birthday trip to New York and whisked her off to the airport in a flurry of excitement and hastily packed bags. On arrival, to Ruby's concern, she realised that in the rush to leave she'd left her contraceptive pills at home which meant relying on Marcus taking precautions while they were away.

On their first night in the Big Apple, following a very lavish dinner and rather too much wine, Ruby sampled the very best that Marcus had to offer in the bedroom department and amidst the passion, forgot all about birth control. Once they realised, Ruby was treated to a fine example of her husband's practised sales technique, smoothly selling her the line that they might already have made a baby, so they may as well forget about contraception and let nature take its course. They *were* thinking of having a family, after all.

What Marcus omitted to tell Ruby was that the missing packet of pills was actually lying in the bottom of a waste bin in the toilets at Manchester Airport. He'd removed them from her case and then slyly slipped them into his jacket pocket. One month later, when Ruby took a pregnancy test and the two blue lines appeared in the little window it came as no shock to both of them that she was pregnant, especially Marcus.

Oliver was born the following August after a long, drawn out and very painful labour lasting eighteen excruciating hours which resulted in a horrendous forceps delivery. All of which Marcus missed when he was mysteriously delayed after missing two flights from Istanbul. The birth *was* witnessed though, by Olivia who, to Ruby's surprise, came running to the rescue and steadfastly held her hand, mopped her brow and whispered words of comfort and encouragement throughout the whole hideous ordeal. Later, once the nurses and doctor had done their thing, Ruby witnessed a rare moment of compassion as her mother-in-law helped her wash and change into a clean nightie, fussing and caring for her like a real mum would. When calm was restored to the private room and Ruby was settled, Olivia held her tiny grandson in her arms for the first time. Wiping away tears she looked up at her daughter-in-law and through misty eyes, spoke with genuine emotion.

'He's perfect, Ruby, just perfect. Thank you so much for bringing him into the world. We shall both have to take very good care of him, very good care. I never thought this would happen, that I would have a grandchild and for that I owe you a great debt of gratitude.'

Looking down at Oliver, she seemed lost in her thoughts for a while so Ruby left her in peace, committing the picture to memory just in case it was the last time she ever saw the softer, kinder side of her mother-in-law.

For what Ruby could only imagine was a reward for bringing her grandson into the world, Olivia made an extremely grand gesture and bought them a brand new home in Prestbury, just around the corner from her. It was a wrench leaving the apartment but Ruby had become isolated and lonely there, especially during the latter part of her pregnancy after completely losing touch with Martine, Kay and Jackie. Even though Rosie was on the phone all the time it didn't make up for a real live person to talk to or share your worries with.

When they eventually moved into their spanking new, four bedroomed home on an exclusive gated estate, Ruby hoped it would be a fresh start, a place where they could put down roots and make new friends. Marcus at first bemoaned the fact that it was too close to his mother and that they'd never be rid of her, a thought that had flashed across Ruby's mind more than once making her feel guilty and ungrateful. As it happened, this couldn't have been further from the truth. Olivia was the soul of tact and discretion and never overstepped the mark, instead, she made sure that she was always on hand if and when she was ever required for babysitting duties but never insisted on or demanded contact with Oliver. All of which was a huge relief to Ruby who needed her more often than expected, especially as she was shattered, due mainly to sleepless nights and after it became crystal clear that Marcus had no intention whatsoever of doing his bit where his son was concerned.

Ruby did manage to make one friend but only for a while because once again, Marcus put the mockers on it. Rather than being able to nurture a friendship which was entirely innocent and within the boundaries of mutual motherhood, Ruby was forced to survive on the scraps that he deemed acceptable and didn't encroach on their fake family time together. She met Liz at the baby clinic where she took Oliver to be weighed and they hit it off almost instantly. With two little girls already and her new baby daughter in tow, Liz was the calming voice of reason and giver of advice where night feeds, teething problems and nappy rash were concerned. It was nice to have someone to call if she was worried about weaning or colic and as they pushed their prams around the park on summer afternoons, Ruby thought she'd found a friend, at last.

At first, Marcus didn't mind because socially, Liz ticked all the right boxes. Her husband was quite high up within the local borough council; they lived on one of the better estates and sent their eldest daughter to a private school. The Olivia connection also helped, she knew Liz's father from church, so Marcus was loathe to ruffle any feathers and kept quiet, for a time. But things soon began to go wrong when their friendship attempted any movement outside the perimeter of childcare. If Liz suggested finding babysitters and a shopping trip into town then perhaps some lunch, Marcus objected on the grounds that Ruby shouldn't be gallivanting off without Oliver. She also shouldn't impose on his mother either because Ruby's job was in the home, caring for their son.

Liz felt desperately sorry for her lonely young friend who seemed to have no family support and little life away from the four walls of her beautiful home, and if she was honest, didn't care much for Marcus or his pretend friendliness. Whenever he popped home early and found them sitting in the garden playing with the children, the atmosphere plummeted and Ruby's whole persona visibly changed. Marcus gave Liz the creeps and she suspected he was spying on them. Still, she stuck at it and rather than abandon Ruby, only suggested shopping trips and excursions that included children, therefore ensuring Ruby's inclusion and the approval of her husband.

When Ruby found out she was pregnant the second time around it really was a huge shock as romantically things hadn't been going too well and their lacking love life had been of concern to Ruby for a while. Following the birth of Oliver, Marcus rarely showed her any affection and whenever she tried to broach the subject he was dismissive and hurtfully blamed his disinterest on her flabby bits or even worse, that leaky breasts and her 'mumsiness' was a bit of a turn off. Ruby worked hard to get her figure back, longing for the days when he couldn't keep his hands off her body, treating her to beautiful lingerie before making love to her for hours. The only time she could remember him being slightly interested in her sexually was when he was drunk and that turned out to be a quick fumble in the dark, satisfying only his needs. So it was with mixed emotions that over dinner one night she told him her surprise news, and it was with a heavy heart and tear-filled eyes that she heard his cruel response.

'Typical! You just start looking half-decent again and then you get pregnant. Only *you* could be that stupid. I suppose it's better to get it over with and out of the way now, but just so you know there'll be no more after this. The last thing I want is a dumpy wife popping out sprogs every five minutes. I didn't marry a baby machine and Oliver never shuts up wailing as it is. Looks like we'll just have to get on with it, but I mean it, after this one you'll have to get sterilised or whatever it is you have done, but no more, understand?' Marcus was pointing his knife at her as he spoke then took a gulp of wine and carried on eating his steak, oblivious to the distress he'd caused his wife.

That night signalled the beginning of the end for Ruby, and her marriage if she was completely honest. They carried on their charade all through her pregnancy, putting on a united front for Olivia and on the few occasions that she came to visit, for Rosie too. Marcus had little interest in Oliver unless they were in company where she had to admit he put on quite a show, playing the proud daddy and family man. Generally, he wasn't actually violent, just moody and belligerent, pushing her off him if she showed affection and using punishment and reward tactics to keep control. He would throw things or smash them up when he was in a temper and she dreaded him having a drink, so in the end, Ruby simply toed the line, grateful for any scrap of happiness or kindness that he allowed into her existence.

If Olivia suspected anything was wrong she never confronted either of them, apart from the odd comment to Ruby that she looked pale, or a bit tired and drawn which she took as a criticism and not the opportunity to tell her mother-in-law what really went on behind closed doors. To be fair to Olivia, she was always available to take Oliver off her hands for a couple of hours while she rested and was also there to welcome Lily into the world after a thankfully quicker and less traumatic labour than the first time.

Once again, Olivia was present throughout and took care of Ruby as if she were her own. When Marcus finally arrived at the hospital with Roman, three hours too late and straight off the London train, semi-drunk and stinking of whisky he interrupted a rare and special moment between Ruby and Olivia. The two women were sitting drinking a cup of tea in the relative calm of the private room when Lily woke from a mini nap and began making hungry noises from her cot.

'Why don't you feed her, Olivia? You can give Lily her first bottle, you only got a quick cuddle earlier and I think she needs a hug from her Granny.' Ruby wanted to offer the hand of gratitude, recognising the fact that had it not been for her mother-in-law, whipping into action and leaving Oliver in the capable hands of Mrs Wallace and Henry, she would have given birth alone with only the nurses for company.

As she watched Olivia feed Lily, Ruby began to doze and must have fallen asleep for a few minutes only to be woken by the sound of sobbing. Opening her eyes, Ruby was stunned to see Olivia gently rocking Lily to sleep as tears coursed down her cheeks and small sobs escaped into the dimly lit room.

Ruby spoke softly in a voice full of concern. 'Olivia, what's the matter, are you okay, is something wrong?'

Looking up, pain was etched all over Olivia's face as she tried valiantly to control her emotions.

'It's alright, my dear. I'll be fine. I was just being a silly old woman and letting my mind run away with itself. I was just remembering...' and then Marcus burst into the room and the moment was lost.

Olivia recovered quickly and returned to her normal self, admonishing Marcus gently for his poor timekeeping and alcohol-laced breath. After assuring Ruby that Oliver would be fine staying with her until she came out of hospital and directing one last, withering look in the direction of her son, she was gone. Ruby never again brought up that night in the hospital and normal relations were resumed once she got home. Maybe what she witnessed may have been the result of a cocktail of gas and air, pain killers and her imagination.

Lily was the perfect baby, never any trouble and settled quickly into a routine which made Ruby's life a little easier because her world had further descended into chaos. Over the next year, Marcus began to spiral out of control. His behaviour was erratic and his drinking bouts worsened while his business trips were more frequent and nights away from home a regular occurrence, staying overnight in his apartment in town which he'd kept as an investment. Ruby suspected that not only was it convenient and within staggering distance after a bender, he probably used it to entertain women because for a while she had suspected he was having an affair. If she questioned his behaviour in any way or stepped over the mark he had clearly defined, whether it was regarding suitable activities for Oliver or visiting her one and only friend, he would fly into a rage and beat away any resistance.

The final straw came when she found the packet of powder in the bathroom. It must have fallen out of his trouser pocket and lay nonchalantly in the bottom of the laundry basket and Ruby knew what it was the second she laid eyes on it. The drinking was bad enough and the womanising, but taking drugs and bringing them into their home, he really had stooped low this time. After a whole morning sat in stunned silence staring at the television, not taking in a word of whatever Phillip and Fern were wittering on about, Ruby realised she was in a deep hole and worse, had nobody to help her climb out.

Olivia was blinded to her son's faults due to his well-rehearsed Oscar winning performances. She wouldn't dream of telling Liz – the shame was too much to bear and what if it got out? Oliver was due to start big school soon and imagine if the headmaster got wind of it, he might lose his place. Even though Liz had remained loyal and kept in touch via texts, apart from chatting in the yard when they dropped off and collected the children from nursery, they'd drifted apart. Consequently, Ruby withdrew into her own private world of secrecy and bruise concealment, marking time and dodging bullets. The only joy in her life came via her children and as long as the mud Marcus threw didn't stick to them, she was determined to find the strength to carry on and in the meantime, hope for a miracle.

***

'*What a mess, what a truly awful mess,*' thought Ruby as she fastened Lily into her car seat. As she pulled away from the house and drove towards Olivia's she wondered, not for the first time either, what her mother-in-law would say if she knew the truth about the monster she'd created. Secretly, Ruby blamed Olivia for most of Marcus's failings; after all, someone had to be responsible for how he'd turned out. Within minutes, they'd arrived at the castle and

Ruby swung the car onto the gravel drive just as Lily began to kick her legs in excitement, chanting 'Golly. Golly, Golly'.

'*I give up,*' thought Ruby. '*This woman must have hidden talents that only my children can see.*' Resignedly, she unfastened Lily and made her way to the front door where Olivia appeared instantly and after making small talk about her precious, hard-working son, took the giddy baby from Ruby's arms, assuring her that she could take as long as she liked and that Henry would pick Oliver up from school.

'If Marcus is going to be late, why don't you make the most of your freedom while I have the children? I can give them their dinner and a bath if you like. I'll have them both ready for seven so you can have some me time, how does that sound?' Olivia was always eager to spend quality time with her grandchildren so on this occasion, Ruby definitely wasn't going to disappoint or refuse her.

'That would be lovely, Olivia, thank you. I might have a look round the shops and I need to pick up some new school trousers for Oliver, oh, and collect Marcus's dry-cleaning on the way back. I'll see you at seven then.' Ruby kissed Lily then hurried back to her car.

Ruby drove away and onto the main road with a huge grin on her face because she now had seven hours of freedom to look forward to. She had no intention of going to the doctors or the opticians and had only made the appointments to cover her tracks just in case Marcus rang and checked up, because she wouldn't put it past him. It was so rude just to not turn up and it was wasting people's time but needs must, and it was a necessary part of her life now – sneaking about and not telling the truth. Instead of being prodded and poked at the private clinics she was really driving over to Cheadle to meet Rosie who was there on a flying visit to see Aunty Doreen who was sick.

They were going to have lunch and spend the afternoon catching up before she flew back to France that evening. The unwitting lifeline Olivia had given her meant she could now take Rosie to the airport and prolong their time together. For once, Ruby's heart was filled with expectation and excitement as she made her way along the country lanes. She couldn't wait to see her cousin again, even if it was only for a few, precious hours.

Chapter 7
Rosie 1998

The train pulled slowly out of the station, taking Rosie away from her forlorn cousin, Cheadle and her parents. Rosie sat alone on a tatty seat looking at her solitary reflection in the window. She hardly recognised the pale face which was distorted and blurred by the vibration of the train as it jiggled along the tracks. Her blonde hair looked tangled and lank, thanks to the persistent drizzle and howling rain that she'd endured as she sat at the bus stop and her aching bones were still chilled from the long, boring wait. The fact that she was a lonesome traveller seemed to be illuminated by the harsh, bright light of the empty carriage. Rosie stared back at the stranger in the glass who'd been forced into the spotlight of a drama, not of her making, but in which she had a starring role. This only made her think of her two co-stars and she wondered how her parents were feeling right now.

Rosie checked her phone just in case there was a message of apology or at the very least a request to return home and attempt to sort things out. But the screen was blank and perversely, Rosie was glad because it proved beyond a doubt that she had been right to leave. The fact she had no desire whatsoever to make things up with her parents meant she harboured not a trace of guilt over her actions. They were both stubborn, cold fish who probably thought they were being clever, hatching a master plan no doubt conceived by her mother, to sit it out and wait for her to come home with her tail between her legs. Well, how wrong and stupid could two people be? No, she was free now and there would be no going back, she'd made her bed and yes, she would lie in it, however hard and uncomfortable it might turn out to be.

The train slowed as it pulled into Alderley Edge station. Rosie stood and grabbed her case, then dragged it to the doors, feeling nervous as they slid open and she stepped onto the platform. Hearing her name being called, Rosie searched among the faces of passengers boarding or alighting the train and spotted Laura and her mum, standing by the exit. An overwhelming surge of unexpected emotions overcame her and by the time she reached them, her nervousness had vanished and was replaced by fatigue as a culmination of the weekend's events suddenly caught up with her. Within seconds, she found herself wrapped in concerned arms whilst being whispered words of comfort as she was ferried to the car in floods of tears. To her relief and eternal gratitude, after she was taken in, listened to and actually allowed an opinion, Rosie's new life of freedom and opportunity began.

Laura's mother Natasha, or Tash as she preferred to be known, was what you would term as 'right on' and of a spiritual nature, believing that children should be free to explore and develop at their own pace and discover their true path through their mistakes and endeavours. Along with being kind, easy to talk to and a very good listener, she also worked for social services and had a degree in psychology. Tash therefore, was well versed in the problems of modern society, family issues of varying natures and in particular, troubled teenagers. Having had the displeasure of bumping into Doreen on many occasions over the years at parents' evenings or school events, Tash was of the opinion that Rosie's mother was a bigoted, obnoxious, stuck-up cow and therefore tried to avoid her whenever possible.

It was with great pleasure when later that evening, she rang Doreen for a chat. It became clear, within minutes that Rosie's parents expected her home before the evening was out and made it abundantly clear that a full apology and subservient capitulation was expected from their daughter. Natasha calmly arbitrated on Rosie's behalf and got precisely nowhere so after consulting her young guest as to how she wanted to proceed, Natasha told Doreen how it was going to be.

Tash said that Rosie was welcome to stay with her and would be kept safe and well for the foreseeable future. First thing in the morning she would ensure that all relevant departments were made aware of Rosie's situation. As for a contribution to her daughters board and lodging, Natasha hinted to Doreen that it might be deemed fraudulent to claim child benefit for a family member if they were no longer in your care and that to be on the safe side, she should post the money on, once a month, until further notice. Rounding it all off nicely, Tash informed a totally dumbfounded Doreen that Rosie would make arrangements to collect any belongings she'd left behind at a mutually convenient time for all concerned and could be assured that her daughter would be encouraged to study hard for her upcoming exams. Ending the conversation on a cheery note, Tash insisted that should Doreen have any concerns she could feel free to telephone at any time for a chat. Then she hung up.

***

Rosie had spent all morning in the restaurant preparing for lunchtime, a task that she found relaxing and rewarding. The tables looked so beautiful with their pale green napkins and crystal glasses. She also enjoyed the buzz of pre-service activity and the gorgeous aromas that wafted from the kitchen every time someone came through the swing doors. She was currently doing a stint on reception which was one of her favourite places to be and loved welcoming the guests, priding herself on being the first friendly face people saw when they arrived at The Fairhaven. It was her job to make every visitor feel relaxed and special at the beginning of their stay and a valued much-missed guest once they'd checked out. In quieter moments Rosie would take time to drink in her surroundings and feel rather smug that after all her angst, things turned out just fine.

***

Rosie came on in leaps and bounds once she left school in June, when the much-anticipated day of freedom finally arrived. After she wrote the very last word in her final exam, ending with a big, bold, full stop, Rosie clicked the lid onto her pen and placed it by the side of the completed test paper. She then let a wave of sheer relief wash over her body, allowing her mind to drain itself of the facts and figures that were imprinted on to her brain. When she walked out of the exam hall and stepped into the sun, Rosie looked down the driveway of the school and saw her whole life spread out before her, just waiting for her to get on and live it.

Alfred had continued to be her mentor and Mrs Amery had also taken her under her wing, so safe and secure under their watchful eyes and tactful guardianship, she was nurtured, encouraged and given the opportunity to thrive. Laura's mum turned out to be Rosie's unofficial guardian angel too, and their home was a welcoming and relaxing place to be during the week, not only that, there was never a dull moment or a pork chop in sight when it came to mealtimes. Tash insisted that this harmonious existence was entirely due to the lack of testosterone in the house and was firmly of the view that since her messy divorce, it was going to remain a man-free environment forever. Rosie topped up her keep from what she earned at The Fairhaven and as far as she was concerned, it was money well spent. Tash had given both girls the hard word where a revision-play ratio was concerned, saying she didn't mind them having a bit of fun as long as they put the hours in. There was no way she was taking the blame for failure especially where Rosie was concerned because domineering Doreen would just love that!

On Friday nights after school, Rosie would make her way to The Fairhaven and work there until Sunday evening. Alfred arranged for her to live-in at the weekend and as soon as she finished school, she'd moved permanently into a small room at the back of the hotel. Rosie would always be grateful to Tash and Laura for making her feel so welcome and for the wonderful blanket of security they gave her when she needed it most. She would never forget what it felt like to be fed tea and toast, wrapped in a warm duvet and told everything would be okay, and actually believe it. It was one of the kindest, most natural things on earth, to care for someone in need and she hoped that if the situation ever arose and she was given the opportunity, she would do exactly the same thing.

For the next three years, Rosie worked hard at The Fairhaven while at the same time studying for her Hotel Management qualifications. Actually working within the industry was a huge advantage and made the tedious, theory side of things much easier. Even though she preferred to be hands-on and at the hotel, Rosie strove to do well at university and justify the faith Alfred and Mrs Amery had in her. Life was never dull and she made great friends with the other members of staff, some of whom lived in while others came and went, frequently moving on to pastures new. One of the constants in her life was André, the fiery French chef who struck fear into the hearts of his kitchen staff, reducing men and women alike to tears on a regular basis. All except for Rosie who knew he was just a big softie at heart.

Their friendship began very early one morning when she crept into the small kitchenette provided for the staff who lived in. It was around 3am and she couldn't sleep. She was worrying about Ruby who'd rung earlier that day in a right old state about another one of Aunty Stella's boyfriends, apparently he'd pinched money from her purse. What made Rosie really sad, and extremely mad at the same time, were the awful things her aunt had said to Ruby – they were below the belt and cruel. Anyway, after advising her to open a savings account and buy some locks for her bedroom door, in an attempt to cheer her cousin up, she had invited her over on Sunday. It was her weekend off and she'd promised Ruby a lazy day of talking rubbish, eating chocolate and a slap-up tea at the local pub. Rosie didn't notice anyone sat at the small table when she walked into the kitchen and automatically switched on the light. She nearly wet herself with fright when a loud voice boomed in the darkness.

'*Sacré bleu*! What the fuck are you doing? *Merde*! I am blind now. Turn that light off before my eyes are exploding.'

The shock of André's voice prompted Rosie to do as she was told and then stood stock still, waiting obediently in the dark. As her thudding heart slowed she plucked up the courage to speak to the fearsome chef.

'Sorry, André. I didn't know anyone was in here. I was just about to make a cup of tea, do you mind if I disturb you? I could make you one too.' Rosie gulped and waited silently for her head to be ripped off again.

'Tea, tea, what is it with the bloody English and their tea? You think it will cure everything. It tastes like the dishwater. No, I will have my wine. Come, sit down and join me, share with me a proper drink.'

André had the knack of making people do as he wished so Rosie nervously pulled out a chair and sat down. Watching him search the cupboards for another glass in the dim light of the kitchen, illuminated only by the half moon and the fact that her eyes had grown accustomed to the dark, Rosie wondered about André. Why had this man, with his mass of wavy, dark brown hair, closely trimmed beard and rugby player physique, who was quite handsome in his own ruggedly Gallic way, ended up hundreds of miles away from home, living in a cramped single room at the back of a hotel?

Everyone said he was gay but seeing as he kept himself to himself, the staff actually knew very little about him or more to the point, nobody dared to ask. Once he'd poured the wine André lit another cigarette. Rosie knew this wasn't allowed but she certainly wasn't going to be the one to remind him so instead she sat and drank, letting the ruby red liquid soothe her. In the silence that followed and while he smoked his cigarette, his watchful eyes burned into her and finally, he spoke.

'So, Mademoiselle, how come you live here at the hotel, did your family throw you away or did you run from your home? I watch you in the restaurant and you are different from the others, more sensible, not stupid. Tell me, what is your story?' André dragged on his cigarette and waited, holding Rosie's gaze.

'It's not exactly a story. It's all a bit boring really. I just wanted things from life that my parents didn't agree with. They had this image in their heads of what they wanted me to be and the fact that it made me unhappy was of no interest to them. All they seemed to care about was what other people would think and that I had let them down by not conforming to what was acceptable in their world. So I left. Simple as that.' Rosie drank her wine and tried to push down the anger that bubbled to the surface every time she thought back to the events that forced her to leave home.

'This does not surprise me. Parents can be very stupid sometimes, but I am interested, what did they want you to be? You are very young to make this decision and leave your family so it must be something horrible.' André's tone was softer now and he was intrigued by the pretty young woman with the golden hair sitting before him in the moonlight, who had the guts to speak to him and not scurry away like the others always did.

In return, Rosie sensed that just across the table, was a slightly lonely kindred spirit who was taking a chance and reaching out to a stranger so she smiled and poured some more wine, then told him her tale and in return, he told her his.

André was born in France, in the small, picturesque village of Saint Pierre de Fontaine. It was nestled in the beautiful countryside of the Loire and had been his happy home until he reached the tender age of sixteen. His parents and grandparents before them owned *Les Trois Chênes*, a small hotel and restaurant, or auberge, as the French called it. The master plan, mutually agreeable to all concerned, was that one day their one and only child would follow in their footsteps and take the reins. At around this time, André made the naive and totally misguided decision to tell his devoted parents that he was gay and to put it bluntly, all hell broke loose.

Rather than the understanding and acceptance he expected in this modern world, he was met with horror and aggression. His mother took to her bed after her husband took his belt to their son, hoping to beat what could only be the devil out of André and rid their family of its shame. When it became obvious to all concerned that neither the priest nor the leather of a belt could rid André of his curse, and that it would only be a matter of time before the rest of the village became suspicious of the quiet, young man who never had a girlfriend, he decided to pack his bags and head for Paris. Here, André could be assured of finding the two things he needed to live his life – plenty of restaurants where he could learn to cook and plenty of men whom he could love.

Free from the restrictions and prejudices of a rural community, André worked and played hard, finding a release in creating beautiful food and spending his spare time with beautiful men. With a lust for life and adventure, as soon as he was qualified André headed for London and after slaving away, working his way up the kitchen ladder, he eventually found himself in Cheshire as Head Chef of a five-star hotel. However, there was one thing in his life that was lacking and that thing was love. There were easy pickings to be found in Manchester and he was never short of admirers or a one-night stand but as he got older and a little wiser, André was beginning to feel the need for something more permanent in his life. He knew that it was unlikely he would ever have children, a fact he deeply regretted as he would have loved to be a father and part of a family. And so it was that on nights like these, André always felt the pull of a small village in France and the love he still had for his parents. He had forgiven them for being trapped in another, less enlightened world, for not knowing any better – and for being scared. André was wiser now and realised that perhaps they were guilty of only one simple thing – loving him too much.

'So, it seems we are the same you and I. Runaways with parents who are blinded by their hopes for us and cannot see that this world changes each time it spins.' André stood and sighed then wandered silently from the kitchen and returned with another bottle of wine and began to open it.

Rosie felt honoured that this huge bear of a man with the reputation of being an ogre had confided in her. André threw the cork onto the table but before he had time to pour the wine, Rosie reached across and placed her hand over his. As his fingers closed gratefully around hers, they silently sealed their friendship and forged a bond. It would last for the rest of their lives.

Sunrise began to bathe the room in a silvery light and realising that André was determined to drink himself happy or into a coma, Rosie slid her glass across the table.

'Well, if we're going to drink that wine I need something to soak it all up. You might be on a late shift but I start work in a few hours and I've never been drunk on duty before. So, how about a fried egg and bacon sandwich? Speciality of the house, my treat.' Rosie stood up, slightly unsteadily and made her way to the cooker.

'Okay, if you insist, with lots of your brown sauce. Breakfast is the only thing you English can do properly. Do you have any sausages? I am in the mood for food.' André drummed his hands on the table, then rubbed them together in anticipation.

As Thursday morning dawned, while the birds sang their chorus and the sun broke through the clouds, the unlikely friends sat in the kitchen drinking red wine and eating bacon and egg sandwiches. Over the years to follow they would often reminisce and laugh, remembering that night and how against the odds Rosie managed her first completely drunken shift. André had woken up at the kitchen table, surrounded by bemused colleagues who quietly ate their cornflakes and wondered who would be brave enough to tell the ogre that he had a piece of bacon stuck to his forehead.

When Rosie finished her degree she was rewarded with the post of Deputy Assistant Manager and rose eagerly to the challenge. There wasn't a square foot of the hotel she didn't know or a member of staff whose name she didn't remember. With a natural flair for putting people at their ease and a way of getting the most out of her colleagues, Rosie was worth every penny of The Fairhaven's investment. Extremely tactful and a practised watcher of people she had a knack for names and faces, doing her best to make sure that each guest who stepped into the foyer felt special.

As Rosie lived at the hotel she was more or less on call for any emergency or crisis and would step in at a moment's notice if they were short staffed. That wasn't to say she was a slave to her job and managed to squeeze in some fun here and there. Rosie could be a bit of a party animal when she wanted to be and aided and abetted by André who had finally come out of his shell and was a little less scary these days, would order a minibus and along with whoever she'd roped in, stay up all night painting the nightclubs of Manchester crimson.

Rosie was also quite a favourite with the male members of staff and finally succumbed to the good looks and undeniable charms of Tony the barista, who it had to be said, was a bit of a let-down. After all their years of speculating about the contents of his spray on trousers, during a giggling confessional to Laura following her first one-night stand, Rosie admitted that she'd lost her virginity to a bloke who obviously stuck a couple of socks down his undies just before he went to work.

There had also been a slight thaw in the relations between Rosie and her parents who, apart from a card to congratulate her on her successful A level results and sentiment-lacking birthday cards sent to the hotel, she had no contact with them whatsoever. It was actually due to some gracious and wise words from André that she begrudgingly changed her mind. He had long since made peace with his parents, mainly because he accepted that they still lived in the land of make-believe and were happy there. They told everyone in the village that their son was travelling the world, cooking in fine restaurants, a roving bachelor who sadly hadn't found the woman of his dreams. André reasoned that if this made them content then it was fine by him. It also allowed him to go home for visits, drink in the bar with his friend Sebastien and sleep under the same roof as his parents. Rather than hate them for their prejudices he loved them for who they were, his beloved

Mama and Papa. To this end, Rosie made the odd, polite phone call to her own parents, observing their birthdays and Christmas but drew the line at spending the festivities with them. The hotel was alive and buzzing and that was where she wanted to be, not at home, cutting through dry turkey and thin ice while watching the clock tick by in *very* slow motion.

One person who remained constant in her life was Ruby. Rosie faithfully kept a close eye on her cousin, maintaining regular contact with phone calls and invites for weekend visits to the hotel, where they would top and tail in her small bed, talking about rubbish and giggling into the night. Continually providing support whenever Ruby needed it (which unfortunately was a frequent occurrence) became a part of Rosie's life. She didn't believe in curses but had to admit that the thought sometimes crossed her mind where Ruby was concerned. Just when she found happiness with her first boyfriend, Dylan, the rug was torn from under her, and her heart was broken. Rosie thought he was a lovely boy and even when he left for Scotland she'd truly believed it would be a happy ending and his love for Ruby would survive, but it didn't and she was left to pick up the pieces.

After the Dylan phase ended, Ruby managed to pull through and seemed happy enough with her job and new housemates so Rosie took her eye off the ball for a while, reassured by stories of mad nights out and the odd, unsatisfactory date. She actually thought Ruby was finally over her bad luck spell and on the track to happiness and would eventually find herself a nice steady replacement for Dylan and then live happily ever after. How wrong could someone be?

Chapter 8

Rosie

Rosie had become accustomed to the occasional guest coming on to her. When she first started working at the hotel even a casual chat-up line or compliment would leave her flustered and tongue tied, wanting the ground to open up and swallow her whole. As time passed, Rosie grew a little more experienced in the ways of the world and developed skills to rebuff flirtatious comments and over-zealous diners with wandering hands; for the most part she easily dealt with tricky situations.

From one week to the next there was always something going on. Rowdy guests, annoying the people in the room next door, wives ringing to check up on their husbands and husbands checking in women who were clearly not their wives. They'd had one hysterical, jilted bride and her equally hysterical mother, then a couple of grooms who were caught quite literally with their pants down, one with a female wedding guest and the other with his best man. Christmastime brought a wealth of goings on within the walls and more often than not, behind the topiary bushes in the garden. Such antics never failed to keep the break room alive with tales of the night before and the high jinx of the guests.

There'd been a few uncomfortable situations with female escorts loitering in the bar and the ensuing hoo-ha when they were asked to leave. They'd had items stolen from the rooms and the awful suspicions it raised amongst the staff, but worse, there had been a nasty assault on one of the chambermaids a few years before which scared most of them to death. No charges were brought because in the end it was her word against his, but the young girl in question was severely traumatised and left the hotel and, rumour had it, the country.

For this reason, whilst maintaining her friendly demeanour, Rosie was always on her guard, which was precisely why the gentleman in room 203 was causing her some concern. Mr Crawley had been pleasant enough when he checked in three days earlier and in passing, mentioned he was on a business trip but apart from the odd walk around the grounds he seemed to spend much of his time alone in the hotel. He was invariably found sitting in the lounge reading his paper, eating in the restaurant or drinking in the bar, chatting to Tony or whoever happened to be on duty. She knew he swam in the pool each morning because Nellie, the Swedish masseuse had seen him chatting with Dawn, the attendant.

There was just something about him that unsettled Rosie. She decided that as with herself, he was a watcher of people and she'd noticed that while he sat, supposedly minding his own business, he was observing everything and everyone. In short Mr Crawley gave her the creeps. Rosie passed on her concerns to André who didn't help matters by telling her he was either a private detective, trying to collect evidence for a suspicious wife or a psycho, eyeing up his next victim. With these scenarios playing on her mind it was no surprise that when she bumped into him loitering in a corridor early one morning, spying on the chambermaids she immediately reported him. If Alfred and Mrs Amery thought she was overreacting they didn't say and promised to keep a close eye on him, but no sooner had Rosie mentioned it, he checked out.

The whole thing was totally forgotten until about a month later when a large party of suits checked in and creepy Mr Crawley (as she now referred to him) was one of them. Two hours later, the owners of The Fairhaven, the Hamilton-Pykes, also arrived after flying over from the Bahamas where they lived, a team of lawyers in tow. The hotel was buzzing with speculation. Alfred bustled about all day in a complete flap, red-faced and desperate to ensure that everything was up to, or above standards during their surprise visit.

The mystery guests and the lawyers spent the next two days locked in the conference room as wild rumours of bankruptcy and closure wafted around the hotel. The most popular theory with the best odds was that Fairhaven was to be turned into a Retirement home, followed closely by the wishful thinkers who hoped it would be the set of a period drama and they'd all get work as extras. On the third day, all of the management team and any staff who could be spared were called into the conference room and as they waited to be addressed by the Hamilton-Pykes, an uneasy tension filled the room. Rosie was curious and worried. No matter how ludicrous the rumours they had unsettled her and glancing towards her boss, she noticed that Alfred looked worried too.

When the bigwigs finally breezed in, flanked by their lawyers, the room hushed and everyone waited expectantly, eyes glued to the front while praying it would be good news. Gregory Hamilton-Pyke looked every inch the ex-pat wearing a starched white shirt and a jaunty yellow cravat under a yacht club blazer, teamed with chinos and deck shoes. Rosie perceived him to be slightly nervous yet faintly smug. His beady blue eyes scanned the gathered audience from his deeply-tanned face, and it occurred to her that he looked like a shrivelled nut as opposed to his wife Miranda who was bleached blonde and swathed from head to toe in Gucci. From the looks of her crease-free face she'd been pumped with enough Botox to sink the yacht that Gregory had probably left moored on the Manchester Ship Canal.

The lawyer got things under way with a dramatic cough and made his grand announcement. It was brief and to the point, well-rehearsed and designed to limit panic, embellished with lashings of optimism and grand designs for the future which would benefit everyone stood before him. The upshot of his enthusiastic speech was that after a century of being owned by the Hamilton-Pyke dynasty, The Fairhaven Hotel was being bought by the Belmonte Grande chain of International Hotels and would, from this day on, be part of their ever-growing family. He had been asked by the Hamilton's to thank them all sincerely for their loyalty and dedication over the years, wishing them every success for the future and promising to pop back to see how they were getting on whenever they were in the country. With that, he handed Alfred a stack of leaflets to give out to the staff which provided any information they required, after which they all shuffled off, the ex-owners a few million richer and leaving a stunned audience in their wake.

Later that evening once her shift had finished, Rosie went in search of Alfred who had disappeared almost immediately after the meeting and had been in his office with the suits ever since. Tapping on his door she inclined her head to listen for his reply and on hearing a voice telling her to enter, she pushed it open and went in. Alfred was sitting at his polished walnut desk, drinking whisky. His face was bathed in the gentle light of a brass lamp. He looked pleased when he saw it was Rosie and with a weary smile, indicated for her to take a seat.

'Well, that was a bit of a shock, Alfred. Did you know about all this or were you as surprised as the rest of us?' Rosie watched her mentor carefully, sensing something was wrong just by his body language and lack of enthusiasm. If this takeover was good news, he certainly wasn't showing it.

'No, Rosie, I had no idea. Not until they all turned up and the Bahamas bunch flew in, then I realised something big was on the cards. They filled me in that same evening but I was sworn to secrecy. Apparently, we have been under scrutiny for some time. It seems there's also been a steady influx of mystery guests secretly checking us out. Obviously, we all passed with flying colours so they came here to dot the 'I's and thrash out a deal. All I could do was keep you all on your toes and wait for the verdict, which I suspect was a foregone conclusion.' Alfred took a sip of his drink and sighed.

Rosie couldn't understand her friend's negativity so pressed the point, mainly in the hope he would share his troubles.

'From the way the lawyer sold it to us the hotel can only benefit. A complete makeover and millions of pounds being invested, surely that can't be bad? They're still going to need all the staff, especially if they expand like they said so why are you looking so fed up, is it because things are going to change? I know you love The Fairhaven just how it is, Alfred, but you will be king of a brand-new castle and I'll be the princess. You know you can rely on me to help you.' Rosie thought she'd done a sterling job of cheering him up with her list of positives but even her jokey royal references couldn't make him smile.

'Well, that's just the point, Rosie, because while I agree with everything you say there's one tiny flaw in your argument. You see, I won't be king of the castle because they're letting me go. It seems I'm not part of the deal and along with the fancy wallpaper and a fresh lick of paint you'll be getting a new manager with a Masters degree and a refreshing outlook that will pilot everyone into the future. No, Rosie, one way or another, my time here is finished.'

Alfred poured himself another drink and let the statement hang in the air, waiting for Rosie to react, which she did by bursting into floods of angry, indignant tears.

Rosie missed Alfred more than she'd ever missed her parents. He had given her a chance when she needed one and was her guide and inspiration but most of all, for the past seven years he had been her friend. That night in his office when she eventually calmed down, he explained that it wasn't all bad and despite his disappointment there *were* some positives to be gained from the takeover, especially for her.

The Belmonte Grande chain had recognised Alfred's value and wealth of experience and had asked if he would remain at The Fairhaven in a supervisory capacity to help facilitate the handover to the new management team. For this, he would be rewarded with a hefty pay-off on top of his early redundancy package. Naturally, he'd run it all by Mrs Alfred (as he lovingly referred to his long-suffering wife) who told him to grab the offer and scarper so that she could have him all to herself, at last. She'd shared him with his other love, The Fairhaven, for over forty years and now it was their time. Alfred painted an idyllic picture of a rose covered cottage in the countryside, lots of golf and perhaps some gardening, plus a nice cruise around the Med. Anyone who knew him well could tell that he was bluffing because the light had gone out in his eyes overnight and the spring in his step was reduced to a resigned waddle.

There wasn't a dry eye at Alfred's leaving party. Mrs Amery looked distraught and confided in Rosie that had they offered her the same deal she would've hit the road as well, but it seemed her time hadn't come so for now her days of linen and laundry were far from over. As for Rosie, it transpired that her star was in the ascendant and due mainly to a glowing recommendation given by loyal Alfred and the observations of the mystery guests – in particular creepy Mr Crawley – she was to be fast-tracked on the Belmonte Management Training Scheme.

Rosie volunteered to help carry all of Alfred's leaving presents and cards, plus the crate of champagne from the Belmonte lot, to his car. He didn't want a big fuss or everyone waving him off but it was Rosie's way of prolonging her last moments with him. Doing her level best to keep a grip she loaded his gifts into the boot, the closing of the lid with a thump signalling the end of an era. Turning to face Rosie, just as heavy drops of rain began to plop onto their faces, Alfred held out his arms for one last hug, folding her into his portly frame while they both forced back the tears.

'Now, you must listen to me, Rosie. I want you to make the most of whatever this Belmonte lot can offer you. Watch and learn but always keep your guard up. They have big plans that you could be a part of so take every opportunity that presents itself, work hard and be the best. I saw something very special in you all those years ago and you have never let me down. Please be a success. It will make an old, rather cynical manager very happy.' Alfred smiled and looked into Rosie's tear-filled eyes for an answer.

Rosie valiantly composed herself and managed a squeak.

'I'll try, Alfred. As long as you promise *me* you will always stay in touch and that you will have the best time in the world with Mrs Alfred.' Rosie gave him a brave smile as the rain became more persistent, forcing their conversation to a premature end.

'Just one final thing, Rosie. Don't let this industry swallow you up. Stay on the ride for as long as you enjoy it but when it starts to burn you out or you no longer feel the thrill of a new day, it's time to get off. Don't go round too many times like I did and miss out on the important things in life. You'll know when, so follow your instinct and act on it. Now get yourself inside before you're soaked. I've got an impatient wife waiting for me at home and we need to get cracking on some of this champagne.' With that, Alfred gave Rosie one last hug and jumped in his car.

As he started the ignition, she tapped on his rain-soaked window and mouthed two words through the glass.

'I promise.'

The first phase of Rosie's fast-track life began when she was sent on a twelve-month tour of the other hotels in the Belmonte chain. This was to give her an insight into how they ran their operations and also, to see how she coped when she was out of her comfort zone. Staying at each hotel for a few months at a time, Rosie shadowed the managers of every department and was frequently left at the helm where she would either sink or swim. Naturally, Rosie swam and faced each challenge head on. She approached every day with vigour and rather than putting mistrustful noses out of joint, was accepted as a fresh-faced, breath of fresh air who slipped easily into their routine. Having worked her way up through the ranks endeared her to everyone from the pot washers to the porters. Rosie returned to The Fairhaven on a crisp September morning, took up her old post and was literally champing at the bit to put her year of travelling to good use in the beautifully refurbished Fairhaven-Belmonte Grande.

During her year away, despite having a full-on workload, Rosie had kept in constant touch with Ruby who had blossomed since moving in with Martine. They managed a quick weekend together when she worked in the York Belmonte, squashing six months of gossip into forty-eight hours where Rosie was adequately assured of her cousin's new-found happiness and consequently, felt at liberty to get on with her own career.

Rosie's triumphant return also coincided with a jubilant phone call from Ruby who had her own wonderful news. Someone called Marcus had arrived in her life. After listening to her animated cousin chatter on about her fabulous boyfriend, Rosie was relieved that finally Ruby had found a replacement for her one-true-love, Dylan. Before replacing the receiver, Rosie promised that once she'd caught her breath and got back into her routine at The Fairhaven they would get together and she could interrogate Ruby about Marcus properly.

However, since then, Ruby had been a bit of a stranger and Rosie had been busy too. They'd only managed phone calls and a couple of days at Christmas after which she left her cousin to get on with her budding romance and thought nothing of it. Therefore, it was a bit of a shock when early one January morning, as she oversaw the removal of the festive decorations, Rosie took an excited call from Ruby who was ringing from Dubai with some amazing news. She was engaged to Marcus!

During Ruby's stay at the hotel over Christmas it was blatantly obvious that she was head over heels in love but there had been no hint of anything so serious and certainly no talk of a proposal. After that bombshell came another, just a few weeks later. Ruby was moving into Marcus's penthouse apartment and giving up her room at Martine's and there was more, they'd be tying the knot in July.

Rosie had yet to meet the man who had swept her cousin off her feet and despite numerous invitations to the hotel or arrangements to meet up in Manchester, at the very last minute Ruby would ring and cancel due to Marcus being unavoidably detained, or some other equally vague excuse. Then he went off to the Far East, then Europe, meaning that their get together was further postponed. Rosie suspected that Ruby's wonderful, posh fiancé couldn't actually be bothered to meet the in-laws, which made her feel insulted and roused her suspicions. That was why, instead of following her instincts which told her to pay them a surprise visit, Rosie had a jealous sulk and decided if that was his attitude she would let him come to her. It was with a certain amount of intrigue and expectation that Rosie finally met Marcus, accompanied by Ruby, just one week before their nuptials for a pre-wedding dinner.

The evening went well, as well as a night could go sitting opposite a man who made your skin crawl while he oozed fake charm and false interest from every scale on his long slimy body. Rosie couldn't stand Marcus and her well-honed instinct kicked straight in. He reminded her of the lounge lizards, a name that the girls at work gave to the men who slithered around the hotel bar trying to pick up anyone available for a night of passion before heading off into the sunset in their company cars. Yes, Marcus asked all the right questions and feigned interest in her answers, yet Rosie still got the unshakeable feeling that he was checking her out and trying to decide where she figured in Ruby's life. The clincher came when she noted his relieved reaction to some exciting news of her own, which she had saved for that evening and wanted to share with Ruby in person.

Rosie had been called into the manager's office a few days before to find Mr Creepy Crawley also in attendance. Alfred had handed over the control of his beloved hotel to Mr Hemming, a nice enough chap who did seem extremely competent in all things managerial, putting his master's degree to good use ensuring the hotel ran like clockwork. The only misgivings Rosie had was suspecting Mr Hemming of looking down his nose at her slightly. Even though she had a degree of her own, Rosie sensed that he didn't admire the way she'd worked her way up and maybe thought she'd had special treatment from The Fairhaven. Whatever it was, Rosie got the distinct impression he also saw her as a threat.

Seeing a thick file lying open on his desk, which Mr Hemming swiftly closed as she entered the room, made Rosie slightly apprehensive. Perhaps Creepy was a detective after all and he'd got something on her. She gave herself an imaginary slap, realising that if he'd managed to dig up any dirt where she was concerned, it would be a miracle, unless you counted a wonderful night of passion with a hot guest in Aberdeen. As it turned out there was no need for concern. The reason for the meeting was an appraisal of her progress so far and the good news was Mr Creepy thought she was performing well, so they had an exciting proposition for her. If she was agreeable, they planned to send her off on phase two of her training which would involve working at their hotels based in Europe. Much to her delight, from October, Rosie would be off to Paris, Berlin, Palma, Madrid and Rome.

Despite her misgivings about Marcus, she decided to give him the benefit of the doubt after talking her observations through with the ever-wise André, who convinced her that the smarmy git (as Rosie described him) might have been very nervous or trying too hard to impress and she'd taken him the wrong way. Rosie resigned herself to the fact that Ruby was old enough to make her own mind up and even though Marcus wasn't her cup of tea, he made her cousin happy and that was what mattered.

No matter what André said, she still couldn't shake off the bad vibes and only hoped that time would prove her wrong. Unfortunately for Rosie, two people were about to rain on her optimistic parade and through no fault of her own she would be left with secrets that in time, one way or another, would cost her cousin dearly.

Chapter 9

Rosie

Rosie shed tears of pride and happiness for her cousin as she made her vows in the pale blue registry office. She knew that Ruby had dreamed of a church wedding but having not been christened and therefore unable to provide a certificate, she was faced with either being baptised at the tender age of twenty-three years old or plumping for a civil marriage. Unable to bear the thought of Olivia looking down her nose at a non-Christian, Ruby put on a brave face and pretended that Manchester Town Hall was her preference. Looking radiant in a Grace Kelly style dress with its lace covered bodice and sleeves, elegant flowing silk skirt and half veil, Ruby quite literally glowed as Rosie's father walked the blushing bride into the room. Before the assembled guests made up almost entirely by the groom's family and friends, Rosie's beloved cousin married Marcus Neville Cole.

Rosie watched with amusement as her mother sucked up to Olivia for all she was worth, and that accent, where *did* Doreen think she was from? She sounded like Hyacinth Bucket and it made Rosie cringe. Following the ceremony she decided to stick with Ruby's ex-housemates as there was only so much polite conversation she could make with her parents and after a quick round of photographs, everyone piled outside into the July sunshine. Led across the cobbles by the joyful bride and groom, the wedding party gradually made their way over to the limousines that were waiting to whisk them off to a nearby restaurant for the reception.

Doreen and Jim bagged a seat with Olivia and her friend Henry, so Rosie was left to organise the rest of the guests seeing as the best man, a handsome but arrogant chap called Roman, was neither use nor ornament and completely drunk. Just as Martine and the other girls were being bundled into the last car, Rosie turned to scan the cobbled square and check that she hadn't missed anybody out. That's when she spotted him, watching from the steps of the Albert Memorial. She would have recognised him anywhere. He held her gaze and for a second Rosie was frozen to the spot until years of thinking on her feet kicked in so turning to the waiting car she told Martine to go on without her, she'd left something inside and would follow in a cab. Instructing the chauffeur to drive on, Rosie hastily slammed the door shut and waved them off before they could protest or ask questions.

The second they were out of sight Rosie looked back to the memorial, he was still there, just as she knew he would be. Taking a long deep breath and then on very high heels, Rosie made her way tentatively across the cobbles towards the despondent face of Dylan, stopping just in front of him.

'Hello, Rosie, fancy meeting you here.' Dylan's sad eyes belied the joviality of his words.

After brushing down the steps to avoid soiling her dress, Rosie sat by his side, and for a moment found herself at a complete loss for what to say, then asked the obvious.

'What on earth are you doing here, today of all days? Is it a miraculous coincidence or did you know Ruby was getting married?' Rosie was still a little in shock and desperately trying to second-guess Dylan's motives.

Resting his arms on his knees, his head looking down on the cobbles, Dylan spoke in a dejected whisper. 'A bit of both really. I came to see Ruby. I arrived this lunchtime and went straight to her house from the station. I was hoping to surprise her but there was nobody at home so I caught the bus back into town and went to the store, thinking she'd be there. I hovered about for ages but couldn't see her so in the end I asked one of the assistants if she was in work today. When they told me she was getting married I nearly threw up with the shock of it. Somehow, I managed to bluff my way through and ask where the wedding was being held. As soon as the girl told me it was at the Town Hall at three, I ran all the way here. I thought my heart was going to explode which it might as well have done because I was too late. I went inside and the bloke in the office said the wedding was under way but I just wanted a glimpse of her, so I sat here and waited. In some ways, I wish I hadn't because it's made it a million times worse.' Dylan placed his head in his hands, deep in thought.

'Oh, Dylan. I'm so sorry, truly I am. But what would you have done if you *had* got here in time? Tried to persuade her that she was making a big mistake? Ruby hasn't seen or heard from you in years and apart from the odd card I thought you two lost touch ages ago.' Rosie was half glad he hadn't got there in time, imagining the scene it would've caused and the dilemma Ruby would've been in.

'That's why I came back. For some reason, recently I just couldn't get her out of my mind. I was full of regrets and "what ifs" so I talked myself into believing that maybe we could start up from where we left off. I've never forgotten her, Rosie, and not one single girl ever made me feel the way Ruby did, but I left it too late and now I've lost her forever.' Dylan slumped back against the cold stone memorial, staring ahead, lost in his thoughts.

'Did it not even occur to you that she might have a boyfriend? Were you expecting her to just drop everything and give you a second chance? And even if she did, there's still the matter of you living miles apart to consider. Talk about wishful thinking, Dylan, you really didn't think it through, did you? If you'd sent her a letter first or even rang, you could have saved yourself a long journey and a lot of heartache.'

There was a moment of uncomfortable silence and then Dylan spoke.

'You're right. I didn't think it through and part of me wouldn't face up to the fact that she might be with someone. I convinced myself that if she did have a boyfriend I'd be able to win her back so I just got on a train and came straight here. It was a spur of the moment thing, madness I suppose. I planned it all in my head and rehearsed what I would say during the journey down. I was going to tell her that I'd move down here or she could pack her job in and then come back to Scotland with me. I would've done whatever she wanted me to, every single thing I should have done five stupid years ago.' Dylan swallowed hard, choked by his emotions and regrets.

Rosie couldn't believe what she was hearing and knew for sure that under normal circumstances, Ruby might have sulked a bit and even made Dylan beg for another chance, but ultimately, she would've forgiven him and took him back. Now, there was Mr Wonderful to contend with and Rosie couldn't call it. Would Ruby have chosen Marcus or her old love, Dylan? All she did know was that Dylan's arrival would cause a furore and ruin Ruby's day and she wasn't going to risk that, no matter how much she disliked her cousin's new husband.

Sighing out loud, Rosie prepared to salvage the day and at the same time, quash poor Dylan's dreams. 'What a mess! Maybe if you'd done all this a year ago, before she met Marcus, you might have stood a chance. But Ruby's with him now and as much as she may have loved you then, I doubt you would change her mind, not on her wedding day.' Rosie felt so sorry for him and a little bit angry at his rubbish sense of timing, as well.

'Is that how long she's known him, just a year? And they're married already. That's a bit quick, isn't it, what's he like anyway, is he a good bloke because she deserves the best?' Dylan looked incredulously at Rosie, waiting for answers.

There was no way she was sharing her innermost thoughts on Marcus with Dylan, that would only give him false hope and after all, they were only suspicions. The creep might just prove her wrong and turn out to be a good guy after all.

'I don't know him that well, Dylan, I only met him a week before the wedding. I travel a lot and so does he, but I can tell you the basics if it makes you feel better, though I doubt it will. He's from quite a wealthy family who have a large import company here in town and they also produce clothing in this country too. Ruby met him last September and things moved quite quickly from then on. He proposed in the New Year and she moved in with him soon after. The girls at the house were a bit upset and thought it was moving too fast and so did I but she's an adult and we had to let her make her own mind up.' Rosie wanted him to know she'd been vigilant but ultimately, Marcus was Ruby's own choice.

'So that's it. I've blown it. He must be mad about her and it sounds like she'd be stupid to leave someone like him for me. Will you tell her I came today, perhaps give her a message?'

Dylan's eyes looked hopeful but Rosie knew she had to be firm and let him down gently.

'No, Dylan, I'm not going to tell her. Whatever any of us think, this is the happiest day of Ruby's life and I'm not going to spoil it for her. She's somewhere across town right now drinking champagne and welcoming her guests and probably wondering where the hell her chief bridesmaid is. The last thing I want to do is put thoughts of you or the past into her head. I will tell her one day, I promise, but not now. Can you remember what her life was like before? Never in her wildest dreams would she have expected to meet someone like Marcus.' Rosie paused to let her words sink in before continuing.

'I used to worry that she'd end up like her mum or some of the other girls she went to school with who were on the dole and pushing a pram around the estate. Maybe I was selling her short but with a mother like Stella and no father figure in her life, anything could have happened. I'm so proud of how she's turned out and that's because she never gave up and worked really hard to make something of herself. Let her have this perfect day without a care in the world and her moment in the spotlight.' Rosie hoped she'd got through to him, it was such a shame but she had to be loyal to Ruby.

'I know. You're right. But I will always wonder what would've happened if I'd got here sooner. It's just another regret to add to my ever-growing list. Anyway, you'd better get going or you'll miss the party. Everyone will think you've been kidnapped.' Dylan stood and picked up his rucksack.

The sight of this made Rosie feel even sadder, he'd obviously packed a few things and had expected a happy ending. 'What will you do now, have you got anywhere to stay?' Rosie didn't want to abandon him but she needed to get a move on.

'I'll walk back to the station and catch a train home. There's no point hanging around now. It'll do my head in if I stay here. Can I ask you one thing before I go? If I give you my number will you promise to ring me if she ever needs me, or for anything really? I don't care if I wait forever for the call. Even if I'm an old man I'll always be here for her.'

Dylan meant every word. Rosie could tell just from the look in his eyes so took his number and gave him hers, just to make him feel better.

'Come on, let's walk together. I need to find a taxi, sharpish, and you've not had a chance to tell me anything about yourself. Send me a text while you're on the train and bring me up to speed with your life. I'd like to know how you're getting on.' As she finished speaking a cab came into sight which she flagged down.

Opening the door, Rosie stopped to give him a hug and felt like she was leaving a lost puppy on the side of the road.

Dylan's body sagged as he let go, weighed down by disappointment, his voice sounding similar. 'Go on, you get going. Give her a secret kiss from me.' And without another word, he waved and walked away.

Rosie knew he was crying.

By the time she arrived at the restaurant the guests were tucking into their gourmet buffet and Ruby was in a flap, wondering where on earth she'd got to and why she wasn't answering her phone. Rosie lied to her cousin for the first and final time in her life, relating a believable tale she'd concocted during the cab ride over. Convincing Ruby that she'd lost her phone in the marriage room and because there was another wedding taking place, she had to wait till it was over before she could search for it. It had slipped down the side of one of the chairs and thankfully, the battery had gone flat, otherwise the ceremony would have been disturbed by Ruby ringing up every two minutes. Ruby believed every word making Rosie feel dreadful. It was supposed to be a happy day but she felt crap. Not only had she just lied through her teeth but the first love of Ruby's life was trudging his way back to Victoria Station with a broken heart and now, she was burdened with a whopping big secret.

'*I need a drink*,' thought Rosie as she stealthily avoided her mother who was monopolising Olivia and hadn't spotted her yet. '*Thank you, God*,' was the silent message Rosie sent heavenwards as she slugged back whatever came to hand from the large silver tray at the end of the buffet table. The last thing she needed was to spend even one second in the company of her mother because it really, really would send her right over the edge.

The following week, Rosie was sitting at her desk in the office behind reception, flicking through the wedding photos and smiling like a fool at her beautiful cousin when her reminiscing was interrupted by one of the chambermaids looking for Mrs Amery.

'Hey, what are you looking so pleased about... ooh, are those the photos of the wedding? Let's have a quick look. She's so lovely, your Ruby.' Rosie passed the pictures to Kelly who'd met Ruby many times when she'd visited the hotel. Much ooh-ing and aah-ing commenced and they both agreed she made a stunning bride. Then, as Kelly flicked to another photo she stopped still and stared silently at the image in her hand as the colour drained from her face.

'Rosie, is this who your Ruby married, him there, the one with the dark hair?' Kelly tapped the photo, pointing to Marcus.

'Well, obviously it's him, that's why they're cutting the cake together. Why, what's wrong?' Rosie watched as Kelly sat down on the chair next to the desk, visibly shaken and staring incredulously at the laughing bride and groom as they sliced through their spectacular, three-tiered wedding cake.

When Kelly began frantically flicking through the other photos fear prickled Rosie's skin as she watched her friend's face and knew instinctively that she wasn't going to like whatever she was about to hear.

'Oh God, Rosie. I don't know how to tell you this. I can't believe it's him. If I'd known I swear I would've told you.'

Kelly's face was ashen and Rosie was beginning to panic.

'Tell me what, Kelly? Just say it, what's wrong.'

Kelly held the photo up and touched Marcus's face.

'This is the man who attacked my friend Magda. Don't you remember, I told you all about it? It happened a few years back, you were away at the time when a guest tried to rape one of our maids, well it was him. I'd remember his face anywhere. He was drunk and came on to her when she took some extra towels in, he really hurt her, Rosie. If it wasn't for the fact that we work in twos and I went to look for her, God knows what would've happened.'

Rosie felt cold ice spreading through her veins, but asked Kelly to carry on.

'Our shift was over but Magda had to go back with the towels so I said I'd wait for her. We always went home together and I told her to hurry up. I knew which room she'd gone to so when she didn't come back for ages, I went looking otherwise we'd have missed the bus. When I got up there I tapped and waited but there was no reply. I sensed something was wrong so I tapped on the door again and called out that it was housekeeping. The next thing I heard was Magda screaming for me to help her. She'd managed to break free. He'd been holding her down with his hand over her mouth but she bit him when she heard my voice and he let go. I burst into the room as Magda was running for the door, her hair and uniform were all over the place and he was trying to do his pants up. She looked terrified and became hysterical. He was saying the vilest things, calling her a whore and a prick tease and then all hell broke loose because the other guests came into the corridor to see what all the commotion was.' Kelly took a swig of water from the glass on Rosie's desk then continued.

'Anyway, Magda was crying, then security and Mrs Amery came and all the time he was ranting about the hotel employing prostitutes. Next thing I knew the police were called and he was arrested. They questioned me obviously, but all I actually saw was what I told you so it came down to her word against his. I felt like I'd let Magda down but I couldn't lie. He got himself a top lawyer and made out Magda came onto him, adamant that she was consenting until I disturbed them and because she thought she'd lose her job, he said she *cried* rape.' Kelly's cheeks were red from the telling of it all and remembering her friend's distress.

'So, he was never prosecuted then?' Rosie looked down at the picture of the dark-eyed man who was smiling into the camera, making her shudder.

'No, he got away scot-free. The police said that there wasn't enough evidence to ensure a prosecution. Poor Magda was traumatised and stayed off work for ages. She even split up with her boyfriend, probably because of the stress and eventually she went back to Poland. It makes me seethe when I think of it. He put on a really good show that night, acting like the injured party who couldn't believe the injustice of being arrested. But I saw him just before everyone arrived, he was steaming drunk and nasty, Rosie. He had this crazed look in his eyes, cold as ice and evil. I'll never forget it. Poor Ruby! I wish I'd have known because I swear I would have told you and then we could've warned her off.' Kelly looked riddled with guilt and worry.

'It's not your fault, Kelly, but what do I do now? She's off on her honeymoon in Mauritius. I can hardly ring her up and give her the earth-shattering news that her husband is a violent weirdo, can I?' Rosie was horrified, confused and worried.

'You're right, and the worst thing is that if she's as loved up as you make out she's not going to take kindly to what you say, she might not even believe you. He wriggled out of it once so he probably will again and you know what always happens to the messenger, Rosie, they get shot. If you go in all guns blazing and she takes his side you risk losing her forever.' Kelly put the photos down and placed her arm round a dejected Rosie's shoulder. 'I'd best get on or I'll be in trouble, but I'll look in on you before I go home. Perhaps we can go for a drink and talk it through after work? Two heads are better than one, or so they say.'

With a quick hug, Kelly left the room and Rosie to her thoughts, along with the terrible, vivid visions of the vile man her foolish cousin had married.

André became the voice of reason and managed to console and wisely counsel Rosie, thus preventing her from making enemies of both Marcus *and* Ruby. He only confirmed what she knew to be true in her own heart, and along with Kelly, convinced her that the best thing she could do was watch and wait – be on hand if Ruby ever needed her. It would have been a foolproof plan had she not been due to jet off to Europe so instead they decided that Rosie would need to match Marcus in the cunning and calculating stakes, and make sure that he had no reason to exclude her from Ruby's life, which was most likely his aim.

It all seemed so obvious now, why he never came to the hotel to meet Rosie – it was because he was terrified of being recognised. He knew Ruby would have shown her photos of him so he'd got away with it to a point, because Rosie had no idea what Magda's attacker looked like, but he was obviously taking no chances and postponed their meetings for as long as possible. He was a cool customer, she'd give him that and he must've wet himself when Ruby told him where Rosie worked. Taking heed of André's words, instead of a full-on attack Rosie decided to be the best cousin-in-law Marcus could wish for. She would keep her distance while maintaining regular contact and most importantly, offer no reason for Ruby to cut her ties. That way if he did step out of line, she'd have someone to turn to.

Rosie loved Europe. Her favourite place was Paris although she couldn't help falling a little in love with each city she stayed in. Not that there was much time for sightseeing in what she called her 'Continental Year'. She worked so hard that days frequently merged into night and when she opened her bloodshot eyes in the morning, for a second she forgot where she was. There was no time for romance either because the last thing she wanted was a reputation for bed-hopping and rumours always spread like wildfire so for twelve months, Rosie behaved herself and got on with her training. It did occur to her that at times the managers of the hotels used her as a dogsbody, taking her good-natured eagerness to please for granted. They would often ask more of her than other staff on much more money were prepared to give. Still, she soldiered on, keeping her promise to Alfred to learn, work hard and make him proud. In her precious spare time Rosie decided to learn French and when her eyes would stay open for long enough, she practiced in her room and listened to her Michel Tomas CD until sleep eventually claimed her.

Sticking to her mission, Rosie kept in constant touch with Ruby and, begrudgingly, Marcus, sending jolly postcards and emails from wherever she landed whilst giving no hint that she was spying. In return, she received loved-up messages back from Mr and Mrs Cole who had recently been on a romantic break to New York. The only thing she did pick up on was that Ruby appeared to have lost touch with her work friends and a quick email to and from Martine soon confirmed her fears. But her year of training was almost up and Rosie vowed that as soon as she was on British soil she would be like a rash they couldn't get rid of, in the nicest possible way of course.

She'd missed André like mad. He'd become her best friend and confidante, they knew and understood each other inside out and were inseparable when she was at The Fairhaven. Apart from enjoying wild nights in town where André would trawl the clubs on Canal Street in the Gay Village while Rosie danced the night away with their friends, she also enjoyed supper nights in the kitchenette. He would cook while she watched and learned. Sometimes, they would take long walks through the Cheshire lanes or visit gastro pubs, scrutinising the menus and giving their own private critique, imagining it was their restaurant and how they would do it differently. Rosie's favourite times were when they'd sit in her room and watch a soppy film, eating crisps and sharing a box of chocolates, then have a good old cry together at the end. By the time her year was up and she returned to The Fairhaven with a glowing report and the promise of a promotion on the horizon, Rosie was looking forward to seeing André and making up for lost time.

She found him in the huge, stainless steel kitchen that had been wiped down and prepped for the next morning's service. He was busy writing lists when she crept up behind him and grabbed his bottom, making him jump two feet in the air then swing round to hug the person he knew would be responsible for daring to touch his bum and scare him to death.

'*Chérie*, you are back and you are early! How I am missing you, let me see you… *non*. You are too thin. Did those Germans feed you only sausage and cabbage? Pah, you need to eat some real French food to put fat on your bones. I will prepare something for you right now.'

André began his ceremonial search for red wine and glasses, fussing around Rosie who noticed instantly that he was avoiding eye contact.

'So… what are these lists that you were so engrossed in before I made you poo your pants? What are you up to?' Rosie flicked through, not really understanding much of what was written in André's elaborate, French-style writing.

When she looked up, André's eyes were wary and she knew he was nervous.

'*Chérie*, please sit down. I have some news and I was waiting for you to come back before I tell you everything. I did not want to send the message. I want to speak with your face to face.'

Rosie giggled at André's use of the English language. It always made her chuckle but on this occasion her mirth was an attempt to cover nerves.

'André. What is it? Are you ill, what's going on?'

Taking her hands in his, he spoke tentatively. 'I am leaving, Rosie. I am going home to France… to my village and my little auberge. These are instructions for the new chef. I'm sorry, *chérie*, but there is no easy way to say this.' André looked sad and pensive as he waited for his friend's reaction.

'André, you can't leave. I don't understand. What will I do without you, when are you going?' Rosie had so many questions, so much sadness and panic in her heart as the flustered chef guided her to a chair and poured two glasses of wine.

Once Rosie was seated and had a glass in her hand, André attempted to answer all of her questions and in doing so, hoped to ease the pain he saw in the eyes of his dearest friend.

His old papa had died. He passed away peacefully in his sleep, in bed at the side of his devoted wife – a perfect way to go, according to André. His mama was unwell and frail and couldn't care for herself alone so he was going back to take up his rightful place in the family hotel. Things had changed in the thirty years he'd been away and being gay wasn't quite such a sin anymore. And after all, the villagers weren't stupid and probably guessed long ago that the son of Monsieur Levron was never going to bring home a bride. He needed to leave as soon as possible to help make the funeral arrangements and console his mama and later, once they had grieved, he would reopen the little hotel as a tribute to his papa and make it a huge success. He even had plans to transform the restaurant and serve some of his own specialities.

Rosie was lost for words then instantly realised that her friend had enough on his plate without having to deal with her snivelling and begging him to stay. He was going home to bury his father, care for his mother and as far as she was concerned, about to enter the lion's den and take up residency as the only gay in the village. Pulling herself together and doing her utmost to hide her dismay, Rosie did what she was good at and went into organisational mode. During the next twenty-four hours she was the best friend anyone could wish for, helping him pack and rewriting his terrible lists, arranging the quickest send-off ever and even though her heart was breaking, she went with him to the airport to wave goodbye. On the drive back, Rosie realised she had never felt so lonely in her whole life and even contemplated visiting her parents, then the moment passed as she wasn't that desperate, so decided the best thing to mend her aching heart was work, work and more work.

Chapter 10

Rosie

Rosie considered herself to have a good life and all things considered, she had done well for herself so, after André left and for the next couple of years, she threw herself into her career. The promised promotion never materialised and to her annoyance, despite flogging herself to death and trying hard to impress Mr Hemming she remained a Deputy. Sometimes, she thought her name badge should really say Dogsbody Assistant Manager. She'd had a few unsatisfying dates with the odd handsome guest that blew in and out on the wind, always ensuring that any meetings were off site and strictly above board. Rosie wasn't really looking for anything serious and even if she was, didn't think she could fit a boyfriend into her busy schedule as well as keeping a close eye on Ruby who was now pregnant.

Her outlook changed in the summer of 2007 when a large car dealership hired the hotel for a VIP weekend. They would entertain potential customers while showing off their range of gleaming vehicles. Rosie as usual, was deputising to Ryan, the events manager, and between them they'd organised the whole shebang whilst knowing full well that none of the credit would go to her.

They couldn't have asked for a more perfect weekend. The sun shone brightly in the cloudless, blue sky, customers parted readily with their cash after a couple of glasses of bubbly and a whiz around the estate in a flash motor, ordering a car they probably couldn't even afford. Rosie had just finished a quick tour of the grounds, checking that everything was ticking over nicely in the catering marquee and was making her way back when she couldn't help but notice a hideous yellow sports car, emblazoned with advertising slogans and draped by two very glamorous promotion girls. Just as she turned away, her attention was drawn to two long legs sticking out from the rear of the car. Worried it might be a guest who'd had one glass of cheap champagne too many, Rosie went to investigate. What she actually found was the car salesman, a really fit one at that, tucking into a venison burger and having a cheeky skive.

'Sorry to disturb you, sir, I was just checking that we didn't have a drunken guest. I'll leave you to eat your food in peace.' Rosie turned to leave but he interrupted her.

'It's okay. I'm almost done anyway. Has anyone else seen me, do you think? I was starving and I've been stuck listening to those two yakking on all morning about Botox and fake tans. They were making my ears bleed so I thought I deserved a break. See if the coast is clear, will you, and then I'll come out?' He scrunched up his paper and waited for Rosie to give him the nod.

Laughing, she scanned the crowd and after checking that the salesmen on the other stands were occupied, she gave him the thumbs up. As he stood and brushed the grass off his trousers Rosie noticed that he was slightly taller than her and had lovely grey eyes which looked amused, clearly enjoying the moment. He had what she always described as a skier's tan, healthy looking, with a scattering of freckles over his nose, and chestnut brown hair that held a tinge of red. For the first time in ages Rosie felt the electricity of real attraction and was reluctant to leave so feigned interest in the banana car. After he gave her a brief rundown of its finer points, none of which meant a thing to Rosie who was quite happy with her little Fiesta, she realised it was time to tear herself away or end up looking like a car groupie. To her surprise, he halted her escape.

'So, how about I repay you with a drink once we've finished here? You did keep lookout for me and I really appreciate you pretending to be interested in this monstrosity. The only other conversation I've had all day is with seven-year-olds, smeared in ice cream and trying to persuade me to take them for a spin. Those two over there are from another planet so I'd be grateful of a bit of intelligent conversation.'

The sales rep nodded towards the girls from the promotion company and then gave Rosie a cheeky grin, leaving her powerless to refuse.

From that moment on, and for the first time in ages, Rosie allowed herself a little bit of fun and thought she might actually be falling in love. Peter was romantic, thoughtful, and keen. He had his own place in Macclesfield and combined hard work with enjoying life to the max which in turn, rubbed off on Rosie. It made a welcome change to be able to spend nights at his flat rather than in her small room and she enjoyed putting all André's cookery lessons to good use, spoiling Peter with her favourite recipes. Now, whenever she was off duty, Rosie would be with him. He was easy-going and made her laugh, sharing the same sense of humour and tastes in music and films. When he suggested they took a quick holiday together, Rosie jumped at the chance and two months later, in August, they jetted off to Greece for a week of love in the sun. Unfortunately, it meant missing Oliver's birth and due to Ruby going into labour early, she wasn't there to hold her hand when Marcus went missing in action. To Rosie's huge relief, Olivia had stepped in.

The second she arrived back in the UK, Rosie went straight over to meet her new second cousin and instantly fell in love with the dark-eyed, peaceful baby. After a million apologies for not being around, Rosie promised to make up with babysitting duties and pram pushing whenever Ruby needed her. She was instantly shot down by Marcus who pointed out that they had it covered – his mother was just around the corner and on hand should they require her. Gritting her teeth, Rosie smiled sweetly and offered her services should Olivia be otherwise engaged, and then let it go. Ruby seemed happy enough in her beautiful home with her equally beautiful baby and from what she could make out, apart from Marcus showing jealous, control-freak tendencies, her cousin looked well.

Despite the close proximity of Prestbury, The Fairhaven and Peter's place in Macclesfield, the juggling act of job, boyfriend and cousin, sometimes meant that Rosie only saw Ruby once a month, if that. Remaining vigilant she stayed in contact by phone and heard nothing in Ruby's tone that alarmed her. For the next few months Rosie's life chugged along happily, despite having a huge row with Mr Hemming. He point-blank refused to take into consideration the fact that she had never, *ever*, had one single Christmas off since starting at the hotel all those years ago, but even so he still turned down her request for leave over the holiday period so she could go skiing with Peter.

Rosie began to feel that Mr Hemming had it in for her when Gordon, the Assistant Manager, transferred to the Edinburgh Belmonte. She confidently applied for his post, one that everyone in the hotel thought she'd earned anyway and it was a dead cert, they all fully expected the job to be hers. Well, it wasn't and she had to endure the embarrassment of an interview panel and await her fate along with the other three external candidates who lined the chairs outside the conference room.

The bad news was delivered one morning by a smug Mr Hemming who informed her in front of Mrs Amery, Ryan the Events Manager, and Head of Catering, Lenny, that they would soon be joined on the team by Jason, an old university friend and general all-rounder who would take up the post within the month. Rosie wanted the ground to open up and swallow her. Not only had he humiliated her in front of her friends, he had appointed one of his cronies too. After all her hard work and dedication it was like a slap in the face, actually it was more of a punch.

The rest of the staff were outraged and threatened revenge, from spitting in his tea to an all-out strike, and while Rosie was grateful for their support, knew in her heart that he was edging her out and by early spring her life at the hotel had become unbearable. He criticised her rotas, found fault with any of the staff she was put in charge of, tersely reminding Rosie where the buck stopped and made sure there was always some urgent task to complete, just as she finished her shift. In the end, Rosie began to refuse overtime, would arrive for work just a few minutes before her shift started and made damn sure she was out of the door the second it was over. The days of giving her all to The Fairhaven were well and truly over.

In a tearful phone call to André who had problems of his own, with a ramshackle hotel and a mother who was nearing the end of her days and needed full-time nursing, she passed on the news that Mr Hemming was shuffling her off to Bristol to stand in for someone who'd had a nervous breakdown. Quite how her name had been picked from a long list of equally qualified and nearer placed employees was anyone's guess, but he probably used his crony network of spies, so her fate was sealed. André said Hemming had the eyes of a green monster and was scared that Rosie could take away his crown and therefore wanted her gone from the hotel. He was destroying the opposition, simple as that. Whether this was true or not, one thing was for sure: Hemming was slowly eroding any joy Rosie had left for a job she once loved.

Not knowing when she would be back, Rosie called to see Ruby who seemed quite tearful at her news, then assured Rosie it was just baby blues and tiredness, insisting she would be fine. On the train journey to Bristol, Rosie pondered on whether she should have delved more into Ruby's personal life. Wasn't it a bit late at nine months to be having baby blues? Perhaps not. But why was she so tired when Saint Olivia lived just around the corner? Suspicion pricked her conscience and she wished she'd done a bit of digging. Her mind was now a whirl of mixed emotions, worry for Ruby, spite-filled thoughts of Mr Hemming, slight nerves at what lay ahead in Bristol and homesickness for a flat in Macclesfield and her lovely, grey-eyed boyfriend. Peter had been great about the whole thing, reassuring her that they would survive a couple of months apart, promising he'd pop down to visit and they'd talk every day. He also told her to sod Mr Hemming and his rotas because as soon as she got back he would take her away for a holiday in the sun.

Her time in Bristol dragged by and for the first time in her life, Rosie clock-watched and wished her days away. True to his word, Peter came down for a couple of days and after insisting she needed a break from anything to do with the Belmonte, defiantly booked them into a double room in a rival hotel. Apart from André, Rosie had never cried over a man before and was distraught when he set off for home. It did cross her mind though, whether she was also venting emotions that were a result of pent-up anger and worryingly, a creeping disillusionment with her life in general.

Finally, Rosie got the news she was longing to hear. Just six weeks into her stint in Bristol she was relieved of her duties and told she could return to The Fairhaven. Her predecessor was on the mend and would be returning to work forthwith, so she was free to go home at the weekend. Rosie couldn't wait to pack her bags and get on the train but decided not to ring Peter, wanting to surprise him by being at the flat when he came in from work instead. Her mind flew into overtime, planning the meal she would make, the wine she would choose and the lingerie she would nip out and buy at lunchtime. It would be perfect and Rosie was going to make him so glad she was home.

Clutching the keys to the flat she arrived just after lunchtime. Struggling with her large case and a carrier bag full of food she'd bought before she caught the train, Rosie thanked the cab driver and trundled up to the block of flats where Peter lived. Giddy with excitement and expectation, she let herself into the foyer and bumped her case up the stairs to the first floor. She hoped the flat wasn't a pigsty and suspected that Peter may have had a mini-holiday from domesticity while she was away, so she wasn't too surprised when she opened the door and saw clothes scattered around the living room floor. What she was surprised to see was the pink lacy bra and a black stiletto, peeking out from under the sofa.

When she heard noises coming from the bedroom, grunts and groans and giggles, her heart actually missed a beat. Rosie knew full well what she would see if she opened the door but morbid curiosity forced her to creep across the carpet and gently push it open. There, in all his white-bottomed glory was Peter, bouncing around on top of what looked like Barbie's sister. When the blonde bombshell spotted Rosie she let out an ear-splitting scream and attempted to cover herself up. All Rosie heard next was Peter saying 'shit' but by that time she was on her way back out of the door. As she bounced her case back down the flight of stairs, tears burned holes in her eyes while he called out her name from the landing, begging her to come back so that he could explain, shouting that he was sorry.

'*Sorry,*' thought Rosie, as humiliation and hurt swept through her body. '*Sorry, is that the best you can do? And why would I go back, so I could have a nice chat while Barbie's sister searched for her knickers? What an arsehole he turned out to be and what a fool you are Rosie Wilson!*' Muttering and cursing, she marched down the path and went in search of a taxi, all the while seething inside.

When she eventually hunted one down Rosie spent the journey to The Fairhaven in stunned silence. Ignoring any attempt by the cheery driver to make conversation, all Rosie could think of was that she'd left two bottles of seriously expensive wine and a bag of gourmet food in that dirty scumbag's flat. To make life worse she was haunted by the erasable image of a huge red boil, situated on the left cheek of Peter's bouncing bottom.

By using the tradesman's entrance and the old servant's staircase, Rosie managed to get to her room without being spotted. The last thing she wanted was for anyone to see her red eyes and know she'd been crying. Dragging her case into the small bedroom she noticed it smelled musty so opened a window to let in some air before flopping onto the bed and looking despondently around the room. Everything she owned was crammed into these four walls. It reminded her of her bedroom at her parent's house and how all those years ago she'd stuffed her worldly possessions into a case and a carrier bag, bravely and expectantly swapping one small room for another. Tears welled in Rosie's eyes as she remembered that fresh-faced girl from the past, full of hope and ambition and drive, and just look at her now. Where had those ten years of hard work got her? She was tired and disillusioned and the sparkle of The Fairhaven fairy dust had worn off.

Rosie knew most of it was down to Hemming because he'd finally worn her down and driven her out. She could hang around and wait for years for her promotion while she was shuffled off like a spare part but there would always be another high-flying graduate ready to come along and pip her to the post. It was about time she took stock of her life and put it into perspective.

She had a very healthy savings account, mainly because, apart from her little car, she never went anywhere or spent money on herself, but what about the things that mattered, friends, and relationships? Peter was just another Jack the Lad, Rosie realised that now; because of her job she'd gone away and he took the opportunity to play the field. Maybe if she'd been here and a bit more available it might never have happened. Rosie accepted that didn't alter the fact he was a cheat and instead, focused her attention on her room. There was one single wardrobe, a chest of drawers and a bedside cabinet, and in those three pieces of furniture, her whole life was stored. She'd grown up between these walls but it wasn't much to show for her time on this earth and dedication to her job, and in that split-second realisation hit; Rosie decided she'd had enough.

One hour later, she calmly surveyed her room and mentally ticked off a hastily compiled check-list. The bed was stripped and held a stack of clothing she no longer wanted. The cupboards were empty and the posters had been removed from the walls and rolled up. The small TV and radio were too cumbersome to carry so she would leave them for Kelly, along with the clothes and a note explaining everything. Maybe one of her kids could have them in their bedroom. In contrast to the last time she did a flit, Rosie had carefully placed all her remaining belongings into her suitcase and a large black holdall. The final thing she packed was Humphrey the bear and the fading photo of her and Ruby, sitting on the front step when they were kids. It had always been by her side and was a talisman, a bond which reminded Rosie that she always had one special person in her life, two with André. Zipping up the bag she sighed, took a final look around then said a bittersweet goodbye to a huge part of her life before wheeling her case out of the door.

Leaving her worldly possessions at the bottom of the servants' stairs, Rosie made her way to Reception and nodded politely to posh Belinda who was busy checking in some guests. Without drawing attention to herself, Rosie went into the office and from her desk removed any personal belongings before placing two white envelopes on the shiny wooden surface. One was a personal goodbye and a heartfelt thank you to Mrs Amery and the other contained her room key and a terse letter of resignation for her nemesis, Mr Hemming. Without a second glance Rosie walked out of the office, smiled at Belinda and collected her cases. She felt bad about not saying a proper goodbye to all her friends but if she was going to go, this was the best way, without fuss and ceremony. Teary farewells would be too much for her; she hoped they'd understand why when Kelly read them the letter. Not only that, if she had to see Mr Hemming one more time, Rosie knew that she'd probably punch him right in his smarmy, know-it-all, superior, eyes-too-close-together, annoying face.

Saying goodbye to Ruby wasn't quite so easy.

At first, she seemed agitated and worried that Marcus might complain about Rosie leaving her car on their drive, so instead, she parked it in their empty double garage and promised to advertise it for sale as soon as possible, asking Ruby to send the money on. Surely he couldn't find fault with that?

Once inside again, Rosie fed Oliver his bottle. Ruby had given up on breastfeeding because Marcus objected to her being sat around with her bits out, as he so gentlemanly put it. Sensing her cousin's sadness Rosie ventured the question if everything was alright at home, with her and Marcus, commenting that she looked pale and very drawn in the face. Batting away any concerns Ruby put her tiredness down to Oliver's colic and teething; not knowing the first thing about babies, Rosie had to take her at her word.

When it was time to go Ruby became tearful so when she clung on for dear life in an extended hug it didn't inspire confidence and for the second time, Rosie felt like she was abandoning a puppy. The honking of the taxi's horn forced them apart and Rosie despondently dragged her bags to the waiting driver. As he loaded up, the two cousins said their final goodbyes.

'Now, don't upset yourself. I'm only an hour and a half away and I will be back and forwards all the time. You can visit me whenever you want. Come on, give me a big smile otherwise I'll chicken out and go back to the hotel.' Rosie was also having trouble reining in her emotions but had to be strong, for her own sake never mind Ruby's.

The taxi was loaded and ready to go and the driver returned to his seat, looking impatiently at his watch and giving Rosie the hint that they needed to get a move on.

Ruby had by this time rallied sufficiently and was able to appear composed. 'I'm sorry, Rosie. I'm just overtired and being a baby, look, Oliver is braver than me. You get off and text me when you arrive. I'll come and see you soon. Just be happy and do something for yourself for once. Go on, get lost before I lock you in the garage and keep you hostage forever.' Ruby gave Rosie a brave smile and a gentle push.

They waved to each other until they were both out of sight and when Rosie turned to face the front of the cab, she let out a huge sigh of relief. *Please God, let her really be okay*, she said to herself as the taxi made its way to the airport. Once she was off the estate and onto the motorway, the tension eased and Rosie felt a spark of excitement in her chest, the faint trace of a smile appearing on her lips. It had been a long and stressful day but it was almost over now and soon, she would be in France, and best of all, she would be with André.

When she'd rang him from her room earlier that day and told him all about Peter and Mr Hemming and how she hated her life, as always, he made everything instantly okay.

'Listen, Rosie, tell them all to fuck off and come and live here with me. You can help me run the auberge. I can't manage by myself and I am sick up to my teeth of it all. I argue every second with my chef who thinks he is the Mr Smart Alex and I miss you very much. So, this is the answer. Book the ticket and come to France.'

The second he said it, everything fell into place and a wave of pure relief and excitement washed over Rosie's body while adrenaline fizzed in her veins. The rest was easy. Rosie booked her flight, stripped her room, packed her case and wrote her letters, just about managing not to take André's advice where her boss was concerned – even though it was so tempting.

The Air France flight to Nantes taxied onto the runway and Rosie waited patiently in her seat for take-off. She'd turned off her phone when she was inside the terminal as there had been a constant flow of calls and texts from Peter and Mr Hemming. It was now 9pm and the sky outside was dark. The engines roared and the plane gathered speed as it hurtled along the runway. Rosie waited for that amazing moment when the wheels lift off the tarmac and you know you are on your way. As the nose of the plane pointed upwards she tilted her head back and rested against the seat, enjoying the thrill of the ascent, feeling the power of the aircraft as it flew higher and higher, speeding her to a new life.

When it began to level off, the plane banked to the right and set its course south. Looking out of the window Rosie could make out the bright lights of Manchester in the distance, then Jodrell Bank and scattered below the homes of Cheshire where somewhere amongst the yellow dots lived her parents and Ruby. There was still a tinge of sadness attached to her actions but at the same time Rosie knew without a doubt she had made the right choice.

The lights soon began to fade and the sky grew black as the plane flew higher into the clouds. Rosie smiled to herself, remembering something someone once said to her. In her head, she spoke to him, wishing he could hear.

'*See, Alfred, I kept my promise. You said I'd know when and you were right, old friend. It nearly burnt me out but I followed my instincts and I think I got off the ride just in time. I hope I've made you proud, one way or another.*' Gazing out of the small window into the starry night, Rosie felt a wonderful sense of peace wash over her.

Deciding that she'd had enough of soul-searching for the day, Rosie looked around for the air hostess. She was going to order a large drink and make herself a toast to the future – to being with André, starting a new life in France and enjoying the important things in life.

Chapter 11

Rosie

Birdsong and bright white light woke Rosie from her wine and fatigue induced slumber. Snuggling down under her blankets she allowed herself to wake up slowly from the deepest, most peaceful sleep she'd had in years. She sort of remembered coming to her room and while she yawned and stretched, she scanned her surroundings in order to get her bearings. After a very late evening of reminiscing and catching up with André, she was so tired she'd barely managed to pull off her jeans before collapsing onto the bed. Checking her watch, which was still on UK time, it said 9am which meant it was 10am in France. Rosie was semi-reluctant to leave the warmth of her bed and relinquish the luxury of a rare lie-in but the urge to explore took over and she was eager to get downstairs and start the day.

The lack of an en-suite meant a dash along the corridor to the bathroom which harked back to the seventies and cried out for a makeover. It was clean enough and the ancient wall heater eventually clunked and spluttered into life, giving up just enough lukewarm water to refresh her. After a sprint back to her room, Rosie dressed quickly and dried her hair. The old-fashioned, three-sectioned mirror was mottled and worn at the corners and the dressing table which it stood on was pre-war, Rosie wasn't sure which one, but crafted from beautiful oak that had stood the test of time. As the drier warmed her hair, Rosie took in her room.

The floral wallpaper was faded, but would probably have been pretty when it was first hung in the low, timbered room, now it was just tired and peeling at the edges and way past its use by date. The carpet had also seen better days, threadbare in places and it didn't remotely compliment or match the heavy chintz curtains. The old-fashioned, mustard, woollen bedspread and the mismatched sheets reminded Rosie of the boarding house where they used to stay in Scarborough when she was a child, making them at least twenty years out of style. The bedroom was spotlessly clean though and a weary traveller wanting fresh bedding and a place to rest their head would have no complaints on that score. On the other hand, you wouldn't exactly be eager to get back to this room in the evening or be tempted to book in for next year, either.

André was waiting in the lounge when she came down the wooden staircase. He was listening to the radio in the corner, drinking his coffee whilst flicking through a pile of paperwork. When he spotted Rosie he immediately left his task and ushered her through to the next room which doubled as a small dining area and a bar. Sitting at one of the traditional wooden bistro chairs, Rosie waited patiently while he fussed about bringing coffee and croissants and shouting orders to someone who was clanking around in the kitchen. Finally he came to rest and after pouring them both a cup of steaming fresh coffee, André relaxed and got stuck into his breakfast.

'We are expecting some guests this afternoon, so after breakfast, I must prepare. Michel is happy for once as they wish to eat here this evening, so he is pushing a boat out in the kitchen.'

André's haphazard use of English phrases never failed to make Rosie smile.

'It's pushing *the* boat out, André, but you were almost right. I can give you a hand with your rooms, that's what I'm here for, remember. Just let me know what you need me to do and I'll get cracking.'

'*Non, chérie*. For one week you are on holiday, I insist. I can manage by myself. Michel prepares the breakfasts, then cooks for our guests in the evening while I have been demoted to the waiter. You, Mademoiselle, will watch and eat and relax.' He gave

Rosie his best stern look and then continued. 'But first, I will take you on a grand tour of *Les Trois Chênes*. Come, it was too dark last night so now I want to show you my kingdom.' With a dramatic flourish, André stood and pulled back his chair, and then gentlemanly, helped Rosie with hers. Beckoning, he signalled that she should follow him through the back of the bar to the kitchen.

'First, I will introduce you to *L'Enfant Terrible*. He is a good chef but wants to run about before he can walk. Come, he is in here somewhere, complaining as usual.' And with that, André bustled off into the kitchen.

At first, Rosie couldn't see anyone but heard the sound of a male voice coming from underneath the sink, over by the window. There was a great deal of noise, the clunking and clanking of metal and then the word '*enfin*,' before a head of dark curls appeared from the cupboard below. When he reversed out and stood up he was surprised by his audience but recovered quickly and smiled at Rosie, then immediately scowled at André, letting off a tirade of angry French that was almost lost on her. Following the heated conversation as best she could, Rosie got the general gist due to a lot of pointing towards the sink and a bucket of water, which she presumed was the cause of the chef's problems. André responded with his own flurry of dramatic hand waving and eye rolling before remembering why he was there so changed the subject and introduced Rosie.

'*Chérie*, this is Michel, our wonderful chef and winner of the prize for finding fault with every part of my kitchen. Michel, this is my Rosie who I tell you everything about. Speak English. She is not so good with French.' André stepped back like a proud father while they shook hands.

'It's a pleasure to meet you, Michel. I'm sure you are not as bad as André makes out and neither is my French, as it happens. I'm looking forward to sampling your dishes and if you need any help in the kitchen, please let me know, I'd be happy to assist.' Rosie kept it short in case he didn't understand English too well and she was finding it hard to concentrate with those huge, dark eyes staring at her.

'Hi, Rosie, it is good to meet you at last. André has told me a lot about you. I will prepare something special in honour of your arrival here in France. I hope you will be very happy with us.'

His smile was warm and genuine and his English was perfect. Rosie felt a little bit odd inside.

'Okay. Enough of this chittle chatteling, we need to get on. I have guests to greet and things to do. Come, *chérie*, let's go through to the garden.' André bounded back through the door, seemingly oblivious to the sparks of electricity that were bouncing around the peeling walls of his kitchen, with Rosie following obediently.

'I think he seems rather nice, your chef. I hope you're not being too hard on him, André. I know what a grumpy tyrant you can be sometimes, oh and it's tittle tattle by the way.' Rosie felt it her duty to reprimand André and correct his English although his mistakes did make her smile.

André continued down the path of the kitchen garden, pretending not to hear while at the same time concealing a wry, knowing smile. He'd seen the sparks.

The grand tour gave Rosie much to think about and she still hadn't been introduced to André's mother, Clémence. They both lived in the end section of the block of three buildings and he had to get her ready, then, after he had prepared the guest rooms, they would all have lunch together. It was clear that in his absence André's parents had struggled and let things go and possibly hadn't invested any money back into the auberge for a number of years. From what Rosie had gleaned from hers, she expected the other seven bedrooms held a similar mishmash of pre-war furniture and a few useful modern additions, probably bought sometime in the seventies or eighties and since then, they'd made do.

Furnishings aside, the hotel setting was perfect, just far enough from the main road not to hear traffic noise yet easy to find on the map. The rear of the building looked out over a patchwork of farmers' fields, spreading as far as the horizon. They were interspersed with the odd cottage roof peeping from between a hill, providing a breathtaking view, which Rosie was sure would be just as beautiful whatever the season.

The kitchen garden was a bit wild and in need of tending but just about holding its own and abundant with salad and vegetables. From there, they followed the winding path that led towards a wooded area which opened into a clearing and on it, stood a large, dilapidated barn. André explained that it was hundreds of years old and had been used to store feed for the animals and farm machinery, some of it was still inside, covered in hay and dust and whatever else they had no use of. Continuing along the path they came to a copse of tangled bushes, squeezing through they ended up in the fields at the back of the hotel and here stood four outbuildings of various sizes. One looked as though it was partially restored but the others were in a poor state of repair.

They had been unused for decades and bought from Clémence and her husband Hugo by two friends from England, some years back. The English pair had intended to convert them all into holiday lets but after a huge row about money and one or the other not pulling their weight, they abandoned the project and sold everything back to André's parents for a knock-down price.

They completed the tour of the grounds by ending up at the back of the hotel and the residential section of the property, which is where André left Rosie while he went to see his mother.

The sun was high in the sky so she sat in one of the rusty iron chairs that were scattered around the terrace, allowing the warmth of the rays to soothe her as she took in the view and embraced the wonderful peace of the place. Lost in her thoughts, Rosie was interrupted by a cough and the silhouette of a tall man. Shielding her eyes her gaze rested on Michel. His white T-shirt was splattered liberally with what she imagined was blood and his apron smeared with God knows what. His baggy, chequered chef pants were teamed with clogs and in his hand he held two glasses of rosé, silently offering her one before sitting in a wobbly chair by her side.

'It is very beautiful, the view from here. I like to sit and look before I start to work. It is a simple and free pleasure in my life. I think it is sad that more people do not come here. It was once full of laughter and visitors. I remember coming here as a child.' Michel drank his wine and looked out across the fields.

'From what I can see I think it all became too much for André's parents and I suspect he is struggling too. I was surprised that he even let you into his kitchen to be honest, you must be doing something right.' Rosie took the opportunity to look at Michel closely and have a sneaky peak at his strong, toned arms and admire his Gallic complexion and chiselled jaw line. She wasn't even going to contemplate what lay under his road-kill T-shirt because she was flustered already so remained silent and waited for Michel to speak.

'Hah! He only lets me in because he is too busy with the hotel and most days we have no customers, so I do nothing. I am here just in case somebody arrives or there is a miracle. This place could be… how is the expression? Ah, like a gold mine. I want to open the restaurant every night and attract people from the villages close by. There is a bar and small café in St Pierre but nowhere else to eat for miles. I feel that André has given up and he has lost his fire so I think soon, if things do not change, I will have to leave and find work in the city.' Anger and resignation flashed across Michel's face as he shook his black curls in annoyance.

'Well, he has just lost his father and all this is a huge change from what he did in England. Perhaps you just need to give him time to readjust and once he's taken stock, he can start afresh. And that's why I'm here, to help him run this place so please don't give up on him just yet.' Rosie had been loyal to André and hoped her words would also cheer Michel up and make him stay, because it occurred to her as she was speaking that she really didn't want him to go anywhere.

'Well, I wish you luck, Rosie, and hope you can make a difference because he does not hear one single word I say. He is a very stubborn man. Now, I am going to make you lunch and if

I cannot impress the boss, then maybe I can work my magic on you.' He held her gaze for a second then gave her a cheeky smile and removed her empty glass before standing and marching off towards the kitchen.

'Don't you worry about that,' Rosie whispered to herself. 'I think you've already cast your spell.' Smiling, she closed her eyes and lifted her face to the sun, looking forward to lunchtime and some of Michel's magic.

When Michel reached the kitchen, he placed the glasses in the sink and couldn't resist sneaking a look through the small window at the golden-haired goddess who was sitting in the garden. That very morning, he had decided to offer his resignation to André and then head to Nantes to find work there, but from the second Rosie walked into the kitchen, his plans changed. Perhaps he would stay on, just a little while longer. It would be worth the leaky sink *and* the useless range if he could spend some time with the beautiful English woman, and maybe, just maybe, she could make André see sense.

André's mother was so frail and tiny that Rosie thought she may snap in two if the wheelchair hit a bump on the terrace, and her heart was in her mouth as he jiggled her out of the back door and towards the kitchen. He was going to leave her in the lounge, listening to the radio while he prepared the rooms before lunch so they wheeled her past Michel who was busy chopping but managed a quick smile and a nod, plus a seconds worth of eye contact with Rosie. They left Clémence in a world of her own in front of the huge fireplace, wrapped in a blanket and nodding off to Strauss.

Upstairs Rosie tidied her room then overcome with restlessness and anticipation, went in search of André. She was going to rediscover the joys of bed making whether he liked it or not. Anything to keep her mind occupied and off Michel.

The warm heat of June soon became the angry, red roar of July and then August arrived. A few guests came and went, none of them promised to return and most had happened upon the auberge by accident or in desperation when everywhere else was full up. The workload was nothing that Rosie and André couldn't cope with on their own but not nearly enough to satisfy the burning ambition of Michel who was desperate to make his mark on the culinary world, or at least the residents of St Pierre.

Rosie had to admit that he was a wonderful chef and looked forward to mealtimes, not just to sample his food; she enjoyed Michel's company as well. He was intelligent and well-travelled and had served his apprenticeship in Paris and London, which is where he learned to speak English. André was good friends with Michel's older brother, Henri. At his father's funeral André was bowled over by the eager chef whom he hadn't seen for many years and offered Michel a job on the spot. Thrilled at the chance to run a kitchen of his own, Michel jumped at the opportunity but it wasn't quite the dream position he had imagined and until the arrival of Rosie, had been summoning up the courage to leave.

Apart from kitchen politics they all rubbed along with each other quite well, although what surprised Rosie the most was the change in André. She remembered him flying around the kitchen in England, barking orders, doing a hundred things at once, creating new menus each season and basking in the glory of his reputation at The Fairhaven. The change was unbelievable. He hadn't given up exactly, but seemed content making beds, doing laundry, pottering about and most of all, relaxing in the sun with a glass of wine or playing pétanque with his buddies. There was a constant stream of acquaintances at the hotel to distract him. Old school friends and neighbours from the surrounding farms would drop by, who thankfully had no problem associating with the only gay in the village, which in some ways, made André a bit of an attraction and a change from the norm.

His closest friends were Sebastien who owned the bar and café in the village; Henri, Michel's very smooth, extremely handsome brother; and Dominique, who lived up the lane with his Polish wife, Zofia. None of the men needed much encouragement to wile away the hours drinking and playing cards, or pétanque on the dusty drive at the front of the hotel. Rosie once commented to a frustrated (in many senses of the word) Michel, that even if a coach load of guests pulled up and wanted rooms for the night, André would probably prefer to play cards and be most put out if they ruined his game. To be fair though, Rosie didn't begrudge André his new-found way of life because he had plenty to do just looking after Clémence. Apart from a nurse who came each afternoon to do the necessary for his mother, he lovingly cared for her by himself.

Their summer days had taken on a natural, contented routine. Once Clémence was wheeled out in the morning, Rosie would take her for a stroll along the lanes. Here, the frail old lady would chatter away to nobody in particular, pointing to various things along the way to which Rosie would always respond in her improving French and attempt some conversation in return. Whether she heard or understood, Rosie couldn't tell, but Clémence seemed to enjoy her little stroll and always had a bit of pink in her cheeks when they returned home.

The four of them would eat their lunch together, a task slightly more demanding for Michel than the continental breakfast he prepared each morning for the guests. Now and then Rosie would catch Clémence watching her son, love written in her eyes and the rarest flicker of a smile when he cracked a joke. Sometimes, she would ask Rosie where Hugo was, or tell André to save some food for Papa which made everyone feel sad because somewhere in her lost world, she was still waiting for her husband to come home. One evening, as they sat on the terrace, in the most uncomfortable chairs in the world, Rosie broached the subject of the hotel and André's plans for the future.

'So, André, what do you plan to do once the autumn arrives? I've got quite a few suggestions for the bedrooms, nothing too scary but I think they need updating, and the kitchen needs some work too. Maybe we could get Michel involved, what do you think?' Rosie saw not an ounce of interest in his eyes.

'We shall see, Rosie, for now, we are ticking like a clock, there is no hurry. We are not poor or starving, we have a nice life and good friends so why should we rush about? Slowly, slowly, *chérie*, we have all the time in the world.' André presumed the subject was closed.

'Yes, but soon, you will want to get back into the kitchen, won't you? If we get cracking and work through the winter we could have this place looking like a new pin by the time we reopen in the spring, and André let's not forget, I came here to work. It's been a lovely few months pottering about, but now we need to make plans.' Rosie was being firm but saw that André wasn't entirely convinced or bothered.

'Okay, *chérie*. I will hear your ideas and if it makes you happy to work like a mad woman, then so be it, but tonight, let us enjoy the sunset and our wine.'

Rosie huffed and rolled her eyes at her friend but she couldn't be cross with him for long, so resolved to pin him down with her lists in the morning. However, when she came downstairs the next day Rosie found a note saying he'd gone to the sea with Dominique to fetch the oysters, the nurse would see to Clémence and he would be home later that evening. Now Rosie knew exactly how frustrated Michel felt, with his head full of ideas and hopes for the future. Well this time André had met his match, two heads were better than one and whether he liked it or not, with the help of Michel she was going to put *Les Trois Chênes* firmly back on the map.

Rosie loved village life and had managed to make a few friends whilst soldiering along with her French. She had realised quite quickly that if you had a go at speaking their language, regardless of how badly it all came out, most people appreciated your effort and helped you along. Zofia, Dominique's wife, who mercifully spoke excellent English was her closest friend and ally and introduced her to the great and the good of St Pierre. Within a few months she had been welcomed into the fold and was now on speaking terms with Renee from the patisserie and Florian who owned the pharmacie. There was also an amusing hierarchy within village life and any scrap of gossip or news would be passed along the grapevine and spread like wildfire. Not a lot went on in the countryside, so any little snippet was well received.

André was old news so the arrival of the pretty English girl with golden hair perked things up no end. Once they knew she was staying *and* working alongside the single and equally good-looking Michel, rumours were rife and tongues wagged like crazy. Zofia's neighbour, Hortense, was the queen of the village and not one nugget of information passed her by. If you wanted to know what was going on, whether a rumour was true or who said it, she was your woman. Her family had lived in the village since it was hewn from the earth and her ancestors had fought in every single French war or uprising, sending their brave men-folk off to die in battlefields around the world. The very powerful Mayor turned out to be Michel's uncle, who was in turn Hortense's brother-in-law (also of ancestral stock). Her younger brother was the chief of police, her son was the notaire and her daughter was the headmistress of the local school so between them, they had the village sewn up.

Rosie was given the once over by Hortense during morning coffee, which took place in Zofia's kitchen, where she acted as translator when things got a bit confusing and helpfully jollied the conversation on. It was possible that she gilded the lily here and there to spice things up, but in the end, the queen of the village seemed suitably impressed with what she had heard and seen and so she went away with enough information to begin spreading the word.

After their initial meeting, Hortense and Rosie soon became good friends and chatted along quite happily with albeit stilted conversations and the use of a dictionary. It was during one of Zofia's coffee and cake mornings that Rosie had a moment of inspiration. It would be Hortense's birthday at the end of August, not a special occasion, but enough for her to require a nice meal and a get together with her friends and family. Seizing the moment, Rosie volunteered the auberge and not only that, she also volunteered Michel's services free of charge, along with herself and André who would be the Maître d' for the evening. All Hortense had to do was pay for the food and wine. She would get Michel to draw up a choice of menus which the queen could ponder on and they would all ensure Hortense had a birthday to remember and was talked about within a ten-mile radius for the foreseeable future. Naturally, Hortense agreed immediately which thrilled Rosie who could hardly wait to get back to the kitchen to tell Michel because at last, this was his chance to shine.

Chapter 12

Rosie

Rosie was like a woman possessed and made list after list of things to do. Michel was also on a mission to impress the whole department of the Loire Atlantique while André took himself off on an impromptu cycling holiday with Dominique, announcing that he would be gone for a week. While he was away, they planned Hortense's birthday meal as if it was a military exercise and after perusing the menus she decided they all sounded wonderful and much to his delight, left the final choice to Michel.

Meanwhile, Rosie decided that a dip into her savings was required if she was ever going to get anything done. Her first job was to advertise the hotel. It was nearing the end of the summer holidays therefore unlikely that there would be any new custom from families on their way to or from the south. Still, there were many couples who waited for the kids to go back to school before they took their well-earned break and also, those who didn't worship the sun might fancy a bit of sightseeing in cooler temperatures.

Rosie remembered the programmes she'd seen in England where Brits were packing up and looking for a new life overseas and with an abundance of run-down properties still left for the taking, France was a popular house-hunting destination. After a long day of research, she placed adverts in two glossy property magazines and emailed British estate agents who ran tours and viewings of houses for sale in the area. Taking Zofia with her for backup, they drove to Chateaubriant and engaged the services of a printer who made fliers, and then spent a whole day sticking them in every shop, bar and garage they passed en-route to the hotel. Utilising her bubbly personality, Rosie also left their details with all the estate agents in the area whose weary clients may want a comfy bed and a good meal after a day trudging around renovation projects. The added assurance of English speaking staff would hopefully put them at their ease because it was a nightmare making a reservation by phone if you didn't speak the language.

That still left the problem of where she would put her potential guests because there was no time to rip out the one and only bathroom in the hotel, so she had to take a chance. Rosie decided to re-vamp two rooms quickly – anything would be better than how they looked now. If both of the new bedrooms were occupied then any extra guests would just have to use the old facilities and dowdy rooms, but at least she would be able to show them what they could have next time, once the whole hotel had been refurbished. The facilities downstairs would just have to wait because if she was catering for people who were out all day sightseeing or on their way back to the ferry port, then the most important thing would be to provide a lovely room in which to sleep, not worry that the armchair smelt of dogs or the lumpy, threadbare sofa was stuffed with the original horsehair. This was where knowing the queen of the village came in handy and Hortense soon put Rosie on to a couple of builders and plumbers who could be relied upon to do a quick, professional job, otherwise her majesty would hear about it and they wouldn't risk that.

Rosie picked the two large, central bedrooms which had the best views and were bright and airy. While she scraped off ancient layers of wallpaper, Christophe and Bernard constructed a small en-suite in each room, installing a modern white toilet, sink and power shower with shiny chrome fittings and a lovely tiled floor.

When he finally returned, André was encouraging but left Rosie to her own devices. He was charged with bringing them refreshments in between caring for his mother, who was now his number one priority. The doctor and the nurse were becoming ever more frequent visitors and Clémence spent most of her day in bed. Rosie called in each afternoon to hold her tiny, frail hand and listen to her muttering. It was all she could offer but it gave André a break and some time outside in the sun.

Michel had surprised Rosie by turning up at the crack of dawn on day one of her makeover and offered his services, labouring for the builders, scraping walls and rubbing down skirting boards. As they slopped soapy water onto the peeling paper, Rosie was enjoying the close proximity to Michel and the chance to spend some time with him.

'I didn't expect you to help, you know, Michel. I'm sure you would rather be in the kitchen than here but I do appreciate it. I haven't a clue what those two are saying half the time. It's like being on another planet when they get going and they argue constantly about everything.' Rosie inclined her head to the two men shouting and cursing at each other as they dragged a large piece of plasterboard into the room.

'Just ignore them. They are like two children and have always been the same, like Henri and me. We fight all the time about football, rugby, women, anything really. But I wanted to help, like you will help me with Hortense's party. We are a team now, you and I.'

He didn't look at her when he said it but had he done so, Michel would have noticed the stupid grin on Rosie's face and her pink cheeks, flushing with happiness.

Michel carried on scraping, waiting to see if his words got any kind of reaction while his heart hammered in his chest. Rosie had no idea of the effect she had on him. Since the day she arrived his life had changed. As he served breakfasts, his only thought was of when she would appear and when she did, her sunny face would kick start his day. While he chopped vegetables and prepared for dinner he listened constantly for her voice on the terrace or footsteps in the corridor. The hours ticked by too slowly until they would eat lunch together, then she would be gone too quickly on some errand or visit and as he lay in bed at night, she tormented his thoughts and dreams. He wasn't lying either when he said he and Henri argued about everything and Rosie was the subject of their most recent altercation. Michel was incensed when his brother hinted he was going invite Rosie out for dinner one evening, whether Henri was teasing and trying to wind him up he didn't care so had warned him to stay well away.

There was no way Michel would let his older brother muscle in this time. He was convinced Rosie had been sent to France especially for him so he needed to pluck up the courage to tell her how he felt – and soon, but was terrified that if the feeling wasn't mutual he would scare her off and she would pack her bags and leave. The cogs of his mind turned constantly, waiting for his opportunity, watching for signs and dropping hints the size of bricks. If André guessed that Michel was in love he didn't let on and there was no way he was going to confide in his boss who was over-protective of Rosie and quite obviously adored her. What if he didn't approve and sent *him* packing? No, he would wait and keep it to himself.

The two cumbersome iron beds from each room were dismantled and taken into the courtyard and repainted antique white. The carpets were ripped up and then the floorboards sanded down then varnished and after the walls were given a few coats of emulsion, Rosie was ready to put the finishing touches to the bedrooms. André reimbursed her for every centime she spent and let her have free rein with regards to decor, mainly because his mind was elsewhere, concerns for his fading mother outweighing everything.

Two days before Hortense's party, the bedrooms were ready so Rosie threw open the doors for the grand reveal to the curious faces of André, Michel, Dominique and Zofia. There were oohs and aahs and an avalanche of compliments. Rosie basked in the glory of a job well done and enjoyed a huge hug from her old friend, who seemed genuinely pleased and slightly overwhelmed at the transformation.

The freshly painted sash windows and off-white drapes, which were speckled with tiny blue flowers, framed the view across the fields while the little en-suite was functional and took up the minimum amount of space in the bright, white room. The adjoining wall was painted in duck-egg blue and complimented the quilted, patchwork bedspread and crisp white sheets. The antique furniture now blended into the room and stood elegantly on the varnished wooden floor. The bedside tables that Rosie had stripped, repainted and distressed were unrecognisable; they held a vase of country flowers and a pretty lamp. The room screamed country chic at the same time as being functional and easy to maintain. While the others went next door to inspect the almost identical bedroom – the walls inside this one painted a dusky, rose pink – André held back and gave her a kiss on the cheek.

'You have done well, *chérie*. I am proud of you. I wish Mama could come up here and see how beautiful all this looks. We should take a photograph and show her, it will make her happy I think.' André gazed around the room and Rosie noticed a tear in his eye and for a moment her pride turned to despair for her friend.

'Are you sure she will like it though, André? This has been her home for so long. What if she hates it and thinks I've interfered? I don't want to upset her in any way.' Rosie felt the joy and confidence she felt a few minutes earlier evaporate. Had she been totally insensitive and disregarded Clémence?

André was standing by the window, lost somewhere in his thoughts, staring at the fields in the distance when he turned to quell Rosie's concerns.

'*Chérie*, believe me, this will bring joy to my mother's soul. She likes you very much. Mama says to me that you are the wind of fresh air and have brought new life to this place. I am only sad that you could not have met her when she was full of energy, like you. You are very similar and you remind me of how she was when I was a boy, always laughing and running about, making people welcome with her smile, bringing them inside and caring for them. I miss those days more than I can say.'

Rosie saw André wipe a tear from his eye and she took his hand in hers.

'Come on then, no time like the present. I'll go and get my camera then we can show her what we've done. Tell the others not to bounce on the beds while I'm gone, I want it to look perfect.' With that, she pulled him from the room and left him to check what was going on next door. His words had at first made her sad then more determined than ever to turn this place around and honour the legacy of Clémence and Hugo.

It was party time and Michel had spent the day before constructing a large wooden pagoda on the terrace. Rosie had been busy all morning, weaving artificial flowers and fairy lights around the frame and down the legs. The tables underneath had been placed together in a long line and covered with starched, white linen and decorated with floral displays from the shop in the next village. André had washed and polished all of his mother's and grandmother's finest cutlery and tableware and done a wonderful job setting the table. It looked spectacular and Rosie was sure Hortense would be over the moon with the result.

Dominique got in on the act as well. Having had his own restaurant in London for many years before he retired to his homeland, he volunteered to help choose the wine after matching it to Michel's menu. Then it was all hands on deck as they prepared a feast for thirty guests, amongst whom would be the great and the good of the village, plus assorted acquaintances and family members, all hopefully well-connected and ready to be impressed.

Clémence sat under the pagoda in the shade, watching with interest the comings and goings as they all flapped about. She had been overjoyed when André and Rosie came to show her the photos and kept tapping the pictures then holding them to her heart, talking to her Hugo who she thought was in the room and then beaming at her son and his friend. The snapshots were now placed on her bedside table where she could always see them and when she found out about the party, she insisted on being brought outside to watch.

Rather than use the only available option of bringing their guests through the kitchen or around the back of the hotel and past the vegetable garden, Rosie and Zofia had cleared a path along the side of Clémence's living quarters and now, everyone could park in the drive and walk round to the terrace at the back where they would be met by the sight of the beautiful pagoda. As André served aperitifs to the birthday girl and her appreciative guests, the late afternoon sun bathed the terrace in burnt orange light while Rosie and Michel beavered away in the kitchen. They worked together in intense harmony. Both aware of how important this meal was and at the same time, how comfortable they felt stood next to each other or moving around the kitchen, passing knives and bowls, touching hands briefly and wondering if the other had felt the fizz of electricity and their heart beat faster on contact.

The plates that contained the warm duck salad came back scraped clean and the fish course of fresh sea bass in a light cream sauce was savoured by each diner. The fillet of steak, cooked to perfection and served on an artistic nest of crispy onions, drizzled with jus and complimented by the garden vegetables (pulled fresh from the earth that morning) went down a storm. During the lull that settled while the cheeses were passed around, Rosie and Michel peeped through the window, observing the diners and trying to judge their mood. The four panes of glass were very small and required them both to squash together in order for them to see out. Rosie could feel the heat of his skin through his T-shirt as his muscled arms pushed against her bare skin. She could almost hear him breathing and fought an incredible urge to hold his hand which was splayed out on the draining board, right next to hers. Eventually he spoke and turned his head to look at her, their faces were only inches apart.

'We did it, Rosie, you and I together. Look what we have made.' His eyes flicked quickly to the terrace then straight back to her. 'This is all because of you. Since you arrived, my life has changed and I want you to know that I thank God every day for bringing you here.' There, he'd said it, almost. All he had to do now was kiss her. She was right there waiting, he could tell from the look in her eye.

Then Zofia appeared.

'Michel, where are you? Congratulations! The food was superb… *magnifique*. They are all saying such wonderful things. I am so proud of you both. Hurry, you must come outside and shake hands with your guests and sit for a while, you are amongst friends and we want to say thank you.' Zofia was oblivious to crashing the party and the moment was lost.

Gathering their senses, Rosie and Michel did as they were told and walked out to the terrace to a huge round of applause.

The party, as predicted by Zofia, went on into the early hours of the morning. After their dessert of pears poached in Marsala wine and infused with the heady fragrance of star anise, vanilla and cinnamon, and served with a swirl of crème fraîche, the diners got on with the important business of dancing the night away under the fairy lights, the moon and the stars. Eventually, the food and the wine caught up with the less hardy of the bunch, including Zofia who wasn't a huge fan of the Frenchman's penchant for alcohol. Along with most of the other guests she parted company with her husband just after midnight and left them to drink themselves under the table.

Most of the clearing was done and soon, André was alone with his band of very merry men. Rosie was exhausted and after their brief moment by the window hadn't spent a second alone with Michel since. He had been summoned to the terrace by an extremely chilled out André and was now drinking brandy and resting his aching feet. Rosie knew she would be the only female and the odd one out in the crowd and had no desire whatsoever to see in the dawn with a glass in her hand, so went outside to say goodnight. Remembering the almost-kiss by the window, Rosie didn't want to let the special moment fade away and needed to send Michel a message, to remember how they felt during those precious seconds. As she approached the table the men hushed slightly and waited for her to speak. She stopped, just behind Michel and boldly placed both hands on his shoulders, then addressed the bleary-eyed gathering.

'Well, I'm going to leave you all in peace. Try not to make too much noise and wake Clémence, and if you can't make it home feel free to use the sofas or one of the guest bedrooms, but *not* room three or four, or you'll be sorry, okay?'

As she spoke, Michel placed one of his hands on top of hers and the feel of his skin almost made her lose concentration.

'Anyway, enjoy yourselves and I will see you in the morning for a full English breakfast, if you're men enough to face it.' She gave them all a cheeky wink and just for Michel, gently squeezed his hand. When she felt him respond, Rosie thought he'd got the message.

Rosie lay in her bed with the windows open, letting the moon cast a silvery glow over the walls as she listened to the voices down below and willed Michel to come to her room.

Michel sat on the terrace, frequently glancing up at her window, wondering if she was asleep and if he should creep up the stairs and knock on her door.

André sat at the table and drank more wine and wondered if Rosie and Michel were not the most stupid young people on earth. How much more was he expected to do to get them together? He really was losing his patience with them both and somehow, would have to speed things up.

Chapter 13

Rosie

September arrived and with it, more bookings for the restaurant and a few unexpected arrivals who were shown to their spanking new rooms by a very relieved Rosie. The thought of all her hard work going to waste had given her nightmares, imagining the creep of autumn and the demise of the holiday season leaving her lovely rooms unoccupied all winter. For the first time since she arrived, the departing guests promised to return; her fliers also began to work.

Rosie was busy sweeping the porch one Monday afternoon when a motorbike roared into the courtyard, flicking up a cloud of dust and disturbing the tranquillity of the early autumn day. Not one to let a bit of muck, or the fact that she'd have to start all over again get her down, she abandoned her broom and went to greet the stranger. A heavy Dutch accent surprised Rosie and once he removed his crash helmet, he introduced himself in English as Wilf.

'My motorhome is being repaired at the garage in Le Pin and I saw the paper with the name of your hotel on the wall. I am wondering do you have any vacancies. The mechanic must order the parts so I will need to stay for three days. Is this possible, Madame?'

Rosie was impressed with the polite, well-spoken biker and pleased as punch he'd noticed her fliers. She estimated that Wilf was somewhere in his late fifties. He was dressed in jeans and a tan suede jacket with long tassels hanging from the sleeves. Underneath she spotted a check shirt and knew before she even looked down that he would be wearing cowboy boots. He had fair hair, swept off his face and sported a greying moustache, the type that curls up at the side of the mouth and goatee beard.

'Well, as it happens you are in luck and by the way, I am a mademoiselle. I have a lovely room with your name on it so if you would like to come inside I will take your details and show you around. But first, would you like a drink? Come and sit in the bar and I will get our André to look after you.'

As she ushered him inside she had no idea that once her old friend clapped eyes on Wilf, he would be more than happy to ensure that the friendly Dutch biker-boy enjoyed every minute of his stay.

It had been a while since the party and to Rosie's disappointment and despite her feeble attempt to give Michel some encouragement, he seemed to have cooled off. He was still friendly but it was as though the moment had passed and she wondered if it was gone forever, or maybe she had just imagined it all. To be fair, he had been a lot busier since the grand meal, reasoning with herself that along with the extra bookings for the evenings and the steady flow of guests, maybe it was just a case of him concentrating on his cooking and her being occupied in the hotel.

Michel was also in a dilemma. He had looked up at the bedroom window all night, hoping to see her face and receive a signal but none came. The men were all so ill the next day that a whole twenty-four hours were lost to a hangover and then the week began and he was consumed with work, not resting on his laurels and desperate to keep up momentum. Rosie had been friendly as usual but there had been no more hand holding or close contact, so maybe he had imagined it all.

André thought they were both completely mad and decided that straight people were extremely boring. He wouldn't have waited this long to make his feelings known – life was for living and too short for pussy-footing around. It was an ethos he firmly believed in and put his theory straight to the test, the minute he clapped eyes on Wilf.

Wilf extended his stay for another week, and then another. He parked his motorhome in the field at the back of the hotel and camped out. André was a regular visitor to the four-wheeled love-mobile and sometimes didn't return home until first light when he would check on Clémence. If she didn't know better, Rosie would have said that André was in love but he played it very cool and was extremely careful when he was around his mother.

Clémence could observe the entire goings on of the hotel from her bedroom window which looked over the terrace, and from behind the net curtains, the wise eyes of a loving mother tenderly watched her precious son. Rosie was sitting with the old lady, holding her hand as they listened to the radio, watching André and Wilf who were sitting on the rickety iron chairs outside, chatting and drinking coffee. Clémence averted her rheumy eyes from her son to look at Rosie and as she did, the old woman gently shook her hand to gain her attention. Turning away from the inconspicuous lovers, Rosie smiled down at Clémence and asked her if she was okay. Pointing her shaky hand at the window she spoke in short, raspy sentences as her chest rattled and her breathing was laboured. Clémence took her time but managed to get the words out.

'*Laisse le aller, chérie, il est amoureux, qu'il soit libre. Quand je suis allé, lui donner ma benediction. Dis lui d'etre heureux.*' Tears filled her eyes, the exertion of just saying the words left Clémence exhausted and once she knew Rosie understood, drifted instantly into a deep sleep.

Rosie stroked Clémence's head and let the hot tears flow from her own eyes. As soft music flowed from the little brown radio she took in what the sleeping woman had said, understanding completely the simple words that were spoken from the heart of a mother who loved and adored her only son. Rosie knew it was almost time for Clémence to be with her Hugo. As her tears subsided she wiped her eyes and looked through the net at André who was laughing at something Wilf had said, knowing that when the time was right she would pass on his mother's words. That time came sooner than anyone expected.

Clémence Levron departed this world sometime during the early hours of the next morning. After waiting for so long she went off to be with her Hugo and bring him up to date with the goings on at *Les Trois Chênes*. She wanted to tell her beloved husband how well their wonderful son had done for himself and that he had returned home, just in time to say goodbye and give her hope for the hotel's future.

That's what Rosie told an inconsolable André when she found him sobbing on the terrace that morning, but he wouldn't listen and was completely lost in his own private world of grief.

A dark cloud rested over the hotel for days as the funeral was arranged and kind, concerned callers came to sit with André and offer their condolences. Wilf was a tower of strength and Rosie noticed that he seemed to be the only person who could give André any comfort. He would talk to him quietly in his easy, rhythmic accent, knowing when to melt into the background and not embarrass the visitors or his lover with open gestures of tenderness or love, saving this for when they were alone.

After the funeral and the wake, the area of low pressure lifted slightly and André insisted that Rosie take bookings if any came along, which was unlikely as it was well past the peak season. Wilf encouraged André to get out and about but even the thrill of speeding around the country lanes on his huge motorbike and the chance to spend some time away from the depression that still hung around the hotel, didn't tempt him.

Rosie watched André closely, saying nothing, because she had a feeling that her friend was fighting demons deep within. He was thoughtful, introverted and very quiet. She could also tell that Wilf was starting to lose patience and she feared he would move on, breaking André's heart all over again. It was with trepidation and concern for her oldest friend that Rosie waited for a quiet moment and as the sun went down, asked him to join her for a walk along the lane before it got too dark.

As they strolled together arm in arm, Rosie realised that she felt closer to this man than she had any other in her life, even her own father. For that reason, she knew she had to try to reach him but it was hard to know where to start so she decided to just ask him straight out, taking the direct approach that André always seemed to understand.

'André, you have been my friend for longer than I can remember so I feel that I've earned the right to tell you off now and then or expect an honest answer if I ask you a question. I also know you quite well and I can tell that something is troubling you deep down. Apart from losing your mama, is there anything else you need to talk about? I'm so worried about you and there's nothing we can't say to each other, is there?' Rosie rubbed his arm and waited for a reply.

André slowed his pace in order to kiss Rosie on the side of the head before answering.

'Oh *chérie*, you do know me well but I don't think anyone, not even you, can help me sort out the mess that is in my head. I don't know where to begin. I am confused, I am torn and I am sad. I have reached the part of my life where I must make decisions, wise choices and not waste what is left of my time on this earth. But I owe so much to the memory of my parents that I cannot dishonour them, not now.' André stopped to lean on a gate, weary from just saying the words.

Rosie sensed that he wanted to unburden himself and she could only hope he would tell her, and then something occurred to her – instinct kicked in.

'André, you need to tell me why you are torn and confused. I know why you are sad. If you could decide your future right now, at this gate, even if it's a crazy plan, just say it. Tell me what you would do with your life.' Rosie looked up at her grumpy bear who was shrivelling as each day passed by.

André continued to stare straight ahead, then took a deep breath and spoke.

'Okay, this is what I would do. I would get on Wilf's motorbike and drive with him to his camping car, then he would fix it onto the back and we would go on an adventure. There are so many places I want to see. We could drive through Italy or Spain or maybe across the Swiss Alps. How beautiful they will look in the snow. When the weather is warmer, we might take a boat to Corsica then across to Greece or Turkey, we could go wherever the wind takes us. I don't want to cook anymore, Rosie, unless it is for two people. I want to spend the rest of my days with one person, not pretend I am content to sleep with men I don't know and will never see again. I have waited years for someone to love and now he is here, at last. My heart says go, right now but my head says I must stay and fulfil the destiny my parents had planned. I cannot let them down and everyone in the village will think I am a bad person for throwing away my birthright.' Tears flowed down his face, wetting his chin as he looked across the barren, brown fields.

When Rosie started to laugh as she turned him to face her, wiping his cheeks with the cuff of her cardigan, he thought for a second she was laughing at his dreams, until she spoke.

'Oh André, you old fool. Why didn't you tell me all this without me having to drag it out of you? If you had then perhaps I could have saved you a little bit of heartache and you'd have both been on the road to paradise by now.'

André looked at Rosie, confusion in his eyes so she continued.

'The night before Clémence passed away, I was with her in her room. She was watching you and Wilf through the window. She had such love in her eyes and I noticed that she smiled along with you each time you laughed. She was very tired but she still managed to speak to me. What she said, well it was clear as anything. She gave me a message and made me promise to tell you. It gave me goosebumps and I just knew that the time would come, but it had to be just right, for me to pass it on.'

André was transfixed and looked into Rosie's eyes which were swimming with tears as she kept her word to Clémence.

'This is what she said... "let him go, *chérie*. He is in love. When I am gone, give him my blessing and tell him to be happy".' Rosie remained silent, letting the words sink in.

Without speaking, André enveloped her in a hug and they clung on to each other for dear life. Rosie let him cry and as he sobbed, she knew that soon, just like Clémence had said, she would have to let him go.

Later, after they had walked back to the hotel and André came to terms with the fact that he was free to leave with Wilf, he came to look for Rosie and asked her to join him in the bar. He needed to speak to her urgently. Rather perplexed she obeyed but when she got there, was surprised to find Michel sat at the table along with three glasses and a bottle of André's best wine, uncorked and waiting to be drunk. Motioning for Rosie to sit, Andre poured the wine and told them he had an announcement so they should drink and listen, and not interrupt.

'My dear young friends. I will be leaving the hotel at the end of the week with Wilf. We are going on a grand tour of the world, or as far as we can get in a camping car. I am not going to beat my bushes so... I would like you to buy the hotel from me, both of you. We can settle on a price another day, there is no rush. As long as it keeps me in diesel and wine, I don't care. You have both proved that you can manage without me so I am leaving you to get on with making *Les Trois Chênes* everything my parents hoped it would be. There, I am finished, now you may speak.'

Nobody said anything for what seemed like an eternity then Rosie piped up, the shock was wearing off and reality was setting in.

'I think all this is a bit hasty, André. Why don't you go off with Wilf and in the meantime Michel and I can run the hotel? What if you decide that travelling in a one room van isn't for you, or what if you fall out with Wilf? You haven't known him for very long and it's a big ask, being confined to one small space for long periods of time. I think you should just leave us in charge and see what happens.'

Then Michel piped up.

'What would you do, André, if your dream didn't work out and you have sold the hotel to us? You'd be homeless and we'd feel terrible. And what if we can't raise the money to buy it? We need time to consider your offer and you need more time to think, too.' Michel took a swig of his wine and waited.

'Pah, don't you think I have spent the last two years thinking. When I arrived, I thought everything would be simple but soon I realised that I am sick up to my teeth of cooking. I do this all my life. I want something different and to see the world. But I understand your fears and for that reason I will make you a deal. We will give each other six months, a year if you prefer. I will decide if I am the great explorer and you will decide if you can manage alone and raise the cash. If we are all lucky and happy, we can proceed. If I get fed up with life on the road then I will return and I will either buy a house in the village where I can walk to the bar of Sebastien, or I will rent a room from you for the rest of my life. I will be able to afford it so I am not worried about both options. But I warn you of this, I am not coming back to run this hotel, ever. If I do not sell to you, I will sell to somebody else.'

André looked from one shocked friend to the other, watching his words slowly sinking in.

'Okay, I see a cat has eaten your tongues so I am going to find Wilf. We are planning our route tonight, oh and when you have both stopped looking at me like I am the mad person you can plan my going away party. I want to go out with some big bangs.' With that he drained the last of his wine, placed his glass on the table before dramatically clomping off up the stairs.

They sat there for a few moments, deep in thought, lost for words, both desperately trying to work out what the other was thinking. When Rosie finally plucked up the courage to ask, she didn't get the answer she was hoping for.

'Well, that was a bit of a shock to say the least. I wasn't expecting André to drop a bombshell, but he seems adamant that he's going. What do you think, do you fancy buying this place and giving it a go? I'm sure we could make a success out of it if we work hard. I'm willing to take a chance if you are.' Rosie sat with her hands on the table, nervously twiddling the cork from the bottle.

Michel sighed and shook his head sadly. 'No, Rosie, I am sorry, it is not enough for me, perhaps for you but I want more.' The statement hung in the air as he saw tears fill her eyes.

He had waited too long and missed too many chances so tonight he would get things right and make her understand exactly how he felt, otherwise there was no point in any of it. 'You see, Rosie… I have been trying to tell you this for so long, what I want isn't this hotel, it is you and if they don't come together then I'm not interested, no deal.' Michel let his words settle, giving them time to sink in before continuing.

'So, what do you say, will you be my everything, will you love me like I love you, do you want to work and sleep together, side by side, under this roof?' Michel focused on Rosie as he held out his hand, palm open and rested it on the table, waiting for her to respond.

When she placed her hand in his, Michel's heart leapt for joy as he folded his fingers around hers.

'Okay, you're on. Me and you against the world and yes, I do love you like you love me. I've been trying to tell you for ages so will you please stop dilly-dallying? Otherwise I'm going to explode!'

Rosie let herself be pulled into his arms and finally, after waiting far too long they sealed the deal and signed their own legally binding, private contract, with a kiss.

Upstairs, André listened as Wilf chattered on about where they would go, what they should buy for their journey and so on, but now and then his mind wandered, thinking of the two young people downstairs. *'Please let them agree,'* he prayed to himself.

Apart from banging their heads together he didn't know what else to do. André was sure they would accept his offer, they were made for this place and they were made for each other. He had seen it the moment they met. It was their destiny, but it just took them longer than expected to realise it for themselves. Even his own dear mama had noticed. She had known that love was in the air from the beginning and he'd heard her muttering in her dreams about their *chérie* and *L'Enfant Terrible*. Perhaps Mama saw more than she let on through those net curtains and in her wise and loving way, she'd worked out the grand plan all by herself.

André looked out of the window at the blackening sky emblazoned with twinkling stars and thanked heaven for sending the fresh-faced girl to the kitchen all those years ago, and yes, even for Michel who drove him crazy sometimes. But most of all he thanked his beloved mama, for letting him go.

Chapter 14

Rosie

After André's leaving party where Rosie, Michel and most of the village ensured he went out with lots of bangs, he drove off into the sunset to explore Europe with Wilf. After swearing an oath to keep in regular contact, Rosie tearfully let her friend go and then got on with ripping the hotel apart and putting it back together again.

Both Rosie and Michel had many things in common, the most useful being that they were savers and had amassed healthy sums of money to invest in the hotel. Pleased as punch that their youngest son would soon be the proprietor of their local auberge, Michel's parents also offered to lend him any money he needed to fulfil his ambitions. André agreed a price for the hotel over the phone from Switzerland where he and Wilf were busy sampling the delights of fondue, Swiss chocolate and Grappa brandy, and having a whale of a time.

After sitting up for hours writing their business plan, the eager couple paid a visit to the bank manager who just happened to be best buddies with Michel's uncle, the Mayor. By some miracle, he was also second cousin to Hortense, queen of the village, therefore they had an easy enough ride when they applied for a mortgage. After setting a budget for renovations and handing over their deposit, the two young lovers signed on the dotted line and, brimming with energy and barely controlled excitement, began the next chapter of their lives.

They re-enlisted the services of Christophe and Bernard who got on with transforming the remaining bedrooms to the same specification as the first two. Once they were all complete, the tiny communal bathroom was to be ripped out and turned into a housekeeping storeroom, where they could keep all their linen and cleaning products, Mrs Amery style. The small rooms in the single storey, end building where Clémence and André had lived were gutted and opened up into one large space that would be the brand-new dining room. They installed French doors which led onto the terrace at the rear and large, airy windows to the front which overlooked the gardens. They also intended to use this room for functions such as weddings and christenings and hopefully, not too many wakes. The kitchen was torn out and a brand new, all-singing, all-dancing replacement was installed. Here, Rosie left Michel to his own devices and for weeks he was lost in brochure heaven as he designed his dream workplace. The lounge was stripped of all its furniture and they bought two new, comfy sofas and Queen Anne chairs which would be positioned around the large fireplace. Any antique furniture deemed to be re-usable was lovingly sanded down then painted or varnished by Rosie and re-installed in its rightful place.

The large disused bedroom above the lounge was commandeered by Rosie and Michel as their living quarters and turned into, what most would describe as, a bedsit; but they upgraded it in their heads to an apartment. It was adequate for just the two of them with a bedroom and small en-suite, a lounge and a tiny kitchenette which reminded her of the one in The Fairhaven where she met André. It was the last thing to be finished and for months they slept on a mattress on the floor, surrounded by bare plastered walls and building supplies. Most nights they were too tired to speak, never mind make love but they didn't care because they were together, turning dreams into reality, side by side, and that's all that mattered. The final part of the plan was to install a small swimming pool, scheduled for construction in very early spring, just before they fully re-opened.

Although the hotel looked like a bombsite, Rosie decided that as the two new rooms were ready for action, they could still take guests but warn anyone before arrival that they should take them as they found them. A continental breakfast was all that was on offer, the bar being the only room in one piece yet still adequate for a quick coffee and a croissant. Even one or two paying guests could be potential re-bookers and if they could see that the hotel was on the up, they might just spread the word.

They did in fact have a steady stream of customers, who, as predicted by Rosie, were travelling to or from England after visiting relatives or house-hunting. The extra income bought nice bits and bobs for the hotel. The fact that the owners spoke English was also turning out to be a definite plus and most apparent when Rosie took calls from travellers doing their best to speak in pidgin French then hearing the relief in their voice when they realised she was a Brit.

One cold November night as they were washing brushes and trying to scrub paint from their fingers, the telephone rang and on the other end was a very tired gentleman who was in need of a room. He was catching the ferry the next morning and had the crazy notion to drive straight to the port and sleep in his car, but it was far too cold so instead decided to look for a warm bed. Their impromptu guest arrived fifteen minutes later, introducing himself as Daniel and instantly Rosie spotted the look of relief on his face when he stepped into the lounge warmed by a roaring log fire.

As with all her guests, she invited him into the bar for a complementary drink and, as he was their only visitor and they could hardly eat dinner while he sat in his bedroom alone, Rosie asked him to join them. Years later, Rosie would look back on that night and smile, remembering the lovely evening when the three of them drank wine, ate a simple meal of soup and bread, shared their plans for the hotel and heard all about Daniel's daughter and her family who lived in Limousin. When he checked out very early the next morning for the drive to St Malo, he promised to return when he was next in France. Daniel kept his word and had since become a close friend and regular customer.

During the long and ridiculously chilly winter months, Rosie thought she would freeze to death during the night and dreaded getting up in the morning, preferring the warmth of her duvet and woolly socks to the sprint to the bathroom and a wash down in ice cold water. There had been a hitch with the plumbing so they had to endure below zero temperatures and no hot water for two weeks. Marie, Michel's doting mother, had kindly invited them to stay at her house until it was sorted, however, having managed at last to escape the clutches of his mama, there was no way Michel was going back. In fairness to Marie, she was a godsend with regards to washing their clothes and keeping them fed and would arrive most mornings with a pile of fresh laundry and something delicious to eat for lunch.

Although Rosie had claimed her baby boy, the two women got on well and Marie fussed and cared for her 'almost' daughter-in-law in the same way she did her son. Sometimes, as they swept or moved bags of rubbish for the builders they chatted and laughed and took sneaky breaks, during which time, Rosie compared Marie to her own mother who, despite being kept informed of her new life, showed little interest or pride in what her daughter had achieved.

***

Even though her days were long and busy, Rosie's mind would often wander across the Channel and her thoughts would turn to her parents and Ruby. She sent Doreen and Jim a letter when she arrived at André's, letting them know where they could find her and to inform them of her decision to leave The Fairhaven. It was more out of politeness rather than the desire for approval. Her father had managed a formal reply, wishing her well from both of them and she received a similar response when they heard the news that she was buying the hotel. It was obvious that they had no intention of visiting nor expected her to visit them so she left it there, her daughterly duty done. It also made her appreciate the love and acceptance of Marie and her husband, Yves, who strived to secure their own family bonds and more than adequately compensated for the inadequacies of Rosie's parents.

Ruby, however, was an entirely different story. Since arriving in France, Rosie had made it her duty to ring her once a week and have a chat, passing on news of day-to-day life on the French side of the Channel and eager for updates on Oliver and begrudgingly, she always asked after Marcus. It didn't take long before Rosie realised that their conversations were a one-way street. After they'd dispensed with baby talk and the weather, Ruby had nothing else to say. Not wanting to be tactless, Rosie never enquired if she'd been out for dinner, to the theatre or to visit her friends because it was blatantly obvious that apart from another mother called Liz, Ruby had nobody and no life outside the home, as far as she could tell anyway.

Rosie was perplexed, because there was no reason why, with Olivia around the corner to babysit and stacks of cash in the bank, that Marcus and Ruby shouldn't be enjoying married life and their lovely son. Even though the hotel was in a state, she repeatedly asked Ruby to fly over for a weekend and tried to pin her down to booking for the spring when they re-opened, but there was always a weak excuse. Oliver had a cold, Marcus wouldn't be able to spare the time and he didn't like the thought of her travelling without him, or any old rubbish Ruby could think of. Rosie had to bite her tongue and blurt out to her cousin that the last person on earth she wanted to see was Marcus so just leave him at home. Had it not been for the fact that she was mad busy with the hotel Rosie would have got on a flight to check things out for herself, but she didn't, and unbeknown to her, Ruby was floundering – just about managing to keep afloat.

Apart from André, who was now in Austria yodelling and drinking *bier*, Rosie wrote frequently to Alfred who was overjoyed with her new-found way of life and promised to visit them the minute they were up and running, looking forward to seeing her mini empire. There was one other face from the past that she'd heard from since her arrival in France – Dylan. A promise was a promise and once they'd parted company on that bizarre and sad day in Manchester, he'd sent her a text from the train during his long, lonely journey home to Aberdeen. As she'd requested, he brought her up to speed with his life, ever since the day he left Ruby behind in Manchester.

The first good news was that his mother had recovered from all her treatments, was in remission and doing well. Along with Dylan, she had always felt guilty that they hadn't taken Ruby along with them but she was so sick at the time and terrified of what the future held, so her own family and her recovery had been a priority. Dylan said his mum often asked after Ruby and like him, wondered if she was okay. He had studied Civil and Structural Engineering at Aberdeen University and after graduating took a job with a firm who were contracted to offshore drilling platforms. He was continuing with his studies, specialising in hydro and thermodynamics and was lucky enough to be sponsored by his company. The only downside was that Dylan was terrified of flying and had to endure frequent trips by helicopter across the North Sea to the oil rigs. He enjoyed his work once he finally arrived, and found life on the platforms interesting and exciting, overseeing rigging and lifting operations, writing risk assessments and ensuring the rig was safe. Being busy was a bonus as he said it focused his mind away from the dreaded chopper ride home. At the end of the text he asked Rosie to keep her promise and store his number, just in case Ruby ever needed it, and to ring him if Marcus ever let her down because he would always be there to pick up the pieces.

When Rosie received a text from him, just before Christmas, saying he was changing his phone contract and informing her of his new contact details, she was impressed, not only by the letters after his name but by his loyalty and diligent attention to detail. Following their conversation on Ruby's wedding day, Rosie thought he was being slightly naive and fully expected that as the years passed by, Dylan's love for Ruby would fade along with his promise. Well, this time Rosie had to admit she'd got it well and truly wrong. With a smile on her face, laced with a tinge of sadness as she remembered the earnest young man who sat dejectedly on the steps of the Albert Memorial, she replied with a very quick message, saying she was living in France and hoped he was well and then stored his number in her phone and scribbled his email address on a Post-it note. Rosie didn't encourage further conversation as she had nothing to say regarding Ruby that would cheer him up or give him hope, but at least she had kept her promise.

***

The rapid drop in temperature as Christmas approached was offset by the warmth and love that surrounded Rosie, and as the festivities approached it also brought back memories of the past.

At the Fairhaven she had always thrown herself into the preparations for one of their busiest times of the year and would be rushed off her feet from the beginning of December until the start of January. Being busy was a welcome distraction as it aided and abetted her heart in its avoidance of the truth. She wouldn't allow herself one single minute to yearn for a family Christmas or a welcoming home to go to, or even parents who would genuinely appreciate the gifts she had bought them. Instead, The Fairhaven gave her a sense of purpose and bizarrely, it also gave Ruby a place stay, otherwise she would have been cast adrift and alone at supposedly the most wonderful time of the year.

The only time Ruby didn't come to Rosie was when she was with Dylan, but apart from then it was just the two of them. Alfred had always allowed Ruby to stay over and once Rosie finished her shift they would squirrel themselves away in her room and watch the small television and eat their selection boxes, which was a tradition they saved from childhood. When they were young, and while Stella and Doreen spent the evening bickering and bitching downstairs after too much gin, they would sneak off upstairs and eat turkey sandwiches and chocolate in Rosie's room. Her father wasn't allowed to drink on Christmas Day – he had to drive Ruby and her mother home because there were no buses. Therefore, to his great regret, Jim had to remain sober while enduring through gritted teeth a very dry dinner, his overbearing wife and her tarty, drunken sister.

To her surprise, not expecting Doreen to spare the cost of a stamp to France, Rosie had received a Christmas card from her parents which included a short note from her mother informing her that her father was ill. He had suffered a mild heart attack but was recovering well at home so there was no cause for alarm, or a visit. The information brought with it mixed emotions and huge conflict within Rosie's soul. Should she ignore her mother and go home? But if she did, she felt she barely knew the man she called Dad and had little to say to him – even his letters were formal and lukewarm. The thought of sitting by his sick bed and holding his hand was as alien as being hugged by her mother and the realisation of this making Rosie angry, then extremely sad. Deciding to heed her mother's advice she ordered them a festive hamper and posted a card. Then, merely out of duty, Rosie rang her mother once a week for a brief update on his condition and a one-sided and stilted chat with her dad but apart from that, she left them to it and got on with her life with Michel.

Now she lived in France, for the first time in years and years, Rosie felt a childlike fizz of excitement when she thought of Christmas. Even though the supermarket was festively decorated and brimming with delicious food and drink there wasn't the same commercial pressure she'd experienced in England. There were still adverts on the television, flogging toys and the joy of Christmas but nowhere near as hard sell and in your face as the advertisements in England. Away from commercialism, the simplicity of country life and the gentle pace of rural affairs provided a barrier and allowed you to turn off the TV, enjoy some peace and find something more rewarding or satisfying to do with your time.

Friends and neighbours were always popping in, but as the big day approached there was an even more jovial atmosphere about the place as visitors dropped by with a special bottle of something they had brewed, or a brightly coloured gift of marshmallows adorned with sweets, or just a sack of winter vegetables. Everybody swapped or borrowed things in the country and if you didn't have it, then your neighbour probably did, otherwise they would know someone who had just what you were looking for then get straight on the phone to organise things. The community spirit was definitely alive and kicking in St Pierre and it made Rosie feel at home for the first time since she was seventeen years old. But the one who made her come alive, the second he walked in the door was Michel and with every day that passed, Rosie fell more and more in love with him.

Their days were long and full with renovating the hotel and if they weren't careful, there was a chance that fatigue and stress could make them overtired or grumpy and neither wanted the shine to rub off their happiness. With that in mind, Rosie made a rule that they would stop work at seven o'clock every night, unless there was a major incident like when Bernard flooded one of the bathrooms and water cascaded into Michel's newly plastered kitchen. They would shower and change into clean clothes then share a bottle of wine and some food together, either sat in the bar or in their bijou apartment and while they waited for the electrics to be completed, ate by the light of the moon or candles.

On Sundays they took it easy and walked through the lanes to Marie's house and allowed her to fuss over them. Afterwards, they would make their merry way home and sometimes call in on Dominique and Zofia or just go home to bed and enjoy being alone in their castle.

Michel made Rosie laugh when his stroppy chef persona took over – like the time he discussed menu ideas with Dominique or he had a diva moment on the phone to the kitchen suppliers and he won a gold medal in the rant Olympics when the floor tiles turned up in totally the wrong colour. She had also learned a few new French swear words over the course of the winter. Knowing when to back off, Rosie just left him to it and waited for him to calm down because the kitchen was his domain and the food he would cook there was his passion. There was a roaring fire in his soul and that was part of why she loved him so much. He was also observant, kind and acutely aware of her worries regarding Ruby which is why he suggested many times that she go home for a quick visit but always got the same reply, that this was her home now and he said hearing this made his heart soar.

In return, Michel admired Rosie for her strength of character, her love of people in general, and her hard work and commitment to their hotel, but most of all he just loved to look at her. He didn't care whether she was covered in paint and dust or overtired and irritable at the end of a long day. His favourite time had to be when he watched her laughing, maybe at something he had said or done, or welcoming in a new guest because that's when he saw kindness and the purity of her spirit lighting up her face. In the mornings while she slept and the sun burst through their curtain-less windows, bathing her face with its rays, he would silently watch her and tell himself he had done well because his Rosie was perfect.

Christmas Day arrived and Rosie and Michel gave themselves two days off to recharge their batteries and enjoy being together and with family. Rosie's gift to Michel was a set of aprons embroidered with the name of the hotel and a brand new box of terrifyingly sharp knives which gave her goosebumps. There was also a case of fine wine to start off his cave and a truffle that cost more than the rest of the gifts put together. They opened their presents in the apartment, sitting on the mattress wrapped in blankets, drinking fresh coffee.

Rosie's gifts from Michel made her chuckle and were a testament to his erratic train of thought and the inner workings of the deluded male mind. There was a beautiful set of L'Occitane bath oils which smelled divine but would be of no use whatsoever, seeing as though the hideous green tub had been ripped out and taken to the *déchetterie*. The gift voucher for the *Salon de Beauté* would have made most women wonder if they were being given a huge hint, especially as her nails were completely worn down and her hair was permanently ingrained with dust but she knew he adored her and meant well so would save it for the grand re-opening. What Rosie presumed was her final gift left her with no other alternative than to draw on her acting skills and feign great pleasure at her new book, written in French, which when translated said – *A Beginner's Guide to Pickles and Preserves*. She realised her error instantly, remembering a conversation with Michel which obviously resulted in the gift that now lay in her lap. They had been given an array of food-based gifts from their friends and neighbours on the lead up to Christmas and Rosie had felt extremely lacking and caught off-guard so in passing remarked to Michel that next year, she would find something to make and give to them in return.

As Rosie showed willing and flicked through the pages, Michel interjected with words of encouragement. 'See, *chérie*, now you can make wonderful use of all the leftover fruit and produce from the garden and make everyone presents. I am sure you will enjoy it. This way, we will not waste anything and you will find a hobby and make our friends smile. *Parfait!*'

The thought that crossed her mind, straight after where he could stick his pickles, was that she wouldn't have time for peeling kilos of soggy fruit with a hotel to run but Rosie couldn't be mad at him for long – his earnest face and chuffed expression melted her heart. However, he was still annoying her slightly, for the past half hour he hadn't stopped checking his watch and couldn't sit still.

'Michel, are we going to be late for your mother's because you keep looking at the time? I thought you said we should be there for one.' Rosie began to tidy away the bits of wrapping paper, just in case they had to get a move on.

'*Non, chérie*, everything is fine.' Then, hearing the doorbell ring his face lit up and he rushed to leave the room before turning to point at Rosie. 'Wait here. I have a surprise, you must stay... do not move. Okay?' Then he dashed out of the door and bounded down the stairs.

There was the sound of muttering voices and Rosie strained to hear what they were saying, then she heard the front door slam and Michel making his way back up the stairs, a little slower this time.

'Close your eyes, *chérie*. Do not open them until I say. I have a very special gift for you.'

Rosie was thrilled but then cautioned herself just in case it was an industrial vacuum or a sewing machine. So far, Michel's gifts were bordering on the practical side so she shouldn't get her hopes up. Then Rosie felt him kneel on the mattress and place something in front of her.

'Open, *chérie*. There, what do you think?'

Rosie looked down and low and behold, she saw a wicker hamper and presumed it was either a picnic set or empty jam bottles, nothing would surprise her. Then the box moved slightly.

'Hurry up, Rosie, lift the lid. I have been waiting for weeks to give you this.'

Tentatively she opened the box which contained a pale blue blanket and four tiny eyes, blinking into the light.

'Michel, oh Michel, they are perfect! Come here little ones, come and meet your mummy.' And as she picked up the two tiny puppies, one a golden Labrador and the other, what looked like a raggedy terrier of some kind, she could hardly speak she was so full of emotion and love. Not only for the two giddy dogs that licked and wiggled in a frenzy but for her wonderful Michel, who got it right in the end.

'I have always believed that a home is made by children and animals so I thought we would start with a dog, there is time for children when we are both not so busy. I was only going to take one but the man who sells the Labradors had this little thing also and I could not leave him behind. They will be brothers for each other I think, and not feel lonely if we are away.' Michel tickled the ears of the puppies and watched Rosie intently who had already fallen in love with her boys.

'I love them, you are so clever. I've never had a pet or someone as wonderful as you. Happy Christmas, Michel, you three are my best presents ever.'

Later, they walked over to Marie and Yves' house with Bill and Ben, wrapped in blankets and stuck down their coats and once they arrived, Rosie had the happiest Christmas Day of her life. The focus of the day was family, food and obviously wine, so along with Henri and the grandparents, Rosie and Michel sat back and let someone else do the cooking and the fussing for once. As they made their merry way home that evening they resisted the urge to visit their neighbours, especially as they had the dogs with them. Michel confessed he'd left the puppies with Dominique and Zofia overnight but they'd both disgraced themselves on her spotless floor (more than once) so for now, they might not be too welcome at the inn.

That night, as Michel snored by her side and Rosie resisted the incredible urge to go downstairs and bring the crying puppies into bed with her, she watched the clouds skim across the moon and thought of home. The same silvery light was also shining down on Ruby and Oliver and she hoped with all her heart that her cousin's Christmas had been as joyous as hers.

Looking around the half-finished room from her mattress on the floor, it was hard to believe that since her arrival in summer her life had changed beyond recognition. Maybe everything that had happened was in her destiny and she had been moving towards her Michel all the time. Perhaps he had been orbiting her planet and when the time was just right, they both landed here and found each other. She also realised she had no regrets either. Yes, she could wish for different parents but then she would never have left home. She had learned so much from Alfred and her time at The Fairhaven and would put it all to good use here. In a few months, the tiny auberge would re-emerge as a fully-fledged hotel and restaurant. All they had to do was what they were good at. Michel would make glorious food and she would provide a cosy room in a welcoming, peaceful environment. But most important of all, they had to keep the magic alive and for the rest of their lives, just keep on loving each other. It was as simple as that.

Chapter 15

Rosie 2010

Rosie waited impatiently in the restaurant of John Lewis as they'd arranged. She was eager for Ruby to arrive and her eyes constantly scanned the shoppers for a glimpse of her cousin's face. After a strained morning in the company of her mother, Rosie was ready for some light relief and an afternoon of shopping and catching up. Doreen had sent a short message to France from her sick bed, saying that she'd had a fall and broken her hip but there was no need for concern and she was being cared for by her many friends and therefore a visit wasn't necessary. Once again Rosie then spent the next twenty-four hours trying to decipher the coded message and work out what it actually meant. Was Doreen really okay and politely informing her out of propriety, or was it a cry for help from a hard-hearted, lonely old woman who was reaching out to her only daughter in her hour of need?

When Rosie arrived in Cheadle it dawned on her instantly that her mother was in fact just being polite, or more than likely, hoping for a gift in the post and a bit of long-distance sympathy. Her subconscious also told Rosie that once and for all, she needed to wake up and smell the coffee where Doreen was concerned. As well as the lovely ladies from the church, who seemed to genuinely like her mother and rallied round with a rota for wheelchair pushing and hot meal deliveries, she had a devoted cleaning lady and a newly-installed stairlift. Rosie therefore was definitely surplus to requirements.

Doreen still hadn't mellowed over the years and not even the death of her husband managed to thaw her frozen heart. Rosie accepted that her parents' marriage probably died the day after she was conceived because no matter how hard she tried, she just couldn't remember them ever showing warmth or love towards one another. Rosie saw their life together as an example of how not to be and vowed to make sure that what she had with Michel remained as fresh and exciting as humanly possible.

During their first season running the spanking new hotel they had managed to combine work with pleasure and muddled along together as they got to grips with their new life. They were always shattered so when winter came, they managed to slow down a little, concentrating more on the restaurant while the hotel was quiet. They were now in their second season and almost fully booked. Rosie really could have done without the trip to England but on the up side, at least she could see Ruby.

As for Michel, she missed him already and knew this was a good sign. Most couples would dread working and living together, however, she thought they'd got it just about right. In between watching for Ruby, Rosie chanced a quick glance out of the windows at the dark curves of the Pennines in the distance. They were mesmerising and moody, covered with low rain clouds which reminded her of the cold, grey November day when she flew in over their peaks for her father's funeral.

***

Jim suffered a massive heart attack after chopping wood for the Scout bonfire and the fact that he died in pursuit of helping their church had given Doreen a strange sense of comfort. Rosie received the news via a short and to the point conversation with the vicar who, along with the great and the good of his flock, was caring for the needs of the bereaved widow. She remembered feeling no sorrow on hearing the news, just a strange emptiness that replaced the standard emotion of grief. Two days later, as she prepared to fly to England for the funeral and a dreaded stay at her mother's, Ruby rang from hospital to announce the early arrival of baby Lily which cheered Rosie up no end. The prospect of tea and sympathy with Doreen was enough to depress anyone but now she would be able to see her new second cousin. Harsh as some would deem it, Rosie's journey across the Channel had suddenly taken on a happier purpose.

After the funeral, which was well attended and provided Doreen with an excellent opportunity to be the centre of attention, Rosie boarded the plane home to France with very mixed emotions. She couldn't wait to be back with Michel and her safe haven, yet at the same time her conscience tormented her all the way to the check-in desk. Ruby was desperately unhappy. Rosie had seen and heard it for herself and now she didn't know what the hell to do.

At the time of the funeral, Lily was six days old and her father, the delightful Marcus, had flown out to India on a business trip leaving Ruby alone with a toddler and a newborn. Olivia had apparently been a godsend and was doing her best to help out in her own stand-offish sort of way, but at least it allowed Ruby to attend and pay her respects. At the wake, the two cousins managed to escape upstairs to Rosie's old bedroom and in the familiar surroundings of their childhood confession box, Ruby unburdened herself and told Rosie the truth about her failing, troubled marriage.

None of it surprised Rosie but still she wished that it wasn't true and that all her fears and doubts had been misplaced. Sadly, on a gloomy November afternoon as they sat on her shiny pink chintz bedspread, Ruby admitted that she'd married a monster. They talked it round the houses and the obvious thing to do would be to kick him out, divorce him and tell his mother what her precious son was truly like. Ruby panicked at the prospect because she was terrified of being a single mum – look what happened to Stella.

Ruby wanted the best for her children and all that Marcus could offer, but most of all, she wanted him to be the man she fell in love with. Uncertainty and her fear of the unknown conned her into thinking that now he had a beautiful daughter and a complete family, and once she'd lost her baby weight, they could put the sparkle back into their marriage and pick up where they left off. Ruby was convinced she'd be able to turn things around and begged Rosie not to intervene in any way.

Rosie thought it was more likely that Doreen would convert to Islam before Marcus would change his ways, however, Ruby was tired and overwrought. She also had enough to cope with at home and didn't need anyone stirring things up and pouring hot water on an already volatile situation. Instead they made a pact. Ruby swore that she would be honest and tell Rosie if things got worse and in return, Rosie promised to be there at the end of the phone, day or night to help in any way she could. That's how they had left it. Over a year had passed since that day in her bedroom and as far as she was concerned, Rosie had kept to her side of the bargain. Whether the same could be said of Ruby, she would soon find out.

***

Realising she had been lost in the moment, fixated on the distant peaks and the many soulless and bleak conversations she'd had with her cousin since that day, Rosie dragged herself back to the present. Nothing on this earth could convince her that Ruby's life had improved. She could hear it in her voice, those flat, tired tones of a broken spirit. Rosie snapped her head around and searched the crowd. Where was she? She just wanted to see her in the flesh.

Then she spotted her amongst the sea of bodies, her long fair hair swept into a pony tail, pulled away from her pale, drawn face. The beautiful swan that drank champagne on her wedding day had been reduced once again to a sparrow, thin and fragile, with dark sad eyes encircled by shadows. Rosie waved to attract Ruby's attention while trying to ignore the brick that had landed in the pit of her stomach, leaving her winded and in shock. As she hugged her cousin's tiny frame the tears that Rosie shed were not of joy, they were barely held in sobs of frustration and guilt laced with unbridled hate for the man who had reduced her precious Ruby, to this.

When Ruby pulled away she made a joke of Rosie's blubbing. 'Hey, what's with the tears? I didn't think you'd missed me that much.' Ruby's eyes were also wet, yet she was able to control her emotions better.

At the same time, Rosie had sensed that keeping a lid on her feelings was something Ruby was practised in.

'Sorry, all I can say is that I've just spent twenty-four hours with my mother and that would make anybody cry. Anyway, I'm fine now so let's get something to eat. I'm starving and it looks like you could do with some food in you. How much weight have you lost? You look like a stick!' Rosie wanted to make the point that she'd noticed Ruby's altered appearance.

'I can't win, can I? I've got Marcus telling me I'm fat and now you're saying I'm too thin. I'll have an extra-large portion of chips with my lunch if it shuts you up, anything for a quiet life.' Ruby smiled and rolled her eyes, then looked down quickly and fiddled with the salt and pepper.

'*You don't fool me, Mrs Cole,*' Rosie thought to herself. She could hear the thinly veiled strain in Ruby's voice and knew when she was being diverted but decided to give her a break – until after they'd eaten at least.

During lunch, they chatted about Lily and Oliver and avoided the subject of Marcus entirely. Rosie didn't even press her as to why she didn't want to meet at the house because she really would have loved a cuddle with her little cousins. Instead, she'd gone with the flow when Ruby suggested meeting here, suspecting she just wanted time to herself, away from home. Rosie brought Ruby up to speed with how the hotel was doing and the progress of her gîtes. The first one was almost done and only needed painting while the other three were also taking shape. None of which would have been possible without the surprise gift from her late father.

***

It had been one of the greatest shocks of Rosie's life when, just after her father's wake, Doreen handed her an envelope. On the front she recognised her dad's handwriting.

185

Once her mother's friends had tidied up and left, they sat together in the lounge listening to the tick of the clock and the sound of deafening silence as they both struggled for something mildly useful or comforting to say. Suddenly, Doreen stopped mid-sip, as though she had just remembered something. Placing her cup and saucer on the nest of tables by her side she walked over to the small mahogany writing bureau and slid open the top drawer.

'Here, your father left you this. I found it in his paperwork. There's no note, just the documents and the cheque. Perhaps you will have use for it if things don't work out in France.' Doreen stood in front of Rosie, holding out the envelope.

The coldness of her stare told Rosie that she begrudged her daughter whatever it contained. Instead of opening it in front of Doreen, Rosie decided to deprive her mother the satisfaction of witnessing her reaction. With slightly shaking hands, she took what was offered then stood. Holding the white envelope tightly to her chest Rosie made rushed excuses to her expectant mother.

'I think I'll open it in my room if you don't mind? I'm tired and I'm sure after today you'll need some time alone. Give me a shout if you need anything, otherwise I'll see you in the morning.' Rosie didn't hug or even try to give her mother a peck on the cheek because affection had given up, packed a case and left the building many years ago.

Within the privacy of her bedroom, Rosie opened the envelope. It had once been sealed by her father's hands but since then, she could tell that it had been steamed open, invaded and pillaged by her mother when she discovered its existence. Inside was a cheque for £50,000, typed in her name and dated the week before he died. Along with it came a covering letter from the insurance company who had arranged the endowment policy. It had matured in September on her birthday and her father must have taken it out when she was around three years old.

Hot, sad tears swam in Rosie's eyes, as a thousand questions pinged around her brain. Why had he not told Doreen about the policy? Because she would probably have put a stop to it, that's why. She would have been jealous or said Rosie didn't deserve it. Doreen was a spiteful old cow and wouldn't want her daughter to take precedence over her. That's how she was. But despite her mother's controlling ways, Rosie's dad had paid this policy every month for twenty five years. All that time, he'd known that one day he would give her this and that mere fact, his little secret, showed unexpected defiance. For once, he'd gone his own way and taken control but most of all and incredibly precious, was it told Rosie that he loved her. In his own timid, back-seat way, he was still looking out for her and in giving her this gift he had sent a special message.

Pulling back the covers, she kicked off her shoes and slipped out of her black dress, then got into bed. She read and reread the words from the insurance company, it was all she had. Maybe her dad *had* put a letter in there for her. She wouldn't put it past her mother to have removed it but here was no point in asking because Rosie knew her mother would never admit to it, not while she had breath in her body.

An overwhelming sadness began to slide over her bones, dragging her back in time to her childhood and from amongst the sombre memories she'd stored in her head, filed away in the wrong category, Rosie pulled out forgotten images of the past. Lots of snapshots emerged, no longer in sepia or black and white, they were in vivid colour and all of them were of her dad.

They were both on the beach, not a Doreen in sight. Jim had his trousers rolled up and his white ankles poked out as they splashed along the shore, picking cockles and jumping waves. He held her hand tightly to stop her from falling over and getting soaked. Afterwards, they went to a beer garden where he had a sneaky shandy and Rosie sipped Coke straight from the bottle. They ordered a plate of chips, smothered in salt and vinegar, and ate them with their fingers, both knowing that Doreen would freak if she knew.

Then, there was her first Christmas card from school. Rosie made it herself – it was a house with cotton wool snow and half a ton of glitter on the roof. When her dad came home from work she almost burst with pride when he said it was the best card he had ever seen and insisted it should take centre stage on the mantelpiece. Doreen complained daily that when she dusted, the glitter went everywhere but Jim put his foot down and said it had to stay where it was.

Blue Peter appeals flashed up next and Rosie remembered squashing up to him in his chair and watching telly while he smoked his pipe. They had their own Bring-and-Buy sales in the garden and she recalled collecting spoons and coins which they sent off to be melted down to buy hearing aids or support the Lifeboats.

Rosie smiled in the dark, remembering being terrified of *Doctor Who*. She'd hide behind a cushion or the settee while it was on, then her dad would chase her round the front room pretending to be a Dalek until inevitably, Doreen appeared and told them to calm down and spoilt their fun.

Then there was the time her mum had to go into hospital overnight for an operation that to this day was known only as 'lady troubles'. She'd left them a shepherd's pie in the fridge but instead of warming it up, Rosie and her dad went into town and got a kebab each. It was heaven. They sat and ate it in the car as their lips were set on fire from the spicy sauce. Their old Volvo smelled terrible and they had to spray all sorts on the seats before he went for Doreen the next day – they even scraped the pie into a carrier bag and chucked it in next door's bin, just in case she spotted it amongst their rubbish. Then, they had to sit and eat a whole packet of mints in the hospital car park to disguise their garlic breath because the woman struck terror into both their hearts and they couldn't face her wrath if she cottoned on.

Then the images faded away, perhaps around the same time as being married to her mother started to wear her dad down. Somewhere along the line, he lost his spirit and his fight and began to blend into the background, merging with the furniture until he was barely noticed. Rosie sobbed into her pillow, crying for a lovely dad who somehow got erased, whom she would have missed if he'd been given the chance to be himself. There was no point in wishing he'd tried harder or stood up to Doreen. She couldn't change the past but with his money she would make damn sure she changed her future. This gift was a silent message from him to her. It meant independence, choice and free will. In honour of the good memories she had left, that night Rosie made a pact with herself to do her very best to make him proud.

***

Under the watchful eye of her cousin, Ruby had dutifully polished off everything on her plate as she listened to all the news from France. On the opposite side of the table, Rosie had decided that the time for idle chit-chat had passed and wanted to confront the looming spectre of Marcus, head on. She was only here for a few more hours and could see the whites of Ruby's eyes and therefore couldn't be fobbed off down a phone line. It was time for some home truths.

'So, how are things between you and Marcus? And don't start telling fibs. I'm not stupid, Ruby, and I can hear it in your voice when you ring me that you are unhappy. Have things not improved since Lily was born?' Rosie was slightly nervous, dreading what she was going to hear but still hoping that Ruby would tell her the truth.

Rolling her eyes, Ruby attempted a casual response that belied the seriousness of her situation. 'Okay, I give in. I can tell you've wanted to ask since I got here and you've never been one for pussyfooting around so I may as well get on with it. The answer is no, he hasn't changed at all. In fact he's got worse. He's bad-tempered, moody, drinks too much and as far as being a husband and father are concerned he's a complete waste of time. I've finally faced up to the sad and pathetic truth that I was just a baby-making machine and now I've done my duty, I'm of no interest or use to him. There, does that sum it up for you?'

Ruby's eyes were cold and this surprised Rosie. Under the circumstances and owing to the nature of her confession she would've expected tears.

'Bloody hell, Ruby. Why didn't you say before? I've given you enough chances. I thought we could tell each other everything. It's been what, sixteen months since I was here last and you're telling me that all that time you've been unhappy and kept it to yourself? Just tell me what he's been doing. From the state of you it looks like you're starving to death but I expect that's just stress. I hope to God it is. Is he still controlling what you spend and where you go?' Rosie was fuming.

'Yes, yes, it's just the same. I have to ask for extra money for myself. He's almost ruined my friendship with Liz and now I only see her at school. The only person that seems welcome at ours is Olivia but even that irritates him. He barely communicates with me and sometimes I think he just about tolerates Oliver. Lily gets on his nerves if she so much as gurgles and as for me, I'm no better than a live-in nanny and housekeeper. I asked him to go for counselling and he laughed in my face. What else can I do apart from carry on and hope this is a phase, or pray for a miracle that one day he will miraculously turn into a decent human being?' Ruby picked up her cup and sipped her coffee while Rosie continued her interrogation.

'You know how you said he drinks too much and is bad-tempered, well, he doesn't hurt you does he?' Rosie prayed she was wrong but nothing would surprise her where Marcus was concerned.

On hearing such a direct question Ruby looked up and studied Rosie for a second, deciding what to say, how truthful she could be.

'Rosie, can we just not talk about this today? I'm fine, honest. I can cope with Marcus, I really can. It's just that I've been looking forward to seeing you and for a few hours I want to forget about home and the Dark Lord and have some fun. Please, for me, just drop it. I'm okay.' Ruby's eyes pleaded with Rosie.

'Alright, but you're not totally off the hook. I'm sure there's something you're not telling me but I agree, I'm not letting him spoil our day. Come on, we'll go and do some shopping and the first thing I'm going to do is buy you something cheerful to wear. You're starting to look like a frump. Let's get a move on, it's my treat. And that's a cracking name for him by the way... at least he's not managed to smother your sense of humour.' Rosie picked up her rucksack and scrutinised her cousin.

Ruby was visibly relieved at her reprieve and looked like she couldn't wait to get out of the restaurant as she shrugged on her dowdy beige jacket. Plain Jane, that's what came to mind as Rosie watched her. Ruby was turning into Jim, fading away into insignificance, blending in and trying not to draw attention to herself. She wasn't weak though, she was actually quite strong. To get through a day with Marcus must take it out of you. Putting on a brave face for your kids, holding back the tears and not passing the tension on to them required a certain amount of steel. Still, Rosie wondered just how long someone could cope like that, with two small children to look after and no support.

Picking up her bag, Ruby tried a chirpier tone and pasted on a bright hopeful smile that almost lit up her peaky face. 'Right, let's get going. I saw a nice dress for Lily on the way in so shall we start off in the children's department?'

'No, we will not! We're heading straight to Womenswear, no arguments.' And to show she meant business, Rosie grabbed Ruby's arm and steered her in the right direction but as she did, noticed her cousin wince.

As they marched off, Rosie pretended she hadn't noticed Ruby's reaction but it didn't prevent the spread of anxiety, or allow her to ignore the sense of foreboding which had taken a firm grip on her very suspicious mind.

They browsed the array of garments on display, laughing and teasing each other about their respective terrible dress sense and eventually made their way to the changing rooms with armfuls of clothes for Ruby to try on. Rosie stood guard outside the curtain and was the hanger-upper as she bossed Ruby into trying on the bright, youthful outfits she had specifically chosen to jazz her up. Rosie had also purposely picked a few tops with short sleeves because she wanted to tactfully check Ruby's arms for bruises. Her chance to look came a lot sooner than expected.

'What *are* you doing in there? Hurry up and let me see what you look like. If you don't like that flowery dress I'm going to buy it for myself.' Rosie had picked a pink floral shift dress that would've complimented Ruby's skin tone had it not been a deathly shade of grey.

'I can't get the zip up… just hold your horses will you?' Ruby sounded flustered.

'Well, let me do it otherwise we'll be here all day.' And without waiting for a reply Rosie flung back the curtain to lend a hand.

Ruby stood stock-still and stared into the mirror, frozen to the spot, eyes filled with horror and a tinge of shame. Rosie felt her legs go weak and her face go hot before a cold rush of fear swept through her veins. Her eyes moved from Ruby's body then back to her reflection in the mirror, before returning to look over her bruised and battered skin. Taking in the plum coloured bruises, red-raw scratches and the fading weal marks that covered her pale flesh, separated only by Ruby's protruding spine, Rosie covered her mouth because she thought she was going to scream, or be sick.

As she suspected, Ruby's left arm held a huge bruise, exactly in the place where she had grabbed her. As she scanned downwards, there were more dubious marks on her legs which had previously been covered up by black trousers. Pulling herself together, Rosie swung the curtain closed behind them. They stood silently for a while until Ruby crumpled onto the chair by the mirror, head held low and here she began to cry, quiet heart wrenching sobs that tore at Rosie's heart. Kneeling down in front of Ruby she held her fragile cousin in her arms while she cried. The only words that they could think of, in-between the tears, turned out to be exactly the same. They both said they were sorry.

'I'm sorry for lying, Rosie. I'm sorry I didn't tell you what he's really like. You are so far away and so happy. I didn't want to ruin your life too. I knew you would worry and come home if I did, but there's nothing you can do. My life is a complete mess but that's no reason to spoil yours. I miss you so much, Rosie, and I don't know what to do. Look at all these lovely clothes. Even if you did buy them for me I couldn't wear them. He doesn't even know you're here. My life is one big secret joke.'

Ruby clung on to Rosie who was actually scared to hug the shaking body too hard in case it hurt or she snapped in two.

'Shush now, it's me who's sorry. I knew something was wrong. Deep down I knew you were in trouble but I've been selfish and should've acted on my instincts and come back to check on you. I feel like I've let you down and I will never forgive myself for all this. Good God, Ruby, look at what he's done to you.' Rosie wiped away Ruby's tears.

'It's not your fault, Rosie, so please don't feel bad or guilty. I'm a big girl now and need to learn how to sort out my own problems. I can't come running to you every time Marcus loses his temper.' Ruby had regained her composure and stopped shaking.

Rosie was having none of it. 'Right, you get dressed and I'll take these clothes back, then we're going to get out of here and find somewhere to talk and see if we can't work something out. Okay?' Rosie smiled bravely at Ruby who nodded, and then left her to get changed.

When she closed the curtain behind her, Rosie leaned back against the walls of the changing rooms and took deep breaths. If she could get her hands on Marcus Cole right now he would know exactly what it felt like to be beaten, then she'd dig a big hole, chuck him in, and bury him. Dead or alive, she didn't really care.

Chapter 16

Ruby

Ruby drove them to a pub which was off the beaten track and close to the airport. Rosie's flight wasn't until eight so they still had a couple of hours before she had to collect Oliver and Lily. The pub was almost empty and they found a secluded spot in the corner where they could talk without being overheard. Despite her initial embarrassment at being found out, Ruby felt a huge sense of relief now that Rosie knew about Marcus. At last she could talk about it with another human being, instead of having the same conversation in her head, night after night. Ruby had faced up to the truth that no matter how much she wished for it, nobody was going to come and rescue her because that only happened in fairy tales. Now, she could unburden herself without having to bear the guilt of forcing her problems onto someone else because Rosie had discovered her secret. They stuck to soft drinks, Ruby was scared that Marcus would smell the alcohol and Rosie said that the way she felt, if she started drinking she wouldn't be able to stop. There was no avoiding the issue any longer, they needed to talk it through and this time there would be no holding back.

Once they were settled, Ruby began explaining how, since Lily was born, his disinterest in her became even more apparent and his mood swings ever more frequent. There was no communication other than what was necessary between them; apart from wanting to know where she'd been, order what he wanted for his dinner or send her on an errand, they hardly spoke. The only time things were semi-normal was if Olivia came to lunch or, as with the previous evening, he had invited people for one of his fake dinner parties.

The violence began one night when Lily was just a few months old. He'd ranted and raved all week about needing his sleep and Ruby dreaded hearing her daughter cry so, to keep the peace, she moved into Lily's bedroom where she could comfort her the second she made a peep. On the night in question, Lily just wouldn't stop crying and couldn't settle, prompting Marcus to storm into her room, swearing and cursing loudly, inevitably waking Oliver who joined in with tears of his own. Ruby was tired too and uncharacteristically she just snapped, pointing out that he was the one doing all the shouting and making everyone worse. When the slap made contact with her face, for a millisecond she didn't register what had happened and when it sunk in, shock and fear took over. Marcus simply turned and stomped off to their bedroom, shouting that she should never speak like that to him again. From then on things escalated gradually, beginning with aggressive pushes and hard prods, then more slaps that led to punches. Now, there was no stopping him. The slightest thing would cause him to lose his temper and her life was merely a case of constantly treading on a path of eggshells and being used as a punch bag.

'So, there you have it, the truth, warts and all. I have tried everything I can to keep home life calm and running smoothly then bam, for the smallest of things he just goes berserk. Drink makes it worse but he doesn't even need an excuse these days.' Ruby sipped her orange and waited for Rosie's verdict.

'You've got to leave him, Ruby. If this carries on he is going to seriously harm you. You could have him locked up, tonight. For a start, we need to take photos of those bruises for evidence. You should tell his mother too, let her know what her precious son has done. The time for playing happy families is well and truly over. I'll come with you to the police. I can ring Michel and say I'm staying a few extra days to help you get sorted. I'm not leaving you alone, Ruby, not now I know what he's like.' Rosie was mad as hell and wanted to punish Marcus herself, with her own bare hands.

'Rosie, listen, you don't know what he's like. Please let me think things through. I need time. Do you think that I want to be a single mum? I want a family, a nice house and the man I married. I know you think he won't change but he might. Let me give him one more chance. I'll tell him that if he hurts me again I'll go to the police. I'll even tell Olivia. That will shame him, I'm sure. If he thinks he will lose us, maybe it will shock him into getting help for his drinking and anger, and if his mother knows then he will have to give it a go. I should have done this a long time ago and now you're in the loop it's given me the courage to face up to him.' Ruby's pale face was flushed and frightened.

'You're kidding yourself, you know that don't you? He's been like this for years and he won't change. People like him can't. I should have told you this a long time ago. I found something out about Marcus, just after you were married but I stupidly gave him the benefit of the doubt but now it looks like I was wrong.' Rosie couldn't believe how stupid she'd been, not telling Ruby there and then.

Ruby swallowed, her face was ashen and her lips felt numb but they managed to tell Rosie to continue.

'He attacked one of the maids at The Fairhaven. He tried to rape her and got really nasty. I didn't tell you in the hope that it was a drunken one-off. He hasn't changed, Ruby, and he never will.' Rosie felt awful for keeping a secret in the first place, then having to tell the truth. That was why she had to give it to Ruby straight this time, to make her see sense.

They talked everything through, over and over but it was clear that Ruby was not only terrified of Marcus; she was more petrified of becoming her mother. Stella's life was like a vision of hell which had haunted Ruby for years, and there was no way on earth that she would jeopardise the future for Lily and Oliver. If there was any way to get through to Marcus, any tiny scrap of hope that she could mend her marriage then she wanted to give it one last go. In the end they called a truce, with the conditions set firmly by Rosie.

First, Ruby had to promise to tell Olivia exactly what was going on and show her the bruises, immediately. If she didn't, then Rosie swore she would do it for her. Secondly, they were going straight into the toilets to take photos of her injuries and keep them as evidence. And finally, if Marcus didn't agree to get help and stop the violence then Ruby had to swear that she would go to the police.

Rosie also wanted Ruby to come to France for the half-term break, whether Marcus came or not, preferably not. It would be a test of his commitment to their marriage and apart from that, Ruby and the kids needed a holiday, seeing as the only person who ever left the country or had fun was him. She agreed to everything and knew that Rosie meant business. Especially when she promised she would ring Olivia at the end of the week to check progress and have a little chat about her vile son's behaviour, that way, there would be no going back or making excuses.

By the time they got into the car and headed for the airport they were both wrung out. Ruby sensed that Rosie was on the verge of cancelling her flight and staying, but that would just add to her problems. Now, she had a plan and a way forward and could manage things by herself. If Rosie stayed it would only get Marcus's back up and she wanted to do this her way, show him she meant business and could stand up to him on her own. As they pulled into the drop-off zone at the terminal, a tearful Rosie reminded Ruby of all her promises and clung on to her hands, squeezing strength into them, scared of letting go.

'Rosie, go on, you'll miss your flight and I need to get the kids. I want to be home and in bed by the time he rolls up and then tomorrow, I'll go and see Olivia while Marcus is at work and Oliver is in school. I promise you, I'll be fine. If it makes you feel better I'll send you a text so that you know I'm okay and safe. Please don't make this harder than it is – or set me off crying again.' Ruby was filling up and losing her resolve.

'Okay, don't let me down, or I'll be back on the next flight. Love you, Ruby, please take care and give the kids a big kiss and a hug from me.' And with a quick peck and a squeeze, Rosie leapt from the car, hooked her rucksack over her shoulder, waved goodbye and turned towards the terminal building.

Inside the car, Ruby knew Rosie was crying and it made her feel so bad. She watched her until she was out of sight and then turned on the engine, indicated and drove away.

Inside the airport, Rosie watched Ruby through the darkened glass, keeping her face pushed against the window so that passers-by wouldn't see her tears.

Never in her whole life had she been as torn in two as she was right at that moment and the urge to jump in a taxi and follow her cousin waged a war within her heart. She wanted to be at home with Michel, safe in his arms in their own little world but how could she do that knowing what Ruby was going back to? Hearing the nasally voice on the tannoy making an announcement broke into her thoughts. No, she was going home to Michel. And if by the end of the week progress hadn't been made then she would come back and kick arse, but for now, she had a flight to catch.

When Ruby pulled into the cul-de-sac later that night her heart plummeted. Marcus was home early. If that wasn't bad enough, Lily hadn't stopped crying all the way home and Olivia suspected she was coming down with something. There was a nasty bug going round and neither of the children had eaten their dinner which wasn't a good sign – Oliver was known for his hollow legs. As she bundled them both into the house, the smell of Chinese food wafted up the hall which meant he hadn't eaten in town, and not being home in time to cook dinner would mean a black mark against her name.

'Marcus, I'm taking the children upstairs to bed. We've been at your mother's and I don't think they're well. I'll be down in a minute. I'm sorry I'm late. I didn't think you'd be home this early.'

Just as they made their way up the stairs he appeared in the hallway, eating from a silver carton and glaring at her.

'I know exactly where you've been. I rang my mother. Glad you've had a nice evening and not had to get your own food. Keep those two upstairs if they're ill, I don't want to catch whatever they've got.' And right on cue, just as he turned to go into the kitchen, he remembered.

'Oh, and where's my dry-cleaning? Don't tell me you've forgotten it, I reminded you enough times. Christ, you really are totally useless!' Marcus sneered before sauntering back into the kitchen, dropping noodles onto the floor as he went.

The blood drained from Ruby's face. Now she'd annoyed him even more but at least Olivia hadn't dropped her in it. 'I'm so sorry, Marcus.' She spoke to his back. 'I'll go and get it first thing tomorrow.' Then to add insult to injury, as if she didn't have enough to cope with, Oliver threw up all over himself, the carpet and the walls.

Ruby rushed upstairs to care for two poorly children, while at the same time, worrying about the carpets she had to scrub and that Marcus was going to be on the warpath. Turning on the taps to run a bath for Oliver, Ruby sighed, knowing full well she was in for a long, hard night.

By the end of the week, Oliver and Lily were on the mend and over their stomach bug. Ruby caught it next and had spent a hideous few days trying to look after everyone, especially as Olivia also succumbed to the dreaded virus and couldn't help out. Marcus got off scot-free, most likely due to the fact that he didn't lift a finger to help or come within a foot of any of them. Ruby was actually glad he wasn't ill because she was worn out and truly didn't have the patience or the inclination to look after him as well. Rosie had never been off the phone but had begrudgingly given her extra time to speak to Olivia, only due to them all coming down with the plague. Still, Ruby knew that she couldn't put exposing Marcus off forever, and soon, Rosie would be back on her case.

The thing was, when there was a lull in the storm and he left her alone, the fear and anger eased for a while. She was still unhappy and spent her evenings on pins but it was bearable. For that reason she began to lose her resolve and dreaded her confession to Olivia. What if she didn't believe her? What if she took her son's side? They could gang up on her and say she was lying, or mad and unstable. They might get custody of the kids. They were rich and would hire a fancy lawyer, and then she would end up alone and with nothing. These fears had haunted her for a while and were one of the main reasons she had kept things to herself in the first place. Now, they tormented her every waking moment and prevented Ruby from going to sleep at night. While the stranger in the other room snored his way through until morning, she laid awake, remembering Stella, the dreary cold flat and having nothing. Ruby couldn't bear to go back to that, she just couldn't do it.

That Friday, when Rosie called to check up on her, Ruby fobbed her off with her latest stalling tactic. Marcus was due to fly to Hong Kong on Monday morning so once he was out of the way, she would confront Olivia and tell her everything then hopefully, by the time he got back, she would be onside.

Ruby wasn't totally convinced by her own story especially as Olivia had never liked her and hadn't wanted them to get married in the first place. How could she expect to rely on this cold, aloof woman who had remained distant for the past five years, or even expect her to take sides against her own son? Ruby was losing momentum and as the day drew nearer, she knew in her heart that she was on the verge of chickening out of her promise. However, the events that were to follow took the decision firmly from Ruby's hands and in the end, her husband more or less did the hard part for her.

Monday morning arrived and Marcus was up with the lark, faffing around with his cases and checking his paperwork. Ruby was so glad he was going away because her mind was fixated on her upcoming confessional but in a last-ditch attempt to extract a smidgen of hope, tried valiantly to make conversation with him before he left for the airport. Oliver and Lily were still sleeping so she brought him his coffee upstairs and sat on the side of the bed while he rearranged his packing.

'Marcus, I know you've said no before, but I just thought that as you are going to be away for two weeks and it's half-term on Friday, well I was wondering if you might let me take the children somewhere for a holiday, maybe to the seaside?' Ruby's heart hammered in her chest as she waited for a reply.

He totally ignored her and continued with his task.

'Marcus, did you hear me, can I take the children away for a week? I could even ask your mother to come along if it would make you feel better.'

Finally he looked up and smirked. 'Why on earth would she want to go anywhere with you? Haven't you realised yet? She can't stand you. The only reason she tolerates you is because you are the mother of *my* children otherwise she wouldn't give you the time of day. The answer is still no. Don't ask again.' With that, he picked up his cases and dragged them onto the landing.

Ruby followed and had one last try. 'Marcus, this is so unfair. They have never been on holiday. *We* have never been on holiday for that matter. What is the point of you working so hard if they can't benefit from all those hours you put in? They deserve to have some fun. I know things aren't right between us but please, don't punish the children. Let me take them for a little holiday, they'll love it.' Ruby trembled and half-wished she hadn't pushed it so far.

When Marcus eventually turned to face her, pure hate glistened in his eyes. 'Are you fucking deaf as well as stupid? What part of no is too difficult for you to comprehend? You are not taking them anywhere, now or ever. Got it?' Then he turned to walk down the stairs, dismissing her out of hand.

Ruby didn't expect to hear her voice answer him back or for her hand to reach out and angrily grab his shirt. Maybe there really was a red mist somewhere inside your body and invisible lines actually do get crossed but right there and then, both occurred simultaneously and something snapped in Ruby's brain. She'd had enough.

'Please remember they are my children too, Marcus, and I am sick and tired of you telling me what I can and can't do. I have rights. I am their mother.' Then there was silence.

It was only a short sentence, nothing over the top or too dramatic but perhaps her tone was sharper than normal or merely the fact that she would not let go of his shirt, which finally sent Marcus over the edge. The first angry punch knocked her head backwards, cracking her skin and spraying blood up the walls as her skull made contact with the doorpost.

In her semi-conscious state, Ruby felt the blows and punches rain over her body, like a boxer, trapped on the ropes by his opponent, taking hit after hit. As she slumped to the floor trying to catch her breath, in searing agony and too petrified to move, she waited silently. Ruby saw his black, polished shoes make their way down the stairs and as he drew level with her, he turned and leant on the top step.

'Just remember this, Ruby. I found you in the gutter and I can put you back where you belong whenever I want to. So in the future, do as you are told otherwise you'll end up just like that common whore you call a mother. Now clean up this mess before Oliver sees it.'

Ruby was trying hard to focus. The edges of the picture were going fuzzy and as he disappeared from sight, his words seeped into her brain, staining it with his hate, destroying her soul and any last remnants of hope. Then the room went black.

'Ruby, Ruby darling, wake up, it's me, Olivia. Come along my love, open your eyes. It's alright… you're going to be okay. I'm here now.'

Ruby could hear a soothing voice, it was saying nice things and a hand was stroking her head. The voice sounded like Olivia, but it couldn't be, Olivia hated her so she must be dreaming.

Then another voice filtered through the mist, small and scared, and it was calling out to her.

'Mummy, Mummy, please wake up. It's me, Oliver. I'm scared, Mummy, I want you to wake up!'

Ruby fought the fog that was engulfing her, dragging her back to sleep and oblivion but she must open her eyes, Oliver needed her.

When she did, seeing the frightened, concerned face of Olivia gazing down at her threw Ruby into confusion. She could barely move her head but urged her weak muscles to work. Where was he, where was her son? And then Ruby felt it, a tiny hot hand in hers, holding very tight. Turning her head to the left, she focused on two huge dark eyes. Oliver's little face was terrified and streaked with snot and tears and on seeing it Ruby's heart broke in two.

'It's okay, Oliver, Mummy's okay. I'm fine, please don't cry, sweetheart.' Ruby barely managed to speak, the pain in her head was so intense and she couldn't see properly through her right eye and her lips stung, her chest hurt too and it took her breath away when she tried to move.

Another voice interrupted. 'Ruby darling, listen to me. The ambulance is on its way and Henry is downstairs with Lily. Just try to stay still and calm. Everything will be alright. I'm going to look after you now, I promise.' Olivia stroked the hair from Ruby's face and smiled kindly as tears dropped from her eyes onto her daughter-in-law's blood-streaked pyjamas.

'Where's Marcus, has he gone?' Ruby panicked as the images of his fists pounding down on her body flashed through her head.

'Yes, he's gone, Ruby. Don't worry about him anymore. I won't let him near you again. Shush my love, just stay still.'

The sound of a siren wailing in the distance and then the rush of footsteps pounding up the stairs was soon followed by caring hands and kind voices.

Ruby reassured Oliver who was trying his hardest to be brave and promised him she'd be home very soon, then she let them wrap her in blankets and carry her away. On the journey to the hospital as the ambulance bumped and sped along the streets, the siren wailed above her head, someone held her hand, never letting go. Each time she winced in pain, a familiar voice eased her fear and when she opened her eyes to check she wasn't dreaming, Ruby saw the anguished face of Olivia.

Chapter 17

Ruby

It was early evening by the time Ruby returned home with Olivia. Despite having stitches and the risk of concussion she had insisted on discharging herself and told the doctor very politely that whether he thought it wise or not, she was going home and would catch the bus in her pyjamas if necessary. Olivia promised the medical staff that she would stay overnight to keep a close eye on her, and march Ruby straight back in again if she took a turn for the worse. Eventually, after a lot of huffing and puffing and shaking of heads, they let her go. It was also abundantly clear that they didn't believe one single word of her hastily made up story.

Ruby told them that she had tripped and fallen down the stairs then somehow, managed to crawl back up because her daughter was crying. When she reached the top, she must've passed out and as she fell, whacked her head on the doorpost. The concerned nurse waited for Olivia to leave the room before asking if her if she wanted to call the police. In hushed tones, she kindly told Ruby that she'd never seen anyone with a black eye and a split lip after falling down stairs, broken arms and legs perhaps, but not a whacking great shiner and punch marks all over their ribs.

Despite the offer of help Ruby was adamant it was all true and stuck to her story, she just wanted to go home to her kids then she could decide what to do next. The taxi driver had obviously seen all sorts and didn't bat an eyelid when he picked Ruby and Olivia up from A&E. He did have the decency to cut idle chit-chat to the minimum and after asking where they were going he contented himself with listening to the radio and swearing at rush hour commuters.

When they pulled into the cul-de-sac, Olivia paid the fare and helped Ruby shuffle up the path. She still felt groggy and a little unstable but the desire to get inside and out of sight of prying eyes helped overcome the pain. Soon, they were in the hall of her eerily quiet, thoroughly depressing house.

'Come on, let's get you settled. I'll put the kettle on and then perhaps you'll want to get out of those clothes. Henry will be here soon with the children and we don't want them seeing you like this. Do you want to go upstairs and have a shower or shall I bring you some clothes down here? If you can't make it, we can get you changed in the lounge?' Olivia's face was pinched with strain and fatigue.

'I think I'd like to stay down here for a while if that's okay. Can you bring me some clean pyjamas and something to wash with? I feel dirty.' Ruby couldn't face going upstairs just yet.

The thought of what happened up there sent spikes of fear through her heart. She could picture the blood on the door and just the thought of it made her feel sick. It reminded her of that night years ago when Barry the Perv tried to get into her room, leaving streaky blood stains on the grimy woodwork.

Ruby eased herself onto the sofa in the lounge and waited while Olivia bustled about, flicking on the kettle and clattering about in the kitchen, then she heard her clip-clopping down the hall and up the stairs. Who was this strange woman who had stayed by her side and helped her through the day? It was as though she had been transformed. Either that or the body snatchers had been in overnight and replaced her with an alien lookalike. Whatever the reason, the person who was marching around upstairs fetching clean knickers and acting like Florence Nightingale was a huge improvement on the frosty mother-in-law of old.

***

Earlier, while Ruby lay on the hospital bed, cocooned inside a green, candy-striped cubicle there had been moments when suspicion and mistrust pricked and nagged, reminding her of the cold, aloof woman she met five years ago. Did Olivia really have Ruby's best interests at heart? Or was she merely there to protect her son, keeping an eye on developments and ready to fend off any accusations of abuse.

Perhaps she was out there now telling the doctor a pack of lies about her, insinuating that she had thrown herself down the stairs because she was unstable and unfit to look after her children, communicating in secret with Marcus, giving him time to get out of the country or create an alibi. Bile and fear swirled around Ruby's stomach and she was just about to ring the buzzer to ask the nurse to fetch the police when Olivia came back, her face ashen and dark circles were appearing under her red-rimmed eyes.

'Right, I've just spoken to Henry. He stayed at the house with the children for a while to do a bit of cleaning up, but he's back at ours now so they can run around the garden and let off a bit of steam. Mrs Wallace will hang on and give him a lift and make sure they're both changed and fed so we can relax and concentrate on you for a while.' Olivia placed her black patent Gucci handbag on the end of the bed and dragged the plastic chair over to Ruby's side.

Paranoia was beginning to unsettle Ruby who suspected that Henry had been busy removing evidence and scrubbing away blood stains while she lay here, well and truly out of the way. As her mind wandered to her children, her worst nightmares came back to haunt her. She imagined them being spirited away to a foreign country and straight into the arms of their callous, cruel father. Just as hysteria and her vivid imagination began to get a firm grip, Olivia's voice broke into her erratic thoughts.

'Oliver was so brave today, Ruby. We should all be extremely proud of him. I will never forget the sound of his trembling voice at the end of the line. He must have been scared to death but still, he had the courage and common sense to go downstairs and get your phone from your bag. He stayed with you until we got there and then came downstairs to let us in. He looked like a little ghost when he opened the door and refused to leave your side while we waited for the ambulance. I will never forgive Marcus for putting him through that, let alone what he's done to you. Oliver will probably remember it for the rest of his life, seeing his mother covered in blood like that. It breaks my heart, it really does. Well, I'm certain of one thing, Marcus won't get away with it, Ruby, and if you decide to involve the police I will back you all the way, that's a promise.' Olivia sounded indignant and thoroughly heartbroken at the same time.

In that moment it became clear to Ruby that Marcus had affected everyone, and as she looked at the tired, unusually dishevelled woman by her side, realised that, in some ways, they were all his victims. Holding out her hand towards Olivia who immediately accepted the gesture, Ruby spoke quietly so that they wouldn't be overheard.

'You will never know how much those words mean to me, but I don't want to involve the police. Marcus will be long gone now and on his way to Hong Kong. I don't want Oliver knowing his father has been arrested and possibly jailed because, like you said, he's had enough to cope with. What I do want, more than anything is to go home and be with the children so can you get me out of here, Olivia, the sooner the better?' Ruby smiled and squeezed her mother-in-law's hand, knowing instinctively that she would do as she asked.

Visibly moved, Olivia took a huge breath and nodded.

'Okay, if that's what you want. Let me go and find that doctor and tell him to get a wriggle on. With a bit of luck we should be back in time for tea, how does that sound?' And with that, she stood up, smoothed down her skirt and shot off with her designer handbag hooked over her arm, on a mission to track down the doctor and get Ruby home.

***

After a quick wash down and a change of clothes Ruby felt a hundred times better. Henry had called to ask if he could take the children to McDonalds for a treat which made Olivia chuckle, knowing full well how much he enjoyed a sneaky burger and was just using her grandchildren as an excuse.

The two women were sitting in the lounge, both thoughtful and lost in amiable silence. Ruby couldn't face the toast Olivia had made so just sipped her tea instead and wondered what must be going through her mother-in-law's mind. Twenty-four hours ago, Olivia most likely thought she had a wonderful son and now she'd found out he was a wife beater. As if reading her thoughts, Olivia put down her cup and came to sit beside Ruby on the sofa, taking her free hand in both of hers before placing them on her lap.

When she spoke her voice was soft and sincere. 'I think I owe you an apology, Ruby. This is all my fault and I feel that I have let you down.'

Ruby attempted to speak but Olivia shushed her.

'I was always afraid this might happen but I did try to protect you from Marcus, I really did, right from the start. It's clear that I failed dismally and now look at you. I made a huge error of judgement and because of that, in the long run you *and* Oliver both ended up paying for my mistake.'

Ruby could hardly breathe. What on earth was Olivia getting at and why did she think this was her fault?

'Olivia, I really don't understand. You can't be held responsible for his actions. *I* kept everything a secret. I hid the truth from everyone and even deceived myself so it's not your fault, really it isn't.'

'Well, I will let you be the judge of that, my dear, but first, listen to what I have to say… then you can decide. All I know is that I can't bear the pretence any longer and I need to tell you all about my son, something I should have done on the first day I met you.'

***

Olivia was used to Marcus tipping up uninvited at social events. He would almost always be drunk or at least well on his way and quite possibly fuelled by some drug or other – she'd been told his favourite was cocaine. Without fail he would be in the company of some brainless, inebriated bimbo whom he'd picked up at one of his haunts. His activities were notorious and she'd had reports from sources inside their company that he was becoming a liability, living the life of Riley at the expense of contracts and credibility. The incident at The Fairhaven Hotel was the tip of the iceberg and enough was enough. He got away with it by the skin of his teeth and had cost her a small fortune in legal bills, not to mention the hefty payoff to the maid in question. It ensured her silence and a one-way ticket back to her family in Poland but the shame and deceit of it all made Olivia ill and she vowed that if he ever crossed that line again, she would cut him off and hang him out to dry. His behaviour hadn't come as a total shock because, where her son was concerned, she admitted defeat long ago, but up until the hotel debacle, he'd just about managed to stay out of trouble.

He was always a strong-willed, highly-strung child, prone to temper tantrums if he didn't get his own way and could sulk for days. Nothing was ever good enough despite never wanting for anything. Olivia pandered to his every whim, mainly in the hope that just once she would see a ray of sunshine emanating from the child she loved so much. She also prayed that the 'phases' she was constantly being assured he was going through would soon end. They never did and by the time he reached junior school it was evident that he was getting worse.

Olivia was convinced that none of the teachers liked him and neither did most of the parents, especially those whose children had suffered at the hands of his bullying. Her husband, Nigel, was neither use nor ornament and cut from the same cloth so, in the end, Marcus received a pat on the back from his father after a dressing down in the headmaster's office. When he asked to go to boarding school, Olivia was at first devastated then somewhat relieved, knowing Marcus would be someone else's responsibility for months at a time and she would only have to control him during the holidays. Consequently, he wreaked havoc in every single school year and the exorbitant fees they paid were a complete waste of money as he had no intention of doing well *or* going to university. Olivia was used to hearing his arrogant theory when she admonished him for appalling school reports – why waste time working when I've got a ready-made job waiting for me at Cole's the minute I leave school?

Olivia realised that boarding out gave Marcus the freedom to run riot, just within the boundaries and never enough to be expelled. She knew full well that he bullied and coerced his way through life, making lesser souls as unhappy as possible. Her son's favourite pastime was finding a quiet, lonely victim – a geek was the word she'd heard him use – then he, along with his cronies would make the poor child's life a complete misery. Once they'd had their fun, all of a sudden, they'd allow the terrified boy to be their friend thus ensuring a relieved, grateful slave for the rest of the term.

Marcus had a dreadful reputation in all aspects of his life and used his undeniable good looks on the girls at school, sailing close to the wind on many occasions, breaking their hearts after he'd taken from them exactly what he wanted. Olivia knew all this because she had insider information. Her old love, Henry, was a master at the school and kept her informed of Marcus's appalling behaviour even though half the time she really, really didn't want to hear.

Once the storm died down following his arrest at The Fairhaven, Olivia told Marcus in no uncertain terms that he was on very thin ice. The board of directors were extremely unhappy with his 'burning the candle at both-ends' lifestyle and if he didn't curb his antics immediately he would find himself removed from the import section and be permanently based in the UK. This would mean an end to his jollies with Roman and for the foreseeable future he would spend his days driving the length and breadth of the country liaising with their knitwear factories.

Olivia also reminded him of the perks of the job, which at present included: his flash company car, travelling Business Class to far-flung corners of the globe and sticking whatever, or whoever, he fancied on expenses. She then compared it to the increasing likelihood of a bog-standard Mondeo, motorway service station food, and cheap motels. The choice was his. Either he pulled his socks up and avoided the embarrassment of being downgraded or she would feed him to the directors and let them punish him in their own way.

Her final caveat was with regards to his choice of women. She was sick to death of him turning up half-cut or too hung-over to eat Sunday lunch, with some rich, shallow daddy's girl in tow, who was more interested in what her boyfriend was worth than any meaningful relationship. It was time he sorted himself out. He was thirty-five and if he didn't slow down and settle down he would most likely end up wrapped round a tree or die a very lonely old man.

Marcus hated every second of being told off by his mother but for once, her words sunk in and worked. He did indeed pull his socks up and the reports from the company were promising. Olivia knew it was more the fear of having his toys taken away than an act of obedience and, as always, he was simply looking after himself.

Olivia vividly remembered the day Marcus told her about Ruby. He had called in on the way back from the gym one nippy November afternoon and casually announced that he had met someone special. Olivia was instantly suspicious. It had been four months since her ultimatum and she was surprised that in such a short space of time he'd changed from a drunken Lothario into a man on the verge of love. By the time he had told Olivia all about his shop girl from East Manchester, who'd had a tough life and hardly any family to speak of, she knew he was up to no good. Going from the sublime to the ridiculous in the space of a few months set Olivia's nerves on edge and warning bells began to ring. Knowing how devious and manipulating her son could be she suspected that whoever this girl was, he'd hand-picked her with one aim in mind, total control. Olivia had seen it before and knew it was just a game, keeping his mother happy by obeying her rules and rubbing her nose in it at the same time. Marcus was trying to irritate her while staying within the boundaries and worse, had bagged himself a new toy into the bargain.

The day Olivia flung open the doors to meet her son's new girlfriend, all her fears were realised in the space of a few short hours. Ruby was beautiful, fresh-faced and eager to impress. A blank canvas on which to do his work and with each question she asked this lovely, friendly human being sitting before her, Olivia's heart sank a little deeper with each reply.

Ruby was estranged from her mother and had no father around to protect her, either. Her closest relative was her cousin who travelled a lot and worked at The Fairhaven. Olivia nearly passed out with shock when she heard the name and she also caught the smirk of enjoyment her distress gave Marcus. It added a twist to the tale and gave him extra pleasure, getting away with it, again. Olivia knew instantly that she had to get rid of Ruby, for her own good otherwise Marcus would make the girl's life a complete misery. And because she had made the rules, Olivia felt utterly responsible.

The only thing Olivia could come up with, was to give Ruby the cold shoulder and make the poor girl feel so unwelcome and unworthy that she may just end the relationship herself. From that moment on, Olivia did everything she could do to dissuade Marcus from his choice, insisting that Ruby was common, beneath him, uneducated and from poor stock. As she said the words she felt thoroughly ashamed because if there was one thing Olivia was not, it was a snob.

Whenever they met she was purposely cold, disinterested and slightly condescending but no matter how hard she tried, Marcus didn't take the bait and neither did Ruby. On New Year's Eve, when Marcus informed her he was taking Ruby to Dubai and intended proposing, Olivia nearly blew a gasket. She was livid and instantly forbade him yet despite this, her protestations fell on deaf ears and just as she knew he would, he went ahead and asked Ruby to marry him. Her fate was sealed.

Olivia was left with only two choices, to confront Ruby and tell her that the man she was marrying would not make her happy and didn't really love her; that his true motives were selfish and a means to an end – merely a way to silence his detractors and ultimately provide him with a family and a convenient air of respectability. But Olivia feared that Ruby wouldn't believe her and think her just a controlling, jealous mother who wanted better for her son. There was no way she could risk exposing Marcus as a sexual predator or even hint at the goings on at the hotel because he could end up in jail for attempted rape and she for perverting the course of justice. So instead, Olivia stuck with Plan B. All she could do now was observe them from a distance, look for signs that Marcus was behaving badly and if he did, then she would be there to help.

Things appeared to be running smoothly at first, yet she suspected Marcus was slowly taking control of Ruby's life as she rarely went out alone and had lost touch with her flatmates. Once Oliver was born, Olivia spotted her chance to get closer to Ruby and at the same time, have a better idea of what was going on behind closed doors. That was why she bought them the beautiful house, just around the corner from her.

Olivia still had to tread carefully, knowing full well that if she took sides with Ruby or appeared to be interfering in any way, then she would be given the cold shoulder by Marcus and the connection would be lost. For that reason, Olivia offered to help in any way she could but remained aloof and impartial whenever she was invited for lunch or in their joint company. Still, you didn't have to be a detective to work out what was happening to Ruby. Olivia could see it with her own eyes. The once radiant young bride was slowly but surely losing her glow. She was nervy, subdued and wore frumpy clothes, had little or no conversation and seemed lost somewhere in a world of her own with no friends or life other than Marcus and her child.

Olivia was surprised when she found out that Lily was on the way and detected that the parents-to-be also had mixed feelings about the news. By the time her granddaughter was born, Olivia knew for a fact there was trouble on the horizon. Tales were filtering back from the company that Marcus was back to his old ways and there were rumours of womanising and wild parties at his apartment in the city.

Fortunately, the fact that Oliver was growing up and starting to talk allowed Olivia to gain vital inside information and by the time he was four and attending nursery, he became a regular little chatterbox and an unwitting ear on the ground. Body language aside, it was clear to Olivia that her cherished grandson wasn't too keen on his father and for the most part had little or nothing to say about him, which actually told her rather a lot. From her solicitous observations, it was clear that Oliver gave Marcus a wide berth and changed from an eager, inquisitive child into a timid, introverted mouse in his father's company, actions which only confirmed Olivia's fears.

There were also little snippets here and there which she picked up on and stored away. Oliver told his grandmother that he'd heard Daddy shouting at Mummy, and crashing and smashing noises coming from their bedroom which made him scared. Mummy was crying a lot last night and sleeps in Lily's room now. Daddy didn't come home so we were allowed to have eggs for breakfast. Mummy fell down and had a bump on her cheek, and so it went on and on. Olivia always felt terrible when it was time for Oliver to go home. She could see that he was far happier with her and Henry and she felt so sorry for Ruby who she knew was a wonderful mother and would be devastated if she cottoned on.

Olivia had also begun covering for Ruby and tried to give her as much free time as Marcus would allow. She knew the situation couldn't continue any longer and after an upsetting, soul-searching chat with Henry, he convinced her that she should act on all the information she had received from her little mole and confront Ruby, offer her support, laying her cards on the table before it was too late.

Ironically, the night Ruby returned from her meeting with Rosie, intent on speaking to Olivia the very next day, Olivia had resolved to do the exact same thing. Oliver had told her that he'd seen a big red mark on Mummy's arm that morning and he heard the bumping noises in their bedroom again, and then Mummy was crying in the downstairs toilet. This was the final straw and Olivia knew it was time to act.

Unfortunately, the virus that laid them all low for a week thwarted any well-intentioned plans and in the end, they both left it too late. That morning, when the phone on her bedside table began to ring, Olivia knew it was a portent of doom. As she grabbed the receiver and heard the sobbing, terrified voice of her grandson, begging her to come quickly because 'Daddy's hurt my Mummy', her world crumbled on the spot and she knew she only had herself to blame.

***

'So, there you have it. Now do you understand why all of this is my fault? If I'd just had the guts to tell you five years ago what Marcus is truly capable of, then you wouldn't be sitting here in this state. I feel so ashamed that I let him get away with this and so many other things. I am a terrible mother and a terrible person.'

Olivia looked so weary and incredibly sad. Ruby was tired too, so rested her head on her mother-in-law's shoulder. This was the closest they'd ever been and if she was honest, it felt nice and gave her comfort.

'You said it all at the beginning, Olivia. If you'd have told me about Marcus before we were married I'd have been convinced that you were doing it out of spite and just wanted rid of me because I wasn't good enough. I felt like that anyway. I thought that was why you didn't like me and even though I was shy and timid, I had a stubborn streak too and would have stuck with Marcus just to defy you.' Ruby heard Olivia sigh and knew she wasn't convinced so soldiered on.

'The past is over and done with now. We can't change any of it, but you know what? Even though I ache like hell and I've had the worst time living here with Marcus, knowing that you don't actually hate me eases the pain. Finding out that you were watching over me and trying to do the best for us all, well, it's priceless and wipes away the past. I swear you have nothing to feel guilty about. You did what you thought was right at the time and you're here now, aren't you? And now is when I need you the most.' Ruby couldn't hold it in any longer and began to cry quietly. She was overcome with so many emotions, but the thing that was making her cry right now, was sheer gratitude and relief.

Olivia's voice cracked as she took Ruby in her arms.

'My dear girl, you don't know how much that means to me. Things could have been so different for us. We could have had a happy life, all of us together and now he's ruined it. Perhaps you are right, we can't change the past but we can make the future brighter and if there's one thing I want you to know and remember forever, is that I don't hate you. I never have, and if I'd had a daughter like you I would be the proudest mother in the world.' Now it was Olivia's turn to give way to her emotions.

Tears that she'd held back for so long, flowed from Olivia's tired eyes as she hugged Ruby, realising sadly that this was also something she should have done, a long, long time ago.

The sound of the front door opening and then Oliver's voice brought them back to earth and as they wiped their eyes and composed themselves, the little man himself warily entered the room. When he saw his mummy's face, his own began to crumple because her eye was very swollen and the skin around it turning purple-black, her lip was cut and puffy and there was a line of stitches on her head. Before he got too upset, Ruby opened her arms and requested the biggest hug in the world from her brave boy.

They sat there for a while, just holding on and relishing the feeling of being in each other's arms until Henry burst in with a box of chicken nuggets and a whippy ice cream. Apparently, Oliver thought it was just the thing to cheer Ruby up so they'd brought some home. Recovering quickly and returning to his chatty self, Oliver began telling everyone that Henry had been very greedy and gone up for seconds and thirds and even had two apple pies! He soon had them all laughing whilst force feeding Ruby nuggets as Lily contentedly spooned ice cream all over herself and the sofa.

'Come on, Henry. I think you should make us all a nice cup of tea and I'll see if I can rustle up something a bit more sensible than chicken nuggets for Ruby and I. You stay here Oliver and keep Mummy company. Then it's upstairs for a nice hot bath, you've had a long day.' Nodding in the direction of the kitchen, Olivia dropped Henry the hint that they should leave mother and son alone.

Lily instinctively followed her grandmother and crawled off in the direction of the kitchen and more food so once her feet had disappeared from view, Ruby spoke softly to Oliver.

'Are you okay now, sweetheart? Granny said you were so brave today and if it wasn't for you I wouldn't have got looked after at the hospital. I'm very proud of you, I hope you know that!' Ruby brushed a lock of hair from his pale, serious face.

Oliver answered in barely a whisper, as though he wanted to keep what he said a secret.

'I'm not really brave. I saw what Daddy did but I was too scared to stop him. I hid under my bed and waited till he went to work and then I came out. You didn't move and I thought you were a dead person. Archie's Grandad in my class is a dead person and he can't talk to Archie anymore. He's under the ground at the church. Please don't let Daddy hurt you anymore, Mummy. He scares me and I don't want you to be dead. I will miss you too much. Will you promise?' Oliver wrapped his arms around Ruby's neck and held on tight.

She could feel his little hands squeezing her skin and even though his bodyweight made her wince as he lay on her bruises, she hugged him back tightly and whispered into his hair.

'I promise you that Daddy will never hurt me again and I won't let him scare you anymore, Oliver. I promise, I promise, I promise.' And if Ruby knew one thing for certain, right there and then in that life-changing moment, it was that she would keep her word.

Marcus had gone too far and Oliver had seen too much. The cruel, heartless words he had spoken on the stairs, telling her how he really felt would stay with her forever. If that wasn't enough, her precious little boy had witnessed the whole thing and to top it all, thought his mummy was a dead person. Ruby knew the truth now, their marriage was finished. With Olivia's help she could be free of Marcus but exactly how she would do that could wait until the morning. For now, she was safe and he was thousands of miles away. That fact alone would allow them all a peaceful night's sleep.

Chapter 18
Olivia

I t was 11pm. Olivia watched over Ruby who snored gently as she lay on the sofa under her duvet. The children were bathed and in bed, and thankfully, fast asleep. Henry had gone home and would return again in the morning with clean clothes for her and then he was going to take Oliver to school. Even though she was worn out, Olivia couldn't sleep. There was too much going on in her head and it was making her restless. There was a black and white home movie playing in her head and she couldn't find the switch to turn it off. Instead, she sat there in the lamplight, resting her aching feet on the footstool and let the memories do their worst. Earlier, she'd told Ruby all about Nigel, hoping that the fact she had also suffered at the hands of a spiteful, bully of a man would make things clearer and prove that you can survive it and if you are strong, your life can change.

***

Olivia had been brought up by her devoted father and two equally devoted nannies from the age of eight, after her precious mother lost her long battle with cancer. The household was bereft but keeping his promise to his dying wife, Maurice Bootle dragged himself out of mourning and got on with the business of looking after his little girl. Having known the love of a mother and all the gifts that brings, along with the precious memories they made before her passing, gave Olivia solid foundations on which to build the rest of her life. Her father was her hero and she was blessed with a childhood surrounded by love because no matter how busy he was at work, Maurice always had time for her. They ate dinner together every evening and he helped Olivia with her homework at weekends. He also ensured they took a holiday every year, just the two of them. Along with their housekeeper, Olivia had her loyal guardians, Nanny Polly and Nanny Tess, who cared for her every need, twenty-four hours a day. They also provided friendship and stability when Maurice was away on his long journeys to the Far East or had to stay late at the office.

Knowing they were there and she was never alone allowed Olivia to blossom and grow into a grounded, kind, loving and generous human being. She did well at school and made her father proud. Olivia enjoyed learning and Maurice encouraged her in all aspects of her life, fully expecting his clever daughter to go off to university and study, or maybe follow him into the business, whatever she wished, as long as it made her happy. When her teenage years arrived, Maurice organised his business trips to coincide with her school holidays where they combined work with pleasure and education; she accompanied him to Hong Kong, Thailand, Malaysia and most of Europe. These were the best times of Olivia's life – having him all to herself while they visited museums and saw the wonders of the world, or just swimming in the hotel pool, eating in exotic restaurants and jetting off around the globe.

When she was eighteen, Olivia gained a place at the University of Manchester where she studied history and her dream was to be a teacher. She was happy to remain close to her father while enjoying life on campus, which is where she met Henry, who it had to be said, was possibly the shyest boy in Lancashire. He was in his final year, studying engineering and intended to join the Royal Air Force. He was due to begin officer training the minute he graduated, however, until then, they enjoyed a perfectly polite and above-board romance, totally approved of by her father and encouraged by her semi-retired nannies who absolutely adored him. Henry, as expected, joined up and began his military life, therefore in a typically British, no-nonsense type of way, they both agreed to continue on their respective career paths but remain in touch and meet up whenever he was home on leave.

Olivia loved receiving his letters which between them spanned thousands of air miles. Henry wrote religiously from wherever he was based. Some of the countries, like Malaysia or Singapore, she had visited with her father, but the Persian Gulf sounded so romantic and for a time, she harboured dreams of being an officer's wife and following him around the world. In her final year at university, fate, with ideas of its own, played its hand. Olivia returned home one evening to find her father in his study, chatting with a group of business friends, amongst them was a handsome, fresh face.

Nigel Cole had recently joined Bootle & Co. and Olivia was at once smitten by the suave, mature man who was witty and clever and a rapidly rising star at work. To say he swept her off her feet was an understatement and soon, Henry and any thoughts of being an officer's wife were almost forgotten. Despite his best efforts her father just couldn't take to Nigel, fearing the fifteen years that separated him and his daughter were too great and besides, the nannies still hankered after the wonderful Henry and Maurice always deferred to their judgement. Olivia, who had been brought up with a mind of her own and was encouraged to be true to herself, batted away any unfavourable comments where Nigel was concerned so, blinded by his charm, she carried on regardless.

As Britain began to withdraw its squadrons from the Far East, Henry found himself based in Cyprus. With a spring in his step and a diamond ring in his pocket, he returned home on a long leave with the intention of finally proposing to Olivia, only to discover on arrival that he'd been well and truly cuckolded. Henry returned to Cyprus broken-hearted and eventually married a lovely woman called Elizabeth who did in fact become an officer's wife and, for the next twenty years, followed him loyally around the world.

Olivia felt terrible and cried for hours when Henry left. It wasn't until he was gone that she admitted to herself how much he meant to her. Poring over his letters, reading again and again the words of undying love brought forth a realisation. The many hours they'd invested in each other from the other side of their worlds had now, due to her stupidity, been a terrible waste. He'd looked so handsome and mature in his blue officer's uniform and she would never, ever forget the look of hurt and disappointment in his eyes when they pulled up outside her house and he came rushing out, only to find her mid-embrace with Nigel. Her father was outraged and it seemed to further fuel his rejection of Nigel.

No matter how many letters Olivia sent, trying desperately to explain, or the transatlantic calls she attempted to have put through hoping that once she spoke to him, she could make him come back and forgive her, Henry ignored them all. He was a proud man and he was gone.

Unable to face Nigel as it only reminded her of Henry's hurt, Olivia had no alternative other than to pull herself together and focus on her finals. Thankfully, along with the nannies, her father was there for her graduation ceremony, and he was the proudest man in the room when she received her first-class honours degree. It was a happy day and an occasion she would never forget because two days later, Maurice was killed in a car crash on the M6 and she never saw him smile again.

Olivia's world fell to pieces. Her precious, devoted father was gone and a cavern of grief opened up and swallowed her whole. The nannies had never moved out of the large mansion in Prestbury once Olivia had no real need for them because they had become part of the family; they lodged free of charge in their old rooms but remained on hand if they were needed. They had promised Maurice long ago that they would always watch over Olivia should anything happen to him. Keeping their vow, they were vigilant in their care of her, never leaving her side, and tried everything they could to give comfort. The doctor came and went. Olivia refused any pills or to listen to his droning psychoanalysis and really didn't care if she would get over it one day. The most important person in her whole world was gone and for that reason she saw no point in anything anymore. Olivia lost any motivation or ambition and refused to leave the house, preferring to spend her days in her father's study where the smell of his cigar smoke had penetrated the curtains and upholstery and his shape was moulded into his leather chair.

Almost a year passed by in a house practically shrouded in darkness, where time was marked by the grandfather clock in the hall and the ritual of three, sombre mealtimes where her food was barely eaten and any conversation kept to a minimum. Olivia shunned all invitations from kind well-wishers and flatly refused to speak to Nigel, who, it had to be said, tried his hardest to coax her back into reality with flowers, letters and phone calls.

The nannies were at their wit's end and running out of ideas when an unexpected letter arrived – the postmark said Cyprus and they knew it had to be from Henry. Praying he was writing to say he was coming home to drag Olivia back into the land of the living they scurried up the stairs and tapped on her door. The room was, as usual, in darkness even though it was the middle of the afternoon. Their ward was lying on her side pretending to be asleep, so they left the letter on her bedside table and silently closed the door.

The nannies waited hopefully in the lounge and decided to give her an hour then they'd take a tray up and see how the land lay. Ten minutes into their wait they heard a dreadful screeching followed by her footsteps on the stairs. Rushing from the room they found her crouched halfway, shaking and sobbing and holding out the letter. Nanny Polly took it from her with trembling hands then read out loud the words which had caused Olivia such anguish. It seemed that news had only just reached Henry of her father's death and he sent his sincere condolences and apologies for not writing sooner. The information had come via his wife who'd heard of Maurice's passing from a mutual acquaintance who lived in her home town of Alderley Edge.

It was the word 'wife' that finally catapulted Olivia from her world of mourning. During the long hours she'd spent waiting and praying for Henry to come home and make things right, she'd convinced herself that he was the only man she loved, after her father. Now, he was married and her hopes were shattered. The nannies were just as devastated, knowing their remaining life line was gone so they resigned themselves to another period of gloom and isolation. Both nearly died with shock themselves when Olivia appeared at breakfast the following morning, showered and dressed, wearing a bright blue twin set and casual trousers, her hair was washed and styled and her thin face had been cheered up by a touch of make-up.

It had been a night of soul-searching and remonstrations but as the first chink of light broke through the gap in her curtains, summoning a new day, Olivia had shed her demons and freed herself from grief. Henry had balanced the books. She had hurt him and he had done the same in return. It was a level playing field and now both he and her father were gone so it was time to move forward. Flinging open her wardrobe doors, Olivia chose something bright and cheerful and after realising that most of her clothes were far too big, decided that later she would go on a shopping spree. She was a wealthy young woman with her whole life in front of her and she intended to live it. The first thing she was going to do was ring Nigel and ask him to take her out for dinner. Then she would surprise the nannies at breakfast and take them both to lunch to say thank you for being so patient. Olivia was going to book a holiday, buy a new car and commission a portrait of her father, all in one afternoon if possible so with everything settled in her mind and a spring in her step, she headed for the shower.

Once Olivia's prolonged period of mourning ended, her romance with Nigel reignited and was given the seal of approval by the nannies who, after seeing her in such a state, were just relieved that she had recovered. They even went so far as to speak on Maurice's behalf when Olivia faltered slightly after remembering her father's disapproval of Nigel. They assured her that all he ever wanted was for her to be happy and he would've been sad to see her so distraught. Therefore if Nigel brought a smile to her lips, then he would have given his blessing.

Olivia married Nigel Cole two days before Christmas in a thoroughly glamorous affair attended by the glitterati of Cheshire and most of her father's oldest friends and colleagues. The ceremony was conducted at St Peter's Church in the village of Prestbury and the lavish reception was held at The Fairhaven Hotel. Nestled in the heart of the countryside it was a picture-postcard setting for the wintry wedding photographs of the happy couple.

Her husband was climbing quickly up the ladder at Bootle's which was now run by the directors and their newly appointed Chairman, Harold. All of her father's shares, property and UK factories had been left in trust and in their entirety to Olivia and would become hers when she reached thirty years of age. Unfortunately, this and a few other important issues had been made clear to Nigel on his stag night by an inebriated, loose-lipped chairman. Harold pointedly informed the stag that even though he was marrying the boss's daughter he needn't think it meant an automatic seat on the board, he would have to work his way up, just like everybody else.

Nigel inwardly seethed, then mentioned the conversation in passing to Olivia in the misguided hope that she would indignantly rule against Harold and bat for his team. He certainly didn't get the answer he was looking for because Olivia only confirmed that there was no way the rules could be changed for him and his connections wouldn't guarantee position on the board, and anyway, what pride was there in that? Her father believed in hard work and just reward but after all, why should he worry? They had everything they needed – a beautiful home, her very generous allowance and his good job. There was plenty of time for him to work his way up so, in the meantime, they should just have fun.

Unbeknown to Olivia, working hard *or* his way up wasn't on Nigel's agenda. In his grand scheme, marrying the boss's daughter was supposed to lead to control of the company along with free and unfettered access to her wealth. He'd also planned on making a few changes at home once he got his feet under the table and he was going to start by getting rid of those two decrepit old hags. It was like living in a retirement home and there was no way on this earth he was going to spend the rest of his days watching those witches dribble their way through mealtimes. It was bad enough wondering what the two of them got up to in their rooms. Just because everyone else was happy to brush under the carpet the fact that they were clearly much more than good friends, he on the other hand thought they were disgusting.

The portrait of Maurice which hung at the foot of the stairs, piously glaring down at him day in day out was second on the list. In the meantime, it gave Nigel a perverse sense of pleasure to give the old fart a two-fingered salute as he made his way upstairs each night to have sex with Maurice's little princess. But Nigel was a patient chap. He'd proved as much when the silly mare spent a year crying in her bed while he waited for her to pull herself together. Some of what his dear wife said was correct because there was plenty of time, and if he had to endure being married to a spoilt, pampered daddy's girl then he would damn well make sure he made the most of it.

When Marcus Maurice Cole entered the world, Olivia was overjoyed. Her days were spent cocooned in a haze of love for her baby boy while the nannies were on hand to give advice. Both being well into their seventies meant they were mostly useful in a spiritual sense and far too tired to be practical, so Olivia threw herself into being the perfect mother and wife. Any teaching aspirations she had flew straight out of the window along with the lullabies she sang to Marcus each night.

Nigel was an affectionate husband who appeared to dote on his wife and baby son, mainly from afar and without getting his hands dirty thanks to their own private army in the form of ancient nannies, an efficient housekeeper, gardener and a doting mother. All of them were available around the clock thus allowing him all the freedom he required to do whatever he wanted, with whoever he wished.

All Nigel had to do was keep up the charade until Olivia hit thirty, then her inherited wealth would be shared with her devoted husband, and then he'd show that pompous Harold exactly who was going to be the boss. Once he had control of his wife and her shares, not to mention the factories which they needed to produce knitwear for the ever-growing demand from catalogue companies, he'd have the perfect bargaining tool to negotiate or demand a seat on the board. Then it would only be a matter of time before they were doing things his way and he was running the company.

A huge great spanner was thrown into the works just before Olivia's 30th birthday bash, when rumours of her husband's infidelity filtered their way into her home. Their gardener, Jed, heard it in the pub from the bloke who cut the grass at the golf club. He had it on excellent authority from Pete, the security guard, who'd seen Nigel and the pretty barmaid up to no good in the back seat of his car, one evening when he was doing his rounds. Over a cup of tea and a slice of cake, Jed told Mrs Hunt, the housekeeper who then felt duty bound to tell the nannies.

The old ladies pondered and fretted over the information for days and were stood at the foot of the stairs, staring up at the portrait of Maurice waiting for some divine intervention from the kindly face of their beloved boss, when they were spotted by Olivia who asked them what they were doing. Caught in her glare they tactfully and nervously related the dreadful (if not unexpected) rumour. There was no way they could tell a lie right in front of Maurice and therefore had no alternative other than to let the cat out of the bag. Olivia swore them both to secrecy and not to let on to Nigel that they knew, assuring the nannies that she would deal with him in her own way.

In possession of new-found knowledge, Olivia acted as though nothing was wrong and did her best to enjoy her party while she watched her husband guzzling champagne and lording it up in front of their friends. She smiled for the camera and blew out her thirty candles and even held his hand while they sang 'Happy Birthday' but all the time, deep inside, her disappointed heart was breaking.

One week later, along with her very eager and supportive husband, Olivia attended the offices of her solicitor, Lionel, one of Maurice's oldest friends and confidantes. They were there to hear the finer details of her father's will and sign the necessary papers for the transfer of shares and properties. Lionel only worked part-time these days and had come into the office to ensure all went well and keep his promise to Maurice that he would look after his little girl. As the list of assets was read out, along with the whopping balance at the bank and the value of worldwide shares were revealed, Nigel thought all his Christmases had come at once. He knew he'd hit the jackpot the day Olivia walked into her father's study but this was well and truly beyond his wildest dreams – he was set for life. That was until the crisp pile of paperwork was slid across the desk towards Olivia and Lionel pointed with liver-spotted, wrinkled hands, to where she was to sign.

Nigel watched impatiently as she scribbled away on each of the sheets that Lionel passed and then, when the final one was complete he stacked them together neatly and Olivia gave him back his pen. Nigel was non-plussed for a second and waited for Lionel to invite him to do the same. Surely his signature was required for something, after all he was now entitled to half of his wife's assets so when it didn't occur, he boldly enquired. The wily old lawyer sat back in his chair and regarded Nigel sagely over his glasses for a while before taking great pleasure in informing the greedy, unfaithful beggar sitting before him that his assistance would not be necessary.

One of the stipulations in Maurice's will was that his estate should remain in his daughter's sole name, even after marriage and if at any time she attempted to sell any of her assets, the profits must also remain hers alone, to do with as she saw fit. Maurice entrusted Olivia to respect his wishes and the nod of her head confirmed her agreement. Therefore, the only way that

Nigel was going to get his grubby little hands on Maurice's money was through hard work and his pay packet. Maybe, he might occasionally profit from the generosity of his wife should she feel so inclined or as a beneficiary of her will, which conveniently, his client had just signed amongst the stack of papers in front of him.

Olivia quite enjoyed the part when Lionel rhymed off the 1870 Property Act when Parliament dissolved a man's immediate right over his wife's fortune and sarcastically reminded Nigel that 'this isn't the Victorian Era, old chap, we've all moved on'. He didn't actually call him greedy, grubby or unfaithful but it was exactly what Lionel was thinking as he watched the smile being well and truly wiped off Nigel's puce, perspiring face.

Lionel was in his element and so glad he'd come into work that day. He was even more pleased that Olivia had called him a few days before to go over the terms of her father's will, just to make sure she remembered it correctly. She also told him about the rumours regarding dear, confused Nigel who was now seated opposite, looking decidedly perplexed, and asked for Lionel's advice. By the end of the call Olivia had been relieved to hear that her husband wasn't entitled by marriage to any of her inheritance so taking Lionel's advice, had given permission for him to draw up a watertight will, fastened with very tight knots – all within the law of course. Consequently, apart from the required settlement for a spouse, Olivia had left almost everything to her son.

After closing his file and kissing Olivia on the cheek, not offended in the slightest that Nigel refused the proffered hand to shake, Lionel politely showed them both out of his office then booked a table at his club for lunch. He felt he deserved a pat on the back, a juicy steak and a very large brandy to celebrate a job well done.

Nigel didn't speak a word on the way home. Olivia could tell he was livid and assimilating all the information. On reaching the house she asked to speak with him privately, so he followed her to her father's study. Once inside with the doors firmly closed Olivia told him about the rumours and asked if they were true. He denied everything and swore it was the work of sour, spiteful people who were jealous of their marriage. He was incredulous and couldn't understand why she would believe this of him. Hadn't he always been the most loving, supportive husband? It was he who stood by her, waiting patiently while she grieved, then guided her through the years after Maurice's death and had done everything possible to make her happy again.

Changing tack when he sensed she wasn't falling for it, Nigel said he had felt neglected and pushed out since the arrival of Marcus and admitted he'd been spending too much time away from home, drowning his sorrows. He assured her that everything would change and they could still put the sparkle back into their marriage and show the world how in love they really were. Nigel hinted that Olivia wasn't entirely blameless and was wrapped up in motherhood at the expense of her own husband. He put on a wonderful show and Olivia desperately wanted to believe him, not only that, they had a four-year-old son and she didn't want this to be the end.

Despite the warning bells in her head and deliberately casting her eyes away from her father's portrait as Nigel led her seductively up to bed, she gave her husband one more chance and stored away her doubts and fears. That night, as she lay with his arms wrapped tightly around her, Olivia truly believed that their troubles were in the past and they could get on with living a happy life of luxury together. Sadly though, this was to be just the first in a long line of fresh starts and broken promises because while Olivia smiled in her sleep, Nigel lay wide awake all night and seethed.

Chapter 19
Olivia

For a time, Nigel toed the line and was a faithful and loving husband, although this may have been due in part to the new set of golf clubs, a no-expenses-spared holiday to the Caribbean and the delivery of a brand new Jaguar, all arranged by Olivia and designed to soften the blow after the visit to Lionel's. By Marcus's seventh birthday, Olivia had enough on her plate dealing with her horrible little boy who, once he started school, seemed to have changed overnight from an angel to a mini-devil. They were forever in and out of the headmaster's office where Nigel was no help at all. He took delight in being obnoxious and condescending to the point of embarrassment and to make matters worse, he appeared to condone his son's behaviour and saw his bullying as a positive characteristic.

Olivia's marriage had also become a rollercoaster ride because when they were happy, she was on top of the world, then there'd be the dip and she would come hurtling down to earth and spend months wrapped in misery and despair. She suspected he was seeing other women again but he'd become adept at covering his tracks and any proof was hard to come by. It was as though he wavered on the precipice, taking pleasure from hurting and goading her into divorcing him, then he would reel her back in, making her so grateful that he was home and playing the loving husband that she always forgave his bad behaviour.

Nigel's failings came in many forms and the worst of them was his drinking because when he drank too much he became abusive, which led to all sorts of atrocious accusations and hurtful home truths. He openly told her on many occasions that he despised her, that she bored him sexually and had only married her for her money, and actually, couldn't bear her overbearing, self-righteous father and was glad he was six feet under. One evening, in the midst of one his rants, Olivia saw Nigel gesticulating at her father's portrait and when she screamed at him to stop he threw his whisky all over the canvas. The next day, as usual, he was full of self-loathing and heartfelt apologies, blaming everything on the drink and his feelings of inadequacy. He was a kept man and she'd taken away his pride and no matter how hard he tried, he felt he could never live up to the legend that was Maurice.

Marcus went off to boarding school when he was eleven and Olivia cried for days for the little boy she'd held in her arms, had loved unconditionally and was devoted to. She certainly wasn't crying for the horrid child he'd become, who stomped and sulked his way around the house when one of his black moods settled and had almost been expelled from his lovely private school for throwing the headmaster's cat off the roof. For this reason alone she was glad of the temporary separation that the school term brought while at the same time, it shielded him from the worsening treatment she endured at the hands of his father.

It began when Nigel was passed over for promotion at work and Harold had appointed a fresh-faced graduate to manage the accounts department. Over lunch the week before, her loyal and honest chairman quite openly told Olivia that he wouldn't trust her husband with the petty cash, never mind the keys to the safe and the company cheque book. So when Nigel heard the news officially, he came home to take it all out on Olivia who he accused of being disloyal and plotting in secret to keep him in his place. It was the first time he'd actually hit her and it turned out not to be the last. For almost a year they teetered back and forth on the brink of divorce and humble apologies, living a life of mistrust and last-ditch efforts to repair their failing marriage.

It must have been on one of these desperate weekends away while they were papering over cracks that Olivia became pregnant.

She was thirty-seven years old and had thought her chances of conceiving were long gone, not only due to her age but the turbulent state of affairs at home and their almost non-existent love life, in her case at least. Despite her initial concerns Olivia was overjoyed and saw the baby as a good omen, a fresh start and another human being in her life for whom she could love and care. She also vowed that this child would be nothing like its brother. When she told Marcus the wonderful news that he would soon have a sibling he said she was disgusting. To add insult to injury, her husband couldn't have cared less, telling her that as far as he was concerned she was just as useless to him fat and pregnant as she was every other day of the week.

Unbeknown to Nigel, Olivia had finally faced up to the fact that he would never change and resigned herself to the inevitable. The divorce papers were already drawn up after instructing Lionel's son, David, of her situation and he was on stand-by for the next time Nigel raised a hand to her. Ironically, the news of the baby gave Nigel an unwitting reprieve and for a while during her pregnancy, he was almost bearable and kept his fists to himself.

Olivia was now eight months pregnant and in full bloom. The impending birth had brought an air of excitement to the house and even rejuvenated her aging nannies, who knitted baby clothes like women possessed while decorators repainted the old nursery. On the evening her world came crashing down, Olivia was reading in bed when she heard the screeching of brakes and the unmistakable sound of smashing metal and glass as Nigel's car crashed into the rockery. Her heart lurched and it occurred to her that he may be injured or even dead, so she got up to investigate perhaps hoping for the latter. By the time she'd put on her robe he was inside the house and making his way up the stairs. Olivia met him at the top and could see by his unsteady gait that he was extremely drunk.

If only she hadn't admonished him for drink-driving or even reached out to steady him as he wobbled precariously on the edge of the stairs. Many, many times afterwards she wished with all her heart that she'd given him an almighty shove and sent him toppling down the sweeping staircase to his death. Nobody would have suspected her due mainly to the state he and his car were in, and those that knew him probably wouldn't have blamed her either. Instead, it was an unsuspecting Olivia who was punched violently as he swore and cursed and unleashed his vile venom.

In the years to follow, her recurring nightmare always began at the stairs, then a hard push and his vengeful face as he sent her flying backwards. Strangely, she always remembered the scene as being filmed in black and white, and slow motion, falling silently through the air as his image receded. Then there was the thud. It would always wake her from the dream but in reality, on that night Olivia had lain motionless on the cold marble floor, looking up into the kind, wise face of her father. As she drifted in and out of consciousness, waiting in vain for someone to save her as unbearable pain raged deep within and blood seeped onto her nightgown, the soul of her unborn baby quietly left her body.

Afterwards, whenever Olivia opened her eyes there was a faceless figure sat in the chair by her bed. It spoke to her but she couldn't hear what they said. The room was always dark but she preferred it so, the blackness eased her back into her subconscious, to a place where her heart didn't hurt so much. There was sometimes a voice screaming or crying, she would swallow a pill then the terrible sound would stop and she could drift away again to a peaceful place. Olivia loved to sleep because in the land of dreams her baby girl was waiting and here, she could hold her in her arms and sing lullabies. Sometimes, her daughter was older, with curly blonde hair and the bluest eyes. She would grasp her little hand and walk through swaying yellow fields, the sky was always blue with white cotton wool clouds. The two of them would laugh and smile as the sun warmed their skin. Olivia never wanted to wake up again.

Eventually, the figure in the chair became more recognisable and she began to hear words, then the curtains were opened and she couldn't slip away so easily. When she heard crying, Olivia recognised her own voice but the pills didn't come as often and the pain in her heart just couldn't be ignored. After months of living in a land of dreams, Olivia emerged into reality and as always, the nannies were waiting to meet her. But this time, the cut went too deep and the hurt was too raw. Her mind was damaged and Olivia's tortuous road to recovery would take much longer than when her father died.

Nigel was never charged with causing Olivia's accident because he played the part of a distraught husband who had lost his unborn child to perfection, describing tearfully the dreadful shock at finding his precious wife at the bottom of the stairs when he came home. He hid his damaged car in the garage and by the time the ambulance arrived he had covered his tracks by slugging back a few stiff whiskies – to calm his nerves. Not wanting to risk Olivia blabbing while she was in a semi-drugged state, he took his turns with the nannies and sat by her bedside, whispering false words of love laced with meaningless apologies, which fell on deaf, uncaring ears.

Once Olivia returned to the land of the almost living she was unsurprisingly diagnosed with depression and despite suggestions otherwise, never moved from her room, from which Nigel was forever banished. Marcus came home for holidays and was a trial in himself, completely unmoved by his mother's plight and irritated by her sickness. Desperate for allies, Nigel donned his fatherly cap and over-indulged his errant son just to keep him on side. He lived the following twelve months on a knife edge, smoking and drinking himself into oblivion, terrified that when Olivia came to her senses she would have him arrested and that he'd lose everything. He kept up the pretence in front of the nannies who were privately unconvinced by his charades and barely tolerated his existence. They knew full well he'd always wanted them gone but were thick-skinned and would rather die than abandon their charge to someone like Nigel.

Olivia remained fragile and knew that the antidepressants were the only thing that kept her going. On the positive side, the long hours she had spent in bed grieving for her baby daughter weren't entirely wasted and she'd had plenty of time to plot her revenge for the death of her child. She'd named her little girl Annabel and she was buried in the grounds of the village church. Here, Olivia would sit for hours by her grave, talking to the daughter she would never know, who had given her so much to look forward to and in whose unborn life she had invested a multitude of hopes and dreams. They could have been best friends and just as she had done with her father, they could've travelled the world together and visited all the places she'd seen with Maurice. Olivia had planned it all in her head, visits to the opera and the ballet, shopping sprees, lunches in town and even her birthday parties. Now, it had all been taken away so in return she would take everything from Nigel and deprive him of the only thing he cared about – money.

Olivia eventually confronted him in the garden one Sunday afternoon in May. The bright sunlight highlighted the cracks and shadows that defined his sallow, swollen face and she noticed that his eyes had an unhealthy yellow tinge. She could barely stand to look at him but wanted to witness the effects of her words because she had planned them carefully in order to cause maximum distress. They were like strangers now and she couldn't even remember loving him, so it was quite easy to impose his sentence and feel nothing but joy as she watched him squirm.

Olivia confessed to Nigel that just before she found out she was pregnant she had already decided to divorce him. She had even been prepared to accept the price of the settlement just to get rid, because paying him off with hundreds of thousands of pounds was preferable to having him anywhere near her. Wasn't it ironic that had he not lost his temper and pushed her down the stairs, and in doing so killed her baby, then he would be sitting pretty right now with a small fortune and the freedom he so desperately craved? Unfortunately for him, circumstances had now changed. She was quite sure he had no desire to end up in prison for wife beating and attempted murder, therefore the price of liberty would be foregoing his undeserved life of luxury and making do with whatever scraps she threw for him. Olivia then went on to explain in great detail, exactly how it was going to be.

He would not dare ask her for a divorce because if he did, she would go straight to the police and tell them everything about that night. She was quite sure the chap at the garage who repaired his car would be happy to corroborate her story; he wouldn't be too hard to find. And the nannies would testify in great detail to hearing and seeing him beat her, and then pushing her down the stairs. Oh, and not to mention the Polaroid photographs that were stored in her solicitor's safe as graphic evidence of his previous handy-work. Rather than upset Marcus who was due to sit his exams and already batting on a sticky wicket, and in order to keep up appearances, he would be allowed to remain in the house and occupy only one room, at the rear and as far away from her and the nannies as possible. She would not have her family name or the reputation of Bootle's tarnished in any way by becoming the hot topic amongst the gossip-mongers of Cheshire. If he stepped out of line just once she would have him thrown out and if need be, face the scandal of being married to a philandering, wife-beating murderer, head on. And should he still chance his luck and ask for a divorce, Olivia painted a picture of the posh chap, fending for himself in prison and then once he was released, more than likely when he was older and more decrepit than he was now, he'd end his days in the big bad world of Poorsville.

From that day forth he was nothing to her, apart from a rent-free lodger. How he fed himself and what he did with his time was his business. He had a wage so he could use that to satisfy any of his pathetic needs as long as he didn't bring trouble or rumour to her door. Nigel listened intently and didn't flinch, he just took it all in. He knew when he was beaten and would have to accept the terms, either that or wind up penniless and in jail.

After a trip around the world, Olivia threw herself into charity work. The Women's Institute became her second home and the church was her favourite place to be. Not especially just to worship although she did enjoy the singing and contemplative prayers, but it gave her purpose and friendship and most importantly it kept her mind occupied. They continued to live together under the same roof for two long years, like strangers. Nigel was an unwelcome lodger who kept himself to himself and ate his meals alone, truly understanding how it really felt to be a kept man, without pride and at the mercy of his wife. They did not socialise together and any functions she arranged were staged whilst he was on business trips or at the office. His presence was not required, nor his absence noted. Nobody really liked him anyway.

Olivia would have preferred not to attend parent's days because she rarely heard anything positive about Marcus but in order to keep up appearances and be seen as a dutiful mother, she travelled to Shropshire alone to endure another earbashing from his masters. It was a lovely sunny July day as she walked around the grounds of the boarding school, admiring the neat, brightly-coloured borders and browsing the stalls of the garden party, which were manned by pupils eager to sell their crafts and cakes.

She didn't mind being a lone parent amongst the well-to-do visitors, knowing she would rather suffer the odd stare and inquisitive look than spend one minute in Nigel's company. Olivia was lost in thought, trying to work out what the hideous handmade pot was supposed to resemble when from behind her someone coughed, the polite kind that draws attention to oneself. Dreading having to make small talk with another parent, Olivia braced herself but before she had chance to turn, the voice from a thousand memories spoke her name. For a second, she didn't think she had the nerve to look but the urge to see his face again was too strong so gathering her wits and calming her nerves, Olivia turned to meet Henry.

It was a day that changed her life. After they overcame their shyness, Olivia and Henry politely brought each other up to speed with their respective lives as they took a walk along the riverbank, pretending to watch students in their canoes when in reality, they only had eyes for each other. At the age of forty-five, Henry had retired from the RAF and was now teaching in the science department at Marcus's school. He lived with his wife Elizabeth in the village and they'd made the transition from military to civilian life relatively easily. The only cloud that floated above their marriage was the lack of children but they had coped and now, he was surrounded by hundreds of the little blighters. At the end of their walk and after a brief foray into the past they reluctantly tore themselves away to do their respective duties as master and parent, but agreed to meet later in a small restaurant on the outskirts of town, well away from prying eyes.

Here, Olivia apologised in person for her treatment of Henry all those years ago and he in return confessed to knowing that she was sorry because he had read and kept every single letter she wrote, but had been too pig-headed and proud to reply. One thing they did have in common was the knowledge that they had both made mistakes and not being together was the greatest regret of their lives.

Olivia was honest and frank about her situation with Nigel, and Henry in turn gave her an insight into his marriage. In stark contrast, he could not lay blame or fault for anything at his wife's door. He may have harboured an unrequited love for Olivia but Elizabeth had always been a loyal, loving and constant companion and for that reason he could never leave or betray her, no matter how he felt about the woman sitting opposite. That said, neither wanted this to be goodbye so after talking things through they decided there was only one thing for it. Just as they had done so many years ago they agreed to go their separate ways, get on with their lives but keep in constant touch.

By the time Olivia returned from parents' day her life had become illuminated once more. It was as though the sun had come out. Its gentle rays were warming up her heart and shining a light on a brighter path. Henry was back in her life if only in the form of letters and phone calls but she didn't care. To her, he was stability, a nod to the days when things were calm and easy, not a weary, constant battle to make her way through the day. The first person Olivia told was Annabel, who she knew would be pleased for her, and as each of Henry's letters arrived, her confidence grew and just hearing his voice on the phone made her heart sing.

Henry always rang in a professional capacity to update her on the monster (which didn't take long) then, they would spend the rest of the conversation chatting about anything and everything. Olivia knew that they were just friends and that he was married to a loyal, devoted wife so their frequent and longed-for communication was all he could offer. Henry had said so in his letters but that's all she expected from this decent, honest man who would never betray his wife, and that's why Olivia adored him. Her own life was far too complicated to look for love elsewhere and at forty-three years old she wasn't prepared to be hurt again. Olivia was content with their long-distance platonic affair the second time around, but she wouldn't let him down again and if need be, would wait for him forever, in this life or the next.

When she took the call from the hospital a few months later to say that Nigel had collapsed on the golf course and was extremely poorly, Olivia didn't rush to his side, instead, she finished her game of bridge and then made her way to A&E via the longest route. She attempted a look of grave concern as the doctor gently explained that her husband had suffered a stroke and then tried equally as hard to hide one of disappointment when told he would most likely make a full recovery. The attack had left him with a slight speech defect but apart from that, he'd got off lightly. The doctor advised a complete change of lifestyle should he wish to avoid a repeat performance. The wise words fell on deaf ears and consequently, eight months after his first stroke Nigel copped for the big one which left him bedridden, paralysed and unable to speak. His unfortunate predicament meant that he was now totally at the mercy of Olivia and the private nurses who cared for him in a solitary bedroom prison, entirely of his own making.

Their friends and acquaintances thought Olivia was a saint, providing care for a man who everyone knew had let her down on many occasions and certainly didn't deserve the devotion of his long-suffering wife. What they didn't know was that Olivia was neither devoted to nor interested in her husband and didn't give two hoots if he lived or died. She did revel in turning the tables and just as he had done, put on a twice daily show of love and affection purely for the benefit of the two nurses who could happily scurry off and pass on tales of how much Mrs Cole loved her invalid husband.

A look of pure hate emanated from Nigel's eyes each morning when Olivia popped in to say hello and ask if he slept well. Then she would tell him where she was off to and who with, before giving him a tender peck on his balding, perspiring head. It made her skin crawl but it was worth it. Olivia returned at six in the evening, just to let him know how well her day had gone and have a little chat about this and that, telling him what delicious creation she was having for dinner while the nurse blended his soup. He would mumble something under his breath, glaring at her from beneath the sheets as she patted his hand and wished him sweet dreams. She would close the door behind her then wipe her lips and him firmly from her mind.

Nigel died (presumably peacefully) in his sleep at the age of fifty-nine. His service was conservatively attended but Olivia knew that most of the mourners were there to support the grieving widow, owing mainly to the fact that Nigel had no real friends to speak of. Marcus was eighteen years old and appeared unaffected by his father's passing or that he had abysmally failed every single one of his A levels. He was, however, champing at the bit to start work at the company so just when poor old Harold thought he'd got rid of one huge, pain in the neck, another good-for-nothing Cole was ready to make his mark on the world of import and export. As the Chairman despondently sipped his sherry at Nigel's wake, watching Marcus as he sneered at his dead father's colleagues and made lewd comments to the waitresses, Harold couldn't wait for the day he received his gold clock and cheque. He'd be straight out of the door without looking back because the young man who'd just pinched the waitress's bottom was going to be trouble.

Once Olivia purged the house of any last reminder of Nigel she got on with her life, shedding forever the shackles of her marriage and locking all the painful memories away. Henry took early retirement and returned to his wife's home town of Alderley Edge where he was within touching distance of Olivia. Despite their unspoken love for one another they always behaved impeccably and conducted themselves as old friends whenever their paths crossed. His wife was given no reason to suspect they harboured deep feelings so when she passed away suddenly after a mercifully short illness, Henry could face the future with a clear conscience knowing he had remained faithful to Elizabeth until the end.

For an appropriate and decent period of time, Henry and Olivia kept their distance and observed the fact that Elizabeth's impeccable life and untimely passing must be respected. Eventually, they felt the time was right and once again embarked on a perfectly respectable, above board romance but this time, both vowed not to make any mistakes.

Olivia marvelled at how a grown man who had served in the armed forces and travelled the world, then suffered daily at the hands of precocious schoolboys, could still be as shy and slow on the uptake as Henry. But for her, that was his charm and she adored him just the way he was. Finally, and not before time, after years of letter writing, romantic dinners and precious stolen moments while the nannies snoozed, Henry threw caution to the wind and took Olivia to Rome for a weekend of passion. After storing up their love for over thirty years, overcoming loss and heartbreak along the way, it had to be said that it was well worth the wait. They continued to live separately, just a few miles apart, until it became impractical to keep both houses and in truth, they wanted more from life than being a 'plus one' at social events. Craving permanent companionship and the opportunity to make up properly for lost time, Olivia endured the wrath of Marcus and moved Henry into her home.

As for the nannies, they both hung on as long as they could, well into their nineties, and were convinced that their little charge had at last found true happiness. Once they knew she was safe in the arms of their beloved Henry, Polly and Tess were happy to accept that their days of nursery-nursing were over. With clear consciences they could finally depart this world knowing that they'd kept their promise to Maurice and their contract of love was fulfilled. Nanny Polly dozed off in her chair by the window and set off first, to check out their new accommodation in heaven, followed closely a few months later by her broken-hearted soulmate, Nanny Tess. Olivia was beside herself but couldn't allow a return to the dark days of depression because this would be letting them down, and besides, neither would be there to hold her hand and make things better. So with all the strength and love they had both invested in her for more than fifty years, Olivia let them go.

***

Olivia's thoughts were interrupted by Ruby, stirring. She was tired now and needed to lie down. Wiping a tear from the corner of her eye she heaved her stiff legs from the stool and waited until Ruby was fully awake.

'Come on now, sleepyhead. We need to get you upstairs and I need my bed. There are decisions to be made tomorrow and those two little terrors will be up at the crack of dawn, raring to go. Let's conserve our energy and call it a day, shall we?' Olivia smiled and held out her hand.

'I'm sorry I nodded off and left you sitting here. I bet you're shattered.' Ruby let Olivia heave her forwards before picking up her duvet and turning off the light.

The two women made their way slowly upstairs together, one was very weary and the other was bruised and battered although for the first time in years, not entirely alone. Whatever Ruby had to face in the morning she would do it with Olivia and for that reason, when they reached the landing and the scene of Marcus's final act, they were able to pass by unaffected. Both women had suffered separately at the hands of cruel men at the top of the stairs. Neither would forget, nor let it happen again.

Chapter 20

Ruby

Oliver bounced right back and straight off to school the next morning. He was especially thrilled that his granny was there when he woke up. Henry arrived with clothes for Olivia that didn't match each other or her shoes, but she let him off despite having to spend the whole day out of her very chic comfort zone. As they sat across the kitchen table from one another, watching Lily mash cereal all over her highchair table, Olivia tentatively broached the subject of Marcus and what to do next. During the night, Ruby had laid wide awake, going over her options and had arrived at only one conclusion – she wanted a divorce. Apart from that she was unsure of what steps to take next and thoroughly terrified of what would happen when he returned from Hong Kong.

'So, have you had a chance to decide what we should do about Marcus? I am appalled that he hasn't rung you even once to see how you are. He knew the state he left you in and you could be dead for all he knows. Henry says he hasn't contacted our house so I presume he's either too ashamed or too drunk on complimentary in-flight drinks to check on you.' Olivia was furious.

'He very rarely rings me anyway so it's nothing new and to be honest, I'm glad because I don't think I could bear speaking to him now. I have decided that I want a divorce but I'm scared of what he will do when he comes back. How will I tell him and more importantly, how will I keep him away from me?' Ruby quailed at the thought of it all, he would go mad, she just knew it.

'Well, why don't you come and live with me? It's not as though we don't have the room. It really won't be a problem, Ruby. We would love to have you and I'm sure I can keep you safe.' Olivia spoke softly.

Ruby, however, remained wary. 'I'm not so convinced of that, Olivia, even though the thought of being away from here and protected by you is very tempting. But I'd be bringing trouble to your door and I know we will disrupt your life. From what you told me last night you and Henry have waited long enough to be together so I'm not going to move into your home and ruin it. And if Marcus kicks up a fuss Henry will feel like he has to protect me and there is *no way* he will be able to stand up to him when he's riled, trust me, I know. The last thing I want is police cars at your house and all the neighbours gossiping, plus it will upset Oliver again, seeing him in a rage and causing a scene at his granny's.' All of this had crossed Ruby's mind the night before and still, it got her precisely nowhere.

Olivia nodded. Everything Ruby said was true and nothing she hadn't considered herself. She would hate Henry being dragged into this, the neighbours, however, were the least of her concerns because she really didn't give a monkey's what people thought anymore.

'Well, what do you suggest... is there anywhere else you can go? What about your Aunt's in Cheadle, could you stay there until the dust has settled?'

'Honestly, Olivia. That's not an option. Aunty Doreen is an odd one and definitely wouldn't welcome me or anyone with open arms, unless it was the Archbishop of Canterbury and then he'd have to book well in advance.' Ruby smiled, at least she'd made Olivia laugh, and then a thought occurred to her.

'There is somewhere I could go, somewhere he'd have trouble finding me and I know that I'd be made welcome but I don't think you would be too happy about it.'

On hearing this Olivia paused and put down her cup. Looking apprehensive, she asked Ruby to continue.

'I could go to France, to my cousin Rosie's. I've wanted to visit her for ages but Marcus wouldn't allow it. We could stay there indefinitely until he calms down. Oliver finishes school on Friday for half-term and we could be long gone by the time he gets back from his trip, but it's so far away from you. The children will miss you too much and I know you will miss them, so maybe it's not such a good idea after all.' Ruby's heart had lifted when she had the idea but seeing the look on Olivia's crestfallen face it had plummeted back down into its usual resting place.

Olivia picked up the crockery from the table and began taking it over to the dishwasher. She was thinking intently and trying to control the frenzy of emotions which raged in her heart. After a few trips back and forth where Ruby sat in anxious silence, sensing she needed to give her mother-in-law time to think, Olivia sat back down in her chair and spoke.

'You're right, about everything. You should go to France. You all deserve a holiday and it will put enough miles between you and Marcus so that you feel safe. I'm quite sure Rosie's husband will be able to deal with him should he turn up, which I'm hoping he won't. I *will* miss the children and you, Ruby. Don't think for one second that I don't have a special place in my heart for you but this is not a time for being selfish, it's a time for action and I think we should get the ball rolling straight away. Once you are all settled I'll come and visit you for a few days, it's not a million miles away, is it?' Olivia was being brave even though her heart was breaking.

Ruby's heart leapt on hearing Olivia's words.

'It's just a break, some time well away from him and if I'm truthful, this house. It's felt like a prison for so long and I'm desperate to escape. I really have had enough, Olivia.' Tears pricked the corners of Ruby's eyes and a huge lump was forming in her throat.

'I can imagine how it's been, Ruby. I'm sure the headmaster will understand and as long as the fees are being paid but we'll cross that bridge when we come to it.' Olivia smiled bravely and was glad when Ruby grasped her hands and held on tightly.

'Are you sure you don't mind? I know how much you love the children and I swear I will only go if you promise to come and see us very soon. I mean it.' Ruby's heart pumped wildly while her mind raced. Thoughts of freedom and images of being safe were already forming in her head.

'Ruby, many years ago I knew what had to be done with Nigel but left it too late. I gave him so many second chances and ended up losing something precious. I almost died that night. I lost so much blood while Nigel scurried about, hiding his car and drinking whisky to cover up the fact that he was already drunk. By the time he rang the ambulance and woke the nannies, I was almost lost as well. When I saw you at the top of those stairs and blood everywhere, it all came flooding back and I thought I'd left it too late again. Marcus abandoned you the same way as Nigel left me. I will not allow my son to hurt you again or be responsible for my grandchildren growing up without their mother. So, you will go to France and we will teach Marcus a lesson he will never forget. Now I want you to ring your cousin and make some arrangements then you and I shall get organised, is that a deal?' Olivia was choked with emotion and holding back her tears.

'Okay, Olivia, it's a deal. I wouldn't be able to do this without you though. I will never forget this, not ever.' And with that Ruby wiped her eyes and let go of Olivia's hands.

'Right, I'm going to ring Rosie and explain and then we can make a list of what needs to be done. Oh, and can you scrape Lily clean? She's made a proper mess with that cereal.' Ruby grinned and pushed back her chair then went into the lounge to make the call and as she picked up the receiver, could feel her chains loosening already.

Following all of Olivia's advice and allowing herself to be instructed in the fine art of teaching someone a lesson, Ruby began packing all their belongings into boxes. To make life easier while at the same time giving Olivia and Henry as much time as possible with the children, Ruby agreed to stay at theirs until they left for France.

It also made her feel safe; she was terrified that Marcus would return early from his trip and prevent her from going. Owing to the state of her bruised and battered face Ruby was unable to do the school run so Henry did the honours while she and Olivia spent their days at the house, wiping away any trace of Marcus's family. It was Olivia's intention that the day he breezed in from his travels expecting everything to be forgotten, presuming his misdemeanours had been swept under the carpet and ready to begin another reign of terror, Marcus would instead return to a dark, empty house and find that his wife and children were gone.

The nitty gritty was left to Olivia. She would make sure that all the legal ends were tied up and deal with the school, then be waiting to pronounce a fitting punishment for her son, the details of which were of no interest to Ruby who just wanted to be gone by the time he flew in.

Once the beds were stripped bare, the children's rooms looked like they had never been occupied. Their toys and belongings were all stored at Olivia's and three suitcases were packed with essential items for their trip to France. No firm plans were made, or the potential length of Ruby's stay discussed. One thing she was sure of was she had no desire to live in a house that held such bad memories. Ruby also didn't trust Marcus to stay away if she lived alone so for now she would just enjoy the space that the English Channel could put between them.

They had a lovely week at Olivia's. It was like seeing someone through brand new eyes. Ruby watched her mother-in-law with Lily and Oliver, running around in her stocking feet, playing hide and seek and making fish fingers for their tea. In the evenings when the children were asleep they would sit together in the lounge and Olivia would talk about her father and her lovely nannies, going through photo albums which Ruby had never set eyes on before, bringing to life her children's heritage and making sense of the past. Oliver had not been told of their impending flit, just in case he blabbed to one of his friends and the old school tie network got word back to Marcus. Olivia meticulously covered every eventuality and planned for any minor setback. She was good at this.

They were surprised by a letter from the police which arrived one morning as they were making a final sweep of the house. It seemed that the lovely nurse had passed on her concerns to a duty officer at the hospital, consequently, a standard letter was sent out offering advice and support from the Domestic Violence Unit. The police officer gave a phone number should Ruby require it so Olivia stashed it away in her handbag knowing it would be put to good use by her solicitor.

As Ruby took a final look around her quiet, soulless home and glanced nervously at the letter she'd left on Marcus's desk, she felt not a trace of sadness. It had once been a symbol of her rising status on the ladder of respectability. On the day she moved in, she was no longer scruffy Ruby from the council estate, another kid who didn't know who her dad was, with a mother who didn't care about anyone except herself. The private estate in Prestbury and everything it stood for had, once upon a time, made Ruby almost burst with pride and relief. How odd it felt now that she was more relieved to be bursting through its gates, as fast as she could, in the opposite direction.

Saturday morning arrived and over breakfast they told Oliver that the very next day he would be going on a holiday adventure to France, to see Rosie and stay in her hotel. He was beside himself with excitement and naturally asked could Granny and Grandad come as well. He was crestfallen for a second or two but once he was reassured that they would be there as soon as possible he raced upstairs to find Henry, who would have books with pictures of where he was going. At no time did he ask about his father or when they would be going home. Everyone packed as much fun and laughter into that day as possible but before they knew it, the five of them were standing at the gates of the departure lounge, two of them preparing to say brave goodbyes.

'Right, young lady. I don't want to see any tears because Oliver has his antennas on full beam and will pick up that something isn't quite right. Give me a hug and I'll see you soon. Text me the second you land and let me know when you arrive at Rosie's.' Olivia held on to Ruby tightly for a few seconds then let her go.

Turning to Oliver whose eyes were busy scanning the airport, taking it all in, Olivia produced two small brown envelopes from her pocket. She had given a larger one to Ruby earlier that day and inside was more than enough to tide them over until her finances could be sorted out and Olivia insisted she accept it.

'Oliver, this is for you and Lily, one each. Inside is some funny money called euros and it's what they use in France. It's for you to spend on anything you like once you go through those doors. I'm sure Mummy will let you buy whatever you want because today is a very special, exciting day. Perhaps you could help Lily choose something but not a car or one of those robot things?' Olivia winked at her grandson.

Oliver was over the moon to be given free will *and* an envelope full of money so hugged his granny and said thank you.

Ruby could barely speak but pulled herself together for the sake of everyone. Still, there was something she needed to get off her chest that if left unsaid she would always regret.

'Thank you for saving me, Olivia. Thank you for being brave enough to set us free. I feel like I've just found you and now I've got to go. I wish we hadn't wasted all those years living around the corner from each other like strangers. I wish I could have been a proper daughter to you because I know you would have been a lovely mum to me. Please don't break your promise and make sure you come and see us soon because we will all miss you so much.' Ruby flung her arms around Olivia's shoulders and held in a sob.

Olivia patted Ruby's back while keeping an eye on Oliver. 'Let's not waste time on regrets, my dear. We have the future to enjoy and I won't break my promise. And just so you know, as far as I'm concerned, and anyone else for that matter, from this moment on you *are* my daughter and I will look after you for the rest of your life. So, will you please go before I ruin my make-up and you miss your flight?' Olivia pushed Ruby gently away and pointed to the official who was waiting patiently to take their boarding cards.

Unable to speak, Ruby kissed Henry on the cheek, grabbed Oliver's hand and then pushed Lily's buggy towards the doors. To shouts of, 'See you soon Granny' and, 'I'll send you a postcard, Grandad Henry', Ruby managed to ferry the children through the body scanner, which Oliver was fascinated by, and once they were on the other side all three turned and waved through the glass. The figures on the other side waved enthusiastically back until Ruby could take no more so turned and walked away, pointing Oliver in the direction of the shop and herself on the road to freedom.

The plane taxied to the end of the runway and Oliver finally sat still but only because he was waiting with bated breath for take-off. He had a bag of toys and numerous treats stored under his feet which he'd bought in the duty-free shop. Once they were seated he'd inquisitively pushed every button on his armrest and was now wearing his pilot's earphones, pretending he was flying the plane. Oliver was also dying to go to the toilet, just to see what it was like but Ruby said he had to wait until they were in the air. Lily was almost asleep on her knee and Oliver was busy peering out of the window at the other planes when he suddenly turned to face his mum and removed his headphones. Reaching over he placed his small pink hand over his mother's and looked up, huge brown eyes wide with concern. Ruby's heart lurched. Was he frightened or about to kick up a fuss at the last moment? Then he spoke.

'Don't be frightened, Mummy, I'll hold your hand.' Then in a whisper. 'Thank you for taking us away from scary Daddy. Everything will be okay when we get to Rosie's cos he won't be able to hurt you anymore and make you cry. We will have the best time, Mummy, I just know it.' He held Ruby's gaze for a second and then his eyes went as big as saucers when he felt the engines begin to rev underneath him and the plane begin to move forward.

If Ruby had any doubts in her mind as she boarded the aircraft about what she was doing, hearing those few innocent words from her son was the only confirmation she needed.

'Here we go, Mummy. Get ready, hold on tight!'

And as the jet hurtled along the runway and the wheels lifted off the ground, Ruby felt Oliver's little hand squeeze hers. As her lock and shackles fell loose, scattering across the runway, she recognised a feeling which she thought had abandoned her forever. For the first time in years, Ruby felt hope.

Chapter 21

Rosie and Ruby

After Rosie had replaced the receiver following her long, traumatic conversation with Ruby, she then sat on the sofa and sobbed her heart out. She knew she shouldn't have left her. She should have followed her instincts and not gone running home to be with Michel. She had been selfish and because of that Marcus could've killed Ruby. Thank God little Oliver had been sensible and saved the day and hats off to frosty Olivia who had surprisingly come up trumps and helped Ruby in her hour of need. It was a lot to take in at first and then to top it all off, Ruby had asked if they could come to France. In a heartbeat, Rosie naturally said yes.

By the time she had composed herself, hurt and anger were beginning to fuel the adrenaline in her body. She had four full days to prepare and get everything ready. Her mind whirred into action and the professional hotelier inside her came to the fore as she began composing 'to do' lists in her head. The guest rooms were almost fully booked for the season and she needed to leave them free so the only other option was the attic. They had intended to use it as an overspill room but never got round to finishing it. Instead, they stored bits and bobs up there and apart from having been repainted, the room remained a bare shell but was ample for the needs of Ruby and the children. The first thing she was going to do was find Michel and fill him in, and then she would ring the terrible twosome and ask Bernard and Christophe to come round and empty the attic.

Rosie washed her face and pulled herself together before she went downstairs to speak with Michel. Gathering her thoughts she picked up the photograph on her desk of her and Ruby sitting on the step. It was the only one she had of them together from their childhood and she'd always kept it close. A huge lump reformed in her throat then fresh tears began to burn her eyes as she stared at the faded image of a scrawny little girl with pigtails, dressed in scraggy clothes, linking her elder cousin's arm and smiling into the camera. Rosie remembered that day so clearly. She'd promised Ruby that she'd always look after her and be best friends forever. Well, now was her chance to come good on that promise and by the time they arrived on Sunday she would have a safe haven ready and waiting, then she could tuck them under her wings and look after them all.

Michel's mother and Zofia were marvellous because once they heard the tale, both were eager to help out. Between them, while Rosie split herself between her guests and the preparations in the attic, they mopped, polished and hung curtains. Bernard and Christophe stayed late each night and installed a tiny en-suite which would be adequate and save her cousin's nipping downstairs to her apartment if they needed the loo. Rosie found a wardrobe, a chest of drawers and two cast-iron beds at the *brocante*, one double and a single that nestled perfectly underneath the wooden eaves of the room.

The three women clucked around the room, made up the beds, fluffed the pillows and vacuumed the rug that they'd placed on the scrubbed wooden floor. By Saturday evening the attic looked cosy and inviting with new duvets and matching quilted throws, plus two brand new teddies sitting on top, just waiting to welcome their new owners to their secret hideaway.

Later that evening Michel came upstairs to find Rosie and insist she have something to eat. It was almost midnight and he knew she was worn out.

'You have done a wonderful job, *chérie*. Now come downstairs and have some food. Everything is perfect here and you need to rest before tomorrow. Soon, the place will have children running about and you will need all your energy to look after them, and Ruby.' He wrapped his arms around her waist and kissed her cheek. He was so proud of the woman he loved, her heart was kind and he never stopped marvelling at her desire to care for everyone.

Rosie picked a stray thread from the rug before answering. 'Okay, you win. I just wanted to check it one more time. I need them to feel safe and secure. I hope it's not too cramped but the children may find it strange at first so at least they'll be with their mum. I'll just be glad when they are here and away from *him*. But you're right as usual and I am tired. Come on, show me what's for supper, I'm starving.'

Following her husband, Rosie closed the door on the attic and went downstairs with Michel. Tomorrow would be a new day and a fresh start and at last they would be safe. Her little family, all together under one roof.

Oliver thought he was in paradise from the second he stepped off the plane into the warm June sun. Rosie was waiting for them at the arrivals gate and was jigging about with excitement as she eagerly scanned the crowd, searching for their faces. Oliver spotted her first, waving frantically while jumping up and down to attract her attention. He barely remembered Rosie but the way his mummy spoke about her, he imagined she was a kind fairy princess with golden hair and a beautiful smile. Oliver recognised her instantly from photographs in his mummy's purse and knew straight away that he was right, Rosie was just lovely.

Michel welcomed them all with open arms when they arrived just after 2pm and had prepared a feast of homemade pizza and chocolate mousse which they ate on the terrace. Ruby's sunglasses hid her bruised eye which was starting to fade slightly but they all steadfastly ignored her injuries. This was a special day and they wanted it to be one they remembered always, talking about happy things and filled with laughter. After lunch, Oliver was desperate to explore so they took a walk around the grounds while Rosie gave them a guided tour. After laughing at Oliver's sheer delight that they had their own swimming pool *and* the fact they didn't have to queue up or pay to get in, then being mithered to death because he wanted to go for a swim straight away, they managed to divert his attention by showing him his room at the top of the hotel. Oliver loved his room, announcing to everyone as soon as he saw it that he was a big boy now so would sleep in the single bed and let Lily cuddle up to Mummy.

In the weeks that followed, *Les Trois Chênes* seemed to blossom with the sound of children's voices. Barking, giddy dogs chased after Oliver as he ran free in the garden and through the woods – Bill and Ben followed him everywhere like devoted servants. Lily enjoyed toddling around barefoot, hot on the heels of her favourite person, Rosie, who adored her little cousin and seemed to have her strapped to her hip, day and night.

Oliver went swimming every day, sometimes twice, but his other favourite things were helping Michel in the kitchen, popping peas or washing carrots and walking up to Dominique's with Mummy where he would look for eggs and put them in a basket. He was proud as punch the first time he came back with six eggs covered in chicken poo and said they were the best he'd ever tasted when he and Michel cooked them for his lunch. Then there was the park in the village where he could play with the other children. They all spoke funny but played tig just the same as in England and afterwards, they'd go to the café and have a glass of pop and talk to a nice man called Sebastien. Bernard and Christophe said they'd help him make a tree house in the large oak just behind the kitchen garden and he spent hours designing his wooden retreat.

But the best thing of all was that when they went to bed at night, he was right next to Mummy. She didn't cry anymore and when he opened his eyes she was just there, across the way with naughty Lily, and that scary feeling he'd had in his tummy for ages had just gone away.

When it was too hot outside, Oliver would spend the afternoon in his bedroom where from the two small attic windows they could see for miles. He said it was like being in a secret place where you could spy on everyone. Each day, he would sit on the window seat, looking through an old pair of binoculars that Michel had given him, watching cars travelling along the winding country roads or tractors making their way back and forth across the stripy fields. Most of all he loved counting all the different types of birds. He had seen an eagle, a hoopoe and an owl, and was currently looking out for a friendly grizzly bear which Dominique had told him roamed the pine woods on the edge of the village. Despite his vigilance, Oliver hadn't spotted it yet but assured everyone that he was keeping his eyes peeled and would give them a shout, the second he saw it.

To Ruby, the room at the top of the house symbolised freedom and with Rosie and Michel just below her, guarding the stairs, she slept peacefully each night, safe and sound with her children by her side. Rosie was always very busy so when Lily slept Ruby helped with the chores around the hotel. There was bed-making and housekeeping to be done and also the terrace and the grounds needed to be kept tidy so without having to be asked, she got stuck in. Secretly, Ruby loved working in the hotel and being useful. Her days flew by in a haze of white sheets, chasing after Lily, watching Oliver in the pool, glorious mealtimes but the icing on the cake was being with Rosie.

She had met so many new people who immediately accepted her as one of the family and part of their community. Ruby loved going into the village where everyone would say hello and goodbye when you went into the shops. The mothers in the park did their best to make conversation and even though they couldn't really chat, they always invited her to sit with them and share their picnics. The hotel was constantly buzzing with activity, diners arriving in the evening and hotel guests coming and going. There was Océane, a lovely girl from the farm up the road who worked in the kitchen with Michel and her handsome older brother, Pascal, who worked in the restaurant and ran the bar.

Depending on how busy it was, Rosie would be on hand to chat to the guests (her favourite pastime) but now and then she got the evening off and would sit with Ruby in the apartment and share a bottle of wine, eating crisps and watching French TV. Sometimes they would chat about when they were children but both had agreed that neither wanted to talk about Marcus because for now, he was the past and they were enjoying the present too much to have it ruined for one second by The Dark Lord.

They had been in France for almost a month and although Oliver was enjoying running wild and had plenty to occupy him, he needed friends and Ruby was concerned that he might fall behind so did her best to keep up with his reading and writing, making sure she spent time with him each day attempting to get him to sit down and concentrate. It was during a Sunday afternoon barbeque at Dominique's that Ruby met Sylvie, the headmistress of the school and the eldest daughter of village royalty, Hortense. Luckily, Sylvie could speak excellent English and was chatting to Ruby about the future – her mother had already filled her in on the whole horrible business of the evil husband and although Ruby confessed to having no firm plans, mentioned in passing that she was worried about Oliver missing out on being with other children.

'I have an idea, Ruby. Would you like to bring Oliver to school for a few days next week? Perhaps he will enjoy playing with the other children and taking part in our activities. I'm sure he will enjoy it, what do you think?' Sylvie had been watching the small boy laughing and playing pétanque with the men and could tell that he was polite and very bright.

'Is that allowed? I don't want to get you into any trouble. What about the language barrier? He won't understand anyone and I don't want him to feel uncomfortable.' Ruby was anxious but knew how much Oliver loved going to school. In England he'd not had a day off since he started.

'Pah, how can I get in trouble? I am the headmistress and my mother and uncle are both on the board of governors. My niece is in charge of *école maternelle*, that is what I think you call nursery school and anyway, nobody will object to a new face. You will be surprised, Ruby, how quickly children can pick up a new language. I have two English pupils in my school who now speak fluent French. Oliver will be fine and I will take care of him… we can start with a few half days if you like, to see how he goes. It is almost the end of term so we are slowing down and having a little fun, you should let him join in.' Sylvie smiled encouragingly at Ruby.

'He's almost five though. It's his birthday in August. Isn't he a bit big for nursery school?' To Ruby, and as much as Oliver protested, he was still her baby and letting him go made her anxious so maybe she was looking for excuses to keep him close.

'No, not at all. In France you can begin nursery at two years old, but school is not compulsory until the age of six when you begin *école elementaires*. We still teach a structured programme *d'études*. How do you say it in English? Ah yes, curriculum. So I think Oliver will enjoy it.' Sylvie poured herself another glass of wine and waited for Ruby to think it over.

'Okay then, if you think he will be okay and you won't get in trouble by sneaking someone in, then perhaps we should ask the man himself.' Shielding her eyes from the sun Ruby searched for Oliver and called him over once he'd played his last boule. After wiping his sweaty forehead she then explained all about Sylvie's school.

She should have known the answer before she even asked and finding out that he got Wednesdays off as well, sealed the deal. Not only would he make some new friends, he still had a whole day to himself at the hotel doing whatever it was he did from the second he woke up until his tired little head hit the pillow. It was all arranged and he would start the very next day, just for the afternoon to see how he went, then they would take it from there. Hearing Zofia calling for him to come and get some cake and strawberries, he was off like a shot.

Ruby almost didn't recognise her son; her little caterpillar, who was once frightened of his own shadow was turning into a butterfly right before her eyes. She was so proud of him, throwing himself into life around the hotel and being brave enough to try out school in a foreign country. Ruby decided to ring Olivia later that evening and tell her the news but for now, she was going to sit back and enjoy the company and keep her eye on Lily who was becoming a terror and currently wiping mushed up ice cream all over Bill's tail.

Rosie was savouring her afternoon off. They had made it a rule when they took over the hotel that Sunday would remain a family day, as was the tradition all over France. They worked hard enough all week and put in the hours so once breakfast was served and cleared away, it was their day and a time when she and Michel could enjoy the fruits of their labour and each other. She'd been watching Ruby chatting to Sylvie, and Lily feeding ice cream to the dogs. Oliver was just a joy and not a moment's trouble to anyone. Michel had taken to him straight away and enjoyed their time together in the kitchen where Oliver would help him in all sorts of simple but *extremely* important tasks. Michel had confided in Rosie that he could not understand how any man could not love this clever, affectionate child or be stupid enough to throw away a complete family, either.

Then there was Ruby. She really was a changed person, who, with a bit of sun on her face and some fresh air in her lungs was beginning to glow again, slowly shedding her old self and finding her feet. Rosie had no doubt that St Pierre had lots to do with it and the hotel just oozed calm and tranquillity; everyone who visited always said they never wanted to leave. This brought Rosie round to wondering what Ruby was going to do about home and where she was going to make it, and more to the point, for how long they could tip-toe around the subject of Marcus. Olivia had kept them posted on developments there and true to her word, she had managed to control her son and keep him away, but arrangements needed to be made and Rosie had something up her sleeve. That was why if everything had gone to plan with her friend Sylvie, stage one of her mission was already in progress.

As far as Rosie was concerned they could stay forever, because that's what she really wanted. All their life, she and Ruby had been apart, mainly due to the faults of their mothers and now Rosie just wanted her family to be together, not on the other side of the Channel. She knew it sounded slightly selfish, wanting everything her own way yet she was convinced that France could offer Ruby and her children a happier way of life. What could be better than growing up surrounded by the countryside and breathing in fresh air every day with your family all around to give love and support? It was a shame about Olivia but she had loads of friends and activities to occupy her, and Henry of course, plus stacks of cash in the bank so could visit whenever she wanted. One day, when Olivia was gone, Ruby would be alone again in England with no family and in the meantime, Oliver and Lily would just be holiday visitors to France. Ruby had finally managed to escape and after seeing how happy she was, Rosie thought it would be a pity for her to go back, so she had come up with an idea.

The hotel already had plenty of repeat bookings for next season and they had ideas for cookery courses and painting holidays and even a bit of a change from French food during the winter months when they were quiet. They had decided to host speciality nights in the restaurant, which was really Rosie's idea but she let Michel think it was his. After the hoo-ha when she suggested serving English food on their menu she realised that she had to tread carefully where the Gallic ego of her wonderful chef and partner was concerned.

***

Rosie wanted a few simple English choices to be available, just in case someone like her mother turned up and hated anything remotely foreign. Michel didn't get it at all and couldn't understand why anyone would come to France and not want to eat French food. No matter how much Rosie tried to explain that even though people loved the country, they didn't necessarily want to eat frog's legs, chicken stuffed with truffles or foie gras. Her way of thinking was that if a couple came to dine in the restaurant, while one of them may adore everything Michel had to offer, if the other sat there with a face like thunder, picking at salad and nibbling on a bread roll, the experience would be ruined for them both and they wouldn't come back. If, however, Mr or Mrs Fussy Pants could have steak and chips or an omelette – even a slice of sodding ham with an egg slapped on top would do, then everyone would be happy. Michel stomped and fumed, and Rosie waited to be proved right which thankfully occurred when a party of four couples from Norfolk booked in for Easter week.

Pâques was an extremely holy period in France and many places closed down completely to take advantage of the long Easter weekend so not being particularly religious (except when he was around his mother), Michel decided that he would keep the restaurant open to feed their guests and any other chance bookings. On the first night, the Norfolk contingent all trooped down, dressed in their finest and looking forward to a slap-up-meal. Unfortunately, only two of the diners could understand the menu and when Rosie translated it for the rest she was met with mainly blank, unenthusiastic faces. After what seemed like an age they finally managed to choose something they thought they might like, Rosie, however, knew deep down that the evening was going to be a disaster.

The devout Francophiles in the group, which amounted to three, plus one adventurous soul who decided to give it a go, all had a lovely meal while the other four diners picked and prodded their way through each course, scraping off the sauce and sending plates of uneaten food back to the kitchen. Michel was incensed and insulted while Rosie put a tick in her 'I told you so' box. The eight guests didn't eat in the restaurant for the next two evenings, and over breakfast a jolly chap named Stan tactfully told Rosie that they had been to McDonalds (twice) because almost everywhere else was shut, and the others didn't want to waste money eating French food they didn't like. Consequently, he was getting blooming sick of cheeseburgers, fries and Coke, and in turn, Rosie decided that enough was enough and marched off to speak with Michel.

'Do you know that our guests would rather have burger and chips than eat in your first-class restaurant just because you are too pig-headed to listen to my advice? We have missed out on two nights takings while our customers have been eating fast food when they could be here, enjoying the atmosphere of the hotel and *your* cooking. They probably won't come back now, and it's got nothing to do with my rooms. So, smart arse, what do *you* suggest we do because as far as I'm concerned we may as well close for a few nights and put our feet up?' Rosie was livid and already knew the answer to the problem; she was just praying that Michel would take the hint.

'Well, perhaps they are just stupid or have very bad taste. I do not know, but if we are losing money then I will need to think of something.' He pretended to think for a while as he chopped garlic before sighing dramatically and offering a solution. 'Perhaps I could prepare some food that is a little more English, only a few dishes though, and I am *not* making pies. I have not the time to be pandering to the wishes of ignorant people but if it makes you happy *and* them, well I suppose I am prepared to lower my standards. Will that stop you from shouting like a madwoman?' Michel knew he was beaten but thought he'd done a damn fine job of wriggling out of being wrong.

'What a good idea, Michel. I wonder why I didn't think of that. I'll nip back and tell the poor, starving man out there he can expect something delicious for his dinner. You really are a genius, you know that?' And off Rosie marched to tell Stan the good news at the same time as wondering just how hard it could be to bang some frites in the fryer and rustle up a bloody omelette.

It worked like a dream and the eight guests dined in the restaurant each evening for the rest of their stay. They almost drank the bar dry which resulted in a hefty profit and a generous tip for Pascal, but more importantly, they had firm bookings for a return trip at the end of summer – for Stan's 60th birthday.

***

Rosie brought herself back to reality and the task of fine tuning her cunning plan. They were going to have themed nights once a month, including Italian, Spanish, and American cuisine and if she was really lucky, might be able to slip in the odd curry because she could murder a nice tikka masala every now and then. If they hoped to promote the restaurant, Rosie would require extra help during the day with the hotel, that way she could conserve her energy for the evening. This was where the permanent post of housekeeper came in. She'd noticed that Ruby was very efficient and it would look more professional to have someone deliver towels in a nice uniform, rather than Rosie, who wore so many hats that sometimes she didn't know whether she was coming or going. A permanent housekeeper would mean they could devise a rota and each take days off, which would be essential, especially now she wanted to focus on the gîtes. The minute the main season ended it was going to be all systems go because this was step three of her attempt at world domination and also, conveniently, it included Ruby.

The first gîte was complete apart from having the kitchen installed at the end of the month. Number two was hot on its heels then after that, Bernard and Christophe could crack on with three and four. The money her father gave her had been set aside specifically for this purpose and Rosie wanted them ready ASAP. The room in the attic was cosy but lacked facilities and wasn't suitable for the long-term, however, gîte number one was perfect for a small family. It had a lounge and an open plan kitchen, a bathroom with shower and a double bedroom. It was compact but ideal for Ruby and the kids and just as cosy as the room they were in now. It would also give them a bit of independence while at the same time, not be too far from her and Michel. Therefore, if Oliver liked school and they continued to be happy during the summer, if Ruby had a job and self-esteem, and as long as Olivia didn't kick up a fuss, Rosie prayed that they could be convinced to stay.

The afternoon of eating, drinking and playing pétanque rolled on into the evening. Lily was fast asleep in her pushchair. Zofia wrapped Oliver in a blanket under the green gazebo and fed him Polish chocolates while he watched the grown-ups chatting in the garden. The tiny lights that were strung around the house twinkled in the night and Oliver thought they looked like fairies, sprinkling magic dust over the flowers and the whole of France. The dust made everyone smile and the sun shine, but best of all, it made his mummy happy. Tomorrow, he was going to school with Sylvie and while he was away he wouldn't worry about anything like he used to. When he came home, Michel would be waiting with something yummy to eat and then he could see Golden Rosie who always gave him cuddles and smiles.

He really needed to tell Mummy something important as well. He needed her to tell Granny to come soon and share the magic with them because he missed her and Grandad Henry so much and it made his heart feel funny and a bit sad. But what he needed to tell Mummy most of all was that he never, ever wanted to go back to the shouting house or see Scary Daddy. He just wanted to stay here in France, forever.

Chapter 22

Olivia

Olivia was in a strange, mixed-up mood by the time she put down the phone after a long chat with Ruby. They spoke every few days and she looked forward to hearing her voice and the information packed conversations with Oliver, which made her smile on hearing his effervescent happiness fizzing down the line. Her heart had dropped slightly at the news that Oliver was going to try out the village school. Ruby had sold it to her as a way of keeping him occupied and making some friends but deep down, Olivia knew that it also signalled the increasing possibility they would settle there permanently, and selfishly, it made her sad. There was no denying that Ruby had made the right decision in going to France. Not only were they a lot happier, they were safe too and after witnessing the mood Marcus was in when he found out they were gone, they were better off as far away as possible. Olivia had never seen her son in such a rage than on the night he returned from Hong Kong, however, she was more than ready for him and well and truly prepared to hand out his punishment, which he so rightly deserved.

***

When Marcus pulled into the cul-de-sac just after 9pm, he had no inkling what awaited him, or not, as the case turned out to be. As his home came into view from where he was sitting in the back of the cab, Marcus was slightly put out that it was in complete darkness. His first thought was that the useless cow had forgotten he was coming home today and might be at his mother's. He wasn't aware of her plans, mainly due to the fact that he hadn't bothered to ring her while he was away; having nothing to talk to her about and the same went for his mother. The last thing Marcus wanted was to hear Ruby snivelling or expecting an apology for his mood before he left and anyway, she needed to be taught a lesson so his silence was part of her punishment.

Marcus stepped out of the taxi and paid the driver, then as he turned he spotted the 'For Sale' sign in the front garden. A nerve twitched in his jaw but he showed no other reaction, just in case the silly bitch was inside, watching him and hoping for some indication that he was shocked. Instead, he dragged his cases up the path and rang the bell. His keys were at the bottom of his hand luggage and if she was asleep then she could bloody well get her arse out of bed and open the door for him. God help her if she hadn't made him anything to eat because on top of that pathetic sign, she was already in deep trouble.

The hall light didn't come on so in temper, Marcus kept his hand on the bell and began thumping on the front door. After a few minutes he stopped when it finally dawned on him that she wasn't actually at home. The bitch had taken the children on holiday after he expressly forbade it. A million thoughts raced through his jet-lagged brain, none of them good as he unzipped his bag and angrily rummaged for his keys, swearing under his breath and promising retribution for her actions. When he finally found them, he pushed the key into the lock and for the briefest moment, pre-empted the scenario of her having changed the locks. Maybe his tantrum before he left had been a little extreme and as a result she'd grown some balls but when the door swung open, the rage in him subsided and he smirked as he let himself into the dark, quiet house.

It smelt strongly of disinfectant and there was a chill in the air. Marcus flung his keys on the hall table and proceeded into the kitchen which was as clean and sparkling as the day they moved in. He was desperate for a drink so flung open the fridge to grab a beer and see if she'd left him anything to eat. When he encountered the empty shelves which were usually stocked to the brim with all his homecoming requirements he stood stock-still, taking it in, thinking. The smooth white, bare interior signalled trouble and for a second Marcus was on the back foot. He moved to the cupboards which were also totally empty, not even a cornflake or a teabag graced their high gloss shelves, without a second thought, Marcus turned and left the kitchen. He walked cautiously up the stairs, his mind on overdrive. If she'd taken the children on holiday, then why had she also taken the entire contents of the kitchen cupboards? Questions ticked away in his brain. His legs didn't run or take the stairs two at a time, because that's what men who loved their families did the moment they realised that their whole life had gone, that they'd pushed their loved ones too far and the consequences of their behaviour was about to be felt. Marcus, however, experienced none of those emotions, only that of anger and the unwillingness to believe she would have the nerve to leave him.

He stopped at the top of the stairs and had the grace to remember the bloodstained carpet which held no trace of his actions, then, his attention was drawn to the five doors which bordered the landing. All were firmly shut, taunting him, daring him to open them and see what lay behind. The nerves ticked again in his jaw and a pulsing vein in his temple responded to the surge of boiling blood as it raged through his body. Stepping forward, he grabbed the door handle and walked inside.

The bare mattress and neatly folded duvet with the pillows stacked on top told him all he needed to know. There was no point in opening her wardrobe doors as he knew they would be empty but he looked anyway, just for confirmation purposes. Calmly, he turned and walked over to his son's room and was met by a similar sight. The walls and shelves which were once adorned with brightly coloured toys and stacks of books were barren as was the room. Lily's pastel-pink room was in the same state, stripped, cold and soulless.

Marcus turned and walked slowly downstairs and into the lounge where here, everything looked much the same as before he left until he noticed the photo frames. They were all in exactly the same place but the images that told a false tale of a happy family, with smiling babies and doe-eyed toddlers had all been removed. Even their wedding photo bore a blank canvas where the picture of a beautiful bride and her handsome groom had once lain.

Marcus felt stunned. His body was left numb from the shock of her actions. Never in a million years would he have imagined that the pathetic creature would have the audacity to leave him and he was having trouble taking it all in. The final place he looked was his study and he was certain of one thing, that if she'd left him a note then that's where it would be. Sure enough, as he entered the room and switched on the light he saw it, resting against the computer screen, goading him, daring him to look and read her words of defiance. Angrily, he grabbed the crisp white envelope and tore it open, hastily unfolding the pages of her note because that's all it was, a few short words. No simpering homage to a marriage that she still wanted to save, no begging for change or hints of a return if he complied, just a terse message and final instructions, and certainly not one scrap of lingering love.

Marcus,

As you are probably aware by now, I have left you and taken the children away. If and when we do return it will not be to this house, or you. I have filed for a divorce and you will be hearing from my solicitor in due course. Your mother is aware of the situation and has further instructions which she will convey to you on my behalf. The keys to the car and this prison are in the kitchen drawer. Do not try to find or follow us as nothing you can say or do will ever be able to persuade or force us to return. Ruby

After reading and rereading the note, Marcus began to shake. Somewhere inside his body a volcano was about to erupt as molten lava surged through his veins and his hands trembled with barely controlled rage. Scrunching the note between his white-knuckled fists he tossed it onto the floor and then flew into the hall, grabbing his keys and slamming the front door shut. He had never noticed before how bloody slowly the electric garage doors opened and was so wound up as he revved the engine of his car he felt tempted to just drive through and smash them to pieces, like they did in films.

As he sped out of the estate and then onto the peaceful Prestbury roads, all he could see was her face which he wanted to smash into a thousand pieces. His only thought was to get to his mother's and find out what she knew and ask her why she hadn't contacted him. Maybe she'd only just found out and was waiting for him to land. Marcus consoled himself with the knowledge that she hated the bitch as much as he did and would help him do everything she could to punish Ruby and get his children back. Smiling as he imagined their revenge, Marcus drove wildly on. Within minutes he'd arrived at his mother's and swung into the drive, relieved to see the lights were still burning. Jumping out of his car Marcus ran up to the front door which was swiftly opened by Henry before he even had time to knock. After being told Olivia was in the drawing room, Marcus stormed past the stony-faced old fart and barged into the pale-yellow room to find his mother standing in front of the fireplace, calmly sipping her drink. She showed little reaction to his arrival and placed the glass delicately on the table as she waited for her son to speak.

'Can you believe what that bitch has done? She's left me and taken the children! She says you know all about it. How fucking dare she leave me and when did you find out, why didn't you ring me?' Marcus was almost purple with anger and spitting venom as he spoke.

'Hello, Marcus, nice to see you too. For a start, we'll have less of the language if you don't mind and yes, I did know that Ruby had left you. I found out over a week ago. I helped her pack and gave her my blessing. And I didn't tell you because quite frankly you didn't deserve to know!' Olivia left the words to hang in the air and sink in slowly as she watched her incredulous son's face become bathed in pure, unadulterated shock and horror.

'What the hell do you mean? You helped her and gave her your blessing. For fuck's sake, Mother, I know you hate her but I didn't expect you to go this far to get rid of her, and what about the kids, why did you let her take them? You should have kept them here.' Marcus was pacing like a caged animal.

'Please watch your foul mouth, Marcus. I have asked you once to curb your tongue and for the record, and so we may be clear as we continue, I do not and never have, hated Ruby. I think she is a wonderful mother and a beautiful human being who was unfortunate enough to cross paths with you and consequently, has led a very miserable life ever since. Hence, when it became apparent to me that she was in danger and that my grandchildren were living with a monster, I encouraged and helped her seek sanctuary elsewhere. So, instead of standing there ranting and raving I think you should sit down and listen to what I have to say. Ruby has left me in charge of her affairs and whilst you have been away, certain things have been set in motion which you should be aware of.' Olivia waited for Marcus to assimilate the information and feeling the need to retain momentum and her position of power, she chose to remain standing.

'No, I will not sit down. I'm not twelve and I won't do as I'm told, especially not by you. Do you expect me to listen like I'm a pathetic child while you chastise me? Not a chance. So, go on, Mother, get on with it. Tell me what you and that cretin have cooked up between you. God, who'd have thought it? My own mother taking sides with some common shop girl. This really is a sick joke. I'll try not to laugh too loudly. I wouldn't want to spoil your moment in the spotlight, Mummy dearest.' Marcus marched over to the drinks trolley and poured himself a large whisky, the brown liquid sloshing over the sides and onto the silver tray below.

'If that's how you want to play it, Marcus, that's fine. I've tried to ignore what you are and in my own deluded way I hoped that one day you would change. I know now that you never will so what I'm going to tell you next, I believe with all my heart that is exactly what you deserve. Ruby has filed for divorce on the grounds of your unreasonable behaviour which is considerable. We have photographic evidence of her injuries not to mention witnesses which include me, Henry and your own son so any attempt to deny what you did will be preposterous. Ruby was contacted by the police and may at any time bring a prosecution against you, and owing to your previous unpunished misdemeanour and the evidence that lies in the solicitor's safe you will be in serious trouble. Luckily for you, your soon to be ex-wife has no intention of having you arrested as long as you play ball.' Olivia took a sip of her drink because even though she had rehearsed her speech over and over, looking into the dark, hateful eyes of her son was extremely unnerving so she needed to stick to the facts and get this over with.

Marcus held his glass to sneering lips as he spoke.

'Blackmail, Mother, again? You're getting good at this and now you're even passing tips onto my lovely wife. Very commendable I must say. So, what exactly am I expected to do in this petty little game of yours?' Marcus was white with rage as he stared vehemently at his mother.

'As I'm sure you noticed, the house has been placed on the market and hopefully it will be sold quickly. Once that is done, fifty percent of the proceeds will go to Ruby, the rest you can do with as you wish. With regards to the children I expect you to set up regular generous payments to provide for their upbringing. This can be deposited into a new bank account that has been opened in Ruby's sole name. Finally, until you are contacted and invited to see the children, you will stay well away and make no attempt to find them. Are all these conditions clear and agreeable?' Olivia observed her son as he mulled over her instructions, noting that he seemed unusually subdued and for a second she actually thought he'd agree until suddenly, he threw his head back and laughed out loud, a long sarcastic snort ended his hilarity.

Then Marcus spoke, staring his mother in the eye.

'If you think for one second that I am giving that tart a single penny from my house you've got another thing coming. You bought it from *my* inheritance, how dare you expect me to give her anything? You should be on my side, why on earth would you give her money? The kids can have it when you're dead but not her. Not a chance is she walking away with a dime, have you got that?' Marcus was actually shaking now. He had never been so shocked or enraged in his whole life.

Olivia stood firm.

'Marcus, let me make something very, very clear to you. Where inheritances are concerned you are batting on a very sticky wicket and have been for a long time. Whom I leave my fortune to is entirely my business. It is for me alone to decide who I think deserves it and at the moment, you are at the very end of the list, just after the cat sanctuary in Chester. So shall we start again? You will do exactly as I say otherwise, the second you step out of line I will instruct David to bring me my will, which for your information has already been amended, and without further ado I will sign it and disinherit you with the stroke of a pen.' Olivia was about to carry on when Marcus spoke under his breath.

'You wouldn't dare do that. I'm your son and you owe me. It's all bluff and I know you couldn't stand the gossip and scandal. It's a joke… this whole thing is a huge joke.' Marcus smirked but underneath his calm exterior he was panicking because he'd never seen his mother like this and had the rising suspicion that she actually meant it.

Marcus had already noticed that behind her on the marble mantelpiece, where once rested a photographic history of his life, he had been replaced by photos of Oliver and Lily and sickeningly, his wife.

Olivia raised her perfectly-shaped eyebrows and continued, ignoring his comments completely.

'Furthermore, I have had a long meeting with the Chairman and made him fully aware of your, shall we say, antics and along with the negative reports he's been having from our offices in the

Far East we are both less than impressed with your performance all round. Consequently, we have decided that it's about time you learned the meaning of hard work and a spot has been found for you at the factory in Leicester. It will be a temporary move and a wonderful opportunity to give someone from the Manchester office a bite at the cherry, plus the chance to sample the delights of first-class travel and move up in the world.' Olivia paused before handing down the remainder of Marcus's sentence.

'Once you have finished in the Midlands you will be off to China. It appears that it's an emerging market and we have some contacts that need chasing up along with plenty of factories that we'd like you to take a look at. You can keep your car for now, so once the house is sold you can scurry off to your bachelor pad and continue the lifestyle you seem to prefer, rather than your lovely home and family. For the time being, I would also like you to stay away from here. I have nothing to say to you and for the foreseeable future, until you have redeemed yourself or at the very least adhered to my conditions, I think that it will be mutually beneficial to get on with our lives separately.'

After taking a sip of her drink, Olivia continued.

'Rest assured that I will be keeping an extra close eye on you, Marcus, so don't think that you can pull the wool over my eyes and if I hear just one negative report, so help me, I will carry out all of my threats. I let the worry of scandal hinder me many years ago, thus preventing me from making sensible decisions which I will always regret. So please be assured that I have no fear of gossip. You can see far more interesting things on daytime television than on the leafy streets of Prestbury, and Cole family dramas are of little interest these days. Now, I'm sure you have plenty to say on the matter so off you go, do your worst.' Olivia was drained from her speech and decided that now was the time to sit down, her legs were a bit wobbly with nerves and she needed another drink to fortify her.

Marcus remained silent for a few moments, watching his mother take her seat and sip her gin and tonic which is when he noticed the tremor in her hands, spotting weakness he changed tack.

'Well, you really have thought all this through, haven't you, Mother? Right down to the last letter. I don't know what that bitch has been telling you to warrant all this but she really has brainwashed you, hasn't she? Has it ever occurred to you that all this time I may have been trapped in an unhappy marriage? Ruby is unbearable to live with and has made my life a misery, did you know that? No, of course not. You have instantly jumped to her defence and believe everything she has said. She's unstable you know, and a depressive. I've done my best to shield you from the truth so that you wouldn't be upset but the past few years have been a nightmare for me and I worry about the children being left alone with her. She hasn't even got any friends for God's sake, what does that tell you?' Marcus waited for a response but when none came, slightly rattled, he soldiered on.

'She even threatened to throw herself down the stairs just before I left for Hong Kong, simply because I wouldn't let her take the children on holiday, but I was terrified she wouldn't care for them properly. I love my family and cannot bear the thought of being separated from Oliver and Lily. I wish I'd come to you now with my concerns and then perhaps we could have sorted this out together, but now you've taken her side and frankly I'm devastated that you would turn on me like this.' Marcus placed his head in his hands and breathed deeply, waiting for his mother to speak.

The sound of slow clapping quickly brought Marcus back from his world of fantasy.

'Very well done, Marcus, nice try, and your little performance bordered on being convincing too, but you see I didn't believe one single word. You don't care a jot about your family. I'm surprised you even remembered the children's names. You've been an appalling father and a despicable husband. Neither I nor any jury in the land would believe those things you said about Ruby. Even your own son has told me how you treat her, and him. We've all witnessed the result of your violence and if anyone is unstable around here, that person is you. Don't ever patronise me with *your* warped version of marriage again. You alone have made it that way and now you will have to pay the price.' Olivia was livid and could hardly contain her anger any longer.

And then Marcus erupted.

'Traitor! You spineless traitor! Ha, but I completely forgot about my father... what should I have expected from a woman who her reduced her own husband to nothing more than a penniless lodger? Oh yes, Dad told me all about how you treated him, forcing him to live here with you and those mad old women, refusing to divorce him and leaving him to survive on the scraps you threw. Well, you won't treat me like that. I'd rather die than do your bidding. I will not be shuffled off to Leicester and I certainly won't be going to China. I am not being swept under the carpet like my poor father so you can just sack me. Go on, I dare you. Then I'll take you and your fucking empire to court and drag your name through the mud. God forbid that the Cole family name should be tarnished by scandal, what would we do, Mummy? You can stick your conditions up your arse. I'm standing up to you like Father should've done years ago then we could have run the company our way and put you well and truly in your place.' Marcus swigged the last of his whisky in one large gulp and slammed the glass on the polished table, triumph glistening in maddened eyes.

Olivia stood to the challenge, visibly shaking with rage and pent up hate for a man whose name she hardly ever mentioned.

'Don't you dare speak that man's name in my house. Your father was even more repellent than you are right now. You have no idea what you are talking about and if you did, then you would know that I wish with all my heart that I had divorced that low life, excuse of a man a hundred times over. He deserved nothing because just like you he expected wealth and wasn't prepared to give anything in return. That leech ruined my life and he killed my daughter. Do you hear me, Marcus, he murdered my baby and I will never forgive him for that, ever. Now get out of this house and do not come back until I invite you. You have twenty-four hours to accept my proposals otherwise I will disown you. Get out of my sight before I ring David right now and have him bring the papers over tonight for me to sign. Just get out, get out, get out!' Olivia was trembling from head to toe and could hear the hysteria in her own voice.

Marcus had never seen his mother so angry and stepped warily backwards, stunned by her threats and finally in no doubt that she meant every single one. As Henry flew into the room to see what the commotion was he barely acknowledged Marcus and centred his concern on Olivia.

When he reached her, Henry turned to face the cause of the anxiety and in his firmest school master's voice and with a death ray stare, banished Marcus from the room.

Marcus was in shock. He sat behind the wheel of his car in the drive, almost hyperventilating, reeling from the viciousness of his mother's words, horrified that she would turn on him like that. Worst of all, he realised that despite his protests and attempts to turn her around she wasn't going to budge. Unless he accepted her deal and toed the line he stood to lose everything. The children were the last thing on his mind because he wouldn't have known what to do with them anyway and as for that bitch Ruby, he never wanted to set eyes on her again. He couldn't imagine a life without his luxuries and there was no way he would risk his inheritance, so that meant he was stuffed. Whether he liked it or not he would have to give in to her demands and allow himself to be exiled to God knows where. Marcus couldn't stand Leicester and the thought of living in China didn't fill him with glee either, but he wouldn't let Ruby win so as long as he was a good boy, he'd be able to keep the lot.

As for his mother, well, she wouldn't last forever and one day, hopefully soon, her empire would be his and then he really would be able to have some fun. Starting the engine he pulled out of the drive and as he turned into the road glanced in the rear-view mirror and noticed the large iron gates slowly closing, locking him out. Any normal person would've felt sadness or regret but Marcus saw it as the final insult and as he drove away, he smirked. He could play the long game too and she was messing with the wrong person. In the meantime, now he was a free man, he might just nip into town and cheer himself up with whichever lucky lady crossed his path first. He was going to paint Manchester red and bang it on expenses, what the hell.

Henry battled to calm Olivia who was inconsolable. So many memories had been dragged to the surface. Deep scars etched into her heart became raw and painful once again. Recriminations and badly made choices tormented her soul while the faces of those departed, haunted her each time she closed her eyes. She longed to hold the visions in her arms and hear their words of comfort once again. It was all too much to bear, facing up to the reality and disappointment that was her son. But what was worse, what caused her physical pain was missing her beloved grandchildren more with each passing day. Being within reach at last of someone who she could love and treat like the daughter she so longed for had been a gift from heaven but no sooner had she found happiness, she had to let them all go.

Henry finally managed to soothe Olivia with assurances that she had done the right thing, along with promises of a visit to France, once the dust had settled he would arrange it all. Eventually, her tears subsided and were replaced by happy images. As she relaxed in the arms of her Henry, Olivia had the strangest thought, she imagined someone was sprinkling magic fairy dust in her eyes and finally, with a smile on her lips, she drifted off into a deep, peaceful sleep.

Chapter 23

Olivia and Ruby

It had been six weeks since Olivia saw her little family off at Manchester Airport and since then she had been living in a topsy-turvy world, confused by ups and downs, highs and lows. Subjected to a continuous torrent of emotions, she battled her own demons and fought with her subconscious on a daily basis. Her highs came after receiving photographs and calls from Ruby and the children, which were reassuringly embellished with giddy tales from Oliver, telling them in great detail about bears and birds and chickens, or whatever he'd done that day. Lily always insisted on speaking to Golly but didn't make much sense, however, she seemed totally enamoured with some doggies so appeared to be quite content. Just hearing Ruby's voice told Olivia that she was on the mend, it was lighter and any strains of tension were gone. She even had something interesting to say each time they spoke, which was a far cry from the mouse-like girl who would timidly drop off her children before scurrying back to her car.

The lows came mostly on the days she'd always set aside for the school run and special teatimes, or when she passed the playroom which was crammed with a vast array of their toys and games. Lately, she'd taken to closing the door on them, just to avoid being reminded. Olivia still had her round of activities and charity work to keep her occupied and most days she thanked heaven for her friends and fellow bridge players, whose companionship kept her afloat, but only just.

Olivia was consumed by so many emotions which had to be overcome and huge hurdles were waiting to slow her down each day, from the minute she opened her eyes and remembered they were gone. The worst emotion, she feared, was hate and a feeling which she had reserved only for Nigel. Now, Olivia attributed the loss of her grandchildren to the behaviour of her son and when she was really low, laid the blame for their departure firmly on his shoulders. The only way she could fend off her black thoughts was by telling herself to have hope, maybe he would change, but in her heart knew it was a fool's errand.

Then there was fear. A terrible wave of it swept over her when she imagined losing touch with the children and Ruby. Sometimes they seemed so far away and she was trapped on a beach and the tide had gone out. The only way to silence the fear was to remind herself that in reality, they were less than two hours away and it took longer to drive to London than get to her beloved grandchildren. Doubt was also a frequent visitor to the inner sanctum of her brain. What if they forgot about her, what if the phone calls and internet chats weren't enough to sustain their bond and gradually, she'd be replaced by others as they grew more independent and needed her less? In her worst moments, Olivia contemplated ringing Ruby and asking her to come back. She'd make an excellent case for why they should return, promise them the earth if that was what it took. She could hint that they were her family too, she needed them and they should be together here, in England.

The summer holidays would soon be upon them and there would be so many missed opportunities, so many things they could be doing together if they lived on this side of the Channel. It made Olivia confused, questioning her actions and her haste in letting them go. Then she admonished herself for selfish thoughts and appeased her conscience with the knowledge that she had come to Ruby's rescue and for that, she should be proud.

The only person with whom Olivia had voiced her thoughts was of course Henry, who listened patiently to her ranting, wiped away her tears and dedicated himself to the service of cheering her up and keeping her going. He missed the little ones too, especially Oliver who was a pleasure to be around and his protégée. He'd had such great plans to teach him all about aircraft and engineering and felt almost bereft when they left. The house always lit up when they arrived and they were the grandchildren he thought he'd never have.

His greatest fear though, was that Olivia's potential to succumb to the deep depression that had reached out and swallowed her whole in the past may once again be reawakened. He prayed it would remain dormant while he watched for the signs and valiantly battled against it on a daily basis. It was for that reason that in the fifth week after Ruby left, Henry concluded that now Marcus was safely ensconced in a small flat in Leicester and had kept to his conditions, the coast was well and truly clear and he could make arrangements to cheer Olivia up in grand style. After a morning spent scouring the internet and making intense, hushed phone calls in Maurice's study, Henry was armed with printouts, timetables, and tickets, ready for action and bursting to unleash his surprise on Olivia.

When she entered the dining room bringing lunch, Henry was given an encouraging wink by Mrs Wallace as she set the salad bowl on the table before tactfully leaving the room.

As Olivia unfolded her napkin she noticed her dining companion was unusually fidgety.

'What are you looking so pleased with yourself about, Henry? Did you beat someone at internet chess again or have you found your spare reading glasses at last? You look like the cat that got the cream. Now, would you like to carve this chicken or are you going to sit there fiddling with whatever you've got in that pile of paperwork?' Olivia smiled as she spoke, none of Henry's little whims really annoyed her but she just liked to tease.

'Actually, m'dear, I have a surprise for you. I think it's time we paid Ruby and the children a visit. We said we would go soon and I think we are dragging our heels a little now. I know you were concerned about Marcus but he seems to have cooled down and is doing as he's told, so I decided to take the bull by the horns and get the ball rolling, so to speak.'

Olivia had replaced the salad bowl and was all ears while two little pink spots had appeared on her cheeks and her eyes were bright with excitement.

'Get on with it, Henry, what have you done, when can we go, where will we stay?'

Henry smiled. 'Patience, m'dear, let me explain. I've checked everything first with Ruby and Mrs Wallace. I think I've covered all our bases, ticked all the boxes and I hope I've found us the perfect place.' Henry shuffled his papers and began looking for something, then lost his train of thought.

'Henry, for goodness sake, please concentrate and tell me or I shall come round there and see for myself.' Olivia could barely hide the excitement and impatience in her voice.

'Oh, sorry, m'dear, lost the plot a bit there. Yes, I was thinking that as the school holidays are almost upon us and to save the bother of to-ing and fro-ing all summer, it might be advantageous to find a long-term rental in the vicinity of Rosie's hotel. They kindly offered to put us up but I think they are rather busy and I thought this way, perhaps, the children and Ruby could come and stay with us now and then and we wouldn't be underfoot at the hotel. We can have it all summer and if we need to pop back here for something or other we could easily book a flight. I've taken the liberty of reserving a car, quite a nice Citroen and big enough for days out, so, if I get the thumbs up from you we shall be off to our luxury countryside retreat by the end of the week. What do you think?' Henry looked up from his notes and saw that Olivia was holding her napkin to her mouth. Perhaps she had swallowed a chicken bone because she clearly couldn't speak.

Jumping up from his chair he rushed over to pat her on the back where, on closer inspection, spotted that she was actually having a quiet sob. Seeing as though he was up, Henry decided he may as well give her a quick tap anyway – just to be on the safe side and as he did so, Olivia reached up for his hand.

'Thank you, Henry. You are so wonderful and kind. You are the most thoughtful man on this earth and wherever you have chosen will be perfect, I know it. However, I think you should pass me that mountain of notes so I can double check we're not staying in a creepy monastery or in the back of beyond, and be an angel and serve the lunch, I'm famished. It must be all the excitement.' Olivia kissed his hand lovingly and awaited the printouts.

Henry's idea of luxury could sometimes be poles apart from hers so she thought it best to make sure. When Olivia came to the photograph of the house her heart skipped a beat. Set on three floors, the cream sandstone walls of the double-fronted house with white-framed Georgian windows oozed charm and sophistication. Set in its own grounds there was a double garage on the ground floor and at the front, the ornate iron rails protected a curving stairway which led to the door from both sides. Photographs of the interior showed polished oak floors, beautiful contemporary sofas and chairs which surrounded the biggest open fire Olivia had ever seen. The kitchen was high-tech and modern with a beautiful range and a long pine table. The dining room was spectacular and tastefully adorned with modern furniture, antiques and high backed, leather chairs. The bedrooms complemented the rest of the décor, with four poster beds which were covered in luxurious linen. It looked like a page from an upmarket, glossy magazine and Olivia couldn't actually believe that her Henry had picked such a gem. At the rear of the house was a lawned garden, abundant with flowers and a decked terrace, complete with a shaded eating area and an all-singing, all-dancing barbeque. Noticing Henry was nervously scrutinising her expressions she decided to put the dear man out of his misery and beamed at him from her end of the table.

'It's perfect, Henry, absolutely perfect, just like you!'

***

Olivia looked down onto the green fields of the Loire as they descended through the clouds. The sprawling city of Nantes was fast approaching on the horizon and as she followed the winding river Loire, she could just about make out the arch of a bridge silhouetted against the sun. She couldn't wait for the wheels to hit the runway and if necessary she would elbow her way to the front of the queue and clear passport control before any dawdlers got a look in. From the moment Henry gave her his surprise it was as though she had been rejuvenated. Mrs Wallace had been an angel, helping her prepare and pack, calmly reassuring her that the house would be just fine and promising to get on with a summer clean of epic proportions whilst she was away. As a special treat and a huge thank you for her continued loyalty and support, Olivia and Henry had left her an envelope in the kitchen. It contained a cheque, along with a note encouraging their wonderful housekeeper to take a couple of weeks off and go somewhere nice with Mr Wallace, their treat.

Olivia had always prided herself in caring for people who cared for her. The nannies apart, once her old housekeeper, Mrs Hunt, and Jed the gardener both retired, she made sure they were comfortable and well cared for in their old age owing to a generous settlement and private health care. Her father had set the standard, always rewarding hard work and loyalty, doing his bit in the surrounding community and contributing to charities all over the world. Since his untimely death, Olivia steadfastly continued in that tradition. It was unfathomable how her own son had turned out the way he had despite having been given the best of everything; she was resigned to the fact that it could only be as a result of faulty genes on his father's side.

They were on approach now and Olivia's heart rate quickened. Soon, she would see them in the flesh and could hold them all in her arms. She just wanted to squeeze them tight and never let go. Oliver had phoned her after school and was beside himself with excitement when he heard the news, insisting that it was the magic fairy dust that made his wishes come true. When he said the words, the hairs on Olivia's neck stood on end, it reminded her of something but she couldn't quite think what it was.

It seemed so long ago now since they left and she'd thought her heart would literally snap in two but now they had eight long weeks together. Two whole months of summer with her family to look forward to and she wouldn't allow the pain of the past get in the way. She glanced to the right and smiled lovingly at Henry who, having spent most of his life flying, now preferred to spend his journey reading *National Geographic* or *The Times*. As they came in to land Olivia looked out of the small windows as the airport came into view and while the plane taxied slowly, she imagined her beloved Oliver waiting inside. He would be popping with excitement and Lily, dear sweet Lily, would be driving Ruby mad and running all over the place. Tears pricked at the corners of her eyes as she pictured them all and if that damn pilot didn't get his finger out and park this plane, Olivia was going to break free, open the door and jump straight onto the runway and make a dash for it.

Inside the terminal Oliver was hyper and on red alert. He'd checked and rechecked the television monitors. Ruby pointed out the word Manchester, so he just fixated on that. His face was presently squashed up against the glass which looked into the arrivals lounge and was now smeared with steam and lip marks and God knows what else that he had stuck to his hands.

They had to set off ridiculously early just to please her eager son. To pass the time they'd eaten in the little bistro inside the airport which thankfully was in full view of arrivals and the riveting telly screen. Oliver's lunch-smeared hands were now pressed firmly against the glass and the imprints he left behind would make a nice job for the airport cleaners. Lily was oblivious to the tension in the air although she understood Golly and Grandad were coming but apart from that was quite content climbing on the waiting area chairs.

Despite the happiness she had found in France, Ruby had to admit she'd missed Olivia and the only way she could describe the feeling was being given a lovely present then having it cruelly taken away. The week they had spent together was a precious memory even though it was tinged with horrible bits. It was a time Ruby would always remember as finding a mother and then it ending too soon, making Ruby feel incredibly sad. When Henry telephoned to run his idea past her and Rosie she was convinced that the summer sun burned brighter that day and her heart was as light as a feather, because soon the missing links would be joined up to make their family complete.

Remembering Olivia's kindness before she left England always brought a lump to Ruby's throat. Not only had she guided her through what needed to be done, she had made sure that she had money to live on and tide her over. Her mother-in-law was horrified to learn that Ruby was almost penniless with nothing of her own and had no access to Marcus's wealth. Just before she left England, they opened a new account at Olivia's bank and not only did she make a hefty deposit to start her daughter-in-law off, she also slipped her an envelope stuffed with euros as they waited in the departure lounge at the airport.

When Ruby related all of Olivia's kindness to Rosie, her cousin was astounded and felt bad that they had got her so wrong for all these years. They'd always joked that between them, they'd been lumbered with the two worst mums in the world in Doreen and Stella, then if that wasn't bad enough, Ruby had copped for the mother-in-law from hell to add to her misery.

Of all three mothers and against the odds, Olivia had turned out to be the best of the bunch. Hopefully though, this holiday would be a chance to get to know each other properly and form bonds. But there were other things on Ruby's mind, apart from Olivia. No matter how hard she tried to push the truth away she knew that eventually a decision would have to be made on whether they should return to England, or make a leap of faith and settle in France. Her thoughts were sharply interrupted by

Oliver's high-pitched voice announcing the arrival at long last, of his grandmother.

'There she is. Mummy look, there's Granny, and I can see Grandad Henry! Wave Mummy, wave so they can see you.' Oliver was jumping up and down and flapping his arms like a bird.

Right at that moment, Lily got her leg stuck between the steel frame of the airport seats so there was a bit of a kerfuffle while she was extracted and then they were at the gate, waiting for the doors to open. Ruby held on tight to Oliver's hand so that he wouldn't get in anyone's way while Lily wiggled on her hip, desperate for freedom. Finally, the dark glass panels moved apart and there they were.

Oliver leapt forward and took a hop, skip and a jump into Olivia's arms and then Lily realised what all the fuss was about and began shouting, 'Golly, Golly, Golly'. Ruby stood back and let them hug themselves silly, forcing down a huge lump that was obstructing her throat as she wiped away happy tears.

Once the children had said their hellos, with Lily busy tugging Henry's ears and Oliver grasping on to his Granny's hand for dear life, they made their way over to Ruby who suddenly felt nervous and the odd one out.

She needn't have worried because when Olivia saw her daughter-in-law, stood on the edge as usual, observing and waiting to be invited in, she immediately abandoned her cases and Oliver. Rushing over with her arms outstretched and in a haze of Chanel No 5, Olivia folded Ruby into a long, warm embrace.

'Ruby, my darling, you look so well and I have missed you so much. I'm so glad we are here. I could hug you all day and never let you go.'

Any reservations Ruby may have had flew straight out of the terminal door, so she breathed a sigh of relief, finally believing the words and relishing the sense of belonging.

'I've missed you too, Olivia. I can't tell you how much. Come on, let's go, then we can start our holiday. It's going to be brilliant having you here all summer.'

And with that, the happy little gang trundled and chatted their way to the car hire desk. Five eager faces, lit up with excitement, love and expectation; their small family unit, tying knots and linking themselves together, forming unbreakable bonds... and that was even before they'd left the airport.

Chapter 24
Ruby, Rosie and Olivia

The late August sun scorched the Loire and *Les Trois Chênes*, bathing the whole of the countryside and the inhabitants of the hotel in a warm glow. It shone life into the crops in the fields which were now in their final stages of growth; heavy and abundant with their fruits, seeds and vegetables and within touching distance of the September harvest. The sound of summer was all around, tractors rumbling along the lanes, dragonflies and bees buzzing in the air, and the roar of the French Air Force jets streaking across the endless blue skies. Other than that, they were surrounded by silence. Its peacefulness eased everyone into their long, hot days, breathing in the scents of summer flowers, swimming in the pool and drinking in the fresh air. Oliver and Lily were thriving, golden brown and freckled after weeks of playing in the field and day trips to the beach or the lake.

There was always a choice of venues. They would either wait for Granny and Grandad to drive over to the hotel where they would all swim together and then eat lunch with Ruby, Michel and Rosie. On other days, they went to their house which was lovely and they could sleep over in the bouncy beds with the swishy curtains. Sometimes, Ruby stayed at the hotel and helped Rosie because they were really busy, so on these days the children were treated to the many sights and attractions of the Loire.

Oliver was in his element at the *Machines d'îles*, set on the banks of the Loire in Nantes, it was a fantasy world of man-made animals, based on the work of Jules Verne and Leonardo da Vinci. It brought intricate mechanisms to life in the form of *Le Grand*

Éléphant: a giant, walking feat of engineering, which took you on a ride around the dockyard and sprayed water at amazed onlookers from its trunk. He loved the *Carousel des Mondes Marins*, a fairground ride on three levels containing giant sculptures of animals and vessels of the sea. Oliver rode on the bouncing boat that breathed steam, then on the back of a sea horse and finally, he sat on a giant crab with Grandad Henry and they worked the legs and claws with special levers as it whirred slowly to the magical sea music. Other days, they would take a picnic to the man-made lake and ride on pedaloes or play in the sandy park. They loved the seaside at La Baule and Pornichet and went to the *Zoo Parc de Beauval*. Henry didn't agree with zoos until he saw this one and remarked to Olivia that it reminded him of being on safari, because here, all the animals were housed in natural habitats and free to roam. Oliver's favourites were the white tiger, the pandas and the huge manatee, but before they left he insisted on having a look at the bears, just so he could get a better idea of *exactly* what he was looking out for in the pine forest.

Ruby and Olivia took time out for themselves and spent many happy hours walking around the market in Angers, buying fruit and cheese from the stalls or drinking coffee and chatting at small bistros, watching the world waltz by and laughing together in the summer sun. Ruby was also the owner of a chic new wardrobe because Olivia had insisted on treating her to something new each time they saw a boutique. The emphasis was on bright and cheerful after Olivia commented that Ruby was in her thirties but had been dressing like a dowager duchess for years and it was time she made the most of herself.

Olivia was no shirker either where retail therapy was concerned, and put her credit card and exquisite taste to good use at every opportunity. She also enjoyed the company of Rosie who made her laugh and whose enthusiasm and energy made Olivia feel quite young again. Along with Rosie, the three women enjoyed a visit to the *Salon de Beauté*, followed by a very merry afternoon at Sebastien's bar in the village, drinking pastis and giggling like schoolgirls at total rubbish. The image of Olivia making her half-pickled way home along the bumpy lane would be forever imprinted on Ruby's brain. She had walked all the way back in stockinged feet (her Manolo's were pinching a bit) and then slept it off on a sun-lounger by the pool, catching flies and snoring like a trooper.

Most Sunday afternoons, Michel took a busman's holiday and they would all de-camp to Olivia's rented house where he would cook on the huge barbeque, which Rosie could tell he lusted after, and here they would all sit in the lovely garden, gathered around the gas-heater, eating and laughing until the sun took a rest on the horizon. It was during one of these evenings as the sky turned orange and the solar lights began to glow along the flowered borders, that the spectre of home and impending decisions inevitably reared its ugly head. Lily was fast asleep on the swinging-seat, Oliver was snuggled in a blanket and out for the count, dreaming away on a steamer chair by Ruby's side and Henry had just announced he fancied a bit of cake.

It was all Michel's fault, because he was the one who innocently wondered what became of the house at the end of the season and then enquired if Olivia and Henry would be coming back to visit in the autumn. In his straightforward way he had assumed and hoped that Ruby was staying and being privy to his wife's secret plan, presumed that enough had been done to seal the deal. Once the words were said an uncomfortable hush filled the space where animated chatter had laced the air and everyone waited for somebody else to speak first. In the end it was Rosie who broke the silence. Things needed to be said so she may as well get it over with and in truth, was glad that Michel had put his foot in it.

'Well, that's left us with a great big elephant in the room but I suppose we have to discuss it sooner or later. Ruby, you need to make your mind up whether you want to stay here in France or go back to England. Either way, plans need to be made, most importantly for Oliver because he can't stay off school forever.' Ruby opened her mouth but holding up her hand, Rosie continued. 'Before you speak, I just want you to know that I will never pressure you one way or another, the choice has to be yours but there's always a place for you here, that's a given.' Rosie's heart was beating in her chest and she wanted to cry out, 'pick me, pick me', but instead she kept quiet and waited for someone else to speak, which turned out to be Olivia.

'Rosie's right and I feel the same way. Whatever you decide I will support you and likewise, there's always a place for you with us in England. So, how *do you* feel, what does your heart tell you to do? Sometimes, and believe me I have experience on this matter, it is better to follow that than your head.' Olivia's heart was also pounding but unlike Rosie, she didn't want to be picked because after much soul-searching and taking so many things into consideration, she thought Ruby and the children should stay in France, however, until Ruby made her move, would keep her counsel.

'If I'm honest, I've thought of nothing else and as usual I've been a wimp and avoided the fact that I need to sort myself out. I love it here and so do the children. I'm scared to death of Marcus and just the thought of getting on a plane and being in the same country as him, well it makes me feel ill. I'm sorry, Olivia. I hope that doesn't offend you, he is your son after all.' Ruby looked up to gauge the reaction of those around her, especially Olivia who spoke next.

'Ruby, please, we've been through this enough times. Marcus deserves all the criticism levelled at him so feel free to speak as you find. I'm truly not offended.' Olivia smiled kindly and meant every word.

'I know you've smoothed things over at school and the headmaster has been very understanding but the thought of Prestbury and all the other parents, staring and whispering, well it brings me out in a cold sweat. Even though the house is up for sale it could take ages to find a buyer and I know we can live with you or rent somewhere, but every time I imagine coming back it's like a huge cloud is hovering over my head. Then, when I think of being here, even in the winter which Rosie has warned me is freezing and nothing like the hazy days of summer, my heart feels happy and there's definitely no cloud.' Ruby was fidgeting nervously with the ties on her shirt but she had to make a decision, so forged ahead.

'But when I picture you and Henry alone in England, that cloud comes back again. It is cruel and unfair of me to separate you long-term from the children because they love you so much and miss you, and I know you miss them. I'm so torn because I know Rosie and Michel have got used to us being here and I love working in the hotel and Oliver can't get enough of the village school. The only way to choose is to put the children first so perhaps we should let Oliver decide, or do you think it's cruel to leave the choice to him? He'll only feel exactly like I do right now but if I have to choose, it's going to be the children's feelings over mine.' Even as she said the words they made Ruby feel sad and worried, about who Oliver would pick and then leaving the others upset.

Ruby couldn't even look at Rosie who she knew desperately wanted her to stay. She'd dropped enough hints and it was obvious that she would offer her a job at the hotel at the drop of a hat. Now she'd let her down by not choosing outright and she could feel tears of frustration and confusion forcing their way up to her eyes.

Olivia spoke next.

'Ruby, please don't cry. There really is no need because there's something I need to say. I have discussed this with Henry and we realise the difficulty that making a choice will cause you. We were going to broach the subject soon anyway so let me set your mind at rest. Of course we will miss you all if you stay here, however, this trip has opened my eyes to many things, most importantly to what a wonderful way of life the children can live in France. I know that they could both benefit from a private education and live in a lovely area in England, but there's more to life than that. We also understand that Rosie and Michel are their family too.' Olivia paused and let her words sink in.

'I don't want you to worry about me and Henry. We are quite set in our ways and have plenty to do back home to keep us occupied and out of trouble. You are only an hour or so away and knowing that we can talk to you on the phone and see you often will keep us going, so this is what I propose. If you want to stay here then I give you my blessing. We can return in the school holidays or any time you need us and maybe once the children are older, they can come and stay with us if they like. However, until that time I am happy to clock up frequent-flier miles, or whatever they're called, to visit you and this wonderful part of France. I also hope that Henry and I can join in with Rosie and Michel and be part of one big family because we have already been made so welcome and it really will be a wrench having to leave you all. So, taking everything into consideration I think you should stay here.'

There was a long pause and it seemed as though everyone around the table was holding their breath, waiting for Ruby to reply. When she leapt from her chair and flung her arms around a smiling Olivia's neck, they all knew she'd made her decision.

'Thank you, Olivia, thank you. But I will only stay as long as you promise to book flights for every single school holiday and then some visits in between, anytime you want. Swear you will otherwise it's no deal.' Ruby swiped away a hot tear and waited for her answer.

'I promise, and if it makes you feel better we will stay until Oliver starts school, just to make sure he's settled. Right, now that's all sorted you need to think about where you will live. Eventually your attic hideaway may become a bit of a squeeze and I'm sure Rosie and Michel could put that room to good use and fill it with guests.' Olivia turned to gauge Rosie's reaction, hoping she hadn't spoken out of turn.

'Well, I may be able to help you there,' Rosie glanced at Michel who nodded for her to continue.

'I've got a couple of ideas I'd like to run by you. I could do with some help at the hotel and was going to offer you the job of housekeeper, if you fancy it. I know you will be getting maintenance from "you know who" but earning your own money will give you self-esteem. As for accommodation, you can stay in the attic indefinitely but there's nothing in the village for rent and I'd like to keep you close for now, so what about the gîte? It only needs the electricity connecting and then it's good to go. We can't really rent it until the others are finished so if you want it, it's yours.' Then Rosie looked over to the little sleeping beauties and continued.

'But first, I think we've forgotten someone very important who we should speak to. What if Oliver really wants to go back to England? We can't ask Lily because she'd pick Bill and Ben.'

Everyone nodded and muttered their agreement, realising that Rosie was right, just as Oliver popped his ruffled head over the top of the blanket.

Peering through the dusk and candlelight with bleary eyes he yawned loudly then spoke.

'That's an easy question, I want to stay here. I like it at my new school because they do lovely lunches and Arno is my best friend. He'll be upset if I leave him behind. Now Granny and Grandad will be coming to see us lots it would be silly to go home. So, can we stay, Mummy, please?'

All the adults looked at each other and realised that their little earwigger, who never missed a trick, had probably been listening for ages. Shaking their heads and laughing, the final word was left to Ruby.

'Okay, cheeky chops, you win. We're staying! But only as long as you go back to sleep, right now.'

Oliver beamed, then his eyes went wide as saucers.

'But what about cake? I remember Grandad said he was getting some and I definitely haven't had any. I'm really starving as well!' Oliver could be very convincing especially where food was concerned.

'Okay, cake, and then sleep. No arguments!' Ruby smiled lovingly at her son.

Thank goodness he wanted to stay because it would've killed her to go back, although she would have made the sacrifice for him and Lily, and their lovely grandparents.

Butterflies were fluttering around Ruby's insides and she felt like an overemotional child, not sure whether to laugh or cry so she decided to embrace the moment and commit the scene to memory. Rosie and Olivia were deep in conversation, heads together, no doubt plotting something to do with her. Rosie's arms were flapping about all over the place describing something in great detail. Henry and Michel were slicing gateau and dishing it out. Lily was still in dreamland and Oliver was staring at the lights, smiling to himself and lost in a world of his own.

And then it hit her, this really was a new world of their very own, to carve out for themselves with the help and support of all her family. It felt real at last, what Ruby had always wanted – her cousin right by her side and a proper mother. The fear had finally gone and worry had lifted its heavy burden from her shoulders and now, she could put down roots and start afresh.

Ruby watched the scene before her. Olivia accepted a piece of gateau from Michel and during the pause, Rosie looked over and smiled then with a wink, she turned back to Olivia and carried on her chattering.

Ruby's heart swelled with happiness and love for the people around her, especially her cousin. Remembering a time long ago when she was a scruffy, timid sparrow, being around Rosie always made her feel safe. She was so utterly scared of losing her best friend that one day, Ruby made Rosie swear to look after her forever. Her golden eagle took a childhood oath and against the odds, despite the miles and the passing of years, through good times and bad, she never let her down. Rosie had remembered her promise to Ruby – and kept it.

Chapter 25

Ruby

Present Day

Ruby was listening to Radio Alouette, daydreaming and singing along tunelessly to Pink as she drove along the quiet country road. Her route was bordered on either side by blossoming hedgerows that were coming alive in the warm May heat and through her sunroof she caught the scent of cut grass from the newly trimmed verges. In the distance she could see another row of windmills being erected, a sight that was becoming a common part of the scenery all across France. She was on her way back from Anna's after a few hours of cleaning. Since their English friend had bought a property in the next village, Ruby found herself another little job as caretaker and always popped over to give it a once over just before anyone was due to visit. Everyone loved Anna and her family who spent their time channel hopping almost as much as Olivia and Henry.

The sun warmed Ruby's arm through the glass and she allowed herself a self-satisfied smile, acknowledging the life she lived now in the land of contentment. This existence provided her with many things. There was friendship, not only from Rosie and Anna but also from the mothers at the children's school, her neighbours in the village and since she bought her house on the new-build estate, Ruby really felt like part of the community.

***

Once the house in Prestbury was sold and half of the proceeds were transferred into her account, Ruby had scoured the local area for something suitable but nothing took her fancy so, heeding Rosie's advice, they remained in the gîte until the right home came along. It had been with great excitement that Hortense bustled into the hotel one cold November morning and shouted up the stairs that she had some urgent news to spread. Halting a curious Ruby and Rosie in their tracks and over the obligatory coffee in the lounge, the beans were spilled.

Hortense explained that at the previous night's council meeting, presided over by her brother-in-law, *Le Maire*, it had been unanimously voted to pass the plans for a new housing estate in the village. The plots were to go up for sale in a few weeks time and therefore Ruby needed to get in quick and put her name down. There was no time to lose and naturally Hortense had already taken the liberty of booking her an appointment. Consequently, just under a year later, Ruby found herself to be the proud owner of a brand new, three bedroomed *maison* after taking the bold step of signing on the dotted line and moving out of the gîte.

The day she collected the large brown envelope from the *notaire*, which contained the shiny set of keys and the attestation that said she was a homeowner, it was the icing on the Cake of Happiness. This was hers and nobody could take it away. It symbolised a solid base, and best of all, the foundations that held the house in place would support them for the rest of their lives. After living in fear of becoming a single mother for so long, or worse, turning into Stella, she banished those thoughts from her mind as she turned the key in the lock and opened the front door to their future.

Ruby had been sad to say goodbye to the attic room and then the gîte because they had been perfectly happy in their little holiday home. It was extremely convenient for work; just a few minutes up the track and, after the arrival of André and Wilf, they had the added security of friends living right next door. It had been a bittersweet surprise for Rosie when she took the call from André, telling her that he'd hurt his back jet-skiing in Italy and was returning to France for treatment and the benefit of the French healthcare system.

As he was in great pain and sleeping in the camping car had become a little too uncomfortable, he was offered gîte number two and they stayed for almost a year whilst André had physiotherapy, plus a lot of TLC from Wilf and Rosie. How they had laughed their way through a very cold winter snuggled round the log burner at night, wrapped in blankets listening to Wilf's exaggerated tales of their voyage of discovery. They all took turns chopping wood and had a rota for keeping their fires going and it was a time that would be immortalised in her memory, along with their first Christmas in France.

The hotel was quiet during winter, apart from the odd guest stopping off for one night on the outward or inward leg of their journey, so Olivia and Henry stayed at *Les Trois Chênes* for the whole of the festive period and along with Ruby and the children, had their first sample of a country-style, French Christmas.

They arrived at Nantes airport laden with gifts and treats for everyone and were soon settled around the roaring log fire. Nestled amongst their extended family and friends, they enjoyed the ambience of the hotel, and the very generous hospitality of their hosts. It was a tradition that had been repeated twice since, and Ruby had no reason to believe that their fourth Christmas in France would be any different. First though, they had to get through the summer and as the hotel and gîtes were booked solid for the holiday period, Ruby fully expected to be run off her feet all season and ready for a well-earned rest by the start of autumn.

Thank heaven for Olivia who had remained faithful and was always there for the holidays to look after Lily and Oliver, who now took it for granted that Grandad and Golly would be on hand to cater to their every need. It was an arrangement that worked well for all of them. Ruby loved her job and as Rosie had suspected it gave her self-esteem and pride, plus a sense of fulfilment each day when she finished her shift. During term time she dropped the children off at school then went straight to the hotel and was always finished by early afternoon, which gave her plenty of time to do her own thing before collecting them at home time. Wednesday was her day off unless she was really needed, then the children would go with her for a few hours and play at Rosie's. During the school holidays Olivia and Henry would arrive and take over where, after a few weeks with their energetic grandchildren, always needed to fly off home for a rest.

Ruby's mind wandered to her duties for the remainder of the day and had just enough time to nip home and let Freddo out before the school bell. Freddo was Oliver and Lily's beloved dog, a bit of jumble with regards to his heritage and a lot bigger than any of them had expected him to be. He was a Christmas present from Michel who it seemed was in the habit of buying puppies and believed they made a home complete. Freddo was also supposed to protect them and make them feel safe once André and Wilf left for more adventures.

It was with much joy and screams of delight that her children opened a picnic hamper on that first Christmas morning to find a wiggly, plump black puppy with tan socks and a matching patch over one eye, waiting to greet them. He was a gorgeous little dog and Michel had been assured that he was a Jack Russell cross, however, looking at him now, Ruby was convinced his father must've been a roaming Labrador because he was huge, but the children loved him. He was a big softie and a useless guard dog, yet utterly devoted to all of them.

It was only a short walk through the village to the school and the journey home was always with other parents and children who lived nearby. Arno was still Oliver's best friend and they were as thick as thieves, endlessly chatting away together in a world of make-believe, superheroes and football. Her son had integrated well and true to Sylvie's words, he had learned to speak French and was now well on his way to being fluent. He even dreamed in French because she'd heard him muttering in his sleep.

Lily was a star and at the tender age of *almost* five (as she frequently reminded everyone) seemed unfazed by anything and anybody. The outgoing, confident member of the family she jabbered away in French at school and then swapped seamlessly into English for Ruby's benefit at home. Lily was clever and wily, arguing in French with Oliver, knowing that she could get away with more if her mother didn't get the gist of what was going on.

Tonight was Zumba in the *Salles des Fêtes* and here, Ruby could practice her slowly improving French with the other women. Ping-pong had finished until the autumn but there was still bingo – or lotto as it was known here, but it didn't really matter what the activity, it was a far cry from her life with Marcus. Ruby didn't think of her ex-husband often, however, it was inevitable that now and then something would jog a memory or cause her to draw a comparison with how she used to live. But as time passed by, the images didn't have the same sobering effect as before and she had learned to brush them off and think of the positives instead. It had been a juggling act with the children at first and she'd tried hard to gauge their feelings and do what was right with regards to their father, because in the end, his existence couldn't be denied especially when his own mother was a frequent visitor. They finally managed to end the dilemma, mostly due to the fact that Oliver spoke up and basically made everything a lot easier for all of them.

Even though Marcus had virtually washed his hands of Ruby and the children, once the quickie divorce came through Olivia insisted that he still sent cards and presents at the required times. It was obvious that his mother bought the gifts as they were well thought out, all Marcus did was fill in the tags. Ruby accepted each one politely because deep down she knew Olivia held on to a mother's hope that one day her son may shock them all and redeem himself, so she did it just for her.

On his sixth birthday Oliver read the tag that was attached to his gift, opened the present from his father then pushed the model plane to one side and continued tearing paper off the rest without fuss or comment. Days later, the plane was still in the corner of the lounge and hadn't been secreted into Oliver's bedroom along with the rest of his birthday hoard. Out of curiosity and concern, Ruby asked him why he hadn't moved it and he simply said, 'Because I don't want it'. He then went on to ask her in his own straightforward way if she could tell Marcus to stop sending him presents. Oliver explained that when he got something from his father it made him fed up, saying with childlike honesty that he remembered all the bad things but he really liked his birthdays. So, if it was okay, he'd rather not have any more presents from 'him' because it spoiled everything. Ruby nervously and sensitively relayed the conversation to Olivia who was upset that Oliver had been affected that way and admitted defeat in her quest to build bridges and passed the message straight on to uncaring, indifferent ears.

Since then, the only contact she had was in the form of maintenance payments which suited them all down to the ground. Lily had never really known her father so therefore didn't miss something she hadn't experienced, and if she was honest, Ruby was glad that she was free from the memories that plagued Oliver. In the interests of fairness and to clear her conscience, Ruby had chosen a quiet moment when they were alone and showed Lily photographs of her father that were kept in an envelope, not the happy family album. Ruby went through each one, giving a short explanation but Lily quickly became bored – she had better things to occupy her mind so showed polite interest then continued to play with her dolls. Since then Ruby had left the photographs in the envelope, they were there if and when Lily ever asked to see them.

From the few, uncomfortable conversations Ruby had with Olivia on the subject of Marcus, she had gleaned that he had served his time in China and was now back on the Far East circuit. Just about managing to behave, he lived a carefree bachelor lifestyle which he conducted from the Quays apartment and was a rare visitor to Prestbury, an arrangement which was mutually agreeable to all parties concerned.

***

Dragging her mind from Marcus and back to the present day, Ruby's attention focused on another unsavoury character – the man who had been prowling the roads in the area and recently robbed and attacked two women. The police had called into the hotel to warn everyone that an unknown male was flagging down drivers then pretending to be hurt or broken down and needed assistance. Once they stopped their cars he assaulted them and stole their belongings. Everyone was on the lookout for a white van and the gendarmes had advised women especially to be on their guard and not to stop for anyone on the sometimes deserted routes around the villages.

It was a big story and had even been on the radio news because things like that rarely happened in the countryside and it was scary to hear that someone was preying on them. Ruby shuddered and drove on, she'd purposely kept her doors locked and windows closed in the car, using the sunroof to let in fresh air. She was approaching the new windmills and some road works so slowed down to wait for the temporary lights to change. A team of workmen who were unloading one of the huge turbine blades distracted her slightly before she turned away to concentrate on the upcoming half-term break and the imminent arrival of the grandparents.

***

When Olivia and Henry came to visit, they would stay at the hotel or rent the summer house if it was available. When Ruby bought her new home, she had presumed they would stay there, but instead they sprang a huge surprise. Henry loved the French way of life and wasn't really one for Olivia's social gatherings but attended them just to keep her happy. He actually preferred pottering, reading and doing his own thing, so out of the blue one morning, decided that they should buy a little piece of France for themselves. That way, they could spend more time over the water and he could craftily escape the rigours of being part of the Cheshire set. It was also becoming a bit of a performance, transporting clothes and hiring a car so if they had a home of their own they could just jump on a plane with hand luggage and Bob's your uncle, they'd have everything they needed waiting for them when they got there.

Without further ado and with a boinging spring in his step, Henry trawled the internet for suitable properties and even bought himself a nice black, rather racy Citroen. The house they previously rented was beautiful but far too big and grand – they had one like that in England, so eventually, they settled on something small, picturesque and manageable. Their little cottage was set in a small hamlet of three other houses and situated on the far outskirts of St Pierre. It had its own apple orchard and a stone well, two bedrooms and a cosy kitchen and lounge. Once they'd had the builders in and brought it up to date and into the 21st century, Henry and Olivia moved into their honeymoon cottage, as they called it, and threw themselves into lighting fires and enjoying the novelty of cooking for themselves on the range.

Naturally, Ruby ensured it was spick and span before their arrival and the children couldn't wait to sleep over in their bunk beds the minute their grandparents turned up. Ruby made a mental note to write a shopping list and do her bit at Olivia's and she would need to buy a birthday present for Sabine. Rosie's little girl would be two at the beginning of June and they were having a big celebration which Olivia and Henry would arrive just in time for.

Michel and Rosie always put on a fantastic party and she was looking forward to it. Everyone would be there, Anna and Daniel and their family, Dominique and Zofia obviously, children from the village school, Michel's family and the inevitable terrible twosome, his brother Henri and partner in crime Sebastien, from the bistro in the village. They still made her giggle as she remembered them both vying for her attention at every single social event they attended together and no matter how hard she tried to give them the cold shoulder or ignore their amorous advances, they just didn't seem to get the hint.

Ruby totally understood that there was a lack of fresh blood in these parts and that a new face, especially someone single and available, sent the testosterone levels of lonely farmers through the roof. But Ruby wasn't tempted. Her heart had been broken twice and she wasn't even remotely interested in repeating the experience. Maybe she'd just have to drag her dowdy, dowager clothes out of the wardrobe and wear them for the party in an attempt to put her admirers off. But as Rosie so eloquently said, they were all gagging for it so even wearing a potato sack and a balaclava wouldn't do the trick.

***

The traffic lights changed so Ruby snapped out of list-making and outfit-planning to concentrate on the road. The radio was blasting out Michael Jackson so she began to sing along as she went on her way. The windmills were receding in the distance and Ruby's mind had moved on to what they could have for tea when she noticed the headlights in her rear-view mirror. At first, her brain didn't register the imminent danger as she watched the lights flashing erratically and then someone stuck their hand out of the driver's window and began waving frantically. That's when the emergency bells started ringing in her ears and the warnings from the gendarmes sent fear coursing through her veins. Realising that the vehicle was also a white van sent Ruby's adrenaline level through the roof and panic took hold of her heart. The only thing she could do was get away. The gendarmes said not to stop so that's exactly what she would do.

Pressing her foot to the floor she gripped the steering wheel and fled. Ruby knew that she was driving too fast and had never hit these speeds before, but terror was in control now and if it saved her from the maniac behind her then she would go with the flow. The van showed no signs of giving up and was gaining on her and this could only mean that the driver really was a madman and intent on doing God knows what to her. Thoughts of Lily and Oliver raced through her brain and tears pricked at her eyes.

Her mouth was dry and the knuckles of her sweat-soaked hands were white from the exertion of gripping the steering wheel and controlling the car. The van was catching up so her only hope was to get to the village, but it was over the next hill and not even in sight yet.

Then Ruby had an idea. She knew this road well and it veered to the right, just along the way and then on the left, was a narrow turning to the farm where Dominique bought fresh milk. The disused bumpy track continued all the way along the fields and right up to the back of the hotel. The locals and the farmers used it as a cut through and if she turned off quickly once she went round the bend, the madman wouldn't see her and might drive on past. Ruby's heart hammered in her chest as she kept one eye on the road and another on the van. Spotting the warning sign indicating the curve in the road, she took the bend and once her car was out of sight hit the brakes and swung dramatically onto the dirt track. The car did a mini skid and swerved from side to side but she managed to keep control and once she'd straightened up, Ruby hit the accelerator pedal and flew off, her heart hammering like a drum. Her logic was warning her that if he'd seen her, she was done for because this road was even more deserted and nobody could hear her scream along here. However, her terrified heart was in control now so driving like a woman possessed, she sped off.

The cows in the fields stared on in amazement as the little cream Fiat zoomed past them in a plume of dust. The farmer's wife thought she saw something flash by as she hung her washing on the line but it was gone before she got a chance to take a second look, while her husband (who was sitting on his tractor just behind the barn, having a sneaky bottle of cider) thanked God he'd not been coming the other way along the lane, otherwise there'd have been carnage. Sweat poured from Ruby's forehead as fields whizzed by in a blur and she concentrated on the track ahead. Twice now, the bottom of her poor car scraped along the earth as she hit deep holes but she kept on going. There was no way she'd stop until she reached Rosie's. To her relief, she hadn't seen any headlights or, more importantly, another vehicle coming in the opposite direction. As she reached the top of the gradually sloping hill, she caught a quick glimpse of the winding track behind her and it was empty. She'd lost him, and as she descended the other side, saw the roof of the hotel peeping from between the treetops and almost cried out in relief. Passing Zofia's gate she slowed down and drove into the forecourt of Rosie's as the panic began to ease.

Ruby sat motionless in her car, fear was quickly overridden by shock and as she undid her seatbelt with trembling hands her only thought was to get inside and ring the gendarmes. They needed to catch this man quickly before someone was killed so on wobbly legs and fighting back the tears, Ruby ran inside to make the call.

Chapter 26

Rosie

osie was worn out. Sabine had run her ragged all day and finally, after the heat of the afternoon got the better of her, the little terror conked out in her bedroom so Rosie crept down the stairs like a mouse, desperate not to wake her. In reality, there wasn't really any other way she could get down the stairs because in her heavily pregnant state, a slow waddle was all she was capable of. At nine months, Rosie was well past full bloom and felt like a pumped-up balloon ready to pop at any second. All she could think now was: bring it on. The sooner her baby elephant arrived the better because she was hot, tired and impatient. It hadn't helped that in the latter stages of her pregnancy they'd finally been able to move into their restored barn but even the walk up the path to the hotel felt like a mountain climb, so today she'd decided to stay home and unpack a few more boxes.

The conversion still wasn't completely finished but the bedrooms were lovely and the open plan lounge and kitchen just needed a few final touches here and there. It was functional and even though Michel thought it was the end of the world, she could live without the wall tiles which were lost in transit and most likely stuck on a pallet somewhere in Spain. Rosie couldn't quite believe that after all these years walking past the rundown barn and stopping to sit on the tree stump while she imagined transforming the old ruin, they were now actually sleeping under the timbered roof. It was an honour to be protected each day by its stone walls that held so much history and had waited patiently for hundreds of years for someone to rescue it.

Taking a glass of water, Rosie lowered herself onto the sofa and took the considerable weight off her feet, then began unpacking a cardboard box that held ornaments and photo frames. On the top was one of her most prized possessions, the grainy photo of her and Ruby, sitting on the step at her parents' house. They were squashed together, linking arms and smiling into the sun. Next, was a more colourful one of her and Michel on their winter wedding day. Rosie smiled lovingly at the picture of her handsome husband as he laughed into the lens of the camera, his arm wrapped around the waist of his new bride, flecks of snow covered his jet-black hair and her shoulders. It had been a wonderful day, full of smiles and laughter, surrounded by their friends and family and despite the haste to arrange it amidst the freezing temperatures, it all turned out perfectly.

***

Once Ruby and the children were settled into the gîte they all commenced a life with order and routine. Michel and Rosie threw themselves into building up the restaurant, while the hotel was ably looked after by their new housekeeper. As far as Rosie was concerned, their life was perfect and she had no reason to suspect that Michel felt any differently. However, despite his previous travels and once independent spirit, he now secretly yearned for commitment and a family of his own. Knowing his parents well – they still thought they were living in post-war France and observing their belief in the sanctity of marriage, Michel decided that he should pop the question to Rosie. On the morning of her birthday she awoke to find the coffee table in their small apartment covered with a crisp white tablecloth and adorned with rose petals. A bottle of champagne was cooling in the bucket and from somewhere, Michel had sourced strawberries, which for him was a miracle as they were out of season and a taboo in the organically-obsessed mind of her little chef. He was making eggs Benedict and as she entered the room, he guided her to the sofa and insisted she relaxed and waited for her food.

Rosie knew something was up because she could tell he was jittery. He cooked every day of his life and breakfast wasn't going to stretch him so that wasn't it, and neither was it a special birthday, so why all the fuss? Then she twigged, he behaved like this when he bought her the puppies so unless she was mistaken, somewhere around the hotel another canine gift had been hidden and was now waiting to be presented. Rosie pretended not to suspect, especially when he did the 'close your eyes, I have a special gift for you' routine, but this time Michel didn't leave the room or move from the spot on the sofa opposite. When he half-shouted 'surprise' the last thing Rosie expected to see when she opened her cautious blue eyes was Michel down on one knee and a box containing a diamond ring.

Rosie smiled to herself and looked at her engagement ring, remembering his terrified face as he asked her to marry him and his relief when she said yes. She still couldn't understand why he was so unsure of her answer because she'd committed herself to him body and soul the day they bought the hotel. Once the kissing and the trying on of the ring was over, Michel boldly announced that he'd already spoken to his uncle the *Maire*. They could be married the following month and they would have the reception at the hotel. He would do the catering as it would be excellent practice, what better place to try out the menu on their guests.

Rosie wasn't quite sure whether she should be offended that her wedding was going to be used as a trial run or pat her fiancé on the back for using his brains. Either way, she loved the fact that he thought for himself and had the courage of his convictions, so she certainly wasn't going to pour water on the fire in his belly or spoil his secret plans. As was their way, Rosie and Michel got straight on with organising their wedding as a team, which had to be said was prone to a few tantrums here and there, but in the end, they got a result and one month later at the end of the coldest November on record, they were married.

Pulling the group photo out of the box filled Rosie's head with a multitude of memories and emotions, ranging from bitter disappointment to the filling up of her heart with gratitude, the true meaning of friendship and unconditional love. Ruby was beyond excited about the wedding, especially that she would be there to witness it *and* be chief bridesmaid – not stuck in England where she would've been forbidden to attend. Once the giddiness wore off they had to get down to brass tacks, which is when the subject of Doreen raised its ugly head. Rosie had accepted the fact that to date, her mother had shown little interest or desire to participate in her life but surely she would want to be there to see her only child get married and meet her son-in-law. With Ruby's encouragement, Rosie posted a hand-written invitation and cautiously awaited a reply.

They had formally announced their engagement and upcoming wedding at a special birthday dinner where Rosie took the opportunity to ask a favour of her dear friend. To her, he was like a father and when she made her request, he replied in a voice cracking with emotion. André said he would be honoured to give his *chérie* away as to him, she was the daughter he never had.

In the meantime, Michel planned his menu and Rosie took a trip to Angers with Ruby where she bought a flowing white gown with long, bell-bottomed sleeves and a full-length ice blue coat, just in case it was chilly on the day. Had she known that the snowstorm of the century was about to fall on the sleepy village of St Pierre and shroud the Loire in a blanket of crisp, deep snow, Rosie would've bought a woolly jumper, bobble hat and some matching wellies.

Placing her photo on the coffee table, Rosie's eyes watered slightly as she looked at the happy family portrait. Ruby looked beautiful in her blue dress which perfectly matched the bride's coat, and Lily would've looked lovely too had she not got paw marks all over her white tights and dress. The only thing that remained clean was the blue sash around her middle. It still made Rosie laugh, remembering the hoo-ha when Olivia spotted her carrying around Ben, the very muddy dog, literally two minutes after getting her dressed. Oliver looked so smart in his grey suit and blue tie and was the proud bearer of the rings, a role he took extremely seriously and he had practised walking around holding a cushion for days beforehand. He revelled in the whole event and when he saw Rosie in her wedding dress, gasped loudly and said she looked like a beautiful snow queen, which made her cry. Her parents-in-law, Marie and Yves were staring proudly into the camera, dressed in their finest and pretending to ignore the snow and plummeting temperature. Henri and Henry looked very dapper and were standing at the back like sentries while Olivia and her huge hat were squashed in next to Michel's tiny grandparents. On either side of them were André and Wilf, the honorary father-of-the bride and his partner.

There was only one person missing and that was Doreen. Her letter arrived almost in the return post, the speed of which told Rosie her mother hadn't even deliberated or pondered on the decision not to attend. It was obviously an easy choice which required no soul-searching or time to collect her thoughts; those that would then enable the writing of kind words to let her only child down, lightly. Instead, the short, terse note told Rosie that it was not a convenient time for her to make the trip overseas – anyone would've thought she was sailing to the Cape of Good Hope, not nipping across the Channel – as she had commitments to the church and hospital appointments that couldn't be broken. Not only that, in her poor state of health it was unfair of Rosie to expect her to travel. Also, having not been taken into consideration previously or for that matter, formally introduced, Doreen would feel uncomfortable around strangers in a foreign land. As she read the letter, anger and resentment raged through Rosie. As usual her mother was deflecting any blame or responsibility. The disappointment had been expected but in a strange way it finally freed her. From that day onwards, Rosie accepted their relationship was well and truly over. Nothing more could be done to build bridges – she'd done her best but was flogging a dead horse and had been for years so without shedding one single tear, Rosie ripped the note and envelope into pieces, then threw them on the fire.

The next photo she came across was of her and Michel, sitting on the back of a farmer's trailer. Rosie couldn't believe her eyes when she woke up on the morning of her wedding and saw the garden. They had listened to the weather forecast the previous evening which said there was chance of a light covering, which thrilled everyone as it would look very picturesque and make for lovely photos. It was obvious that someone at *Meteo France* hadn't done their sums right or were looking at the wrong radar screen, because the white blanket that covered everything as far as the eye could see was most certainly not a thin dusting of snow. What's more, it was still falling heavily and by 1pm the roads around the village were almost impassable by car. The phone hadn't stopped ringing with concerned guests enquiring if the wedding was still on and, more worryingly, how on earth they were going to get there. Michel was in the restaurant, putting the final touches to his feast while Rosie nervously got ready upstairs.

In the bar, a secret emergency wedding committee led by Hortense and Henry, made contingency plans that Mr Churchill and Monsieur de Gaulle would've been proud of. The only way to get to the *Mairie* where the service would take place was by foot if you lived in the village, or by tractor if you didn't, so a map was pinned on the wall and Henry plotted a route that circled St Pierre and the outlying farms. Then they rang the entire guest list and told them to walk to the end of their lanes or wait at their gates, from where they'd be collected at the appointed time and taken to the *Mairie*. Extra troops were rallied by Pascal who with his neighbour, Gilbert, arrived at 2pm on the dot with their trailers swept clean and ready to take passengers. Zofia and Olivia flapped about and tied the flower garlands from the cars around the engines of the tractors and found everyone warm coats or blankets to keep out the cold.

Following Henry's instructions, Rosie rode up front in the first tractor cab with Pascal, followed closely by Michel being driven by Pierre, who had already collected a large number of bemused and frozen guests. Those who were gathered at the hotel climbed onto the back of the trailers and huddled under umbrellas and blankets as they slowly trundled along the country road like a mini carnival parade. Oliver thought it was the most exciting thing he'd done for ages, especially when they picked up his best friend Arno and lots of other people along the way, all dressed in their bright wedding clothes, wearing waterproof boots and holding carrier bags with their dancing shoes inside. The crowd waiting at the *Mairie* hooted with laughter as the procession arrived in the square and the multi-coloured passengers waved cheerily back – even though they all thought they might die from hyperthermia, were suffering from severe cramp and would have sore bottoms for days.

After the service which was dutifully carried out by Michel's uncle and witnessed by the majority of the village, the tractors made the return journey back to the hotel, crammed to the hilt with the whole wedding party, *Monsieur le Maire* and their guests. A party to end all parties followed as the steaming entourage crammed into the hotel and huddled around the fire as large drinks were poured by Dominique and Océane while frozen bones were thawed out. The reception went on well into the night and the wedding was talked about for months to come, regaled as the best knees up St Pierre had seen for years.

How they all got home was another story, best kept from the ears of the gendarmes, (well, the ones that weren't ferried home on the back of a very swervy trailer) and was all down to Pierre, the hero of the hour. He valiantly battled through the lanes, slightly cross-eyed and occasionally seeing double but owing to the fact that he was travelling at one kilometre an hour, managed not to crash and delivered everyone home safely by dawn.

The final photo was of Rosie and André outside the *Mairie*, just before he led her inside. On her wrist was the silver bracelet he'd given her on the eve of her wedding. He had presented her with a small wooden jewellery box which once belonged to Clémence. It contained a collection of earrings, a fine gold necklace, some brooches and the bracelet. André insisted she took them, a gift from him and her adopted grandmother-in-heaven whom would want them passed to their *chérie*.

Rosie missed André so much and was looking forward to seeing him in a couple of weeks time as he'd promised to be back for Sabine's birthday and wait around for the arrival of the baby elephant. As with her first child, Rosie preferred to have a surprise rather than know the sex of her baby. Neither she nor Michel hoped for one or the other, as long as it was healthy... and got a bloody move on.

Baby photos came out next. The first was of the three of them at the hospital, minutes after Sabine made her early morning entrance into the world. Michel quite literally sobbed like a baby himself when she was born and was an emotional wreck for days after. Her second favourite was of Oliver, Lily and Sabine. The three little cousins were sitting together on the sofa just after they brought her home. Lily thought Sabine was a doll especially made for her and there'd been a bit of a to-do when Oliver got to hold her first. Since then, Lily had muscled her way in and was very definitely Sabine's full-time protector and the one in charge. Still, her daughter idolised her big cousin and followed Lily around, copying everything she did. Oliver had since lost interest in Sabine, mainly because she was 'a girl', but he was always kind and looked out for her in his own shy way. As for Lily, she didn't need protecting and could look after herself. When Rosie saw the children playing or eating at the table and chattering away, Rosie knew Ruby had made the right choice in staying because this was where they belonged, all of them together.

Rosie was very proud of her cousin. Ruby had integrated well into the village and the French way of life and was trying hard to get to grips with the language so she could keep up with her children. But as well as that, she was a wonderful, loyal friend to have around and worked hard at the hotel. They were a good team and between them found a happy medium, combining their family lives and work, due in part to a meticulous rota and the flexibility that being related afforded them. Olivia was a frequent visitor to St Pierre and her arrival always heralded much excitement from all three children since she never turned up empty-handed. But most of all, because she was a super granny, they absolutely adored her, and Henry too. Everyone treated Olivia like royalty, possibly due to the grace and calm that emanated from every fibre of her body, however, underneath she was one of the kindest most natural people Rosie had ever met.

Whenever Rosie's mind wandered to Olivia and André and the role they played in their lives, it gave her goosebumps because in some ways, Ruby had found a mother and in return, Olivia a daughter. Rosie had a unique bond with her lovely André, they were a perfect combination – he was her father and friend. And she knew only too well how much he regretted not having children so in many ways, fate had put them all together and made them whole. The only thing that Rosie thought might be missing was some male company for Ruby but she was adamant she preferred to be alone, quite happy just as she was. So for now, Rosie wouldn't interfere or match-make no matter how hard she itched to find a suitable boyfriend for her cousin amongst the eligible, sex-starved farmers of the Loire.

Rosie looked at the clock. She needed to ring Océane and check that she had prepared a table for the large family group who were staying in the big gîte and had booked in for dinner that night. She found it hard to loosen the reins and leave things to other people but was grateful for all the help they received from family and their staff, so Rosie did her best not to interfere. The hotel had gone from strength to strength and their themed nights in the winter months were a big hit, drawing in the locals and even customers from villages further afield, offering something a bit different and a break from the long, dark evenings in the countryside.

The gîtes were also doing well. They'd had the pool fitted and a sandy play area for children, her next project was going to be a camping site at the far edge of the field. It was Wilf's inspired idea, so at the end of this season they'd be making a start on the pitches and intended building a small toilet and shower block. 'Our little empire,' Rosie thought proudly to herself as she folded up the discarded tissue paper and packed it away.

Hearing a car pull up in front of the house, Rosie placed André's photo on the table and made her way to the door before anyone could wake Sabine, another half an hour of peace and quiet was all she asked. Looking through the window, she saw it was Ruby who sometimes called in before collecting Oliver and Lily from school. She'd been stressing about the fact that Rosie was in the house alone in the middle of a wood when a nutter was roaming the area. Since her cousin's off-road, rally car experience as she'd tried to escape white van man, Ruby had become extremely edgy. Rosie pointed out that the gîtes were on the other side of the trees and packed with holidaymakers and she could see the kitchen window of the hotel from the lounge, so she wasn't exactly isolated. Nevertheless, Ruby was having none of it and had taken it upon herself to check-in daily, just in case.

Well, Rosie had some good news in that department because she'd just heard it straight from Hortense's jungle grapevine that her brother, the police chief, had the perpetrator safely in custody after a random patrol had caught him loitering in the lake car park, so now they could all breath easily again. Rosie knew that Ruby's tension was born mostly from bad memories and the stain that violent behaviour had left on her soul. She only hoped that with time she would learn to trust again and with a little bit of luck, find someone who really deserved her.

Chapter 27
Dylan

Dylan sat in his car by the side of the road with a crinkled map spread across his legs. He was staring despondently at the screen of the satnav, waiting desperately for either one of them to give him some divine inspiration. The map was covered with red circles, indicating each of the villages that he'd searched in his hunt for Ruby. He's tried to be methodical but it was like a needle in a haystack and after a week of driving round like a deranged stalker, he had drawn a blank. Folding up the map he knew that he should admit defeat and move on to his next job but the thought that she was here in France, in one of the surrounding towns or villages was driving him crazy. He'd hardly slept since the day he saw her. It must have been a fluke and a complete coincidence that brought her past the field in which he was working, or was it destiny? From that moment on his only mission in life had been to find her and no matter how futile it may seem, he just couldn't give up now.

He was due in La Rochelle in three days time and had intended to spend his well-earned days off enjoying the weather and relaxing, however, since the sighting Dylan was so fired up that he thought he might explode from the sheer frustration of losing her again. It was his own stupid fault that he'd lost contact with Rosie and now he couldn't even ring her up and ask her where to find Ruby.

It had been over five years since he'd sent his last message, passing on his new mobile number plus a short text and then left it at that. A few months later, both his phone and wallet were stolen. In the days before smart phones – and smart people who backed up their contact list on a computer, in one fell swoop he was robbed of his only link to Ruby. He rang The Fairhaven Hotel where Rosie worked but was told she'd left and they certainly couldn't divulge personal information and the only thing the snotty receptionist did say was that she'd heard she had moved to France. Putting two and two together, Dylan now surmised that Ruby must be here visiting Rosie and if he didn't track either one of them down soon, he would go mad.

***

As time passed by, the messages he'd fantasised about in his head from Rosie saying that Ruby needed him, never materialised. When he got a new contract and changed his phone number he finally gave up hope, facing harsh facts and reality – the thread that held Ruby, Rosie and him together was gone for good. Girlfriends came and went but none of them lived up to Ruby or even came near to making him feel the way she did, but that was in the past and it was obvious that her marriage had been a success and she was happy without him.

Dylan threw himself into work and quickly climbed the ladder within his company. He still hated the helicopter ride to the rigs but as he rose through the ranks, the need to dice with death was reduced considerably. That was until he volunteered to take over a Christmas shift as a favour to a colleague who wanted to spend the holidays with his family. The harsh North Sea winds had battered the rig for weeks and Dylan was literally dreading the flight back to Aberdeen Harbour. On what was to be his last ever chopper ride home, as the pilot battled with the storm and forced his way through the pounding rain and howling wind, a Mayday signal was sent from the craft and the co-pilot prepared them for the worst. Miraculously, they made it back to land, but only just. As Dylan alighted the helicopter on legs like jelly and with veins frozen by fear, he vowed he would never step foot on an oil rig, or a helicopter, ever again.

Within six months, Dylan had diversified and found himself alternative employment in another sector of the energy industry. Using his master's degree in thermo and hydrodynamics he embarked on a new career working for a company who built wind farms, however, he studiously avoided those situated offshore. He was interested in climate change and renewable energy so enjoyed his work which was varied and involved a great deal of travelling, and this was how he found himself in France as the senior consultant on his firm's current project. He had been engrossed in the diagram that the plant supervisor was showing him when he was distracted by the music blaring from the radio of a cream Fiat which was waiting at the temporary traffic lights. He was wearing dark, wrap-around sunglasses but even through the black lenses he knew it was Ruby in an instant.

She had turned to look at the turbine blade and in the second he glimpsed her face his heart missed a beat. Time stood perfectly still for a moment and then she was moving off, and as his brain registered this fact he began to call her name. His colleagues thought he'd gone mad as he threw off his hard hat and sprinted to his car which was totally blocked in by the low loader carrying the turbine, so he ran to the nearest van and began bellowing for the keys. Eventually, one of the labourers fumbled in his pocket and passed him the fob which Dylan almost ripped from his fingers.

Dylan drove like a madman onto the road, ignoring the amber light and sped off in pursuit of Ruby. His heart was pumping wildly as he followed her car, flashing the lights and waving his arms out of the window, desperately trying to catch her attention and flag her down. He almost caught up but after she took a bend in the road and he reached the brow of the next hill, he realised he'd lost her. Maybe she'd turned off onto one of the farm tracks, he couldn't tell but he was on the verge of crying with sheer temper and frustration at being so close. From that moment on, the minute he finished work and sometimes before he turned up on site in the morning, he would drive up and down the surrounding roads, scouring lanes and tracks in the vain hope that he would see her car. His supervisor gently suggested that she may have been passing through and could be miles away by now, however, something in his gut told him she was nearby. It was either instinct or wishful thinking, but he could almost feel her presence.

***

Today, his master plan was to ask in all the villages close by if anyone knew an English girl called Ruby. It was a long shot but there was a slim chance that someone may know her, or even Rosie. First, he had to find somewhere to stay because he'd checked out of the hotel his company had booked, but once that was organised he would continue his quest. He had three whole days before he would have to concede defeat but until he'd exhausted every line of enquiry and himself if necessary, he would keep on looking.

After two hours of peering into farm courtyards and driveways of village homes in the vain hope he would spot a cream Fiat, Dylan was feeling confused and frustrated by his inability to read a map properly. Everywhere was starting to look the same; the sneaking suspicion he may have doubled up and visited somewhere twice, didn't help matters. Thirst and hunger finally got the better of him so as he drove into the sleepy village of St Pierre de Fontaine, Dylan allowed himself a break and parked in the car park outside the Norman church then made his way over to the bistro opposite. It was quiet and cool inside so he ordered a *Panaché* and the *plat du jour*. He'd found that in most places, for around ten euros they served a perfectly acceptable three course meal and a small carafe of wine and coffee, so he sat back and relaxed for a while, content to give his brain a rest and watch the world go by.

Two women came into the bistro, one carrying a large basket of eggs which she passed to the owner who they called Sebastien. After much cheek kissing, they declined a drink but had a quick gossip then went on their way and in return, Sebastien bade a loud farewell to Zofia and Hortense. Dylan smiled to himself, thinking it must be nice to live in a place where the inhabitants knew each other, or on the other hand, maybe it became a bit of a pain if everybody knew your business.

This thought prompted him to ask the waiter about Ruby when he brought over his food. Unfortunately, the young lad couldn't speak a word of English and Dylan was rubbish at French so he gave up and instead, got on with his starter of quail egg salad with tiny lardons of bacon hidden amongst the fresh green leaves. When the waiter cleared the table and brought his main course of rabbit stew and potatoes, it was conducted in wary silence by both parties. His dessert of ice cream, decorated with wispy, toffee strands was delicious and the strong coffee made his heartbeat quicken, setting him up nicely for the afternoon's treasure hunt. Dylan hadn't touched the wine as he knew it would make him sleepy and he needed to be alert.

He was ready to pay the bill when the owner came over to his table and jovially introduced himself in basic English. His waiter, Noa, said that their customer wanted some information but didn't understand what exactly. Relieved, Dylan asked if there was anywhere locally where he could stay for a few nights. Sebastien's eyes lit up and then scurried off to the bar, returning with a printed leaflet before giving him directions to the hotel of his good friend Michel, assuring him it was literally minutes away. Dylan was just about to move on to his second question, when a group of men entered the bar and distracted Sebastien from their conversation, he excused himself and went to greet his customers who were obviously farmers and regulars. Seeing that the handshaking and cheerful banter was in full swing and could last for some time, Dylan left payment on the table and slipped quietly out of the bistro. He could ask at the hotel about Ruby and Rosie. Maybe the owner Michel would be able to help him, but first, he needed to find this place and see if there was room at the inn, so he followed the directions from Sebastien, started his car and drove out of the square.

As he pulled into the courtyard of *Les Trois Chênes* his spirits rose slightly; it looked like a lovely place, full of charm and character. He hoped it wasn't full because it would be rather nice to spend a couple of nights here and rest. As he waited at the front door, he could hear the sound of children playing on the other side of the building, then the occasional woof of a dog. When the door finally opened, a young, pretty girl with dark hair greeted him politely and asked in perfect English if he had a reservation. When he told her he hadn't but had been sent from the bistro she invited him in and checked in the large book on the stand at the bottom of the stairs. Smiling brightly, the girl who introduced herself as Océane, told him he was in luck, the attic room was available. She offered to show it to him first but assured him that it was very comfortable and had a small en-suite and tea making facilities. Dylan had been casting his eyes over the extremely stylish, cosy lounge, which was spotless and smelt of beeswax so had no qualms about taking the room, telling Océane to hang on while he nipped outside to the car and brought in his bag.

Once she'd taken his details, Océane showed him to the attic and then after politely checking he had everything he needed, left him in peace. The bedroom was tasteful, clean and very cosy. He presumed that it was used for small families as under the eaves, on either side of the room, were two antique iron beds, one double and one single. The bathroom was compact but looked quite new and more than adequate for his needs. There was a small window cut into the far stone wall and from there, Dylan could see across the tree tops. He spied the roof of a barn as he opened the little pane of glass to let in the warm May air, along with the screeches of the children he'd heard playing earlier. He peeped out as far as his head would reach and could just see the corner of a swimming pool where two young swimmers were splashing each other playfully; one a dark-haired boy and the other, a smaller, fair-haired girl.

Dylan left the window open and lay on the double bed. He was exhausted from his fruitless search and sleepless nights so decided to give himself an hour to recuperate and get his strength back. As his three-course lunch settled in his stomach, the sounds of the countryside and happy children wafted in and out of the room and his heavy eyelids began to close. The comfy mattress eased away the tension in his bones while the tranquillity of his surroundings lulled him into a deep, peaceful sleep.

The last thought he had, just before he entered dreamland was of Ruby. It was there again, that feeling. He could sense her presence, like an aura all around, settling over him like fog, telling him not to give up, to keep on looking. While he slept, his dreams were of a fair-haired girl waiting for him at a bus stop on a cold, grey October day in Manchester. Next, he was sitting beside her on the top deck, holding on to her hand really tightly, just to make sure he wouldn't lose her again. The road in front spread out before them, away from the city and along a winding track towards green hills and fields that went on forever.

Little did Dylan know that as he lay in the attic, snoring gently and smiling in his sleep, the star of his dream was just a few metres away, sitting outside by the pool, watching her children splashing around while Sabine dribbled and dozed peacefully in her arms.

Chapter 28
Rosie, Ruby and Dylan

Ruby was lost in thought; her mind was a confused whirlwind of memories and missed chances, regrets and remembrances of perfect love. She couldn't get Dylan out of her mind and she'd been replaying their time together, step by step from the day they met. All she could see whenever she closed her eyes was his face. Those pale brown eyes, shaded by sandy hair, smiling at her at the bus stop. The piece of paper in her pocket was burning a hole in her linen trousers and the tears of frustration she'd cried all night threatened to return at any moment if she didn't concentrate hard and push them away. The day before had started as a perfectly normal Tuesday, however, by the afternoon it had descended into disbelief and despair as she was consumed by a torrent of mixed emotions.

***

On hearing that white van man had been captured Ruby's mood lightened instantly and her conversation with Rosie turned to Sabine's upcoming birthday party. Naturally, Michel was providing the food and as long as it turned out to be a fine day, most of the activities could take place on the terrace and around the pool. It was now warm enough for swimming so all the other children could bring their costumes and have a splash about. Sensibly, they were thinking of contingencies for rain or easily bored, hyperactive kids and Rosie thought they should have some form of entertainment, like a clown. Ruby said it was a rubbish idea because they were a bit creepy, so instead, they settled on a magician. As her feet were throbbing and Sabine was due to wake up any minute, Rosie asked Ruby to pop up to the hotel and bring her big blue phone book because she was sure that in the back amongst all her bits and pieces there was a number for an entertainer. By the time Ruby returned, Sabine was up and about and running riot in her bedroom with Rosie trailing after her, trying in vain to get her changed.

'I'll be down in a minute, I'm just sorting mademoiselle out. Have a look for that leaflet will you? I'm sure it's there somewhere.' Rosie was out of breath as she shouted over the wooden mezzanine balcony.

'Okay, will do, and I'll make you some tea when you come down. Tell Sabine I've got some *chocolat* but only if she's good for Mummy.' Ruby opened the back of the book and removed the folder which amongst other things, contained leaflets and flyers advertising local events. Tipping them onto the coffee table she began sifting through old postcards and scribbled notes that only Rosie would understand.

Ruby came across the brightly-coloured advert almost straight away and laid it to one side, then decided to sort out the jumble of assorted paperwork into helpful piles before putting them back in the folder. It was one of Ruby's pet hates, keeping useless junk mail that came in the post so she occupied herself by sorting through the adverts for garden furniture which were two years old, amongst other similar bits and bobs. She'd completed the postcards and flyers and was getting started on the various slips of paper and notes, just as Rosie began to make her cautious way downstairs, holding tightly on to Sabine's hand. As Ruby flattened each one out and added it to the heap, she came upon a folded Post-it note which she opened up, fully expecting it to be years out of date but as she read the words and numbers, written in Rosie's bold unmistakable style, her heart almost stopped. There, before her eyes, underlined in red ink, was a phone number and the word 'Dylan'. Her hands trembled as she picked up the note and her mouth went dry. Ruby's heart pounded steadily in her chest and she could hear its drumbeat in her ears. Looking up, she saw Rosie who had paused at the foot of the stairs, Ruby held the note in front of her before asking the all-important question.

'Rosie, why have you got Dylan's phone number and why didn't you tell me you had it? What's going on, why is it in here?'

Ruby waited for her reply and could tell from her cousin's reaction that a million thoughts were racing through her brain and Rosie was thinking carefully what to say.

'I'm so sorry, Ruby, I'd totally forgotten about it. It must have been there for years and if I'm honest, there never seemed to be the right time to tell you about it before or bring up the past. After all this time I suppose it went out of my mind and I just left it alone.' Rosie's cheeks were flushed and she felt terribly guilty.

'What do you mean, tell me about it? I don't understand. How long have you had this number?' Ruby was aware of her shaking hands and the hint of accusation in her tone.

'Look, just let me get Sabine a drink and you'd best give her that chocolate, it will keep her quiet while I explain. I've got a feeling you're not going to like it but before I start, please believe me, Ruby, that what I did was with your best interests at heart, okay?' Rosie shot off and brought her daughter some juice then turned on the TV and settled her down on the sofa.

Once she knew Sabine was occupied Rosie went over and sat next to Ruby before letting out a deep sigh. Then she began.

They both had a good cry. Rosie's fluctuating hormones only added to the problem but mainly her tears were of sorrow at keeping a secret that if told on the day in question, could've saved her cousin a whole heap of heartbreak and definitely a lot of bruises.

Ruby cried for Dylan. She cried for the boy who sat alone on the steps of the Albert Memorial and for the stupid girl in her wedding dress who walked straight past the love of her life and broke his heart. She didn't blame Rosie – how could she? Because all her life she had only ever done what was right and, if the roles were reversed, Ruby had to admit she would've probably made the same choice.

Rosie looked Ruby in the eye before she spoke.

'I want you to know that if at any time, giving you that piece of paper might've made you happy or changed your situation, then I swear I wouldn't have hesitated. But how would you have felt if you'd rung Dylan up when Marcus was at his worst, asked for help and he'd turned you down, or was with someone else? I know he promised to always be there but it was such a bold statement to make and life goes on. I couldn't risk you being let down again. Do you believe me, Ruby? I hate seeing you cry and I feel so bad.' Rosie was exhausted and wrung out but her cousin looked worse.

'If I know one thing, Rosie, there's no point in beating yourself up about the past or wishing you could change it. I've been there and got the T-shirt, so please don't waste a moment on "what-ifs" because it's a complete waste of energy. Of course I believe you, silly, and I'm sorry that you had to carry the burden of a secret. I kept secrets from you so how could you have known to ring Dylan? Or even that I needed his number so he could come and rescue me. It's all in the open now and at least I know he did actually come back for me and best of all, that he loved me, just as much as I always loved him.' And then Ruby burst into floods of tears again.

Later that night, as she lay in her room with the piece of paper containing Dylan's phone number on her bedside table, Ruby turned her whole life over, remembering the tiniest of details, examining all the evidence as she tried to work out whether ringing him would be a fool's errand. Perhaps she should leave things as they were, with bittersweet memories and the knowledge that he had returned to Manchester. She compared this to the risk of an awkward, embarrassing conversation that would probably end in rejection. It was the longest night of Ruby's life and by the time dawn broke and the singing birds started their day, she was no nearer to knowing what to do or how to soothe her aching heart.

Ruby was tired after a sleepless night and not in the mood for traipsing after Lily who was getting a bit too giddy. Her red cheeks signalled she needed a break from the sun and a cold drink. Sabine began to stir so Ruby decided they should all head off down the track to the barn and check on Rosie who had been having an afternoon kip.

When Océane appeared on the terrace she helped Ruby haul the slippery kids out of the pool and wrap them in towels.

'Thanks, Océane. I'll pop back up later to see if you need anything before I go home and I'll move all of these toys. Have you been busy today?' Ruby hoisted Sabine onto her hip as she spoke.

'It's not been too bad. I've restocked the linen cupboard and stripped Room Four ready for the morning. Oh, and we have a new guest up in the attic. He seems very nice... he is only stopping for a few days. His details are in the book so will you tell Rosie? And stop fussing, it is your day off remember!' Smiling, Océane kissed Sabine and waved to Lily and Oliver before heading back inside.

Ruby made her way back to Rosie's with her little ducklings, flip-flopping along the track with their towels over their heads. Oliver told her how *really, really* starving he was and he hoped Rosie had made him his tea, otherwise he was going straight back to the hotel to get something from Michel. Lily stopped a thousand times to get stones out of her toes then Sabine said she needed a wee.

Ruby thought that the sooner the day was over and she could go to sleep, the better. At least then she could get some peace because her brain hurt and she needed to switch it off.

Dylan woke up from the deepest sleep he'd had in a long time. He felt like he'd been drugged and it took him a while to remember where he was and why he was there. Looking at his watch he was able to focus his bleary eyes and saw that it was almost 6pm. He was furious, a whole afternoon had been wasted sleeping so now he had two options – take a quick drive around and chance his luck before it got dark or go downstairs and ask the owner if he'd heard of Ruby and Rosie. There was a restaurant so he could eat there tonight and be refreshed for tomorrow. Yawning, Dylan chose option two and headed for the shower, flicking on the kettle as he went past. It had been a while since he'd had a nice cup of English tea and the little pot on the tray held what looked suspiciously like PG tips.

The children were all fed, dressed in their pyjamas and watching cartoons so Ruby left them with Rosie while she went back to the pool to collect their toys and armbands and whatever else they'd scattered about the place. When she got there, Océane had beaten her to it and already put everything in the basket, ready to carry back to the barn. Ruby loved this time of night. The sun was about to set just over the farthest hill and she could hear the soothing hum of diners in the restaurant. The thought of food turned her stomach right now. It was so full of knots and nerves but she'd promised Rosie that she would eat later, after she'd taken the kids home and put them to bed. It was extremely peaceful on the terrace so Ruby chose a lounger and took a few minutes for herself, watching the sun as it glided gracefully out of sight.

Remembering Rosie's advice from the day before, that even if he *was* with someone, Ruby could still contact Dylan and say hello and perhaps let him know she was okay and tell him she knew that he came back on her wedding day. What was the harm in that? Just a polite, friendly conversation between two people with history. Pulling the piece of paper out of her pocket Ruby stared at it blankly for a moment and then took out her phone. She sort of knew she would ring him when she left the barn because the thought of one more night of not knowing would drive her completely mad. She felt really stupid too, like a teenager plucking up the courage to ring the boy she fancied. Her cheeks were burning with embarrassment and nerves and she hadn't even dialled the number yet.

Taking a deep breath, Ruby began to tap out the code for the UK then slowly and deliberately, she completed the numbers written in red. Placing the phone to her ear she listened with trembling hands and waited for it to connect. When she heard the telltale monotonous tone of a phone that had been disconnected, her heart dropped like lead as humiliation and despair tormented her mind. Hot tears sprang from her eyes and a sob escaped from her throat. She couldn't hold it in any longer, he was out of reach and out of touch. It really was over this time and now, all hope was gone.

Dylan made his way downstairs and past the empty lounge and bar. He waited at the door of the restaurant but nobody was around, apart from other diners who were engrossed in their own conversations and hadn't noticed him. The French doors were open at the end of the room so he followed his nose and went outside to look for signs of life. He was impressed with the stylish cobbled terrace and expensive garden furniture that was arranged in neat sets and looked out towards the pool and the view of the countryside beyond. Fairy lights were strung around the greenery and were beginning to twinkle as the sun started to set. Realising that there was nobody out here either, Dylan turned to make his way inside when he heard a noise. It was coming from the other side of the pool and sounded like someone crying. He was about to make a swift exit when whoever it was, stood up. Even from behind, he could tell that the woman was wiping her eyes and trying to compose herself. Just as she began to turn, the hairs on the back of Dylan's neck started to prickle. There was something familiar about the shape of her body and the way her hair was tied up in a long ponytail and when she finally faced him head on, Dylan knew in that second of sheer relief and joy, that he had found his Ruby.

Ruby stood up and wiped her eyes. There was no point sitting here all night crying. She had to get on with her life and get back to Rosie and the children. As she composed herself and took one last look at the orange orb on the horizon, she had the strangest feeling that she was being watched and sensed someone was behind her. Turning slowly, she looked towards the restaurant and saw the shape of a man, illuminated by the lights from the restaurant. He was standing stock still, staring at her from the terrace. At first Ruby was a little unnerved but it only lasted for a second because there was something so familiar about the shape of his body and the way his hair fell in soft waves around his face. In that second of incredible realisation and pure joy, she knew that her Dylan had come back.

The lights on the terrace twinkled like fairies, flitting excitedly around their heads, just waiting for something to happen, frantically sprinkling magic dust and casting their spells.

Dylan spoke first. 'I've been looking everywhere for you. I thought I'd lost you forever and then I saw you on the road. I chased you but you got away. I was going to keep on searching but you were right here all along. I can't believe I found you. Look, my hands are shaking. I'm so nervous and I don't know what to say next.' He held up his trembling hands and heard her soft laugh from the other side of the pool.

Ruby wiped her eyes as her heart soared. 'I've been sitting here crying. I found the number you gave Rosie but the line was dead. I thought I'd lost you forever too. I didn't know it was you chasing me. I thought you were a nutter who was trying to kill me, and look, my hands are shaking too. So… what shall we do next?' Ruby couldn't see him properly now because her eyes were blurred with tears and her throat was so tight that no more words would come out.

Dylan's whole body ached to hold her in his arms. He'd waited so long and imagined too often how it would be if he ever found her. The thought momentarily crossed his mind that this might all be a cruel dream, and if it was he would drown himself in that pool the minute he woke up. Deciding there wasn't a second to waste he silently walked around the edge of the water and when she was within inches, the sight of her took his breath away. To him, she hadn't changed one bit, she was still his Ruby. As he held out his arms and folded her inside, she clung on tightly and sobbed. While he let her cry and his own tears dropped onto her hair, Dylan made a silent vow that this time they were for keeps. He would never let her down and never let her go. He would spend the rest of his life making up for lost time and move heaven and earth, just to make Ruby happy.

Ruby couldn't think or even speak. Her mind was blank and her heart was hurting from the pain of pure happiness. Her Dylan was here, holding her tight after all these years, and that's all that mattered.

Ruby and Dylan sat on the lounger and held hands. They tried to bring each other up to date as quickly as possible, tripping over their words and laughing when they realised how close they had been and how easily they could have missed each other had he not gone into Sebastien's bistro.

Jolting them from their ramblings, Ruby's phone rang. Rosie was at the other end, wondering where Ruby had got to and checking she was okay, then saying all three children were sparked out on the sofa so they may as well stay for dinner.

Smiling, Ruby placed her fingers to her lips and spoke to Rosie.

'I'm on my way back now. I'll be there in two minutes and prepare yourself for a big surprise.'

When Rosie opened the door to find Ruby stood on the doorstep holding hands with Dylan she thought for a second she'd either been transported back in time or she was hallucinating. For once, she was totally lost for words and just stood there with her mouth open and her hands on her cheeks, wide-eyed with surprise and utterly gobsmacked. After she'd gathered her wits and hugged them both, then ushered them in, she continued to be lost for words as they related the scene at the pool and the events that led Dylan to the hotel.

The atmosphere in the room was electric. Nobody could quite believe Dylan was here or the way destiny had led him to France and then the hotel. Once they'd all calmed down, Rosie rang Michel who ran down the path in between courses to shake Dylan's hand, pat him on the back, then run back up again before anything burnt. Unfortunately, due to the shock of Dylan's arrival and the emotional turmoil of the previous day, Michel was soon running back down the path an hour later when Rosie went into labour and was rushed off to hospital, to finally deliver her baby elephant.

Chapter 29

La famille

Sabine hated everyone singing happy birthday and told them all to stop the second they began. When everyone carried on regardless she burst into tears and refused to blow out her two candles, so Lily gladly stepped into the breach and did it for her. This caused another tantrum and they had to do it all over again. Rosie thought her daughter's behaviour was a combination of overexcitement and a reaction to the arrival twelve days earlier of her baby sister, Odette, so she gave Sabine the benefit of the doubt and a second, third and fourth chance to behave.

It was a beautiful June day and all the family along with their closest friends were gathered at the hotel to celebrate the birthday girl's special day. Michel had prepared a feast and was currently having some kind of disagreement with André about the contents of his sausage mix. Wilf was keeping out of it and continued drinking his *bier*, talking to Henry about a recent trip to Corsica where he and André had a bash at hand-gliding. Rosie told them both they were irresponsible and would have no sympathy for either if they ended up in wheelchairs, and if André hurt his back again, it was his own stupid fault. Her protests fell on selectively deaf ears because the couple's summer plans included diving with sharks and a dune buggy safari. Deep down though, Rosie was pleased her beloved André was happy so keeping her word to Clémence, in the end, she always let him go.

Rosie giggled when she saw what Sabine and Lily had done to Olivia, although she suspected that the pretending-to-be-asleep, chiffon-clad granny knew exactly what they were up to.

The terrible twosome had been making daisy chains with Olivia who had patiently shown them what to do and now both girls were wearing lovely necklaces and bracelets. However, poor old granny's head was covered in daisies, dandelions and tufts of grass, which the two monsters had scattered liberally over her head. Sure enough, Olivia woke dramatically from her pretend sleep and was horrified to find someone had put a garden in her hair, so kicked off her Jimmy Choo's and proceeded to chase the screaming, giggling terrors around the terrace.

Anna was laughing at something Zofia was telling her, probably about Dominique who had fallen off his horse and almost crippled himself. He was in fear of his wife selling Figaro, his wilful, highly strung mare so instead invented a dreadful accident with his ladders. The mistake he made was telling half the village the real version of events and naively, swearing them all to secrecy. Once the tale had done its rounds it inevitably, if not mistakenly, fell on Zofia's unamused ears. He'd been in the doghouse for days now and the horse had been given its final yellow card.

Zofia was terrified of Figaro after she'd spent a whole morning pinned behind a tree where the jealous horse had cornered her after she took him in a bucket of feed. Despite her frantic calls for help, nobody heard because her husband had nipped across the road to their neighbours for a quick one before lunch. Since then, she refused to go near the nasty horse and left its care entirely to her husband.

Dominique was oblivious to Zofia's grumblings and totally engrossed in his task of dishing out the home-made wine he'd made from the vines in Anna's garden. He also had his absinthe and *eau de vie* stashed away for later – he said it eased the pain of his injuries and earache from his wife.

Pascal was enjoying an animated conversation with Dylan about solar power and wind turbines. Many farmers in the area were turning to renewable energy and Rosie knew that her part-time waiter and barman had big ideas for his father's farm and desperately wanted to try new things, so they were both in their element trying to save the earth. Oliver and Arno were playing football with Anna's son, Sam who had recently returned from yet another tour of Afghanistan and was home on leave.

Hortense was holding court with *le Maire* and her daughter Sylvie who was recently separated and had caught the eye of Sebastien and Henri, both were prowling and gearing up for a night of wine, hopefully a woman (depending on who won the heart of Sylvie) and even a bit of a song.

Searching the terrace, Rosie looked for Ruby and spotted her in front of a line of eager children who were waiting for their faces to be painted and adorned with half a ton of glitter. Her heart swelled with pride and love for her cousin. Ruby looked so pretty today, wearing a flowery maxi dress and silver sandals, slim shoulders turning pink from the afternoon sun and her radiant face had a healthy scattering of freckles across her nose. Ruby's light brown hair blew in the breeze, so she tucked it behind her ear and then went back to chatting to the little girl in front of her. She looked so free and happy, relaxed in her own skin and comfortable in her surroundings and even though she was still shy about the whole Dylan thing, Rosie knew that Ruby was in love again.

Océane interrupted Rosie's people watching to announce the arrival of the magician so with squeals of delight, the children scurried about as they were rounded up by Olivia and Anna and arranged in neat lines on the terrace floor so that the show could begin.

Ruby took a break from painting tiger's faces or the current favourite, Tinkerbell, and accepted a glass of cold white wine from their friendly barman, Dominique. She then went to sit on the step of the terrace, a vantage point from where she could observe the goings on. The children were enthralled by the magician, especially Oliver and Arno who were sitting right at the front and had already volunteered to help with two tricks. She knew that her mesmerised son would be desperately trying to work out how the magician did it and predicted that for his next birthday present, he would want a magic set. Dylan and Pascal were pretending to watch the show while furtively talking about organic vineyards in between applauding the tricks. Olivia was sitting amongst the children with Sabine on her lap. The little girl adored her adoptive granny and insisted on addressing her in the same way Lily and Oliver did – Golly – so they all went with the flow as it made her happy and Olivia, who was secretly very flattered, didn't mind a bit.

Ruby was so relieved that Dylan and Olivia got on well. They had only met a few days earlier and what could have been a very awkward moment was handled with ease and charm by both Henry and his wife-to-be, which was another development. On the night Olivia and Henry arrived, everyone met at their cottage for aperitifs and were treated to a surprise announcement because as soon as it could be arranged, they were going to be married. Olivia had confessed that she hadn't told Marcus yet as quite frankly it was none of his business. She wasn't going to let anyone spoil her happiness or put up with one of his histrionic strops either. So perhaps that was why, when Ruby told her all about Dylan's return, Olivia seemed genuinely pleased that the young lovers had been reunited, just like her and Henry.

Smiling, Ruby watched Michel walk over to Rosie and give her a gentle kiss on the head and then pull back the cover of Odette's pram before smiling adoringly at his new baby daughter. He was soon shooed away by his mother and once Michel was out of the way, Marie took over cooing at her granddaughter. Ruby took in the scene and marvelled at how many wonderful new people had come into her life. All families had their ups and downs, she knew that, but from her humble beginnings and Rosie's battles with her parents, they had both managed to find their way here, to this extended, unconventional family. Rosie had her crazy, gay, adoptive father who had been her rock for so many years and had wisely guided her towards Michel and their hotel. No matter where he was on his travels he rang Rosie every week and loved her as if she were his own daughter, and then there was dear Olivia.

Out of three mothers, she had been the hidden gem. Not only had she become the parent Ruby should have had and the complete opposite of Stella, she was just as watchful and caring with Rosie who had yearned in vain for tenderness and warmth from Doreen, and now adequately compensated by the attention she received from Olivia. Her love for both Ruby and Rosie was constant, loyal and reciprocated.

One important thing that life had taught Ruby was that real love has nothing to do with whose blood flows through your veins. When someone truly loves a child, at whatever age, even if it isn't their own, honour could be found in the act of giving; placing them under your wing and making it your duty to care for them. It was something that was given freely, unconditionally and with pride.

Ruby looked up and saw Dylan and her heart flipped over. Every time she saw his face her stomach fluttered and a bass drum boomed inside her chest. Maybe it would wear off, but for now she embraced the thrill of new love, even if it was the second time around. Ruby had been nervous about him meeting Oliver and Lily, however, he had won them over with his casual friendliness and easy-going nature. They were still being discreet and even though she had an inkling that Detective Inspector Oliver was on to them, her son seemed unconcerned and relaxed in Dylan's company. Lily was shy and quiet around him at first but now treated him much the same as she did everyone else, with vague interest and of secondary importance to her dolls and Sabine. It made her glow inside, remembering yesterday at tea, and Oliver's wide eyes as he related something Dylan had told him.

'You'll never guess what Dylan is going to bring for me and Arno when he comes back. Manchester City shirts! They won the Premier League in England and guess what? Their stadium is just round the corner from where you lived when you were a little girl. Why didn't you tell me that, Mum? It's really cool!' Oliver continued to eat his spaghetti which spread liberally all over his face.

'Well, because I didn't think it was that important, but yes, it's true. I used to live in a place called Eastlands. That's how I know Dylan. He used to live just up the road from me and I was his girlfriend.' Ruby had to hide a grin when she saw the look on Oliver's face.

'Oooh, that's disgusting! I'm not going to have a girlfriend, girls are boring. Anyway, Manchester City is mine and Arno's favourite team now, after FC Nantes. Dylan makes me laugh as well, he says funny things like, that's mint, and he calls me dude. Me and Arno say dude all the time now. Did you know he can play the guitar and was in a band *and* I'm going to go inside a wind turbine and up the stairs? I bet you didn't know they had stairs inside, did you?' And there the subject ended as he slurped his pasta and the conversation moved on to Scooby Doo.

The line in Oliver's testimonial which made her glow inside was the part when he said that Dylan was coming back. He'd been down to La Rochelle and then came straight back for a couple of days where they spent every moment they could together. He was currently working in Bordeaux but they spoke each day on the phone and as promised, had driven back late on Friday for the weekend and Sabine's birthday party. Dylan was officially staying at the hotel but she'd waited patiently for the children to fall asleep and then sneaked him in the back door, praying hard that the neighbours hadn't seen. They both felt like teenagers again, yet at the same time, knew that what they were feeling wasn't a silly crush or the madness of youth. It was the real thing and always would be.

The contract with the French energy company was expected to run for over a year, so for the time being Dylan would be in France regularly, even if he was travelling all the time, but had assured Ruby that whenever he had time off he would either drive or walk back if necessary. He still wasn't that keen on flying. They were going to take their time and he was going to get to know Lily and Oliver – the rest would follow naturally, Ruby was sure of it.

The magician had finished and was now off-duty, propping up the bar while the smaller children played with balloons tied in the shapes of dogs and rabbits. Oliver and Arno were bouncing a ball and pestering the grown-ups to play with them. In the end, their perseverance paid off when Dylan gave in and stood up.

'Okay, I surrender. Let's go down to the field and play there. Come on, Sam, and you too, Pascal. The rest of the world against the champions, Manchester City. First ones to the gîtes can kick off.'

Without having to be told twice, Arno and Oliver sprinted away while their semi-willing team mates, jogged behind.

Dylan ran over and kissed Ruby quickly on the cheek before winking and sprinting off, just as Rosie appeared by her side and sat down on the step next to her cousin. They didn't speak for a moment or two, enjoying what they saw and heard – their family and the sound of laughter.

Eventually, Rosie nudged Ruby playfully and spoke.

'Well, I think we can safely say that our Dylan has got it bad. He hasn't taken his eyes off you all day. He looks eighteen again and if I may say so, you look like love's young dream with that gormless smile you've had slapped on your face since this morning. I take it everything's going okay then?' Rosie sipped her juice and grinned mischievously into her glass.

'Yes, thank you, Captain Nosey Parker. All is well, and no, I'm not telling you the juicy bits because I know that's what you're after. I will leave it to your vivid imagination.' Ruby knew that Rosie could get blood out of a stone if she set her mind to it and only a matter of time before she dragged vital information from her.

'Joking apart, you do look happy, Ruby. I'm so glad everything's worked out for you. It might have been a bit of a bumpy ride but you got there in the end, we both did.' Rosie could feel a tear form in the corner of her eye and put it down to fluctuating hormones.

Ruby smiled. 'We sure did! If you'd have told me on that freezing afternoon at the train station when you left home, that one day in the future we'd be sitting here in the sun, in France, with our beautiful children and two gorgeous hunks of men, I'd have thought you were completely mad. Life seemed so desperate, so many times, and all of this was beyond my wildest dreams. I couldn't have done it without you though, if it hadn't been for the fact I had you in my life I think I'd have just given up.' Ruby held out her hand and folded it around Rosie's, unable to speak because her throat was knotted with emotion.

Rosie kissed Ruby's hand. 'Shut up or you'll set me off, and you seem to forget that having someone special in *my* life, that unbreakable connection between the two of us and knowing that you needed me, made *me* strong too. No matter where I was or how lonely I felt, somewhere out there was my little cousin. I always had you, Ruby. So, you're right, I think we made a good team. Me and you against the world and in the end, we won.'

Ruby and Rosie grinned, squeezing their hands tightly together.

Suddenly, Henry appeared with his trusty camera tied around his neck and made them both jump.

'Come on you two. Let's have one for the album.' Henry fiddled about with the lens and then declared he was set. 'Okay, get ready, say *fromage*.'

Looking up from where they sat on the step, their eyes squinting slightly in the glare of the summer sun, Rosie and Ruby linked arms and smiled for the camera. The happy sparrow and her trusty eagle, together at last, best friends forever.

THE END

ACKNOWLEDGEMENTS

My stories are written for and inspired by women from all walks of life. I am continually in awe of your resilience and ability to thrive, sometimes against the odds and in the face of adversity. Whilst telling my tales I hope to celebrate strengths and struggles, triumphs and love – a tribute to you.

This book is about parents who, despite their best intentions, have a child who takes the wrong path. Just like Marcus. Some children are saddled with a mother, just like Stella, or parents who are incapable of stepping up to the mark, yet these youngsters throw off the shackles of their past and live. Just like Ruby and Rosie. This story is for those who made it through. The triers, the brave of heart, the believers who never give up hope and love unconditionally, and the wise ones, who strive never to repeat the mistakes of their parents.

The books in this series will take you to the Loire Valley in France. It is a place close to my heart and the setting for new beginnings where you will meet a host of new characters, all with a special story to tell.

I would like to thank you, the reader, for taking time to read this story. A huge thanks to my French friends who are a joy and provide me with endless inspiration. To my loyal followers who continually astound me with their support, interest and pride in my achievements, thank you.

To the team at Bloodhound and Bombshell Books who are my rock, the best bunch of colleagues anyone could wish for. Huge thanks to Heather my editor who is a pleasure to work with and whose comments and input I have found invaluable. Thanks also to Abbie for her patient proofreading and attention to detail.

Finally and as always I want to thank my family, six wonderful people. Their love, encouragement and unwavering belief in me are the foundations from which my writing grows.

There is one more person to thank and that's my Angel, because I am a believer. She is always by my side, guiding me, keeping me safe.

ABOUT THE AUTHOR

Patricia Dixon was born in Manchester where she still lives with her husband. They have two grown-up children and one grandson, plus the company of a lazy bulldog.

Ignoring her high school reports and possibly sound advice from teachers, Patricia shunned the world of academia and instead, stubbornly pursued a career in fashion. Once the sparkle of London life wore off she returned north and embarked on a new adventure, that of motherhood. Now, almost thirty years later she has acquiesced to the wise words of her elders and turned her hand to writing.

In May 2018 Patricia signed with leading crime publishers Bloodhound Books and their imprint, Bombshell Books.

If she's not at her desk Patricia loves to read historical fiction or attempts recipes that look great on television but not necessarily her plate. And when the penny jar is full she cashes in her coins and heads to France, the lure of red wine and escapism equalled only by the pursuance of her dream job, writing.

Contact Details:
Email: dixon.patricia@icloud.com
Facebook: https://www.facebook.com/pbadixon
Twitter: https://twitter.com/pbadixon

Printed in Great Britain
by Amazon

44008890R00213